PRAISE FOR PETER ROMAN

"[Roman] . . . has created a pulp novel with genuine depth and wisdom, insight and consummate skill. It's not capital-l Literary, but it cannily bridges both worlds."

—*The National Post*

". . . Cross's tale sweeps you up with its gallows humour, whether you're revelling in the pleasures of two-fisted, angel-punching action or the cleverly rendered language."

—*Quill & Quire*

"[*The Mona Lisa Sacrifice*] never lets the reader pause for breath. . . ."

—*Publishers Weekly*

"The author of *The Warhol Gang* and *Please* (writing as Peter Darbyshire) takes urban fantasy to a different level with this tale of conspiracy and confession."

—*Library Journal*

"*The Dead Hamlets* resembles something written by Neil Gaiman with its somewhat mystical imagery, and at other times it reads as a full-blown work of bizarro fiction."

—*The Examiner*

"[Roman]'s big dumb fun book is actually whip smart."

—*The Vancouver Sun*

D1244673

ALSO BY PETER ROMAN

The Mona Lisa Sacrifice
The Dead Hamlets

THE APOCALYPSE ARK

ChiZine Publications

FIRST EDITION

The Apocalypse Ark © 2016 by Peter Roman
Cover artwork © 2016 by Erik Mohr
Cover and interior design © 2016 by Samantha Beiko

Distributed in Canada by
Publishers Group Canada
76 Stafford Street, Unit 300
Toronto, Ontario, M6J 2S1
Toll Free: 800-747-8147
e-mail: info@pgcbooks.ca

Distributed in the U.S. by
Consortium Book Sales & Distribution
34 Thirteenth Avenue, NE, Suite 101
Minneapolis, MN 55413
Phone: (612) 746-2600
e-mail: sales.orders@cbsd.com

Library and Archives Canada Cataloguing in Publication

Roman, Peter, 1967-, author

    The apocalypse ark / Peter Roman.

Issued in print and electronic formats.

ISBN 978-1-77148-377-3 (paperback).--ISBN 978-1-77148-378-0 (pdf)

    I. Title.

PS8557.A59346A77 2016   C813'.6   C2015-908377-X

                          C2015-908378-8

CHIZINE PUBLICATIONS
Toronto, Canada
www.chizinepub.com
info@chizinepub.com

Edited by Samantha Beiko
Proofread by Tove Nielsen

Shelfie

A **free** eBook edition is available
with the purchase of this print book.

CLEARLY PRINT YOUR NAME ABOVE IN UPPER CASE
Instructions to claim your free eBook edition:
1. Download the Shelfie app for Android or iOS
2. Write your name in **UPPER CASE** above
3. Use the Shelfie app to submit a photo
4. Download your eBook to any device

Canada Council   Conseil des arts
for the Arts   du Canada

We acknowledge the support of the Canada Council for the Arts which last year invested $20.1 million in writing and publishing throughout Canada.

ONTARIO ARTS COUNCIL
CONSEIL DES ARTS DE L'ONTARIO
an Ontario government agency
un organisme du gouvernement de l'Ontario

Published with the generous assistance of the Ontario Arts Council.

Printed in Canada

"It is not down on any map; true places never are."

—*Moby Dick*

THE APOCALYPSE ARK

PETER ROMAN

IN THE BEGINNING WAS THE BOOK

The end of the world began with a bible. It's always the bibles that cause problems.

It's a long story. Let me explain it as best I can.

I was walking the dusty trails of the Camino de Santiago, an ancient route for pilgrims that crosses Spain. Other travellers shared the path with me, but in my head I walked alone.

I wanted to be on my own. Make that *needed* to be on my own. I had a lot to think of after that ghost Hamlet business I told you about last time we met. The ghost had nearly been the end of me and all those I cared about, and it wasn't done with the world yet. But that wasn't what occupied my mind.

I thought about Morgana, the faerie queen, my ancient enemy and lover. She and the surviving members of her court had gone their own way after we'd escaped the ghost in the Forgotten Library. She'd freed me from the enchantment that had bound me to her, but still I thought about her all the time, even though I didn't know where she was now. There was something unfinished between us. I wasn't sure I wanted to know what it was.

I knew as I made my way along the Camino's well-worn trails that I'd see Morgana again. We had that kind of history where we always met up once more. Maybe it would take months, maybe centuries. But we would meet again. It was either a benefit or a curse of immortality, depending on the nature of our relationship at the time.

I had no idea what I would say to her when that day came.

At night, I slept on the ground beside the trails, using my backpack for a pillow. I could have stayed in villages along the way, but I preferred feeling the earth under my back while I gazed at the stars overhead. I thought about Amelia, my undead daughter, during those times. She had died with her mother, Penelope, the one true love of all my lives. Penelope, who was the offspring of a mortal and an angel and thus my grace. She was pregnant with Amelia when she died at Hiroshima, after Judas lured us there in time for the dropping of the atomic bomb. We all died there. I resurrected, as I always do. I was the only one.

But then Morgana ripped Amelia from Penelope's womb, long since turned to ash, and birthed her. She raised Amelia in the faerie court, supernaturally aging her into a young woman and teaching her the secret ways of the faerie. Amelia was still dead, but death meant little to the faerie.

And Amelia had yet to discover life. After the two of us left Berlin, where the Hamlet haunting had begun and ended for me, we went to Paris. We spent some time getting reacquainted in the cafes and riverside paths of the city where I had fallen in love with Penelope. Then Amelia set out on a pilgrimage to Hiroshima, to see the place where her mother had died. It wasn't a place I particularly wanted to revisit, and it was a trip she needed to make on her own. So I continued with my wandering, which is how I came to be walking the Camino.

It wasn't the first time I'd followed its path. I'd joined the crowds along the Camino many times over the centuries, just another sinner searching for penance or spiritual salvation or simply to escape the world. Sometimes I was even one or all of those things. I've been many people throughout my lives. I'd never experienced the enlightenment others seemed to find in their travels, but the Camino was still a good way to clear your mind.

I walked for maybe a week or so, hiding myself and my memories amid all the other people lost in their own thoughts, before the angel appeared.

It rose up from the trampled earth of the path ahead of me, a swirling cloud of dust that took the shape of a woman in robes, with great wings stretching behind her and a sword in her hand.

I took several steps back, out of the range of that sword, even before she finished fully forming. I shrugged off my backpack and let it drop to the ground, ready to fight or run. I recognized the angel, despite the fact she was made up of dust.

Sariel.

An angel sworn to kill me for what I had done to her. What I had done to the world.

But I also knew it wasn't her. It was one of her—what? Incarnations? Shadows? Souls? Even I didn't know the true nature of the strange angel now blocking my path.

For a couple of seconds, I wondered if I perhaps had heat stroke and was dreaming the whole thing. It had been centuries since I'd last encountered Sariel, after all. I looked around and saw the other pilgrims staring at her, too. A woman leaning on a walking stick made the sign of the cross. A shirtless man with the faces of a dozen different people tattooed on his chest fell to his knees. A middle-aged man and woman in matching shorts and shirts fumbled for cameras around their necks.

Then Sariel came at me on a sudden gust of wind, her sword driving at my chest. I knew from experience that even in dust form she could be deadly, so I burned some grace to move with superhuman speed, twisting to my right to avoid the sword. I kept moving, grabbing the walking staff from the woman with both my hands and striking Sariel in the back with it.

The staff wasn't much of a weapon against an angel, but it was the only weapon I had. I hoped to throw Sariel off balance with my blow, to give me a few seconds to find a better weapon or to make a run for it.

Instead, the walking staff cut through Sariel like a blade. It sliced through the wings and then her body, and she blew apart, no more than a dust cloud again. I held the staff in a guard position and waited for her to reform, but instead the dust slowly fell back to the earth and was still.

The other people stared at the ground and then stared at me.

"An angel," said the woman whose walking staff I'd taken.

"A visitation," said the couple together, their cameras forgotten in their hands.

"It was nothing," I said. "It was some dust and the wind. I've seen stranger things." Which was true enough, but I wasn't going to elaborate.

"It was a sign," said the man with all the tattoos. He bent down and kissed the ground.

I stared at the last of the dust settling back to the earth, and thought he was probably right. That hadn't been a true manifestation of Sariel, not if she went down that easily. Which meant it had to be something else, like a warning or a message. But of what?

I gazed out at the surrounding landscape and saw it. The mountain in the distance. The mountain I knew held a buried, forgotten monastery.

I sighed. Yes, the angel had been a sign. A sign that things were about to take a turn for the worse. Again.

I looked back at the others and saw them staring at me now. I knew what they were thinking. If that had truly been an angel, then what was I, the one the angel had come to fight? Perhaps another angel. Perhaps the very devil himself.

I picked up my backpack and shouldered it. I just wanted to keep walking the Camino and lose myself in my memories. But I knew that wasn't possible anymore. I tried to hand the staff back to the woman, but she stepped away from me, crossing herself twice as hard now. The couple began to slowly raise their cameras, no doubt hoping I wouldn't notice. The other man laid his hands on his tattoos, as if summoning strength from them.

I dropped the staff to the ground and walked away. I blew out a breath of grace as I went, and the dust rose up all around us again in a sudden storm. I knew the other pilgrims were going to remember this day until they died and probably talk of it to their friends and family. May as well give them something to talk about.

I used the cover of the dust storm to slip away unseen. I stepped off the path and headed for the mountain in the distance, leaving the other travellers crying out behind me. By the time the dust fell back to the earth again, there would be no more sign of me left than of the angel.

I cut through a winery orchard and then crossed a dirt road and a barren patch of land that looked as if it had burned at some point in the past. I went up the slope of the mountain, which was just as barren, and tried to remember how to get inside.

Night was falling by the time I found a big slab of rock that looked about right. It didn't appear that much different from the rest of the landscape, but there was a faded cross scratched into its surface. A cross I'd made centuries earlier, when I pushed the rock there.

I shovelled away the dirt from one side of the rock with my hands, until I'd made a gap between the rock and the mountain face. I wiggled into the gap and tried to push the rock out with my shoulders. Nothing. It was a big rock, after all. I used a bit of grace to give me strength and tried again. This time I managed to push the rock out a bit, widening the gap and exposing the cave behind it. I slid through, welcoming the cool air. It was probably the same air I'd breathed last time I'd been here. I hoped it was the only thing about this visit that was the same.

I went down the cave and deeper into the monastery. I grabbed a torch that had been jammed into a crack in the wall and, with a lighter from my backpack, set it ablaze. Let there be light.

The monks had built upon the natural cave system in the mountain, carving larger chambers out of the rock and shoring up the ceilings and walls with wooden beams. They'd made it as homey as they could, decorating the place with worn rugs and even a few tapestries on the walls depicting the coming return of their saviour. I'd made a mess of that when I'd arrived here the first time.

I came into the dining hall and found it much as I'd left it. The ceiling was largely fallen in, and there was a gaping chasm in the floor that dropped away to who knew where. The tables were overturned, dishes and cutlery scattered everywhere. These were the remains of the battle I'd fought with Sariel so long ago. The real angel Sariel, not some dusty apparition. I went around the edge of the chasm and continued on, searching. I didn't know what I was looking for, but I figured the dust angel had its reasons for making itself known after all this time.

I had to use more grace to clear away great piles of stone throughout the monastery. Sariel had sealed off the different halls from one another when she'd brought down the ceiling. I noted scratch marks on some of the rocks I moved. Someone had been trapped here and tried to dig their way out. But there would've been no moving those stones without grace, and Sariel and I had been the only ones with grace in the monastery back then. And look what we'd done with it.

I found the bodies of a half dozen monks in the scriptorium, scattered among the remains of the books they'd been illustrating. Most of them were on the floor, leathery, mummified bodies in mouldy, dark robes surrounded by piles of yellowed tomes. One of them was still sitting at his work table, though, slumped over a text he must have been trying to finish before he died. He had a quill clutched in his skeletal hand, and I eyed that for a moment. I'd had bad experiences with quills during the Hamlet affair. But I could see the ink pot on the table was dry, and the quill was just a regular writing instrument.

The monks must have come here when they'd realized they couldn't find their way out through the fallen rock. Had they simply wanted to die, surrounded by the texts they loved? Or had they wanted to finish what they'd started? Only the dead knew, and I didn't feel like raising them to find out the answer.

I almost envied their fate. If you had to die forever, spending your last moments in a room full of books wasn't a bad way to go.

The chasm had split the floor in here, too, although it tapered off halfway through the room. I wondered if any of the monks had thrown themselves into it at the end. I passed some time checking out the books on the floor. I blew dust from the covers and opened them, carefully flipping the brittle pages. They were mostly books of hours and other devotional texts, collections of prayers and psalms the monks had illustrated for wealthy patrons. The others were the usual sort of thing you'd find in buried, forgotten monasteries: inspirational tales of noble pilgrims resisting wine, women and wyrms; a copy of the Lost Testaments; a guide to weaving with drawings of naked, lewd women hidden away in its pages.

I set the torch into a sconce on the wall and sat at the table beside the dead monk. There were other tools of the monk's trade near his hands—some brushes, jars of dried, crumbling paint, even a little pot of gold flakes to be applied to the important illustrations in the book he'd been trying to finish. I pushed them aside to make room for my backpack and took out my last bottle of wine. I opened it and drank straight from the bottle. I offered the monk a drink, but he didn't seem interested.

I pushed him to the side a bit so I could see the book he'd been working on.

It was a leather-bound tome with yellowed, crumbling pages. The monk had been finishing a full-page colour illustration when he'd finally died. An illustration of an angel leaping upon a white whale breaching the water, a harpoon blazing with green fire in the angel's hands.

I nearly spat out my wine when I saw the illustration, for I recognized the angel. In fact, I recognized everything about the picture, for I had been there when it had happened in real life.

I closed the book so I could see the cover. The title had been roughly carved into the leather with some sort of blade, the words then filled with a mix of what looked like gold flakes from the monk's pot and blood that had long since dried.

Moby Dick by Herman Melville.

It was a book that never should have been in this monastery, since it wasn't written until centuries after I'd sealed this place off from the world. Unless someone else had been here to leave me a message.

I picked up the book and stared at it. I flipped it open and looked at the first page. The words were written in the careful, elegant script of the prayer books scattered on the floor, but this was not a devotional or inspirational text.

Call me Ishmael, the first line read.

I snapped the book shut, sending a cloud of dust out from the pages. I didn't want to read any more. That was when I heard the giggle from behind me. I turned and found Alice had joined me in the scriptorium.

She was playing with the other dead monks like they were dolls. They'd been moved since I'd sat down at the table. Now they were sitting in a circle on the floor, tea cups in their dead hands. Alice was in the middle of them on a rug made of caterpillars that wriggled like they were very much still alive. The rug stretched over the chasm. Alice was holding a teapot that she used to fill the cups. The teapot was full of dead bugs and rotten fruit and other such delights. She poured some into the cup of the monk in front of her and then pulled on a wire that hung in the air to one side and disappeared into the shadows overhead. Another wire hung down across from her, ending in a fish hook that dug into the monk's arm. When Alice pulled her wire, the monk's arm lifted, bringing the tea cup to his face, its contents spilling into his open mouth and down his robes. Alice giggled again. I saw now that all the monks had wires hooked into their limbs. None of this had been there seconds earlier. That was Alice for you.

Alice always appears in strange ways. Here's how it generally works: you read books in a library. When you find the right one, which usually has been mis-shelved somewhere, Alice will appear. You'll turn around and she'll just be there, watching you while knitting a scarf of cobwebs with bone needles. Or maybe she'll crawl out from behind the stacks of books you've been searching, where she was lying on the shelf like it was a coffin. Or maybe she'll fall from the ceiling, laughing, and you'll look up just in time to see something long and dark scuttle off into the shadows. That's the general scheme of things, but not always.

Case in point—I'd gone through the books on the floor like I was skimming books at a library, and the *Moby Dick* book was certainly mis-shelved, in more ways than one. I'd summoned Alice without even trying.

"Would you like some tea?" Alice asked. "I just made it. I think I just made it, anyway. Sometimes I lose track of time and find myself in the wrong century. Which is terribly confusing if I run into my past self there. What if we forget which one of us is supposed to be in which time?"

I hung on to the copy of *Moby Dick* when I went over to her, stopping at the edge of the chasm. "I've got my own drink, thanks," I said, holding up the wine bottle in my other hand. "And that's why I try to stick to my own time."

"Are you stuck in it like a big pot of glue?" she asked. "Or more like a spider web?"

I didn't want to even think about how to answer that, so I changed the subject. "How's the Scholar?" I asked. I hadn't seen the eccentric, immortal Scholar since that ghost Hamlet business, when he had gone off with Alice after we'd escaped the Forgotten Library. The two usually hated each other, as they had very different views of books. Alice saw each one as its own world to be explored. The Scholar saw them only as his next meal, to be consumed in order to keep him immortal. They'd been on the path to making up the last time I'd seen them, though, courtesy of a very special book.

Alice made a face and all the monks threw their arms up in the air.

"I'm not talking to him anymore," she said. "He made up the most ridiculous stories about a library friend of mine."

So much for that.

"I probably don't want to know," I said.

"The library can't get mad at him because it's a library," Alice said. "It doesn't know how to get mad. So I got mad at him for it."

"I guess that's fair," I said. I didn't really know the protocol for something like that.

"What if the libraries went around saying mean things about scholars?" Alice said. "He wouldn't like that, would he?"

"Can't say as I'd blame them, given the things he's done in libraries over the years," I said.

"You're a fine one to talk after what you did to this place," she muttered, looking around.

"It wasn't exactly all me," I protested. I wasn't surprised she knew about what had happened here. Alice knew about a lot of things when books were involved.

Alice pulled on the wires and all the dead monks turned their heads to look at me. "You didn't have to destroy the entire monastery and trap everyone in it," she said. The monks all nodded in unison, which I admit was rather unnerving.

"The angel started it," I said, then shook my head. "Look, that's all beside the point. I want to know what this is." I held up *Moby Dick*.

"It's a book, of course," Alice said. "What else would you find in a scriptorium? Besides dead monks, I mean."

"I know it's a book," I said. "I want to know why it's here, when it hadn't even been written the last time I'd visited this place."

"I left it for you so you would find it," Alice said. "But you don't seem very grateful." She folded her arms and the monks shook their heads at me.

"Why would you want me to find it?" I asked.

She sighed like I was a child who didn't understand anything. "How was I supposed to know you were looking for me if the right book wasn't here? I left you the book so you'd find it and call me, and that way I'd know you were looking for me. And now here I am. See? It all worked out." She clapped her hands and laughed.

I held my tongue because this was just Alice being Alice.

"All right, I think I understand that," I said. "But why *Moby Dick*?" I wasn't sure if she knew my history with Melville—or even Ishmael—but she could have chosen any book in the world, so it had to mean something she'd chosen this one.

"That's a good question," Alice said, nodding her head thoughtfully. She poured herself a cup of her strange tea and drank it down before answering. "You'll have to ask the book."

"Ask the book," I repeated. I stared down at it. I hoped it wasn't another one of those books that was alive in its own way.

"Books are always trying to tell you something," Alice said. "That's why they're books. This one is about a big fish. So maybe it's trying to tell you what to do next."

"And what might that be?" I asked. The book wasn't showing any signs of trying to tell me anything.

"Go fishing, of course," Alice said. She made a motion like she was casting, and the monks all drank from their tea cups together. Bugs fell from the corners of their mouths. "Who knows what you could catch with a book like that," Alice went on. "Maybe an adventure. Maybe a pirate. Maybe even the end of the world. Why, I'm certain no one has ever used that book to go fishing before."

I opened the book and shook it, hoping some overlooked clue would fall to the floor.

"Not like that," Alice said. "Use this." She pulled a hook from one of the monks' arms and the line fell from the ceiling. She coiled it up and handed it to me.

"I've never used a book to go fishing before," I said. I didn't know what to do with the hook and line, so I just held them along with the copy of *Moby Dick*.

"You can use books for anything, Cross," Alice said. She leaned closer and glanced around, as if someone other than the dead monks might be listening. "But you have to be careful, because sometimes they can use you," she whispered.

"And what if I can't catch anything with the book?"

"Then it must be the other kind of book," Alice said. "It's a book where everyone drowns. So maybe it's trying to tell you everyone is going to drown. But I hope not. I don't like the books where everyone drowns."

"And what would I do with a drowning book?" I asked, which I thought was a fair question.

"I don't know," Alice said. "I've never drowned anyone with a book." Then her eyes suddenly widened, and flames burned in her pupils. "Ohhh, you should ask a pirate!" she exclaimed. "They drown people all the time. Like Blackbeard." She clapped her hands together, and the monks all clapped, too, except for the one she'd taken the hook and line from. "Yes, let's go find Blackbeard and ask him!" she said.

"I never want to see Blackbeard again," I said. "In any of my lives. Not after what happened last time."

But the monks kept clapping. Then the one who wasn't clapping slumped forward. When his face hit the rug of caterpillars, the bugs all gave way before him, revealing the chasm beneath them. The caterpillars fell into it as the rug collapsed, and so did the dead monk. And Alice. I lunged after her, but my fingers closed on air. I looked down at her as she fell, but she didn't appear concerned. She was still sitting cross-legged, only in the air now, pouring bugs into the falling monk's cup.

"We all fall down," she sang, and then she disappeared into the darkness, along with the monk and the caterpillars.

I stared down into the chasm, waiting to see if she would come back. She didn't. But I knew I'd see her again. This was Alice, after all.

The other monks still hung there, suspended over the chasm on those hooks and lines that disappeared into the nothingness overhead. They spun slowly in the air, one after another turning their dead gazes on me.

I put the copy of *Moby Dick* in my pack, along with the line and hook from the fallen monk. They had to be important, even if I didn't know how. There was still too much here I didn't understand. But that was nothing new.

I left the rest of the wine for the dead monks, who continued to spin on their lines, forgotten puppets that they were. I wasn't sure which of us needed the wine more, but I could always make my own. Besides, I owed them.

I went out of the buried monastery and back into the world, which had managed to continue on without me. But who knew how long that would last?

☦

A MONSTER TAKES THE BAIT

After I left the monastery, I walked the rest of the way to the Spanish coast. I didn't return to the Camino route. Given what Alice had done with the dead monks, I didn't feel right travelling alongside pilgrims of any kind. Instead, I took one back road after another, sometimes using walking trails to cut across the land. At one point, a man in a rusting truck stopped to offer me a ride, but I waved him off with a friendly smile. I had a feeling that whatever the book in my backpack meant, it was bad news. I didn't want to involve anyone else in my troubles if I could help it.

Famous last words.

I reached the ocean at dusk. I sat on a beach where a few ancient fishermen were cleaning their rowboats. One of them stretched out a net on the rocks and swore at a long tear that slashed through the middle of it. He gathered up the net and tossed it back in his boat to be repaired another day. None of the fishermen looked at me twice. I knew what they would have seen if they had glanced my way: just another tourist wasting away the sunlight hours. Someone who could afford a day off, unlike most of the fishermen I'd known over the ages. That suited me fine. I watched the sky darken, until the fishermen left the beach one after another, wandering in the direction of the nearby village.

The one with the torn net was the last to go. He didn't look at me, but I nodded at him as he shuffled past.

"I hope that net just got caught on something," I said. "I'd hate to see a fish that could saw a hole that big in it."

I didn't really want to stand out in anyone's memory by talking to them. But I figured it was more important to learn what I could about the ocean around here.

"There are enough wrecks down there to fill a city with the dead and the forgotten," the fisherman said, still not looking at me. "They never give up trying to drag us down to keep them company."

"We'll all join them, soon enough," I said. Some of us sooner than others.

"In the meantime, I'll toast their memory with a drink or two," he said over his shoulder. He kept on walking.

I sat there for a while longer, until the sky was the same colour as the water, and you could barely tell the two apart. Then I got to my feet and went over to the boats, selecting the one that looked the most seaworthy, which wasn't saying much. The boats looked older than the fishermen. I took a knife one of the fishermen had forgotten on the rocks, and then I pushed the boat onto the water. Security was light on beaches like this. What would anyone ever do with a stolen rowboat? I was about to find out.

I was hopeful I'd be back on the beach before dawn without the boat's owner ever noticing the theft. Hopeful, but not optimistic. This wasn't exactly a routine nighttime cruise, after all.

I rowed out until the nearby village was just a small cluster of lights in the darkness. I'm sure Melville would have had something poetic to say about them, but I've never been much of a writer. I settled for taking the hook and line out of my backpack. There seemed to be a lot more line now. Maybe it was one of those Alice things. I jammed the hook through the cover of the *Moby Dick* book, then tossed it overboard on the port side. I wasn't sure if the book would float or not, but it sank like a stone. It was a thick book and all those words were heavy ones.

I didn't exactly know what I was fishing for, so I ran the line through the oarlocks and tied it off on the starboard side. I wanted to make sure that whatever I might catch wouldn't pull me overboard. It was a long swim back to shore. I stuck the knife into the starboard side of the boat, just under the oarlock, where it would be handy. I'd learned the hard way about losing blades in the water when you really needed them.

I stared down over the edge of the boat, but the book was invisible in the depths. Maybe it was among the wrecks now. If there was anything nibbling on it, I couldn't see. I glanced around at the surrounding water. Alice's mention of Blackbeard had made me nervous. The sea was empty of anyone else, though. Not that it made a difference where Blackbeard was concerned. I looked back at the shore and breathed deep of the fresh air, trying to put thoughts of pirates out of my mind. I thought about how nice it would be to have a cigarillo, and maybe even a shot or two of rum. That was when the line snapped taut. Something had taken the bait.

I sat up and reached for the line to pull in whatever I'd caught. But my catch had other ideas. The port side of the boat suddenly dipped down, as whatever it was dove deeper. I caught on to the line and pulled, but it was like trying to pull up the ocean itself. Whatever it was, it was big or strong. Or both.

The side of the boat sank to the water level and stopped there for a few seconds. I threw my weight to the starboard side to stop the boat from flipping, still pulling on the line and trying to coax my catch back up to shallower depths. Then the water surged in and the boat tipped over despite my weight. Whatever was down there was bigger than me—and quite likely stronger than me, too.

I fell into the water and gasped at the sudden shock of cold that engulfed me. The boat sank under the waves beside me, pulled down by my catch. I shook my head at the lights in the distance, where people cheerfully went on with the lives, oblivious. Then I took a deep breath and followed the boat under the water, as it kept sinking.

Luckily, I didn't have to swim down too far. The thing that had sunk the boat rose up now to investigate its catch. I say *thing* because it definitely wasn't a fish.

A pair of long, massive tentacles came out of the darkness beneath me and grabbed on to the bow and stern of the boat. I decided it was time to head back to the beach and kicked away from there.

But another tentacle came up and wrapped itself around my waist. I flailed in the water for the knife before I remembered I'd left it in the boat. I had no weapons to defend myself.

Then the tentacle pulled me down, and I saw a big dinner plate of an eye materialize out of the murk, attached to the head of a giant squid. It pulled me toward its beak, and I saw the mangled remains of *Moby Dick* in its mouth.

Just then, one of the oars floated past. I grabbed onto it like it was a life jacket. I used some grace to give me the strength to snap the top half off, leaving me with a jagged spear of sorts. I used more grace to turn the water around my head into a halo of air, and took a quick breath before it bubbled away. When the squid drew me closer, I stabbed the sharp end of the oar into that great big target of an eye.

Sure, I was fighting dirty, but the squid had a dozen more arms than me, so I figured we were even.

The squid thrashed, jerking me in half a dozen directions in the span of a few seconds. Sometime during that its beak scored the palm of my left hand, slicing it open. Then it dove deeper and a sharp pain snapped through my head, like I'd been shot. I knew it was just the sudden change in pressure rupturing my sinuses, though—experience has taught me you don't actually feel headshots.

The squid released its grip on me and tried to grab the oar, but I kept clinging on to my makeshift weapon with my right hand like my life depended on it. And maybe it did.

I grabbed the squid's mantle with my left hand, then threw my weight against the end of the oar, using my grip on the creature for leverage. The oar sank all the way in, until I was face-to-giant-ruptured-eyeball with the squid.

What's that saying? When you stare into the abyss, the abyss also stares into you.

The squid gave me one last look, and one last thrash, and then it was still. I had done it. I had killed a giant squid in hand-to-tentacle combat. And to think there were those who said I'd never accomplish anything in life.

Not that my problems were over, of course. I was still deep in the sea, with a dead giant squid that hopefully held the answer to the latest mystery in my life. I swam down another couple dozen feet until I found the rowboat resting in the muck of the seabed. I pulled the knife out of the side of the boat and then swam back up to the squid. I dragged it up to the surface, my lungs screaming for air.

An average man wouldn't have been able to drag a dead giant squid up from the depths of the ocean, let alone kill it in the first place. But I've never been an average man, not since the moment I woke in that cave all those ages ago to find myself in Christ's body with no memory of how I'd wound up there. I don't really know what I am. No one does. Maybe not even God, wherever he's hiding out these days. Not that I could blame Him for making Himself scarce. The world's a mess and getting worse by the minute.

Once I was at the surface and had caught my breath again, I let the body of the squid float beside me while I checked the wound on my hand. It was a minor cut, the sort of thing that would heal on its own in a few days. I didn't like bleeding into the water the way I was, but I figured the presence of the squid, dead or alive, would keep the predators at bay long enough for me to make a peaceful exit from the area. I took another moment to reacquaint myself with the surface world. The moon still hung in the sky, the lights of Spain still burned in the distance. I had a little less grace now, but I still had enough to get by. It was like my battle with the squid had just been a dream—except for the fact that it was floating there beside me.

I swam around the squid, inspecting it to see what made it so special. It looked like just any other dead giant squid, nothing but tentacles and rubbery skin and big dull eyes, one with a broken oar sticking out of it. But that was all.

I shook my head at the stars overhead. There was only one place left to look. I pulled myself close to the squid's side and began cutting with the knife. It wasn't the most unpleasant thing I'd done in all my many lives, but it ranked up there.

I found the prize hidden inside the squid's stomach. It was a man's head. The head was perfectly preserved and didn't look at all digested. That was strange, granted, but it wasn't the strangest thing about all this. The strangest thing was that I recognized him.

He had a short beard and a scar down his left cheek. I've met many men with short beards and scars on their cheeks in my time, so that wasn't enough to make him stand out. What really did it was the fact that he opened his eyes and spoke.

"Have you finally returned to deliver me?" he asked. "Or have you come to damn me further?"

I placed the head on the body of the squid and stared at him as I floated there, treading water.

"Antonio," I said. "I didn't expect to see you again."

"Does the devil never return to torment his victims?" he asked.

"Maybe I earned that," I said. "But let me try to explain."

"Save your breath," he said, "for you will soon need all of it."

"I don't think I like the way this is going," I said.

"I have a message for you from Noah."

"Noah," I said. No, I definitely didn't like the way this was going.

"Noah says a great flood is coming," Antonio said. "It will drown the world and all the abominations along with it. Even you."

"That thing with Noah was a long time ago," I said. "Maybe he's over it by now."

"There will be no ark to save you," Antonio said. "There will only be the endless waves that carry you away to the void itself."

"And where is Noah now?" I asked. I scanned the surrounding sea, as if his ark might cut the horizon this very moment.

Antonio laughed and water came out of his mouth.

"He does not seek you anymore," Antonio bubbled. "He seeks the end of the world. And you know as well as I do that nothing can stop Noah."

He laughed some more, but it was the laughter of the mad. I couldn't really blame him for that.

It seemed Alice was right when she'd said maybe the book was a drowning kind of book.

I gazed up at the stars overhead again, which continued to burn themselves out with complete indifference to the affairs of our world.

Noah.

Damn it.

Why did it have to be Noah?

A MOST DAMNABLE VISITATION

I should probably explain how things got to this point, and where the bible comes in.

Let me start at the actual beginning of this tale then.

I was on the run from a pack of demons the first time I sought refuge in the monastery. This was several hundred years ago. The 12th, or maybe the 13th, century. When you've lived as many lives as I have, you lose track of time after a while. The demons were chasing me through the Spanish countryside in the bodies of some nobles they'd possessed. They were accompanied with hunting dogs and armed servants and the usual retinue. I'm sure it was great sport.

I had only myself to blame for my plight. I'd gone after one of the demons in a tavern when I'd seen him hiding there in that fat nobleman's body. I was sure he was the same demon who had once possessed a Viking chief a few centuries earlier, a man who had caused me a great deal of grief when I'd snuck into a different monastery in a different land to search for holy relics I could steal. The Vikings had sailed in and attacked the place almost immediately, slaughtering every monk. It was like they'd been waiting for me. Maybe they had. I barely escaped with my life, if not all my blood, and the Vikings got away with the relics. Who knew what they did with them? Whatever it was, I'm sure the demon had been laughing the whole time, just as he'd laughed when his men had cornered me in the secret tombs underneath the monastery. The warriors had all been looking at me, so I'd been the only one to see the fly buzz out of his open mouth when he laughed. He'd caught it and ripped the wings off it, then popped it back in his mouth before he ordered his men to attack.

I'd recognized him in that nobleman's body centuries later, when we'd wound up in the same tavern. I was sitting in a corner and the nobles and their followers took up the rest of the room. A couple of the men were arguing about some woman and the noble encouraged them to fight right there and then. So they did, rolling about on the tables and even falling into the fire pit at one point. The noble laughed the same booming laugh as the Viking chief, and when he did a fly flew out of his mouth. He caught it, ripped the wings off and popped it back before anyone else noticed. But I'd seen it. And I knew.

So I'd gone up to the room he'd rented to wait. Things went pretty much according to plan until he managed to cry out for help as I was cutting his throat. He used a tongue I didn't know, uttering words the human mouth shouldn't have been capable of forming. The other nobles came running, calling out to him in that same tongue. That was when I knew they were all demons. I'd never seen demons in a pack before. And so there I was, riding through the rainy night on a stolen horse with a dozen demons on my tail.

Eventually I realized I wasn't going to get away from them, so I started looking for a place to hide. I used some heavenly grace to sharpen my senses, and I heard some monks praying in a monastery carved out of a nearby mountain. I jumped off the horse and cast a sleight to make it appear like I was still riding it. The horse with the illusion went one way, and I went the other. I ran across some fields and up the mountain slope, until I came to the monastery.

To call it a monastery is probably a bit generous. It was more a cave network the monks had found and expanded. They'd added a few wooden beams for support, and torches and rugs to increase the cozy factor, but that did little to hide the fact they were living in caves. Monks were always living in strange places in those times, though, so that was nothing new.

There was no guard posted at the entrance, perhaps because it was hidden behind some rocks, or perhaps because they simply never had visitors. Either way, I let myself in. I paused to listen to the demons ride past, in pursuit of my sleight. Then I went deeper into the mountain.

I encountered the first monk in what appeared to be a cloak room. There were robes hanging on pegs jammed into cracks in the walls and muddy sandals lying underfoot. The monk was going through the pockets of the clothing in the room and looked surprised to see me, which meant he was probably looking for something to steal. Given his gaunt features, I suspected he was hoping to find a forgotten crust of bread or strip of jerky.

"I seek refuge for the night," I told him, pretending not to notice his petty theft. "There are demons about."

He nodded like he heard that every night and took me down another tunnel, to a dining hall. There were a dozen or so men with shaved heads wearing threadbare robes in here, slurping up bowls of a thin stew with crude wooden spoons. If they had taken a vow of poverty, they were clearly serious about it. They all stared at me until the monk who accompanied me said I was a weary traveller and repeated my bit about the demons. One of them brought me a bowl of the stew and a hunk of moldy bread, while another poured me a cup of water from a pitcher on the table. They returned to their meals, only casting me sidelong glances every now and then. The monk who'd introduced me went back the way we'd come, no doubt to continue his search for things to steal. I doubted he'd find anything. It looked like the sort of place where everything worth stealing had likely already been stolen, probably more than once.

I ate the stew, which wasn't half bad, and even the bread, which was all bad. I looked around and saw a few other tunnels leading away from the dining hall. I could see a room holding shelves lined with books down one, and a few sleeping mats on the floor of another. The library and the sleeping quarters. I sipped the water, but it was flat and dull and not at all what I wanted after the night I'd had. I asked if there was a prayer room and the monk who'd given me the stew pointed to another tunnel that led into the darkness. I went that way, taking the cup of water with me.

I found a small chapel, which was little more than a chamber with a prayer bench and a couple of regular benches. A plain wooden cross hung on the wall, which suggested the monks were the normal kind of monks, at least. Normal for that time, anyway. A thick, leather-bound book sat on a wooden lectern, and I took it to be a standard bible. Before you get excited, though, this is not the bible I mentioned earlier. That particular book has yet to make an appearance in this tale.

I sat on one of the benches and leaned against the cave wall with a sigh. It had been a long night. I used a bit of grace to turn the water into wine and all was right with the world once more.

Of course, that never lasts.

"My lord, is that you?" someone whispered from the shadows of the hallway.

"That depends on who's asking," I said. "Are you a demon?"

"No, my lord, it is Ishmael." He stepped into the chapel, and I saw he was the one who had poured me the cup of water in the dining hall. He was a gaunt young man—too young to be throwing away his life with this monk nonsense.

If I had known then what he would become, I would have run off into the night, demons or not. Hell, it would've been better to be torn apart by wild dogs than keep talking to Ishmael. But you never know who the players are going to be in a tale until it is told.

Ishmael hesitated in the entrance as he looked at me. He glanced down at the cup and sniffed the air, and I could tell he'd caught the smell of the wine. I wondered how long it had been since he'd had a drink. I offered him the cup.

"There's enough spirits to go around if that's what you're here for," I said.

"No, my lord," Ishmael said. "That is not why I sought you out. I mean, I knew it was you when I witnessed you transform the water. It was your signal, was it not?"

I sipped the cup and looked at him. I didn't have a clue what he was talking about, but I've found it's best never to let on. Also, I was curious. I wanted to find out who he thought I was.

"Well, that would depend on whether or not you know my name," I said.

Ishmael grinned, revealing a mouth of broken teeth. "A test, my lord. I understand completely," he said. That made one of us. "You are the great Sariel, keeper of the lost knowledge, guardian of the word, protector of the pages—"

"All right, close enough," I said. I took a bigger swallow of the wine now. I knew Sariel, or rather I knew the name. The monk was expecting an angel and thought I was it. It wasn't the first time I'd been mistaken for one, and it wouldn't be the last. The real question was what it meant.

"Another lost text has been delivered to you by your agents," Ishmael said. He reached into his robes and brought out a scroll. It looked to be made of hide, bound with a ribbon of what appeared to be hair. There were claw marks in the hide, but it was otherwise unadorned.

"It is one of the lost dialogues between Socrates and the dead gods," Ishmael said. "I believe it will make a most welcome addition for the library in Alexandria."

He offered it to me and I took it, because I hadn't yet learned to be careful with mystery texts.

"Yes, the library in Alexandria," I said. "Quite the place." I had no idea what he was talking about, so I wanted him to keep going.

"The foundation for a new Heaven, to be built on Earth," Ishmael said, nodding so hard I thought he was going to knock himself out. "I dream of one day visiting it myself to witness all the sacred texts and bow before the other angels."

This library sounded interesting indeed. I was always hunting angels for their heavenly grace, which my body needed like a fire needed kindling, but they'd made themselves scarce of late. Perhaps that was because they were hiding out in this library of Alexandria.

"You will never see such a place," a new voice said. "You will never witness Heaven on Earth because you are as much a fool as every other mortal man."

Ishmael and I both turned to look at the newcomer who strode into the room. He wore the dirty clothes of a traveller, but he was filthier than most. He was covered in mud and his face and long hair were wet from the rain. He leaned on a walking staff, like he was weary from his travels. Maybe he was. But there was a smear of blood on his cheek, so maybe he was tired for other reasons.

"I was delayed in my journey here," the man said, looking at me and not Ishmael. "I encountered a pack of demons chasing a ghost."

I smiled and offered him the cup, but he stopped several feet away from me and made no move to take it.

"I'd sooner drink your blood than share your spirits," he said.

"Sariel," I said. "I don't think we've had the pleasure." I knew he was the angel Ishmael had mentioned. I could practically see the grace emanating from him. He was so full of it that his skin nearly shone.

Ishmael's jaw dropped and he fell to his knees.

"My lord," he gasped to Sariel. "I. . . ." But he didn't know what else to say. I couldn't blame him. He'd made a big mistake, and the angels had never been the forgiving type. Ishmael looked at me. "He is. . . ." But he didn't know what to say about that either. Most people didn't.

"He is the devil," Sariel said. That wasn't entirely accurate, but it was close enough that I didn't bother to correct him. "And you have told him where to find Heaven," Sariel added. "Or at least all we have left of it."

Ishmael turned pale as he stared at me. I shrugged at him. "Sorry about that," I said. "You really should give up this monk lifestyle anyway. It's not healthy."

Then Sariel smashed his staff into the ground and the floor of the chapel split open in a great chasm. I had to throw myself back against the wall bearing the cross to stop from falling in. Ishmael dropped into it but managed to catch the side with his hands. He hung there, wailing pitifully. Sariel simply floated in the air above the chasm, like he was still standing on stone. His robes caught fire and burned away in seconds, revealing his naked body underneath. Then his body flamed for an instant, too, blazing with white fire. When it faded away, Sariel was no longer a man. Now the angel was a woman, with shimmering white wings made of mist spreading behind her. I knew female angels existed, of course, but I had never seen one before until now. It was a shame I was going to have to kill her.

"My lord Sariel!" Ishmael cried from the pit. "I beg your forgiveness!" Then he stared up at the angel in shock as he took in her heavenly form.

"You see, this is what happens when you consort with angels,"

I told him. I finished my drink and tossed the cup into the chasm.

"I am no longer your lord," Sariel told Ishmael. "You are as damned as this corrupt soul is now." I figured she meant me even though she was still looking at the monk. There was no one else in the room, after all.

"Don't worry," I told Ishmael. "You'll have more fun with me." I reached a hand to him, to pull him out of the pit.

Before I could save him, Sariel brought her staff down again, this time on Ishmael's fingers. "I curse you for your sins!" she cried. "I cast you out and into the void, where you shall never know rest again!"

Ishmael fell screaming into the chasm. I lunged after him, but then Sariel swung her staff at me, and I had to jump back. It was more of a warding motion on her part than an attack, so maybe I still could have saved Ishmael. But I wasn't the kind soul back then that I am now. I wasn't going to risk my life for some monk I didn't know. And I had other things on my mind. Like all that grace calling to me from inside Sariel.

"You will join him in the abyss soon enough," Sariel said. "Once I am done with you. And may God withhold mercy from both your souls."

I didn't see any point to further conversation, so I got on with it. I ripped the ribbon off the scroll Ishmael had given me and unrolled it. I figured it must have been something of power if Sariel was here in person to pick it up. But the angel quickly moved her hand in a complex pattern through the air, and the scroll burst into flame. I dropped it into the chasm, where it dwindled into a spark before vanishing entirely. Ishmael was still screaming down there somewhere, so it was definitely a deep pit, if not bottomless.

"That was careless," I said. "Do you know what you just destroyed?" I didn't know what the scroll was, but I was hoping Sariel would give me some clue.

"Better to destroy it than to let it fall into your hands," Sariel said, which told me nothing useful at all. "I have heard how you taint everything you encounter, be it divine or mortal."

"Well, I can't argue that," I admitted.

She raised the staff again, so I ripped the cross from the wall and hit her in the face with it. She staggered back, although she looked more outraged than injured. She caught onto the cross and held it with one hand before I could hit her again.

"Must your every action in the world be a blasphemy?" she asked.

"I am how God made me," I said, and then I sent some grace down into the cross and set it alight. Sariel didn't seem to notice, so maybe it wasn't the first time she'd held a flaming cross. But I wasn't done yet. I breathed out more grace, and the flames from the cross flared up into her face. She coughed and staggered back, and I let her take the cross. My move hadn't been so much an attack as a diversion. I needed to find a real weapon if I was to have any hope of defeating her. Even I couldn't kill an angel with my bare hands most days.

I jumped over the chasm and ran down the tunnel, back into the dining hall. The monks were on their feet and clustered around the tunnel entrance, knives in their hands. They were no doubt wondering about the noise and commotion, but were too afraid to venture into the chapel to find out what was going on. They were about to learn the truth of God's mysteries. I threw myself into them and we collapsed in a great pile. When I rose up from the ground, I cast a sleight so I looked like one of them.

The burning cross hurtled out of the tunnel and into our midst, sending a couple of monks careening into the walls. The cross was quickly followed by Sariel, who charged out of the tunnel and into the dining hall. She stopped when she saw what I had done, her eyes flitting from monk to monk as she searched for me. Then she smashed her staff into the floor again and a new chasm opened up. She certainly liked that trick.

The monks fell screaming into the pit, but I hung in the air over it, much like Sariel did. It didn't cost me much grace, which was good, as I didn't have much to spare. And I had to save it all for my next move.

"I'll cast you down one way or another, you know," Sariel said, floating toward me, her wings twisting in the air behind her. "I'm not like the other angels you've met."

"I'm just a simple monk," I said, gesturing at the sleight that covered me. "Why are you so afraid?"

"I fear you less than I fear the lowest mortals," she said.

"Your mistake," I said. I used my grace to reach down and

catch the monks as they fell. I pulled them back out of the pit and threw them at Sariel, a storm of shrieking, flailing bodies. I threw in some of the knives and plates and other utensils from the tables for good measure.

She knocked the monks aside, smashing them into the walls and throwing them back down into the pit. The ones that got through, I spun them in a whirlwind around her. I used my grace to take control of their arms and slash Sariel's face and body with the knives they held. She didn't seem to care.

"I will end the world if I must to destroy you once and for all!" Sariel cried. She clapped her hands together, and the sound was like thunder in the hall. The ceiling caved in then, the mountain collapsing on us. The monks cried out again as great rocks fell from overhead and struck them, knocking them back into the pit. They hit Sariel too, staggering her, which was all the distraction I needed.

I had thrown myself into the maelstrom of monks, and now I latched on to Sariel's back as the others fell into the pit. I had found a knife in the chaos and I plunged it deep into Sariel's neck. The grace spilled out like blood flowing into the air, and I breathed it in, replenishing myself.

"I'll take you to Hell myself, then!" Sariel screamed and threw herself into the chasm, following the monks into the darkness.

I leapt off her back and grabbed on to a torch sconce on the wall as she fell, and then I dropped down to stand on the bit of floor remaining. I waited at the edge of the chasm, knife at the ready. Sariel didn't come back up. I looked into the pit and saw nothing at all. Sariel and the monks were gone.

Then the rest of the ceiling collapsed, and it took all the grace I had left just to keep the rocks from crushing me. I knocked them aside, and I managed to keep a tunnel open to the exit. After a time, the mountain settled down and the rocks stopped falling. I took one last look around and saw the tunnels to the other rooms of the monastery had caved in, too. If there were any monks left in the place, they were trapped. I couldn't save them, but I could still save myself.

I went around the edge of the pit, then climbed through the rubble and left the monastery.

The sun was rising in the distance, and the sky was a beautiful gold. The birds were singing and the air smelled fresh. It was the sort of day where anything seemed possible. It was enough to make you believe in Heaven if you didn't know any better.

I pushed a large boulder in front of the entrance to the mountain so no one else would ever find it. You never know when you might need a secret hiding place. Then I went down the slope and headed toward the sea, to Alexandria.

✢

A SECRET LIBRARY FOUND

I found my way to Alexandria because of Ishmael's words. I wanted to see the foundation for the new Heaven on Earth myself. I wanted to see if there were any more angels in the library he'd mentioned. The problem was I didn't know how to find it. The angels have never liked to share Heaven with the mortals.

I had heard the legends of a great library destroyed in Alexandria, of course. But places like that burn all the time, and I suspected it was not the same one Ishmael had spoken of. The scroll that he'd given me back in the monastery suggested there was still some sort of special library in Alexandria and that was all that mattered.

I came to Alexandria through the desert, drawn by the city's great lighthouse on the horizon. One of the mortal wonders of the world at that time, it rose toward the sky and was crowned with a flame that never went out. The beacon was only partially meant as a warning to ships—it was also a sign of Alexandria's growing might in the world. In that way it was much like the pyramids and the Tower of Babel and all the other monuments that inevitably crumble into dust.

I arrived as dusk was falling. I wore the robes of a desert traveller, which disguised my face from any who might recognize me and report my arrival to the local officials or angels. I made my way to a market square near the water and bought tea and sweets from a vendor. I sat on a worn rug on the ground and let the weight of my travels fall off me. I turned to the cool wind coming off the ocean. There was a storm out there somewhere, but it had not fallen upon land yet.

I sipped my tea and gazed upon the buildings of Alexandria. I wondered where I would hide a secret library if I were an angel. In one of the port's many warehouses, where no one would notice unusual comings and goings? In a home in a residential district, where the angel would know his neighbours and any strangers would be noticed instantly? In a temple dedicated to whatever god was in fashion in these parts at the moment?

My gaze strayed back to the lighthouse as I sat there, and I had my answer. Where better to hide a secret library than in plain sight?

I finished my tea and sweets and left the market, going out into the night. I wandered around the streets for a bit, keeping an eye for signs of anyone following or even watching me. But all I saw were other lonely wayfarers like myself.

Eventually I found myself crossing the spit of land to the island that was home to the great lighthouse. The land bridge was made of rocks and who knew how many human lives, for it had been built up out of the sea by mortals. It was guarded by them as well, with a barracks and gate at the land side. But a simple sleight made me appear like a soldier returning after a night out on the town, and no one bothered to stop me.

So it was I reached the lighthouse and stopped at its foot to behold it for a moment. It stretched four hundred feet or so up into the sky. It was made of three sections: a broad square base of limestone blocks, topped by an octagonal midsection, followed by a cylindrical spire. The great bonfire that always burned crowned the spire, seemingly closer to the sky than the ground, like a second sun. I imagined the different shapes of the lighthouse had some significance, but I had no idea what that might be. I also had no interest in learning. I tried to avoid getting drawn into local customs whenever possible. It was like consorting with the faerie: no good ever came of it.

There was another barracks around the base of the lighthouse, and I knew I would have trouble bluffing my way past the soldiers inside. A sleight that made me look like one of them was enough to get me through a gate, but it likely wouldn't be enough to get me through an entire base full of soldiers who didn't recognize me. I would have to find another way.

So I scaled the lighthouse itself.

It was a simple ascent: there were enough handholds and cracks in the building blocks that I didn't even need to use any grace. I reached the top in less time than it would take your average soldier to down a wineskin. And if any of those soldiers below noticed me, they must have passed it off to the wine, because no one shouted any challenges as I climbed.

I paused a few times to catch my breath and take in the view. On one side, the city was a dark pattern of squares and rectangles, lit up here and there by cooking fires and torches. It fell away to the desert in the distance, a nothingness at the edge of order. When I looked out to sea, I saw only deeper darkness, with an occasional flash of lightning from a storm far out on the horizon. I thought this view must be how the angels saw the world all the time.

I reached the top of the lighthouse, and the heat from the great fire made it feel like I was climbing under the noon sun. I pulled myself up and over the edge of the wall, into the chamber where the signal fire burned. And that was when I knew my hunch about the lighthouse had been correct.

The fire was the size of several funeral pyres. It burned a great stack of wood that towered above my head. A stone walkway circled the blaze, but the flames made the area too hot for any mortal to stand that close. The other creature on the walkway wasn't having any difficulties, though.

It had the body and arms of a man but the legs of a lion. Giant hawk's wings were folded across its back to match the hawk's head atop its shoulders. The hands ended in great talons.

A sphinx. I muttered a curse and shook my head. I hated sphinxes.

It snapped its head toward me as I dropped down onto the walkway. I had to use a bit of grace to harden my skin against the heat. Hopefully I'd be replenishing that grace soon enough.

"Let me guess," I said. "I can pass if I first answer a riddle."

The sphinx stalked toward me like a lion cornering its prey, which I suppose it couldn't help given its nature. I dipped my hand into my robes and pulled out a knife I'd picked up in my travels. I didn't bother trying to conceal the move. I knew those hawk's eyes would notice everything I did. The sphinx stopped just outside the reach of my blade. It spread its wings wide and curled them around me on either side, like a cat boxing in a mouse with its paws.

"What word is a word at the beginning of time, the world in time and—" the sphinx said, but I didn't let it finish.

"Oh, shut up," I said and lashed out with the knife. I didn't target the sphinx's body or even its head, though. Instead, I cut at the wing closest to me.

The sphinx tried to snap the wing back, and it almost succeeded. It was faster than any mortal creature—but so was I. My blade sliced through the wing, and the sphinx let out a shrill shriek. I didn't know if it was a cry of anger or of pain. I didn't give it enough time to make it clear to me. I leapt back along the walkway even as the sphinx pounced. I blew a great mouthful of grace out at the sphinx and then I thrust my hand toward the sea. A gust of wind came from nowhere and lifted the sphinx away from me, throwing it out into the ocean. It disappeared into the darkness, far enough away that I couldn't see where it fell.

"I've never much cared for riddles," I said to no one in particular, because there was no one left to hear.

I knew the fall wouldn't kill the sphinx, and I also knew that it would come back to the lighthouse. But I'd done enough damage to its wing that it wouldn't be flying back. It would have to swim, and that would take time. Enough time, hopefully, that I'd be able to find what I had come for and leave.

Now I just had to find the entrance to the library. I had a pretty good idea of where it was. I'd learned to think like an angel over the ages.

I strode into the fire, using more grace to keep the flames from burning me. I kicked aside the blazing logs, until I found what I was looking for. A stone trap door hidden underneath the fire. I pulled it open to reveal a spiral staircase underneath. I went down the stairs, leaving the door open behind me. I figured the flames still burning around the stairs would be enough to keep anyone else out. And if a sphinx guard was any indication of what the library might contain, I might need to make a hasty exit.

The stairs were made of bone, of course. If you're going to

build the entrance to a secret library inside a giant fire atop one of the marvels of the world, then bone is a natural choice. I wasn't sure what the bones were from, and I decided not to worry about it for the moment. I had other things to think about.

Like the fact that the stairs went down into a vast chamber that spread out around me for as far as the eye could see in all directions. The library walls, ceiling and floor were made of stone, but the rows of shelves that seemed to go on forever were made of more bone. The shelves were covered in every kind of text imaginable: piles of scrolls, stacks of bound books, sheets of wood with inscriptions, even stones with words carved into them. There were tables with more of the same scattered here and there. There was no obvious source of light, but the room was lit up well enough that I could see anyway.

The room was an impossibility of sorts, for I saw right away that it was too large to fit within the confines of the lighthouse. But now was not the time to give thought about how it had come to be. Now was the time to pay attention to the angel who sat at a table near the bottom of the stairs, watching me descend. Sariel. She wore white robes and had the same glowing skin and misty wings as back in the monastery. I looked around but didn't see Ishmael or any of the other monks. So maybe the chasm had led here and maybe it had led somewhere else. The table was a mess of books and scrolls, which I kept an eye on. Sariel seemed to be waiting for me, as if she expected my arrival, so who knew what she had done to prepare?

I didn't hurry as I descended the stairs and stepped onto the stone floor of the library. Sariel would either fight or flee. If she fought, the odds were I would take her, because I usually did manage to beat the angels. Not always, but usually. If she fled, the room couldn't go on forever. That's what I told myself anyway.

"I wasn't sure if I was going to see you again," I said. "I thought maybe you had left this mortal realm for good when you fell into that chasm."

"I yearn for the day when I may finally rest," Sariel said as I approached, her gaze fixed on me. "But I suspect that day is far off while abominations like you still walk the earth."

"You're probably right," I said. "I don't think any of us are getting out of here any time soon." I looked around as I walked up to the table. "This is quite the library you've built up here. You and your friends have been some industrious angels."

"We are not the only ones who work to grow the library," Sariel said. "There are those among the mortals who would salvage the world. You should seek them out sometime." She stood but didn't move away from the table. That could be a good thing or a bad thing. Either she was resigned to her fate, or she had something up her sleeve. "Perhaps even you could seek redemption," she added, "unimaginable as that might seem."

I stopped on the other side of the table from her and looked up and down the row we were in. "I'd heard the great library of Alexandria had been destroyed. I'd heard that a few times, actually. But I guess you just found a way to hide it."

"There were other libraries," Sariel said. "And they were destroyed. For whatever reasons, most mortals can't seem to abide even the thought of bettering themselves."

"It's a lot of work to better yourself," I said. "It's much easier to lose yourself in wine."

"Those other libraries were just decoys," Sariel went on, as if I hadn't spoken. "The texts lost in them were inconsequential in the greater order of things. They burned so these texts could remain hidden." She looked a little sad at the idea of those lost texts. Angels. They could cheerfully slaughter thousands of innocents, but burn a few books and suddenly they get all misty-eyed.

"Not that hidden if I could find my way in here," I said.

"I was hoping you wouldn't but feared you would," Sariel said, looking past me and up the stairs. "Ishmael deserved the curse I delivered upon him for revealing the existence of this place to you."

"To be fair, he didn't tell me how to find it," I said. "I did that part on my own."

"And how did you manage that?" Sariel asked. I knew she was fishing for information, trying to understand me to get an edge. I couldn't help but tell her, though. I was rather proud of myself.

"Once I made my way to Alexandria, I just thought like one of you," I said. "I looked for the biggest symbol I could find, because I know you can't help yourselves. You're like moths to a flame.

And the lighthouse seemed a perfect symbol for angels—both a beacon and a warning at the same time."

Sariel nodded. "I will obviously have to increase the guards once I deal with you," she said. So it seemed she was choosing fight over flight. Well, that was why I was here.

"Yeah, your sphinx wasn't really up to the job," I said. "I mean, all you have to do to pass is answer a riddle?" I shook my head.

"The riddle isn't a test to let you pass," Sariel said, looking back at me now. "The riddle is a test to see how you answer. A lot can be learned about how an opponent thinks by their answer to a simple riddle."

"You can take it up with the sphinx in the afterlife," I said. "I'm a little tired of talking and I'd like to move things along now."

She nodded and her wings spread out like a mist blown by the wind.

"I will give you one last chance," she said. "I am not foolish enough to think you would join our cause. But you may yet leave with life and limbs intact. I would rather not jeopardize the texts of this library in a senseless battle."

I smiled at her. "I think you're being a touch optimistic about your odds here," I said. "It's been a long time since I lost a fight to an angel."

"Rahmiel," Sariel said. "At Pompeii. I have heard the tales."

"Maybe you also heard I hunted him down again after I resurrected," I said. Although I didn't like to think about that particular time I'd come back to life. Digging my way out of the ruins of Pompeii had been . . . difficult.

"Rahmiel did not have the great library of Alexandria at his fingertips," Sariel said. And suddenly the books on the table flipped open without her touching them, and the scrolls unrolled. A couple of them even floated up off the table and hung there in the air between us.

"I have the secret texts of ten thousand priests in the library," Sariel said. "And a thousand gods. Do you really think you can overcome the powers of all of them? You, a minor mistake in the grand order of things?"

"You know, I'm a little tired of hearing about the grand order of things," I said. "And I've got my own tricks."

I likely didn't have as many tricks, though, so I settled for one that had already worked. I summoned a wind like the one I'd used against the sphinx and pulled it across the table between us. Sariel's books and scrolls flew away from her, swirling around me like water around a stone in the river, and up the stairs to the outside.

"Where have you sent them?" Sariel cried, staring after them.

"The sea," I said.

"The sea," she repeated. Her eyes lit up with a white fire.

"I sent them after the sphinx," I said, although to be honest I wasn't entirely sure where they'd landed. Somewhere in the water. Probably. "It can return them here when it finds a way back. Although you probably won't have much need for them by then."

"You fool," Sariel said. She gestured with a hand and the table between us slid to the side. "You ridiculous mortal fool. What did you do with the sphinx?"

I had been planning on leaping over the table and attacking Sariel after the wind carried away her books. Or maybe diving under the table and going for the low blow. I hadn't made up my mind yet. But I held off on either course of action. I didn't like the way Sariel was reacting. There was something going on here I didn't understand.

"I threw it in the water," I said. "But I don't really see what that has to do with us."

"And now you have thrown the sacred texts into the water after the sphinx," Sariel whispered, staring up the stairs, at something I couldn't see.

"Oh come on," I said. "If they were that important, you would have already made copies of them or committed them to memory. Losing them can't be that big of a deal."

"What matters now is not that they are lost," she said. "What matters is who finds them in the sea."

She rushed past me, not even appearing to be worried about the possibility that I might stick my knife in her back and drain the essence out of her. I guess it was a good bet on her part, because I just let her go.

"We must close the door before it is too late," she cried.

But it was already too late.

Something else came down the stairs then, through the door I had left conveniently open. Make that *three* somethings.

The first one was a Roman legionnaire. Or rather, had been a Roman legionnaire. He wore the armour of a Roman soldier and carried a short sword in his hand, but both blade and armour were rusted almost through, and he was so gaunt he looked like a corpse. The man who came right behind him was a giant dressed in furs that had mold growing on them, and long strands of seaweed hung from his head and body, which looked as wasted as the Roman's. He carried a great wooden club that looked as if it had seen some action in its day, which he raised when he saw us. The third and last one wasn't a soldier at all but a priest. He wore the surplice of a Catholic and carried no weapons. His face wasn't visible because it was hidden by the same barnacles that covered the rest of his body.

Sariel stopped at the sight of them and raised a hand in their direction. A scroll lifted off a shelf beside her and burst into green flames. The flames didn't consume the scroll, though. Instead, they seemed to rise out of it and dissipate into the air.

Sariel said something I couldn't hear. Or rather, I heard it but couldn't understand it. It was as if the words slipped through my mind and out again without me ever making sense of them. But they must have meant something, because the Roman legionnaire burst into the same green flame then. The fire erupted from his body like he was a piece of dry kindling. He screamed and fell down the rest of the stairs. He was little more than ash by the time he hit the bottom.

I decided that it was best to sort out the newcomers before Sariel and I settled our differences, so I went after the one in furs. I threw myself past Sariel and up the stairs, leaping over the remains of the Roman. I didn't want those flames to touch me and spread that green fire.

The giant swung the club straight down at my head. He moved like the type who usually let his strength do the fighting for him. I imagined that club had broken many a blade or shield in its time, as well as many arms. I didn't have a lot of room to maneuver, given the spiral nature of the staircase. So I dropped off it, catching on to one of the stairs with a hand. The club crashed down where I had been, and shards of wood and bone went flying. I used my momentum and a bit of grace to swing up behind the giant while he was still bent over from the force of his blow. I put the knife to good use in his back, and then there was one.

I turned to the priest, but he was already gone, fled back up the stairs.

"He must not escape!" Sariel cried. Books and scrolls rose up on the shelves all around us. Sariel began to chant, and again I heard but didn't parse the words. I had the feeling of something moving past me—through me, even—as I ran up the stairs after the priest. There was a sudden shower of blood from somewhere above that rained down on me. I was starting to feel a little thankful that these intruders had interrupted the conversation I'd been having with Sariel.

I burst out into the fire to see the remains of the priest smouldering amid the logs. They burned with a normal flame now rather than the green flame that had consumed the legionnaire, but Sariel's words had found their mark anyway. The priest lay in several pieces, blown apart by something. His arms and hands lay in one side of the fire pit, his legs and feet in another. Parts of his torso were here and there. The head was all that escaped the flames. It had rolled onto the walkway where I'd encountered the sphinx.

Sariel came up the stairs and pushed me out of the way. She threw herself into the air with a beat of those misty wings and hung there, turning in a circle over the fire.

"Are there any more?" she cried.

"I don't think so," I said.

But there was one more. There was something, anyway.

A great tentacle slid over the edge of the tower then, feeling its way about. It slapped onto the walkway, like it was searching for us.

"Beware!" I cried and dropped into a fighting stance. I wasn't exactly sure how to defend myself against a giant tentacle. It was one of the few things I hadn't faced over the ages.

Sariel spun around in the air and spat more words at the tentacle. Green fire blazed along its length and it convulsed. The tip of it brushed the priest's head. It curled back, gathering up the head in a fiery embrace. Then it dropped back down over the wall, out of sight. I threw myself to the walkway and looked over in time to see the tentacle fall into the waves, still holding the head, burning brightly. A line of green under the water shot back out to sea and disappeared in the direction of the storm.

"We are undone," Sariel said as she drifted down to land beside me.

"What in all the hells was that?" I asked, staring out to sea. Lightning flashed amid the storm clouds out there. They looked closer now.

"Noah," Sariel said.

"Noah?" I said. "Of the ark?"

"He roams the seas searching for abominations," Sariel said. "He must have discovered the sphinx in the water. And then the texts you blew out with your unholy wind would have led him here like a trail even a blind man could follow."

"Don't try to blame this on me, whatever it is," I said. "I was only here to kill you."

"Those three were but a scouting party," Sariel said. "Noah will keep the priest alive long enough to tell him of what they saw. And he will come for the library."

"Well, you'd better close the door and lock it this time," I said. I thought about putting the knife back in my robes, but I wasn't sure what to do yet. I was a little surprised I hadn't buried the blade in Sariel already.

"There is no door that Noah cannot break," Sariel said. "All that can be done now is to save what we can of the library."

I turned to her and shook my head. "Look," I said, "I might be feeling charitable enough that I haven't killed you yet, although I reserve judgement on that. But I'm not going to help you carry every damned scroll and book out of your little library."

"We cannot save them all," Sariel said, her wings folding back in and the fire of her eyes fading. "But we must save one."

"I should have stuck my knife in you when I had the chance," I muttered.

"If you had done so, the world would already be finished," Sariel said. "As much as I might enjoy that, I can't simply stand by and let it happen."

I glared at her a moment longer, but it was really just for effect. Finally, I nodded and slipped the knife back into my robes.

"What's so special about this one that you want to save, then?" I asked.

"It is God's bible," Sariel said and went down the stairs.

"Of course it is," I sighed. And then I followed her back into the library, because what choice did I have?

The bible was on a bone table far back from the stairs. The distance we covered would have put us somewhere in the middle of Alexandria, by my estimate, yet we never left the library. The room continued to stretch on, out of sight, after the table.

The bible didn't look like anything special. It was a simple, leather-bound book, sealed with a metal clasp. It was the size of my hand, and as thin as a work of poetry. No words adorned the cover, and the pages looked brittle enough to crumble. It was clear there was something special about the book despite its appearance, though. The bone table was cracked underneath it, and the stone floor sunken, as if the book were a great weight pressing down to the earth itself. That observation was confirmed when Sariel took hold of the top end of the bible and lifted it. She strained with all her strength—and the strength of an angel is not to be taken lightly—and still barely managed to lift it.

"Help me carry the bible from the library and there may be salvation for you yet," she said, although she didn't sound entirely convinced about the possibility of that.

"Why does God even need a bible?" I asked, not moving to help her. "I thought the point of a bible was to pass on God's word to us lowly mortals and all the other damned. Why would he need his own version of that?"

"All the gods have bibles," Sariel grunted, straining with the weight of the book now. The stone under her feet cracked with her burden. "The universe is a complex thing even for a god, and every god comprehends it in a different way. Most bind their knowledge of it into the words of a sacred text. To hold the bible is to hold the secrets of the universe. We cannot let such a source of power fall into Noah's hands."

"I thought Noah worked for God," I said.

"We were all of God once," Sariel said. "Now Noah is mad."

"And the rest of us aren't?" I asked.

But I lifted my end of the bible, because the memory of that tentacle carrying off the priest's head was fresh in my mind. That is, I tried to lift it. But it was like trying to hoist a mountain. I couldn't even get my fingers under the cover.

"You will need to use the grace you have stolen from those who deserved it," Sariel hissed between her teeth, shaking with the exertion of holding her end of the bible. "You cannot carry the words of God without grace."

So I let the grace flow into my limbs and I tried to pick up the bible again, and this time I succeeded. Now it was only like lifting a large boulder. A large, hot boulder, because I could feel heat emanating from the book, scorching my hands.

"We must carry it outside," Sariel said. "While we can still escape."

So we staggered toward the entrance, like a couple of drunks, trying desperately not to drop our precious cargo. I didn't want to think about what might happen if we did. The world would probably crack open.

"Why do you even have this thing?" I said as we went. "Aren't the secrets of the universe the sort of thing God should be keeping close to himself?"

"Perhaps you could ask him that the next time you see him," Sariel said, stumbling into a shelf of ancient scrolls. The shelf broke under her weight and the scrolls fell underfoot. We couldn't help but step on them. One of them burst into flame as my foot crushed it underneath, another exploded into a mass of beetles that scurried away in all directions.

"The bible was abandoned on this world along with the rest of us," Sariel said. "I do not know why, nor do I care. My duty is not to question God's will. My duty is to keep the words safe."

"And what if he doesn't return for them?" I asked as we reached the stairs leading out of the library.

"Then it is especially important I keep them safe from those who seek them out," she said. She looked down at the scrolls scattered underfoot, and one of them rose in the air before her. I half expected it to unroll itself, but instead words drifted out of it in all directions, as insubstantial as smoke but as bright as fire. They were in a language I didn't know and they twisted through each other, impossible to read.

But Sariel had no problem. She read aloud the words floating between us and now they drifted away from the scroll, into the shelves. The scrolls and any texts they touched burst into flame, and the fire quickly spread, racing along the shelves.

"You have a strange way of keeping things safe," I said.

"They are safer destroyed than in the hands of Noah," Sariel said.

We watched the fire turn into an inferno in the space of seconds, and then I looked back at the stairs.

"We're not going to be able to carry the book up and out of here," I said. "We could barely manage to move it along a flat stretch of hallway." I was having to burn more grace by the moment just to keep upright.

Sariel closed her eyes for a moment, thinking. She stopped breathing and bowed her head. Then her wings faded away, like a mist in the morning sun. When she opened her eyes again, they shone with a golden light.

"I have the strength now," she said.

She started up the stairs, lifting the greater share of the bible's weight. It was a neat little trick I didn't know the angels were capable of. I followed her up the stairs and out of the burning library, no doubt to more surprises.

My expectations were met. We went up into the fire, but when we emerged we were not atop the lighthouse, where I'd entered. Instead, we were in the desert, standing in a campfire. A man in a tattered robe that was little more than rags stared at us, his hand holding a wineskin frozen halfway to his lips. The sand dunes of a small gully surrounded us on all sides, sheltering us from the elements. Wherever we were, we hadn't travelled far. I could smell the ocean in the air.

Sariel laid her end of the bible down in the fire, carefully, and I did the same with mine. I thought that perhaps it might fall through the flames and back into the library, but instead it snuffed the flames out. Or rather, drew them into itself. They flickered for a second, then vanished into the book. The bible was left lying on a dead firepit. The wood cracked and crumbled underneath and the bible began to slowly sink into the sand.

"Thank you for tending the fire," Sariel said to the man. "You may have saved the world because of your diligence to such a sacred duty."

"I thought this day would never come," the man said, his voice barely above a whisper.

"I always feared it would," Sariel said. "I release you now from your duties."

She shot a hand out, faster than my eye could follow. When she drew it back, she was holding the man's heart. It was still beating.

The man said nothing, only smiled despite the gaping wound in his chest. He took a drink from the wineskin. Then he toppled back, into the sand.

First Ishmael, and now this poor soul. Let that be a lesson to any of you who consider consorting with angels.

"Where are we?" I asked. "And perhaps more importantly, why are we here?"

Sariel just dropped the heart, which was still now, and climbed to the top of the nearest dune in reply. She stared at something I couldn't see, so I had no choice but to follow.

We were on the outskirts of Alexandria, in the desert beyond the boundaries of the city. Fires still twinkled here and there, but they were dwarfed by the flames atop the lighthouse. It lit up the sea for a distance, and now I saw what Sariel looked at.

The storm I had glimpsed out on the horizon had moved even closer, until it was almost upon the lighthouse and the city. Great clouds stretched from what seemed like the stars all the way down to the water. Lightning flashed deep in the clouds, and the thunder rolled in from the sea and through our bodies. The lightning was not the only thing that moved in the clouds—I could see shapes looming within it, the silhouettes of ships. And something else, something far larger than any ship I had ever seen.

Then the great tentacle rose out of the water before the lighthouse again. It was the limb of a creature so vast I couldn't even imagine the rest of its body. A waterfall poured off of the tentacle as it wrapped itself around the lighthouse, like it was clutching a twig.

"What have the angels done this time?" I asked.

"This is not our creation," Sariel said, still gazing at the lighthouse. "This is God's creature. It is the kraken. Noah has finally found us."

The tentacle pulled on the tower and great blocks came apart, crashing down upon the buildings below. People began screaming throughout the city. I couldn't blame them.

"Now would be a good time to tell me more about Noah," I said.

Sariel said nothing for a moment. The tentacle shook the tower some more. The great structure began to lean out to sea. Lightning flashed in the storm clouds again.

"Noah is no saviour of humanity and all the other creatures as the myths suggest," Sariel finally said. "He is God's warden."

"I don't like the sound of that," I said.

"He is the keeper of God's mistakes," Sariel said. "The ark was meant to be the prison for those things that could not be allowed to live on in this realm."

"Just what the world needs," I said. "Another angel."

"Noah is no angel," Sariel said, shaking her head. "He is a creature like no other. He is less than a god, but he is more than an angel. He is more than all the angels combined. And he has gone mad in God's absence."

"Haven't we all?" I said.

"Now he scours the seas and takes all he encounters," Sariel went on. "There is no logic or law to his actions. He has become what he was meant to imprison."

A sound like thunder came to us then, but there was no lightning. It was the lighthouse falling into the sea as the tentacle pulled it down. The great tower collapsed as it fell, the stone raining down on the soldiers beneath it, and into the waters of the harbour. The tentacle dropped beneath the water and waves surged in all directions.

"What does Noah want with the library?" I asked.

"He wants what we have," Sariel said.

The waves continued as the tentacle moved under the surface. Blocks from the tower erupted from the water and flew hundreds of feet in all directions, some crashing back down into the sea while others fell amid the buildings of Alexandria. The kraken was searching for something.

"He wants God's bible," Sariel said.

I didn't say anything else, but Sariel continued, as if reading my mind and answering my unspoken question.

"Noah wants to end his suffering," she said. "And the only way to do that is to end the world."

✚

THE WORD OF GOD

Sariel turned and went back down to the bible, which had sunk deeper into the sand, so that it was half-buried. "We must leave now," she said. "While we are still able."

That sounded good to me. I gave the scene one last look, as the storm clouds rolled over the remains of the lighthouse, and then I joined Sariel. I put the screams from the city out of my mind for the time being. I'd had a lot of practice doing that, so it wasn't so hard.

"Where do we go?" I asked Sariel as we lifted the bible from the sand.

"I can only hope we are given a sign," Sariel said, shaking her head.

"I think the days of such signs are long past," I said.

"I am afraid you are right," Sariel said.

I gave the dead man another look, and then we went out into the night, staggering under our burden.

As it turned out, there were many signs. For a time as we walked, flames sprang up in our footprints. Sariel didn't seem concerned by them, so I didn't say anything. The flames eventually died out, but they were replaced by showers of shooting stars overhead. When we stepped across a stream of blood that flowed through the desert, I felt compelled to speak up.

"Is this Noah's doing?" I asked. "Or is it more of your tricks?"

"It is neither," Sariel said. "It is the bible. It affects the world around it."

"Is there anything I need to worry about?" I asked.

"Perhaps," Sariel said and left it at that.

At one point we came across a campfire. The man Sariel had killed earlier was sitting in front of it, staring down at his heart in his hands. He didn't look up as we passed, which I figured was just as well for him. I suspected that if he noticed us, Sariel would probably kill him again.

We decided to stop for a rest when the sandstorm hit. One second the sky was clear, except for the cloud of bats overhead, the next the very air became a whirlwind of sand. We had to pull cloths over our faces to breathe, and we could barely open our eyes against the scouring grains, which were like tiny knives upon our flesh.

"We need to rest," I shouted to Sariel. I didn't know if my words reached her through the storm, but she must have heard me, for she lowered the bible to the ground. I put my end down as well—and then I opened the bible.

I'd been thinking about it for a while as we walked. I thought maybe if the bible was a creation of God's, then it might contain the same grace as the angels. Maybe it held more grace than I could even imagine. Maybe opening it was a bad idea. There was only one way to find out.

Opening the bible was a bad idea.

I caught a glimpse of a word, a single word blazing on the page, before Sariel cried out and slammed the bible shut again. But not before that word lifted off the page and into the air.

The letters of the word burned with white fire as they rose over the bible. I don't know what the word was. It was in no language I understood or even recognized. I could no more describe the word to you than I could describe what it feels like to taste the grace of Heaven. For a second it just floated there between us, lighting up our faces with its fire. I could see the fear in Sariel's eyes. Then the word ripped apart and the sandstorm turned the world into night and I could see nothing at all. I took out my knife and waited.

Eventually the storm subsided, and I discovered we were no longer in the desert. That is, we were still in the desert, but now we were also in some sort of building. Walls of hardened sand stretched up to meet an arched ceiling far overhead. The bible sat on an altar of more hard sand, carved to look like a half dozen angels supporting a stone tablet. The rest of the building was empty, but I could tell from its general shape and the altar that it was clearly some sort of temple. I just didn't know why we were in it.

"Where have you taken us?" I asked.

"This is of your doing, you fool," Sariel snapped. "This is what the word made when you let it free of the bible."

I looked around but didn't see the word anywhere. There were no doors or windows I could see. "Where did it go?" I asked.

Sariel walked over to one of the walls and struck it with an open palm. A section of the sand fell away, leaving an opening in the rough shape of a doorway.

"You'll have to show me how to do that," I said. "That would have come in handy once or twice in the past."

Sariel stepped outside without answering. I didn't see any other courses of action, so I followed her.

There were more buildings outside the temple. We stood in a city carved from the sand. Other temple-like structures surrounded us, and streets stretched away in all the usual directions. I could see the sand dunes at the end of the streets, where the desert resumed.

"The word made all of this?" I asked. I was still a little unclear on how these things worked.

"The word made this with its mere passing," Sariel said. She walked down the street and gazed about, at the city of sand. "Who knows what else it makes in the world?"

"What do we do about it, then?" I asked.

"We must track it and find a way to make it return to the bible," Sariel said, right before she turned and struck at me with a flaming sword she pulled out of the air itself.

I'd been expecting it, of course, ever since she'd ripped the heart out of her servant. She was an angel and I was, well, I was me.

I dove to the right to get away from the sword even as she spun about. I left my knife in her ribs, and then I was rolling under the sweeping arc of her strike to come up behind her. I used the grace that spilled out of her wound to sharpen my hands into claws as strong as iron and then I leapt upon her as she kept spinning to face me.

I slashed her face, taking one of her eyes out and marring her perfect features. I used more of the grace that burst from her wounds to turn my teeth into fangs a werewolf would envy, and I ripped at her throat. I bit into bone and cartilage as strong as stone, but my teeth were even stronger. In short, I turned myself into the sort of thing Noah would no doubt want to imprison.

Sariel barely seemed to notice my savage attack. She grabbed me by the back of my head, ramming her fingers through my flesh and into the bone of my skull. If I'd been mortal, she would have shattered it and driven her fingers into my brain. But if I had been human, we wouldn't be in these present circumstances. That didn't stop me from howling a few choice curses, though.

She settled for throwing me across the street and into the wall of a nearby building. I slammed through it and the building collapsed around me in a shower of sand.

I'll give Sariel credit—she didn't run. Maybe because there was nowhere to run to in the desert, maybe because she didn't want to. She came at me, swinging that sword like she was trying to cleave the world in two. I used some grace to kick up a small sandstorm in her face as I put distance between us. I rolled to the side as she hacked at the earth where I'd been. The ground shook like an earthquake, but it didn't stop me from ducking through the doorway of a nearby building. I looked around for a weapon I could use to defend myself against that flaming sword, but the building was empty and my knife was still stuck in Sariel's ribs.

She came smashing through the wall of the building then, so I kept moving, throwing myself through the opposite wall. The building came down upon Sariel, but I knew it wouldn't hold her. There was nothing that would hold an angel for long. Nothing but death.

We destroyed a couple more buildings like that while I searched for a weapon to use, but they were all empty. Except for one. The one that held the bible.

I climbed out of the remains of the latest building we'd brought down and headed back along the street toward the temple. Then it was my turn to get caught in a sandstorm, as Sariel sought to stop me.

I figured the appropriate response was to throw myself to one side or another to avoid her blade. Instead, I stood completely still, not taking a single step after the sandstorm engulfed me. There was a fiery blur on either side of me, barely visible through the swirling sand, and the earth shook some more.

That gave me an idea, at least.

"You can't blame me for this!" I cried, letting her know where I was.

The sword came at me as fast as an arrow, but I was ready for it. I threw myself to the side even before I'd finished speaking and slashed down with my claws, tearing her wrist open. She still managed to score my ribs with the blade, but if you pick a fight with an angel, you're not going to walk away without a few scars, however temporary they might be.

She dropped the sword when I ripped her arm open, but just as quickly she healed her wound and snatched the weapon out of the air again, before it had time to hit the ground. She lunged forward, coming out of the sandstorm at me, and buried her blade in my chest.

That is, she tried to. But the weapon simply turned to sand, crumbling away at the impact. Sariel stared down at the grains running between her fingers. She didn't try to attack me again, because it was too late. I'd rammed her sword—the real one— through her chest.

I'd managed a quick sleight when she'd dropped her sword, exchanging it for one I'd conjured out of the sand. I'd grabbed the real blade. Things had happened so fast after that, Sariel hadn't noticed the switch until it was too late.

Grace spilled out of Sariel's chest in spurts, like the blood of a dying person. She looked at me with an expression I didn't know how to read. Resignation? Sadness? Acceptance? It was hard to tell what angels were thinking.

"You were going to do to me what you did to your servant," I told her. "I just beat you to it."

"The difference between the two of you is that you deserve such a fate," she said.

"We all deserve it," I said.

"Do not open the bible again," she said. "Even the angels cannot contain the words that are locked within it."

"I'm not going to touch that thing," I said. "I have what I came for." I twisted the blade, widening the wound to let more grace escape.

"You must track down the word," Sariel said with what I thought was her dying breath. "It's your responsibility now."

I shook my head. "If God made that word, then he can worry about it." But Sariel wasn't listening because she was throwing herself backward, off the blade. The sandstorm went with her, rushing past me like a river. I lunged after her, but she disappeared into the sand, and then I was stumbling along in a whirling, stinging storm of nothing.

The sand all dropped to the ground at once, and the remaining buildings collapsed around me. Every one of them but the temple. It was almost submerged underneath a dune now, with small dust devils coming in from the desert and fading away on the temple's roof as I pushed myself back to my feet. Soon it would be completely hidden away. Who knew what other mysterious temples and lost cities were also under the sand?

I looked around for Sariel, but she was gone. The flames on her sword had died now, and it was just another mortal weapon. I dropped it. Let the desert have it. I breathed deep of the grace that I'd managed to free from her before she escaped, and felt it fill the void within me.

I climbed to the top of the nearest dune to figure out where I was and what to do next. The desert stretched away featureless in almost all directions. The exception was a trail of disturbed sand that led away from the ruins of the strange city in a straight line. The trail was as wide as a road and several feet deep. Something massive had gone that way. Something larger than Sariel.

The word.

I looked back at the ruins of the city. I didn't like the idea of leaving the bible out here in the desert for anyone to stumble across. But I couldn't move it now that Sariel was gone. And it was already sinking into the sand. I figured it was only a matter of time before the desert covered it completely.

That left the word to worry about. Despite what I'd said to Sariel, her plea echoed in my head. Maybe it wasn't my problem. But maybe it was, seeing as I'd freed it from the bible. Even in those days I wasn't completely lacking in any sense of responsibility.

I followed the trail because I didn't know what else to do. I walked for maybe half the day before I smelled the ocean, then perhaps another hour or so. Eventually I crested a dune and saw the sea stretching out before me. The trail went over the dune and vanished into the waves.

I stared out to sea for a moment, wondering what had become of the word, and what had become of Sariel, for that matter.

Then, far on the horizon, something lifted out of the water before falling back. A white shape. A whale, I realized, even as it crashed down into the waves. A massive white whale.

I waited for it to surface again, but it didn't. Whatever it was, it had vanished as completely as Sariel had.

I looked up and down the coast but saw only desert stretching away to eternity in either direction. I shrugged, picked a direction at random and started walking.

I had a bad feeling about the whale and the escaped word of God and the disappearing angel. I had no idea how bad things were going to get in the centuries to come.

✠

THE ARK OF MADNESS

The next few hundred years are a bit of a blur, and they don't really matter to this story, anyway. What does matter is the first time I met Noah in person. This was a few centuries after Alexandria, when he wrecked the Spanish Armada in the 1600s trying to capture me. He nearly succeeded.

I'd spent the time in between doing the things I usually did back in those days: hiring myself out as a soldier to whoever had the coin, drinking myself to amnesia and getting myself killed. Not necessarily in that order. After a dozen or so variations on this theme, I found myself in the army of the Spaniards during one of their many misadventures on the Continent. We went about happily sacking places like Flanders and Antwerp. Like most good soldiers, I didn't really care about the politics behind it all. The Spanish paid more than their rivals, so I went to war arm in arm with the Spanish. Also, they had the best wine. If you don't think that's important, then you've probably never been a soldier in the 1600s. When the Spanish decided to invade England, I was so drunk I barely registered the news.

I sobered up quickly when the British caught our fleet at anchor in a port I can't even remember the name of now. They sent in the fire ships, which were blazing wrecks designed to light our own vessels aflame. Most of our captains panicked and cut themselves free of their anchors to escape. It was hard to blame them. There's little more terrifying to a seaman than watching a burning ship bearing down on him—except, perhaps, for that burning ship to be loaded with gunpowder. And just like that, we were scattered and on the run.

A good admiral like Nelson might have been able to turn the tide. Hell, a good captain like Drake probably could have done it. He did it against us on more than one occasion, after all. But we were led by a politician, the duke or other of some principality that probably no longer exists. He'd never set foot on a ship before this, and it showed. As a wiser man than me once said, so it goes.

Somehow, we found ourselves sailing along the coast of Ireland to get home to Spain. Don't ask me how that came about. Maybe it was some tactical decision, or maybe it had something to do with ocean currents. I don't really know. I wasn't any more of a sailor then than I am now. I can't even recall the name of the ship I sailed on, which is a major form of heresy among the sailors I've known. It's like not knowing the name of your mother. In fact, I imagine more sailors know the names of their ships than the names of their mothers.

It was off Ireland that Noah came for us. The first sign was the clouds on the horizon. We thought them a storm, and we weren't too worried. The worst a storm could do to us was scatter the fleet and sink a few ships, and we were already scattered.

But the clouds came at us with unnatural speed, and our ship started to rise and fall on the waves. And then our lookout shouted to us that he saw other vessels hiding in the clouds. When the captain called up to ask if they were more British warships, the lookout didn't say anything else, just crossed himself several times. Like that's ever helped anything.

We crowded the gunwales and watched the storm come. As it neared us, we saw the clouds stretch all the way down to the waves themselves. They were black as night, and lightning flickered in the constantly rolling mass. The water in front of the storm churned and swelled in directions that didn't make sense, as if something massive was twisting and writhing just under the surface. I'd seen this storm before, at Alexandria. I was tempted to make the sign of the cross myself.

The clouds parted as the storm bore down upon us, revealing ships heading our way at unnatural speed. They were unlike any vessels I'd ever seen. Or rather, I'd seen them all before, but never like this.

There were English man-of-war ships much like the ones that

had been harrying us along the coast. There were also Roman triremes and Chinese junks. There were longboats and fishing boats. There were even wooden rafts. They were all clustered in a large mass, tied together with ropes or joined with wooden bridges—one giant vessel that bent and warped in many directions as it rode the waves.

And in the centre was the ark.

It was a vast wooden ship, only the bow emerging out of the churning clouds. It towered above the largest galleons in what was left of our armada, but it was covered with barnacles and starfish all the way up to the deck, as if the ship spent most of the time underwater.

Barnacles and starfish and bones. Skeletons hung from the bow like forgotten decorations. It was the sort of thing you saw on pirate ships from time to time, but on pirate ships the skeletons tended to be human in nature. Not so on the ark. There was something that looked like the shell and bones of a giant crab, only it had long arms like tentacles instead of claws. There was a man's skeleton that ended in fins at the hands and feet, and a skull that was more a frog's than a man's. And there was the skeleton of a man with wings, which I took to be an angel. I wasn't sure, though, as angels normally just faded away to wherever it is dead angels go when I killed them. But there was nothing normal about the vision in front of me.

I didn't dwell on the bones anyway. I was too distracted by the living crew of the ships.

They were unlike anything I'd ever seen before, and most of them I haven't seen since. A creature like a black octopus with mouths all over its body that swung from rope to rope in the torn rigging of a galleon. A woman with six arms and no legs who scuttled along the gunwales of the ark, spider-like, stopping every now and then to wave a pair of swords at us. A half-dozen men who could've been Vikings with horned helmets, until the ark drew near enough we could see the horns grew from their heads. The captain of our ship shouted the orders for us to turn and ready our cannons for a full broadside. I suspected they wouldn't make a difference.

"What manner of abomination is this?" said one of the soldiers beside me, a bearded man with a scar running down his left cheek. Antonio. Yes, the same Antonio whose head wound up inside a giant squid centuries later.

"It is the worst of abominations," I said to him. "It's Noah and his ark." I knew that from the little I'd glimpsed at Alexandria.

Antonio looked at me and then back at the ark. I know he wanted to mock me for such talk, but it was hard to refute the presence of the ark bearing down on us.

"Has it come to save us from the British?" he asked.

I didn't answer him. I knew what Noah wanted. He was hunting for God's mistakes, if what Sariel told me had been correct, and he must have sensed me.

The captain shouted the order to fire, and our gunners delivered a full broadside into the ark itself. Shattered pieces of wood and bone flew from it, and our crew gave a cheer. A cheer that quickly died in our throats when the six-armed woman scurried to the bow and waved her swords at us.

Then Noah himself came out on deck.

He was a giant the size of three men. He wore a white robe stained with blood. His long beard was also white and just as stained. Despite the distance, I could see his eyes were as black as the storm clouds. He dragged a trio of angels behind him with a chain he had wrapped around one hand. The chain ran through collars on the angels' necks. They didn't struggle. Their eyes had all been gouged out.

"Find the thing that should not be and bring it back to the ark," Noah bellowed, his voice like thunder. "The one who delivers it, I will reward with death!"

The captain shouted at the gunners to reload, his voice barely audible over the sounds of the rain hammering down on us, but I knew another broadside wouldn't do any good. The ark was too large, and too close. I looked around for some escape, but we were on a ship at sea, and the water didn't strike me as much safer than the ship, given the present circumstances.

There was, of course, the coast in the distance. We had turned in its general direction to deliver the broadside, but we were too far away to reach it before the ark fully overtook us. The monstrous vessel moved too quickly. But perhaps with a little help. . . .

I blew some grace toward our sails, and the ship surged toward shore.

Then the rain came down even harder. It fell upon us like the very sky had collapsed, like we had sailed into a waterfall. It battered us and knocked men to the deck. I caught sight of the lookout falling past, into the sea, and then he was gone. The rain tore open the sails and the ship slowed, and men who were veterans of many a bloody battle cried out in fear at the madness engulfing us.

And then the madness really began.

Noah roared something unintelligible and yanked the angels on their chains. They stumbled past him and to the bow of the ark, moving like they'd been broken in every possible way. They began to chant in unison, but I couldn't make out those words through the chaos.

Something heard them, though.

Tentacles lashed out from under the waves and caught on to our ship, just like the one that had brought down the lighthouse in Alexandria. The limbs of some great beast. The kraken. I didn't really want to see the rest of it. There were things stuck in the tentacles, bits of wood and rope from other ships. Swords and axes that must have been used in a vain attempt to repel boarders. And the bodies of men. They were half buried in the tentacles, like they were being absorbed into them. And then I saw they weren't bodies at all—the men were still alive. They turned their faces to us as the tentacles smashed down onto our ship, seizing it, and they cried out in different tongues. English, Spanish, Greek, Mayan. They all screamed the same thing.

"Kill me!"

The tentacles curled around the mast, caught on to the sides of the ship, even the wheel itself, knocking the man there aside. And then they pulled us toward the ark.

The captain of our ship didn't need to shout orders. The soldiers and sailors around me drew their weapons and hacked away at the tentacles. The limbs of the great creature bled like any other being cut open with a sword, but they bled black sludge. The men caught in the tentacles wailed like an unholy choir.

I looked around to see if the other ships of our battered armada were in the same plight as us, but they were lost in the deluge. I couldn't see them, and I couldn't see the shore anymore. All I could see was the ark and its fleet closing in on us.

And the boarders.

They came along the tentacles to our ship. The spider woman running down one thrashing limb like it wasn't even moving. The men with horns in their heads swinging along another, chopping handholds into the tentacle with their axes to stop from falling into the sea below. A jellyfish thing on bone stilts running across the water. I knew we could no more repel these creatures than we could repel nightmares in our sleep.

I laid my hand on Antonio's shoulder. "I'm sorry, but they seek you," I said.

He stared at me. "What madness do you speak of?" he asked.

"You're dead anyway," I said. "At least I will have a chance to escape."

I let some of my grace flow through my hand and into him. Enough that Noah would be able to sense it, if the grace was how he had found us. Antonio's eyes widened as he tasted Heaven for the first time in his life. But as he was to find out, Heaven is not what it seems to be.

I performed a couple of quick sleights. One to make me look like Antonio. And one to make him look like me, just in case Noah somehow had my description. I even added a bit of glow to Antonio's skin to attract attention.

Then I ran for the bow of the ship and threw myself into the water.

I dove under and swam as far as I could, kicking against the strange and sudden surges that threw me one way and then another under the surface. The water was colder than I had expected. It was colder than I had ever remembered it. I waited for one of those tentacles to grab me, but they never did.

When I finally came up for air, the ship was a good three lengths behind me and barely visible through the rain. I saw the impossible shapes of Noah's crew swarm onto it and converge on the glowing figure on the deck. I tried not to listen to the cries of the men and other things.

I dove back under and swam as hard as I could for land. When

I reached it some time later, staggering up onto a rocky shore, the storm covered the sea behind me. More lightning flashed within the clouds. And then a roar rent the clouds themselves, opening them up to reveal the ark once more. I caught sight of Noah again, standing on the deck. He held something glowing in his hands, something that he tore into little pieces and then tossed aside.

I ran when he turned to look in my direction. I ran from the beach and up into the green hills of Ireland beyond. I ran until I could no longer see the ocean and the ocean could no longer see me.

☦

A FATEFUL MEETING AT A GENTLEMEN'S CLUB

Once I made it back to the Continent after the Noah encounter, I stayed away from the seas. I wandered the lands instead, fighting and drinking my way across Europe. I lingered for a while in London, until that unfortunate business with Will Shakespeare, Christopher Marlowe and a certain demon in a Royal's body meant I was no longer welcome. I kept going east, until one day I found myself clawing my way out of a frozen Russian field after a resurrection and decided that I needed to seek warmer places to live and die. I went south, through Turkey and the Middle East, where I lived in luxury for a while as a prophet, until I ran out of grace and could no longer perform miracles. In that land, you're only as good as your last raising of the dead or cured disease. I left my small palace in the middle of the night and kept wandering. What I was looking for, even I didn't know.

I eventually found myself in Morocco, where many of those who are lost wind up. This was a few hundred years after the Spanish Armada. I hadn't thought of the bible buried in that strange desert city since long before that. There was nothing I could do about it, after all. I could barely lift it on my own, and I'd learned my lesson about trying to open it. It was better to leave it where it was and let the world forget about it. It was just like Beowulf's sword, Hrunting. Some things are better left at the bottoms of lakes and in buried desert cities.

But sometimes things like that won't stay buried.

I'd stayed in Morocco long enough to get comfortable. It was a good place to hide from the Royals after that affair with the demon and the Nameless Book. Lots of people had disappeared in Morocco over the ages, for better or worse. It was that kind of place.

I wasted the days in an opium parlour hidden away in the basement of a wealthy man's home. The ground floor was occupied by a gentlemen's club, where men of means could debate the issues of the day in a smoking lounge. But the club was just there to hide the opium parlour. Most of the visitors went straight through the lounge and down the stairs on the other side without stopping in between. The only people who used the smoking lounge were those who were still coming down from their high and had to sit in the stuffed chairs for a while before returning to their lives outside.

I was drifting in and out of bliss on a divan in the basement one afternoon, as I had so many times before, when a man reclining beside me started talking and brought me back to this world.

"Enjoy this time while you can, my friend," he said, taking a long pull from his pipe, "for the end times are upon us."

"The end times are always upon us," I said.

"I have seen the signs in my travels," he said. "Raindrops made of bone falling from the sky, like the tears of angels. They fell upon my caravan and killed two camels. If that is not a sign, then nothing is." He looked at the ceiling of the parlour, where billowing drapes hung like clouds overhead, as if he could see the rain or maybe the angels there.

"Perhaps I should try your pipe," I said. "It seems more potent than mine." I thought about adding my knowledge of what angels' tears were really like, but there are some things best kept to yourself, even in opium dens.

"If it is a dream, then the world itself is dreaming," he said. He reached into his robe and pulled out a small pouch. He opened the pouch and shook the contents into his palm. A half dozen or so pieces of bone, smooth and polished.

I suddenly felt clear-headed and sober as I stared at them, despite all the opium I'd consumed that day and all the days before.

"Where did this happen?" I asked him.

"In the desert near Alexandria," he said, gazing at the bones in his hand. "A merchant I dealt with in the city told me of other strange occurrences. A river of blood that sprang from the sand and flowed out to sea. A flock of dead birds circling in the sky for a week before they fell back to the ground. A sandstorm that did not move but simply hung in place, as if the air itself had frozen."

"How long ago was this?" I asked him.

The man simply shrugged and slid the bones back into his pouch, one at a time. "What difference will time make once the world has ended?" he said.

Instead of answering him I got up off the divan and went up the stairs, into the empty club. I opened a window and breathed some fresh air to clear my mind, then collapsed into a chair. I knew what those bone tears meant. The bible. It was making itself known again. I had to do something before it drew too much attention to itself. I didn't want Noah or someone worse to find it.

I let my eyes wander around the deserted club as I thought, and then I realized what I needed to do. I didn't know if it was a good idea or a bad idea. I generally only know that sort of thing much later, when a plan succeeds or fails. But at least I had an idea.

I made my way from Morocco back to the Continent aboard a small smuggler's ship rather than a passenger ship. I didn't enjoy the thought of venturing back onto the water, but it had been hundreds of years since I'd encountered Noah, and it was a relatively short sailing. I kept watch the whole time anyway, scanning the horizon for any signs of storms. I don't know what I would have done if I'd seen one, but it kept me busy enough that I forgot my other problems, such as the Royals. If they did happen to be looking for me in this part of the world, then their agents would be keeping an eye on the ports. Smugglers could make land anywhere, though.

I used some grace I'd taken from an angel I'd found in that opium den months earlier to summon a wind that hastened our passage. It made the crossing rough enough that the crew of the ship paid little attention to me as they struggled to keep the boat afloat and on course. When we reached the coast of France, I slipped over the side of the ship unnoticed long before we reached our destination. Hopefully, the crew would simply think

I had fallen overboard somewhere. They'd already received their payment for my passage, and they had cargo bound for other secret destinations. And if anyone was interested in what had happened to me, they'd likely start the search at the destination I'd told the smugglers, a deserted beach nowhere near where I intended to go.

I swam to the shore of France at a different deserted beach. I took off my wet clothes and threw them back into the sea. The moon was high in the sky as I made my way to a nearby village, where I took some dry pants and a shirt from a home where a man, woman and baby boy all slept in the same bed. The boy was wheezing with some ailment or another, so I used a touch of grace to heal him as payment for the clothes. Then I kept on walking with the help of some shoes I found outside another home, until I found a train station as dawn began to lighten the sky.

There was no money in the pockets of my new clothes, so I stole enough from my fellow travellers at the station that I could buy a ticket to Paris. I kept stealing on the train, although this time it was clothing rather than money. I waited until the porter was at the other end of the car and then I went to the luggage compartment where the extra baggage was stored. I blew out a tiny breath of grace that drifted through the car until it caught in one of the curtains at the far end and lit it afire and started people screaming. I used the distraction to go through several suitcases until I had assembled a wardrobe of a fine suit, dress shirt and tie, and even a fancy hat and an elaborately carved walking cane. I looked the part of a true gentleman, even if I didn't act the part. My outfit earned me a few quizzical looks from fellow passengers when I disembarked, but I was long gone into the Paris crowds by the time they checked their luggage and found what I had taken.

I went straight to a certain club in the heart of Paris that was a home away from home to gentlemen possessing a certain intellectual curiosity. It was in a great house on a street of great houses. A brass plaque above the front door said it was called *The Apollo Club*, although it had been called other things before. The club was older than most of its members, but few of them knew its history. Or histories.

It was not a fake club meant to hide something else, as the empty place in Morocco had been. Instead, it was full of men. When I walked through the entrance, there was a lecture taking place in the hall to the left. It was a large but cozy room with a fireplace, stuffed chairs, paintings of naval vessels and ruins on the walls, and servants with trays of drinks. Many trays of drinks. They came from the lounge and smoking room on the right side of the entrance, a room that was attractively empty. But I wasn't here for that, so I stepped into the hall and listened to the lecture.

A man with an eyepatch stood at a podium near the fireplace, relating his tale of a trip up the Amazon. He was telling the audience about his wild escape from the citizens of a city of gold when I entered. The audience was mostly old white men with long beards, although there were a few young men with shorter beards in attendance. And one man with short-cropped dark hair dressed in a strange military uniform, for some reason wearing glasses so black I couldn't even see his eyes. He was standing against one wall, underneath a painting of a ship burning at sea, beside the young man with a short beard I had come here to meet.

He was looking at the speaker and didn't see me come in. I needed to get his attention, so when the man at the podium paused to drink from a glass of water, I spoke up.

"Actually, the people that chased you weren't the citizens of the city," I said. "They were previous explorers who were trapped there by the true residents. You're lucky to be standing here and telling us this tale."

Everyone looked at me now. I made eye contact with the young man beside the man in uniform. Then I left the room without saying anything else. I made my way deeper into the house, toward the exhibits room at the end of the hall. Electric lights burned softly in wall sconces, just enough to illuminate my way. I'd only seen them a few times before, in the homes of rich gentlemen who could afford such luxuries. With each day that passed, mankind was moving closer to the power of angels. I just hoped that we didn't all end up thinking like the angels, or the future would be a bloody time indeed.

I passed a man sleeping in a chair outside the exhibits room.

He was dressed in formal wear even though the lecture wasn't a formal event, as if he had passed out here during some other event days ago. An empty glass sat on a table beside him, and he snored loudly as I went past him.

The exhibits room was currently unoccupied, which was helpful to my cause. More electric lights gave it a pleasant warmth. The walls were lined with shelves bearing artifacts from around the world. A spear decorated with the feathers of a bird that no longer existed, a chipped vase painted with scenes of the destruction of a city, the skull of a humanoid with horns, that sort of thing. There were more stuffed chairs, a bar cart, and a blazing fireplace in the rest of the room, so I poured myself a brandy and sat in front of the fireplace to warm myself while I waited. I looked at a small idol of a fish-man crouching on a shelf while I drank, and he looked back at me.

We didn't have to stare at each other too long before the man I was here to see came into the room and poured himself a drink of the same brandy. I tore my gaze away from the idol as he settled into the chair opposite me and we touched glasses.

"Jules," I said in greeting, for he was Jules Verne, of course. Who else could help me with my problem?

"Cross," he said. "What is of such importance that you had to disrupt the tale of our good Amazon explorer?"

"It's best that I did," I said. "Who knows how many men he would have sent to that city to be trapped if I hadn't spoken up?"

"He is indeed lucky to have escaped," Verne said, sipping his drink.

"If he did," I said.

Verne gave me a look as he considered my words. It didn't take him long to decipher them. "You think perhaps he was captured," he said. "But then released so he could come here to tell us of the city. So we would send more explorers to their doom."

"You've always been one of the cleverest men I've known," I said. "Which is why I'm here. I have news of something much more interesting than a lost golden city in the jungle."

"Well, I daresay if you find it interesting then I am intrigued," he said.

So I told him about God's bible and the strange sand city,

although I left out its location and how I had come to know about the bible in the first place.

Verne knew of the angels, of course, as most learned men of the time did. And they all knew not to speak of them outside of clubs such as this. The angels preferred to move in the shadows, and they did not appreciate any light shone upon them. But Verne obviously didn't know about the bible. He raised his eyebrows and stroked his beard—the closest I'd ever seen him come to appearing surprised by anything.

"Imagine the secrets such a text must contain," he said.

"It's probably best to let those secrets remain secret," I said. "I've been led to believe that opening the bible is not a good idea."

"That is the first word of sense I've heard in this place," a new voice said from behind us.

Verne and I both turned to see the man with the military uniform and dark glasses standing in the doorway. Who knew how long he'd been there and what he'd heard?

"Normally the members of this club run about the world like wild children, opening up every Pandora's Box they stumble across," he said. "It's refreshing to hear someone express some caution for a change."

"He really doesn't know you," Verne muttered into his drink.

The other man came into the exhibits room and poured himself a glass of the brandy. He took a sniff of it and grimaced. "You call yourself a civilization, yet this is the best you can do," he said. He took a sip anyway, forcing the brandy down.

"I don't believe I've had the pleasure," I said.

"No, you haven't," the other man said.

"Allow me to introduce Captain Nemo," Verne said to me. "He is a mariner of sorts and an explorer of a completely different breed." He looked at Nemo with what could only be described as an expression of unease. "Nemo, this is Cross."

I offered Nemo my hand. He looked at it long enough for the moment to become uncomfortable, then shook it.

"I have heard of your various misadventures," he said, looking me up and down. "I must confess, you are not what I expected."

"If I had a swig of brandy for every time I'd heard that," I said and took a drink. "And I must confess that I've never heard of you."

"He is a man of great accomplishment and achievement," Verne said. "As are all of his people. But he will not allow me to write of his feats while he yet lives."

"One cannot swim in the shadows if the depths are lit up," Nemo said to Verne.

"Interesting saying," I said, not bothering to even try to understand it. "Where are you from? America? Russia? Because I don't recognize that uniform."

"Do you insult everyone you meet upon introduction?" Nemo asked. "Or just your betters?"

"It's probably safe to say everyone," I admitted.

"Gentlemen," Verne sighed. "We are here because of shared interests, not our differences. Let us not quarrel like drunken politicians."

"Is there another kind of politician?" I asked.

"Someday your race may advance to the point you don't need politicians," Nemo said. "If I can keep you alive long enough."

"Nemo and his crew are the last survivors of Atlantis," Verne said to me, in a matter-of-fact way. Frankly, I'd heard madder things that had turned out to be true. "He is their greatest scientist and adventurer. His vessel, the *Nautilus*, is the last surviving Atlantean sea craft."

"And its most worthy," Nemo said. "For I designed it myself."

"Indeed," Verne said, with the air of one who is used to such grandiose claims. "I suspect it is the only vessel in the world that can bear the burden of the artifact you have mentioned."

"Why didn't you just say so?" I said and toasted Nemo with my glass.

He regarded me like I was fish flopping about on a deck in need of a blunt object.

"I have to admit, I thought Atlantis was made up," I said. "What's next, you're going to tell me there's actually a Heaven?"

Nemo took off his glasses and gazed at me then. His eyes were silver, the pupils a darker shade of the same colour. They were more the eyes of a shark than a man. He didn't say anything else, because he didn't need to say anything after that.

"There are many myths about Atlantis," Verne said, casting a sideways glance at Nemo. "Unfortunately, myth is all we have of the fabled city now. At least until Captain Nemo decides to share more with us." He didn't exactly look optimistic at the prospect.

"If there is anything this club has taught me, it's that your kind can't be trusted with the wonders of Atlantis," Nemo said. "I dare not say anything about it for fear of someone mounting an expedition there and causing more problems."

I opened my mouth to say something clever, maybe about how the Atlanteans couldn't have been that much better than us if they'd let their entire city sink, but Verne shook his head at me, as if he could read my mind.

"Enough of this idle chatter," Nemo said. "We must talk about what to do with the bible you have so carelessly lost." So he must have heard everything I'd told Verne.

"I didn't lose it," I said. "I still know where it is."

"Somehow, you are not reassuring me," Nemo said, taking another drink and grimacing again.

"I'm thinking we should move the bible to a safer location," I said. "Who knows who or what could stumble across it in the desert? The problem is I can't move it on my own. It's rather peculiar."

"So you came here for help in this endeavour," Verne said.

"I can't think of anyone more suited to such a feat of engineering than you." Verne was younger than most of the members of the club, but he had accomplished a great deal in his short time on the earth.

"You are perhaps forgetting about da Vinci," Verne said.

"Let's not bring da Vinci into this," I said. "That would create a whole other set of problems."

"Once again, I am forced to agree with him," Nemo said, slipping his glasses back on to hide his eyes once more. "Da Vinci has run wild long enough. He needs to be locked up until he's older."

"Perhaps you are correct," Verne said, although I wasn't sure which one of us he was talking to. He continued to study me, as if trying to make up his mind about whether or not he should help me. Or whether he thought me mad.

"And where would you move it to that it would be so safe?" he asked.

"I would bring it back here," I said. "You could add it to your collection." I waved vaguely around the room with my free hand.

Verne stared at me for a moment.

"I can't think of any safer place," I added.

"That's only because you lack in imagination," Verne said.

"And common sense," Nemo added, as if pointing out the obvious.

"I'm beginning to regret coming here," I said.

"I'm sure it's the latest in a long lifetime of regrets," Nemo said. "No doubt there will be more to come."

"*Gentlemen*," Verne said, a little more sharply this time. He swirled his drink and let his gaze wander over the artifacts. I let him have the moment. As annoying as Nemo was, I didn't have anywhere else to be, and at least no one was trying to kill me here. Not yet.

"I am not certain this is the safest place for such an object," Verne finally said. "But I fear that leaving the bible in the desert may be even less safe."

"There are usually no good choices when angels and bibles are involved," I said.

"You will go and retrieve the bible with the help of the *Nautilus*," Verne said. "I will remain here and improve upon our security system. I have recently made a discovery that may be of some use in that regard."

"We may need more than just some sailing ship and a bunch of men with strange eyes to move the bible," I said.

"And you will have more than that," Nemo said. "If the *Nautilus* cannot transport it, then nothing can. I would stake my reputation on that."

"Well, I managed to get it to the desert," I pointed out. I didn't add that I'd a little help of my own moving it there.

"And look how that turned out," Nemo said. He set down his glass on the bar cart and gave the bottles there another disgusted look.

"I will help on one condition," he said. "The bible is to remain sealed. No one must try to open it or read any of what it contains."

"That would be ill-advised," I agreed.

Nemo shot me a look, then turned and headed for the door.

"When do we leave?" I asked.

"Immediately," he said.

Verne pushed me after Nemo, out into the hall and past the

sleeping man, who was still snoring away. "Try not to make matters any worse," Verne pleaded.

"It's not always me to blame, you know," I said.

"It's you often enough," he said, and I couldn't really argue with that.

So it was that I found myself at a dock in the city, staring up at a decrepit old sailing ship that looked to be in danger of sinking into the river when it was calm, let alone windy. I didn't dare set foot on the walkway until Nemo strode up it, then turned to look back down at me.

"This thing wouldn't survive a pond, let alone the open sea," I called up to him.

"The ocean has depths that cannot be seen from the surface," he said, then turned and walked onto the deck of the ship.

"Is that some sort of Atlantean saying?" I asked but followed him up the walkway, onto the derelict ship anyway.

"It is a Nemo saying," he responded.

As it turned out, the sailing ship was just a cover. Nemo led me belowdecks and to a hatch in the hull of the ship. The hatch opened into a metal vessel that was obviously positioned underneath the sailing ship, hidden away underwater.

"Clever," I said. "You might be a man after my own heart after all."

"Well, it's clear I wouldn't be interested in your mind," Nemo said and motioned me down through the hatch. "Come, let me introduce you to the wonder that is the *Nautilus*."

I can't reveal too much about the *Nautilus* because I promised Nemo I wouldn't talk about it. Let's just say Verne and the movies got the general idea right when they tried to describe it later. The *Nautilus* was a submarine with style and the submarines that were to follow it hundreds of years after resembled it as much as a mobile home resembled a Frank Lloyd Wright.

Nemo led me to the control room, which was all gleaming metal, glass gauges, and brass pipes. The chairs were fused to the deck and made of some sort of jelly-like material that glowed with shifting colours—purple, green, blue. Similar strips of the gel ran along the ceiling and floors, providing illumination. There was a great window that circled the control room, offering a view of the murk outside.

The room was populated with men and women wearing uniforms similar to the one Nemo wore. They had the same silver eyes and gave me disdainful looks, so I figured them to be more Atlanteans. Nemo didn't bother introducing them as he went around the room, scanning the instrument panels, and they didn't volunteer their names. I sat in an empty chair by a panel with more gelatinous lights blinking different colours at me. The chair felt like I was sitting on a jellyfish. It was going to be a long voyage.

Nemo took off his glasses and slipped them into a pocket on his suit. "Let us get underway, then," he said.

One of his men spun some metal wheels on his instrument panel. A howling started up somewhere in the depths of the *Nautilus*.

"What is that?" I asked, as the pipes around me started to vibrate.

"That is our engine," Nemo said. I couldn't help but notice his crew looking at me out of the corners of their strange eyes.

"It doesn't sound like any sort of engine I've heard before," I said. Not that I was particularly knowledgeable about engines. But I was a bit nervous about being under the water in a craft like this.

"Do not concern yourself with the workings of the *Nautilus*," Nemo said, more of a command than a suggestion.

"Is it too late to get a drink?" I asked.

"Not at all," Nemo said. "We never set out without our drinks ceremony." He went over to a storage unit that ran along the bottom of one wall. He pulled out a glass bottle holding an amber liquor and a handful of small drinking glasses with abstract patterns delicately etched into them.

He went around to each crew member, giving them a glass he filled with some of the amber liquor. They all held off from drinking right away, which told me the Atlanteans had more discipline than most of the people I usually surrounded myself with. He poured me a glass once the rest of the crew had been served, and then finally served himself last.

"To Atlantis," he said and raised his glass in a toast.

"Atlantis!" the others all said, raising their own glasses.

"Atlantis," I mumbled, and Nemo shook his head slightly, as if I'd committed some social faux pas.

"May we never forget," Nemo said. He raised the glass to his lips and downed the drink in one swallow. The other members of the crew did the same. I followed suit. The liquor tasted like a fine brandy but had the kick of a whiskey. There was some spice to it I couldn't recognize, so I held my glass out for a refill.

Nemo took the glass away instead, then went around and collected all the empty glasses from the crew. He put the glasses and bottle back in the storage unit, then sat in his chair and stared into the empty water ahead. I felt the deck shift slightly beneath me as we got under way. The crew went about their business at the instrument panels in silence.

We set out along the Seine, on our way to the open sea. The *Nautilus* ran quiet and dark and as deep as the river would allow, so as not to attract any attention from people who might be wandering along the banks. No doubt the windows would have offered splendid views if we were on the surface, but there was not so much as a fish to be seen in the depths.

"I take it we are going to Alexandria, and then you will guide us from there?" Nemo asked.

"It's like you don't need me at all," I said.

"Exactly what I was thinking," he said.

A woman with silver hair and scars on her cheeks left her station to come over to me. She pulled a pistol from her belt holster and pointed it in my direction. It was a strange-looking weapon, all brass and panels of coloured glass, but I had no doubt it was as deadly as any other weapon I'd faced, if not more deadly.

The woman, who I decided to call Scars, kept the pistol aimed at me and pointed at the door with her free hand. "We have a nice room prepared for you," she said.

I didn't move. "I'm not surprised at this betrayal," I said. "But I am surprised it happened so quickly."

"It is no more a betrayal than an adult confining a child for its own safety," Nemo said.

"Does Verne know about this?" I asked.

"Verne knows the bible must be rescued from where it was abandoned," Nemo said. "And I concur. But it is not safe anywhere mortals can lay their hands on it, as you have demonstrated. We will secure it where it will truly be out of harm's way."

The crew all glanced at me again, but they were disciplined enough to keep about their duties during all this. They must have had a lot of questions about what was going on, though. So did I.

"What about me?" I asked. "Are you just going to dump me in the ocean when you don't need me any longer?"

"As tempting as that is, no," Nemo said. "We are not savages. But that doesn't mean I trust you. Your reputation precedes you, after all."

Everyone was making good points at my expense today, so I decided to just go along with things. I let Scars take me out of the control room and through the *Nautilus*. "Quite the man you follow," I said as we went. "You and the rest of the crew must have had the patience of saints."

"He is not a man, he is Captain Nemo," Scars said. "And we follow him because he saved us from the fate that befell Atlantis. Without him, there would be no Atlanteans left."

"I'm still trying to decide if that's a good thing or a bad thing," I said.

She took me to a cabin where there were no instrument panels or even a window. In fact, the cabin looked suspiciously like a jail cell, a similarity that was heightened when I saw there was no door handle on the inside. There was a bunk and a desk that had another bottle of that amber liquor, along with one of those delicate glasses. So it wasn't all bad. I'd certainly found myself in worse prisons.

"We'll let you out when we've arrived," Scars said. "Please try to stay out of trouble in the meantime. I'm not sure what's going on, but we don't need you making it worse." She closed the door before I could think of a witty comeback, which was just as well.

So there I was, a prisoner of Atlanteans in Captain Nemo's submarine as we set out on our mission to find God's lost bible.

I poured myself a drink and sat on the bed. Things were going pretty much as I had thought they would.

✠

RAISING THE DEAD

I spent my time in the cabin aboard the *Nautilus* by sampling the liquor and trying to identify the spices in it. There was nothing I immediately recognized, but I've never been the type to let a bottle beat me. I kept emptying and refilling my glass, until the liquor was nearly gone.

During all this, my mind wandered to thoughts of Penelope, and the moment we had shared under the cherry blossom trees along the bank of the Kamo River in Japan. That was when Penelope had told me she was pregnant with our daughter, Amelia. A daughter who never should have been, and so was my miracle. The cherry blossom petals showered down upon us, and I was lost in a storm of them. Then there was a knock on the door, and they all blew away, into the corners of the room and then into nothing at all. The river was gone, too. So was Penelope.

Scars opened the door and came in, the pistol still in her hand. She looked at the empty glass, then studied my face.

"Your Atlantean spirits are potent," I said. I carefully put the glass down on the table and rubbed my face, to wipe away the moisture from my eyes. "I usually turn to the bottle to forget."

"We cannot afford to forget," Scars said. She motioned me into the hall with her pistol. "We've reached Alexandria. It's time for you to sober up."

"On the contrary," I said. "Returning to Alexandria sounds like a good reason to drink some more." But I left the bottle alone and stepped out into the hall. Scars pointed me away from the control room, and I went along with things. Where else was I going to go, after all?

A low moaning echoed throughout the *Nautilus* as we walked along the hallway. Scars didn't seem to notice it, but I've never been entirely comfortable on ships that sail atop the sea let alone below it, so I couldn't help but comment.

"Tell me that's just a normal engine sound and not the hull giving way," I said.

"It is a normal engine sound for the *Nautilus*," Scars said.

"So we're not sinking, then?" I asked.

"We are inside a metal submarine that is kept afloat only by the constant intervention of advanced technology," Scars said. "We are always sinking."

I decided I was better off not asking questions.

Scars led me to a chamber in the side of the *Nautilus* crowded with boats. A lifeboat hung from one wall, a raft made of logs tied down beside it. A small, one-person sailboat with a furled sail was secured in a rack bolted to the opposite wall, and a couple of canoes were in the racks above it. More boats hung from the ceiling overhead, but I didn't look too closely at them. Nemo and another man stood by a small fishing boat. They were looking out an open hatch in the wall before them, and the ocean's surface was on the other side, the waves rising up against the *Nautilus* and splashing in through the hatch. I could see the dark outline of the shore in the distance, the sky a charcoal grey sheet above it. I wasn't sure if it was early morning or early evening. Nemo and the other man were wearing travellers' robes now, with rifles slung over their shoulders. The rifles were made of the same brass and coloured panels as Scars' pistol.

"This doesn't look like the Alexandria I remember," I said.

The man with Nemo turned to look at me. He had only one eye—the left was a fused mass of melted flesh. I decided to call him One-Eye. I wondered what I would have called Nemo if he hadn't already been introduced to me by name.

"We are a few leagues to the south of Alexandria," Nemo said, not bothering to look at me as he gazed at the shoreline. "We can make landfall undetected here, as there is no one in the area to observe us. You will help us scout the location of the bible and its condition. Then we will determine the best way to return it to the *Nautilus*."

"How can you be so sure there's no one out there?" I asked,

looking at the smudge on the horizon. I suspected that even if I used some grace to sharpen my vision, I wouldn't be able to make out someone standing on the shore, let alone someone that might be hiding in the dunes, watching us.

"Because I designed the *Nautilus*," Nemo said, like that explained it all.

"Well then," I said. "Let's get on with it. I take it you have a plan?"

Nemo reached into the boat and tossed another couple of robes to Scars and me. "We will take a fishing boat in," he said. "Once we have reached shore, you will guide us to our destination. We wear the robes in case we cross paths with any locals. I don't imagine they will be too difficult to deceive."

Scars slipped the robes over her uniform, and then caught the rifle Nemo tossed from the boat. She slung it over her shoulder with practiced ease as I put on my own robes. I waited to see if Nemo would give me a rifle, but he just motioned me to pick up a side of the boat instead. There were no more weapons in the boat, only a few travel bags and waterskins.

"What happens to me once we find the bible?" I asked as the four of us carried the boat to the hatch.

"Once the bible is safe, we will drop you off somewhere just as safe," Nemo said. "Although somewhere far distant from the bible."

"Is that Atlantean code for shooting me in the back and burying me in the desert?" I asked.

"Tempting," Nemo said, a small smile playing about his lips. "But I have heard the stories about you and know that would be pointless. Besides, I have no quarrel with you. I simply don't trust you. So you'll remain a prisoner until the bible is safe and we don't need your help anymore. Than you can go back to doing whatever it is you do. Drinking and causing more problems for us to fix in the future, I imagine."

"We've only just met, but it's like you've known me forever," I said. I helped lift the boat through the hatch and drop it in the ocean. One-Eye climbed in and held the boat to the side of the *Nautilus* while the rest of us got aboard. One-Eye and Scars rowed us away from the *Nautilus* while Nemo watched the shore. I heard another moan echo throughout the sub as we moved away from it. Then the hatch closed, a metal door slowly rising up from the bottom to the seal off the opening. A few seconds later, the *Nautilus* slipped under the waves, leaving barely a ripple behind. It was as if it had never been there.

The Atlanteans were as strong as they were dour, and we reached the shore in a few minutes. We pulled the boat up well above the high-tide mark and then left it there. Hopefully no one would stumble across it here on the beach and steal it. I didn't want to have to swim back to the *Nautilus* when it was time to leave. Though I was still half-convinced the Atlanteans were going to bury me in the desert somewhere. I hated resurrecting in the desert.

The others turned to look at me, and several seconds passed in silence.

"Which way to God's bible?" Nemo finally said.

I gazed up at the sand dunes around us. I realized I didn't have any idea. I was reluctant to admit that to Nemo, though, given our current circumstances. "This way," I said, picking a direction at random and striding confidently up the dune.

"Are you entirely certain?" Nemo called after me, but I didn't dignify that with a response.

The sky lightened overhead as we walked, which meant it was day and not evening. That was a good thing, as I was able to spot the shapes circling in the sky in the distance, far to the side of the direction I was leading our merry group.

"That looks promising," I said, stopping at the crest of a dune to watch the shapes. There were five of them and they were moving in a rough circle that looked more vertical than horizontal. They looked humanoid, but the distance made it hard to tell.

Nemo and the others stopped at my side. Scars and One Eye watched the shapes, but Nemo looked at me.

"Do you know where the bible is or not?" he asked.

"Of course I do," I said. I pointed in the direction of the circling shapes. "It's that way."

"Then why didn't we go that way in the first place?" Nemo asked.

"Had to make sure we weren't being followed," I said. I started down the dune before anyone could challenge me. I hoped I was right. I had a feeling that if I led Nemo and the others astray one more time, they might abandon me and try to find the bible themselves.

We made our way across the desert as the sun rose over the horizon and began to heat up the world. It was slow going on account of the sand shifting under our feet with every step, but thankfully we didn't have to travel that far. It didn't *look* like that far, anyway. The desert could play tricks with your mind.

At one point we saw a line of four people walking across a dune in between us and the shapes in the air. Nemo called us to a stop and nodded at Scars. She unslung her rifle and lifted it to her shoulder. She peered through a cylindrical device of metal and glass attached to the top of the weapon.

"Are we going to kill anyone we cross paths with to cover our tracks?" I said. "That doesn't seem very subtle."

"Only if they notice us," Nemo said. "The sand will hide them long enough for us to make our escape undetected."

"Surely we can manage to do what we came for without leaving a trail of the dead behind us," I said.

"I hardly think your kind are worth worrying about," Nemo said.

Scars lowered the rifle from her shoulder and stared at the figures on the other dune. "You may want to look at this," she said.

Nemo and One-Eye both raised their rifles and sighted in on the other group. Scars lifted her rifle back to her shoulder again, which left me squinting against the sun as I tried to make out what was so interesting.

"Is somebody going to fill me in?" I asked.

"It appears to be some manner of optical illusion," Nemo said.

"I could take out the lead one," Scars said. "Then we'd know if they're an illusion or not."

"If they're not, though. . . ." One-Eye trailed off.

"Yes," Nemo said. "That would be interesting."

I muttered a curse and used a bit of grace to sharpen my vision temporarily to the equivalent of a hawk's. The four other figures trudging across the desert were us. I was in the lead, followed by Nemo, with Scars and One-Eye taking up the rear.

"Well?" One-Eye asked. "Should we?"

"Let's not," I said, giving the others a look. I could have sworn there was the hint of a smile on Scars' lips. When I looked back at our strange doubles, they were slipping out of sight behind another dune.

Nemo and the others lowered their weapons. "Would you care to explain what we just saw?" Nemo asked.

"I can't say for sure, but I'd guess it's a sign we're getting close to the bible," I said. "It has a strange effect on the world around it."

Nemo scanned the scope over to the shapes circling in the air and studied them for a moment. "Indeed," he said.

I looked at them, but the grace had already faded from my vision and I didn't want to use up any more.

"What are they?" I asked.

"They are shadows," Nemo said.

"What kind of shadows?" I asked.

"Just shadows," Nemo said.

"I told you we were going the right way," I said and started walking across the desert again. I didn't bother looking after our disappeared doubles. If they were an illusion, they didn't matter. And if they were real, I didn't want to know anyway. I heard the others fall in behind me a moment later.

The shadows faded away as we approached, but we managed to stumble across the city maybe an hour later. It didn't look any different from the rest of the desert around us, except for the small pool of blood in a gully.

"This looks like the place," I said, nodding at the blood from the top of a dune.

"And where is the bible?" Nemo asked.

"Let me show you," I said. I raised my hands with a theatrical flourish and sent some grace out into the world, to raise a wind that lifted the sand up and threw it away from the blood pool, like waves in every direction. We were blinded for a few seconds, and when the sand fell back down we saw the ruins of buildings poking up through the freshly excavated area. The buildings were the same sand structures as when I'd first come here with Sariel, although they were stained with blood now. The pool of blood had widened to cover the area I'd dug out with the sandstorm.

"Another lost city," Nemo said, studying the scene. "How appropriate."

"We left the bible in the temple," I said, pointing to the building that had somehow survived all these centuries. "And that's about all I can say for sure."

"How do you know it's a temple?" Nemo asked. "It looks like the other buildings to me."

"If there's one thing I know, it's temples," I said.

"I would have thought it was wine," he said.

"The two often go hand in hand," I said. I prepared to use some more grace to summon another wind to clear the temple entrance. Before I could, though, a sandstorm I had nothing to do with erupted at the site of the temple and whirled up the dune toward us.

"Now what are you doing?" Nemo asked.

"That's not me," I said.

The sandstorm suddenly coalesced into the form of a woman. Or rather, an angel. Sariel stood before us, made entirely of sand, just like the buildings. Even her wings were sand instead of the mist they had been made of before. She looked rather unhappy about her current state of affairs.

"Well, that's a new one," I said.

But my words were lost in the sounds of Scars shooting Sariel with her rifle. Her weapon didn't make the usual crack of rifle fire. That's because it didn't fire bullets. Instead, it fired a blast of some sort of energy, a bluish green pulse that made a loud hissing noise in the air. It moved as fast as a bullet, though, for Sariel didn't have time to get out of the way before it struck her. A bright flash of the same colour blinded me for a few seconds, and when my vision came back I saw a cloud of sand falling to the ground all around us. There was no sign of Sariel.

The Atlanteans all looked at each other.

"Was that . . . ?" One-Eye asked.

"Yes, it did appear that way," Nemo said, cutting him off. "But let's not worry about it for the moment."

"You don't exactly seem surprised by the angel," I said.

"On the contrary," Nemo said, looking back down at the sand city. "It was entirely unexpected."

"It was also kind of anti-climactic," I said. "No real angel would go down that easy." The Atlanteans just looked at each other again.

"Do you think maybe I could get one of those rifles now?" I asked. "They seem like they come in handy."

"You have to be an Atlantean," Nemo said. "And we'd prefer not to pollute the bloodline that way."

He started down toward the temple, so we followed him. I had no doubt more strange things would happen as we approached the bible, but what choice did we have?

We didn't have to wait long. We hadn't even reached the first building, when I heard the sounds of the sand moving behind us. I spun around, expecting to see people coming over the dune at us. Maybe the doubles that we'd spotted before. Instead, I saw the sand rising up from the ground to reform Sariel. She looked about as happy as before Scars had disintegrated her.

"Hmm," I said.

Nemo and Scars turned while One-Eye watched for an ambush in front of us. Scars snapped off another shot at Sariel, but the angel was already moving this time, springing above the blast. The strange pulse of light sent a geyser of sand into the air where it hit, and then Sariel fell into our midst, swinging a sand sword with a vengeance.

I shoved One-Eye aside, because I knew who my target would be if I were an angel. Sure enough, Sariel's sword struck down at One-Eye's back, or where his back would have been if I hadn't intervened. It hit my left arm instead, and cut deep to the bone, which the impact of the blow also happened to break. I swore or screamed or maybe both and punched Sariel in the ear with my right hand, which was like punching a rock. I thought maybe I'd broken some bones in that hand to top things off. At the same time, Sariel kicked Scars in the stomach with her left foot, sending the Atlantean flying back. Her next shot went wildly into the sky, no doubt alerting everyone in the neighbourhood we were here.

Thankfully, Sariel didn't have any extra limbs to kick Nemo. He shot the angel and blasted her apart once again.

Nemo glanced at One-Eye and Scars, who were both picking themselves up the ground. "That was clumsy," he said. "You're both lucky you weren't hurt worse."

"I'm fine, thanks for asking," I said, trying not to fall to my knees at the pain in my arm and hand. I settled for hunching over and managing not to whimper too much.

"That is why you have the grace," Nemo said. "Put it to a good use for a change." He started toward the temple again. "We'd better hurry," he said. "I suspect the angel is going to come back."

"They always do," I muttered, but I used some of my grace to heal my broken arm and hand and the cut. Just in time for Sariel's return. She sprang up in front of us, clutching her sand sword again, then threw herself between a pair of half-buried buildings before the Atlanteans could destroy her once more. They opened fire, but all they managed to do was blast away the sides of the buildings. Chunks of sand fell into the blood, and some of the spray hit us.

"The angel must be protecting the bible," Nemo said. "Although it's not a real angel, is it?"

"It doesn't really seem like her," I agreed. "I think it's just the bible at work again." Just another strange miracle in a desert of them.

We waded through the pool of blood, which was thankfully only ankle deep. The Atlanteans kept their weapons ready for another attack, but Sariel didn't appear again. We could hear the sounds of the sand shifting here and there amid the buildings, but Sariel kept out of sight, behind cover. We circled the temple but couldn't find the entrance. It was still buried somewhere in the sand.

"Cross, if you would," Nemo said, walking away from the building and motioning for his crew members to follow him.

"Looks like I'm going to have to do everything," I said. I joined the Atlanteans, standing in the middle of their group because they were the ones with the weapons. Then I threw some more grace into the air and blew the sand away from the temple down to its foundation. When the entrance revealed itself, I even carved out some steps for us to take. The effect was ruined a bit by the blood rushing down the steps and into the temple. Then again, it likely wasn't the first temple to be awash in blood.

We went down the stairs and inside. I almost let out a sigh of relief when I saw the bible was still there. It remained on the altar, although the carved angels supporting the altar were half-submerged in blood now. It was up to our waists here. I'll give the Atlanteans credit for not complaining about having to walk through a pool of waist-deep blood. Most mortals I knew wouldn't have set foot in a temple half-submerged in blood. Some of my other acquaintances probably would have been delighted by it. But the Atlanteans never said a word or skipped a step.

We stopped a few feet away from the bible, Nemo and me looking at it while Scars and One-Eye kept an eye on the door and the dark corners. The slab of sand underneath the bible, which I knew was as hard as rock, was cracked and crumbling from the weight of the book. I remembered how heavy it had been when I'd carried it here with Sariel, and how it had taken all our effort to move it.

"We can't afford to leave it here while we return to the *Nautilus*," Nemo said. "We'll have to devise a method to transport it."

"We could really use the help of an angel," I said.

That was the moment Sariel took to attack again.

She erupted out of the blood just in front of the altar, lunging at us with her sword. It was a horrible sight to behold, even if you were used to seeing blood-drenched angels.

I threw myself to one side and Nemo threw himself to the other. Sariel carried on between us and ran her sword through One-Eye's back. I felt a little bad about that. Life was probably hard enough for him with only one eye, and now bloody sand angels were sticking swords into him.

Scars blasted away at Sariel with her rifle so enthusiastically that she almost hit me with her second and third shot, while Sariel was still in the process of blowing apart. I had to drop down into the blood to avoid getting blown apart myself. Sand sprayed everywhere as the shots hit the temple wall, and I was almost blinded. But not blinded enough that I didn't see a new Sariel rising out of the blood behind Scars, even as the old sand angel was falling apart. Sariel's sword was raised above Scars' head and she was already starting to bring it down. I saw Nemo spinning around and bringing his rifle up out of the corner of my eye, but I knew it would be too late to save Scars.

I was the only one who could do anything, and I didn't even have a weapon. The angel statues holding up the altar where the bible rested had given me an idea, though. I thrust my hands out in a flourish and threw some grace into both Sariels in front of me. I used the grace to make the sand turn hard as stone, and suddenly there were two statues in the blood. One stood in front of Scars, fragments of an angel held together by thin strands of stone, where the sand had not yet fallen away. Years later I would see my first Cubist painting in Picasso's studio in Montmarte and think of this day. The other statue stood frozen behind Scars, its sword hovering in mid-swing inches above her head.

Nemo took aim at the statue behind Scars but I knocked his rifle away as he fired, and he blasted a hole in the other side of the temple instead. I was beginning to worry about the structural integrity of the building.

"Would you prefer I shoot you?" he asked. "Because I'm considering it."

"If you destroy her, she'll just come back again," I said. "This way, I think she can't do anything."

Nemo narrowed his eyes as he studied the angels. "I see. For each angel that falls, another rises."

"If she doesn't fall, she can't rise again," I said. It was a guess, but I didn't see any more sand angels.

Nemo looked back at his crew. "You're dying," he said to One-Eye, who was staring down at the stone sword sticking out of his chest.

"I'd like to say it's been a good life, but we all know better," One-Eye said.

"If your people have any last rites or anything, now's probably a good time to do them," I said. It was one of those kind of wounds.

"There's no need for that," Nemo said. He went around behind One-Eye and pulled the sword out of him. One-Eye screamed and fell into my arms.

"You have some secret technology from Atlantis that can save him?" I asked.

"Better," Nemo said. "I have you."

I sighed, understanding what he meant. "I don't have much grace left to spare," I said, which wasn't exactly true. It wouldn't take that much to heal One-Eye. But who knew when I would stumble across a real angel and be able to replenish my grace again?

"We have the bible now," Nemo said. "What use do we have for you if you don't even have grace to spare?"

"Fair point," I said. I looked down at One-Eye, whose eye had rolled back in his head as he gurgled his last breath. I let the grace flow through me and into him, healing the wound. I tried to ignore the growing feeling of emptiness inside me. When One-Eye's eye rolled back down, I pushed him away from me, back to his feet.

"Thank you," he said.

"I'm glad I could help," I lied.

"I was talking to Captain Nemo," One-Eye said.

Atlanteans. They were all the same.

We waded through the blood over to the altar. One-Eye moved a little slower than the rest of us, preoccupied with feeling his chest and back with his free hand. Everyone's like that the first time they almost die.

"Is it safe to touch it?" Nemo asked.

"As long as we don't open it," I said. "As safe as something that causes pools of blood and sand angels to form in its vicinity can be, anyway."

Nemo stepped over to the bible and tried to lift it. He couldn't even get his fingers underneath the edge. Scars and One-Eye moved to help him, to about the same effect. Nemo looked at me. "Perhaps you could make yourself useful for a change," he said.

I didn't bother trying to help them. I knew I could maybe lift the bible with the help of some grace. But then what?

"I can't bring the bible all the way back to the *Nautilus* on my own," I said.

"Then we must bring the *Nautilus* to us," Nemo said.

"And how are you going to manage that?" I asked. "Is the *Nautilus* capable of flight? Or perhaps it can swim through the sand?"

"As capable as I am, there are limits to even my ingenuity," Nemo said. "But I have heard legends of a man named Moses who once parted the sea itself so his people could pass."

"I'm no Moses," I said.

"Clearly," Nemo said. "Perhaps you could manage a similar trick, though. In fact, it wouldn't have to be as grand. All we would need is a channel carved between here and the ocean, one wide enough and deep enough for the *Nautilus* to travel."

"Is that all?" I said. "Perhaps you would like me to raise Atlantis while I'm at it?"

"Atlantis is better off sunk," Nemo said.

That sounded like an intriguing subject for conversation, but the tone of his voice suggested it was best saved for another time, if ever. I considered our current list of options, which was a short one. It was a list with only one entry, in fact.

I shook my head, because it was that kind of day. Then I turned and sloshed back outside.

"Keep an eye on the bible," I said. "I'd hate for someone to sneak off with it while we're not looking."

I climbed the steps and walked back the way we'd come. Scars trailed after me, keeping the gun loosely pointed in my direction, while Nemo and One-Eye stayed with the bible. I stopped on top of the dune overlooking the buried city and gazed at our tracks from crossing the desert. Then I got on with it.

I'd never done anything like this before, but how hard could it be? I bent down and touched my hands to the ground. Then I squinted back along the tracks we'd made, trying to find the sea. I was almost ready to begin when I remembered we'd started off in the wrong direction and had to change paths after we'd spotted the shapes in the sky. I shifted a bit on the dune and turned toward what I hoped was the ocean. Then I let the grace flow from my hands and into the sand. And I let it keep flowing.

The ground opened up before me in a chasm. I used the grace to push the sand up to either side, creating a channel maybe thirty feet wide and twice as deep. I kept going in a straight line in what I hoped was the general direction of the *Nautilus*. I felt the grace flowing out of me like a tide, but I kept going until I felt I was almost empty. I hoped it was enough.

If it had been solid earth, I don't think I could have managed it. But the sand was easier to move than rock and soil. Which meant it would also be easier for the wind to fill it back in. We didn't have much time.

I turned back to the temple in time to see the pool of blood widening. It spread out until the edge of it touched the bottom of the dune that Scars and I stood on. Then it began to wash away the dune. We hurried away from the edge but kept an eye on it. I knew where it was going. Sure enough, the blood cut through the sand until it flowed into the channel I had created on the other side. It quickly grew into a raging torrent. I looked back at the buried city, but the blood hadn't risen any in the ruins. It was one of those bible things.

I staggered back down into the temple while Scars stayed on the dune, keeping watch. I looked around for a place to sit, but there wasn't any. That was the trouble with temples. You never got to rest unless you were the one being sacrificed.

"Well, Moses, have you made your miracle?" Nemo asked.

I shrugged. "If you count a river of blood running out to sea as a miracle, then yes." I leaned against a wall, feeling hollow after using up so much grace. "The question now is how the rest of your crew aboard the *Nautilus* will know to come find us."

Nemo raised his rifle at the ceiling and fired an energy blast through it. Sand rained down upon us as I watched the shot disappear up into the sky.

"How long will that keep going?" I asked. I wondered what would happen if it hit the moon or even one of the stars.

"It will falter before reaching the heavens," Nemo said. "As most things do. But it will be strong enough to be seen by the watch on the *Nautilus*. They will know it is the signal to come to us."

"I think I might lie down somewhere while we wait," I said.

"Don't try to flee," Nemo said.

"Where would I go?" I said.

I went back outside, patting the statues of Sariel on the way. I was hoping to feel some spark of grace in them I could drain, but there was nothing. I climbed the sand dune that overlooked the blood canal and sat down. Scars split her time between watching me and looking down the canal, searching for any sign of the *Nautilus*. I wanted to dry my clothes of the blood that soaked them—hell, I wanted new clothes—but I didn't have the grace to spare any more. I settled for lying down on the sand and closing my eyes. With any luck, I'd wake up and find this was all a dream.

Instead, I woke to Nemo nudging me with his boot. I squinted up at him, shielding my eyes from the sun, which formed a halo around his head.

"This is one of the worst dreams I've ever had," I said. "And that's saying something."

"The *Nautilus* has arrived," he said without looking down at me. "It is time."

I sat up and saw the submarine resting on the other side of the dune. The blood river continued to flow against and around it, but the sub didn't move. It was butted right against the dune, its edges scraping the side of the channel. I didn't think there was room for it to submerge, but then I guessed there was no need for that here.

"Can you carry the bible from the temple to the *Nautilus*?" Nemo asked as I stood and brushed the sand from my clothes. I could do nothing about the blood, so I pretended my clothes were simply wet from a refreshing desert rain.

"Next time we do this, we really need to bring Moses along," I said.

"You know as well as I do that's not possible," Nemo said.

"Yeah, because the impossible matters when you're dealing with Moses," I said.

But Moses wasn't here and I was, so I went down to the temple and I picked up the bible and carried it in my arms back up the dune and down the other side, to the *Nautilus*. I staggered like a drunk, and I may have wept a little as I used the last of the precious grace I had left, but I managed to lift the bible on board. By the time I got to the sub, there was a hatch open in its side, and a metal gangplank extended across the river of blood. I had a close call walking across the gangplank, when the bible felt heavier, as if the blood were pulling at it, and I almost fell over the side. I didn't know what would have happened then. I didn't think I had the strength to lift the bible out of the river of blood. I probably would have been washed away and drowned somewhere. But Nemo and One-Eye and Scars grabbed on to me and kept me upright, and we stumbled into the chamber in the *Nautilus* like a bunch of sailors returning from shore leave.

It was a different chamber than the one we had left from, lined with stacks of crates along the walls, secured by webbing.

There was a large open space in the middle of the chamber, and I lowered the bible to the floor there. I dropped it the last couple of inches, and the *Nautilus* rocked back and forth for a minute. That howling in the depths of the sub started up again, louder this time, but I didn't pay it any attention. I stripped off my bloody robes, which did nothing to help the bloody clothes underneath.

"I am out of grace and patience," I told Nemo. "If we happen to cross paths with any angels, please be kind enough to inform me. In the meantime, I think I'll have some more of whatever that fine drink is you have on board."

One-Eye gave Nemo a look that I couldn't help but notice, given that he only had one eye. Nemo shook his head slightly at him. He took off his own bloodstained robes and then walked past me.

"Let's be on our way, then," he said as the hatch slid shut behind me. "Before the bible drags us down to the bottom of the canal and grounds us."

One-Eye and Scars followed him, discarding their own bloody robes as they went. Neither one of them gave me another look.

"Isn't someone going to guard the bible?" I asked.

"Do you really think anyone is going to steal it from the *Nautilus*?" Nemo asked.

I followed them because I'd had enough of the bible for one day, and I wanted to put some distance between it and myself. I felt the deck shift a little underfoot as we went, and when we reached the bridge I saw the *Nautilus* was already backing up along the channel, as there wasn't enough room to turn around. I looked through the forward window and saw the sand dunes around the city slowly collapsing inward, burying the temple and other buildings once more.

No one said much until we had backed all the way out of the canal and were at sea again. The strange howling that sounded throughout the submarine faded but it didn't stop entirely. Nemo ordered us to descend, and I found myself holding my breath as the water rose over the windows of the control room and the outside world grew dark. I would never get used to that. I wondered what would become of the canal after we left it behind. Would it collapse back into the desert right away? Or would it continue to exist until the sand slowly filled it in again? Would the river of blood ever stop? I hoped no one would stumble across it. That was the sort of thing that started religions, and no good ever came of that.

"Set a course for home," Nemo said, settling back into his chair.

"And where might that be?" I asked.

"Atlantis," Nemo said. "The bible will be safe there."

"The sunken city?" I said. "You're telling me the bible will be safe in a city that sank?"

"The legends of Atlantis do not tell the whole truth," Nemo said, gazing out at the water like he could see the lost city in the distance.

I decided that shutting up was the better part of not getting imprisoned, so I joined Nemo in looking out the window at nothing at all. This went on for a few hours, during which I decided life on a submarine was actually more boring than life on a sailing ship. At least on a sailing ship you could look to the horizon for hope of something interesting. There was no hope of anything interesting appearing under the waves.

Once again, I was proven wrong.

The water started to get rough, and the *Nautilus* rocked in an unseen current. The lights flashed red every few seconds. I looked to Nemo, and Nemo looked to another member of the crew, who I decided to call Bad News on account of what she said next.

"There's a whirlpool forming three thousand metres away on the starboard side," she said, frowning at her control panel. "It was perfectly calm there a moment ago."

"Rating?" Nemo asked, never one to waste words.

"Leviathan class," Bad News said, looking at Nemo. So at least I'd named her properly.

"Three thousand metres sounds far, but Leviathan really doesn't sound good," I said.

"Any life forms?" Nemo asked.

"Just the usual marine life," Bad News said, shaking her head. So she wasn't all bad.

"It must be another effect of the bible," Nemo said. "Forty-five degrees port, full speed." He strapped himself into his chair and all his crew did the same. I sat down in an empty chair and followed suit. I had a bad feeling about all of this.

The *Nautilus* shuddered as it pushed against the newfound current. The howling from the engine increased to a wail. Detritus flashed past the windows of the control room. A long piece of driftwood shot by like a spear. A strand of rope hit the window and slithered along it like a tentacle. A couple of surprised-looking fish swam backwards, failing to make any progress against the current. Then a skull tumbled past, grinning at us.

"Not good at all," I said, but I think everyone already knew that.

Then Bad News continued living up to her name. "Captain, we have a surface contact aft," she said. She stared down at a strange disk of shimmering blue on her panel. A red blob of light was pulsing at one edge of it. "It appeared out of nowhere, just like the whirlpool. Two thousand metres and closing."

"I am somehow not surprised," Nemo said, glancing my way.

"Don't look at me," I said. "I don't have anything to do with that."

"It appears to be a man-of-war," Bad News said.

Nemo looked back at that red light. "A curious place for a warship to be found," he said. "Especially one that just appeared out of nowhere."

"Maybe it was just passing by and got pulled into the whirlpool," I said. "Perhaps we should rescue the crew before it's too late." I didn't really believe my own words, but all the other explanations were most likely worse, so I was holding out hope.

"We won't be rescuing anyone," Nemo said. "We can't risk others learning of our cargo. Take us to port another twenty degrees. Then we'll see what current the ship follows."

One-Eye changed course, and there was a few seconds of silence as we waited. Then Bad News shook her head. "The surface contact matched our course change and is still closing," she said. "Eight hundred metres." She paused as she stared at her control panel. "And now it's sinking."

"Take us down to five hundred metres," Nemo said. "And increase speed to evasion level."

One-Eye moved his hands over his control panel and the

constant background hum of the *Nautilus* grew in volume a little.

"Contact has increased speed to match ours," Bad News said. "Depth is now three hundred metres."

"It's moving away from the whirlpool," Nemo said. "It's not sinking. It's following us."

"Weapons systems ready," Scars said.

I turned to look out the aft window of the control room.

"I *really* don't have a good feeling about this," I said.

"Take us ninety degrees starboard," Nemo said. "Let's see how badly they want us."

"Wait wait wait," I said as One-Eye ran his hands over his control panel again. "Are you taking us *into* the whirlpool?"

"Even the *Nautilus* could not survive the centre of a Leviathan-class whirlpool," Nemo said. "But we will go deeper into its edges and see if our friends are capable of following."

More debris tumbled past the windows. The top of a barrel. The oar of a lifeboat. The broken-away top half of a mast. I knew everyone probably had a bad feeling about this by now.

"The contact has matched course again and is still closing," Bad News announced. "Its depth is now five hundred metres."

"Who else has submarines like this?" I asked Nemo.

"There are no other submarines like the *Nautilus*," he said. He spun his chair around and looked behind us. "Release the glowfish," he said.

"What are the glowfish?" I asked, as Scars slapped a button on her control panel. "Are they some sort of weapon?"

"We are not attacking yet," Nemo said. "Not until we know we are facing an enemy."

I looked back along the long, metallic shape of the *Nautilus* and saw a number of small globes drift out of a hatch that opened up toward the sub's rear. I could only follow them for a few seconds, as they were made of glass and nearly transparent. I quickly lost them in the dark water.

"What do the glowfish do?" I asked.

"They reveal the secrets of the sea," Nemo said.

On cue, the water behind the *Nautilus* lit up as if a handful of suns had suddenly risen back there. The glowfish. Each of them burned with light, and together they illuminated a patch of sea as wide and long as a soccer field behind us.

They also lit up the ship that followed us.

And it was a ship, not a submarine. It was a man-of-war, just as Bad News had said. It somehow impossibly chased after us hundreds of metres deep in the water. It sails were fully extended and gave off a greenish glow that trailed after the vessel, like a fog. The man-of-war was as black as the night, and the light from the glowfish seemed to dim near it. The ship's sides bristled with cannons and shards of bones stuck in the wood. The figurehead was a skeleton, but not a human one. It was the skeleton of a siren. I heard a wailing sound then, but it didn't come from inside the *Nautilus*, like the howling I kept hearing. It came from the ship behind us, the sound somehow making its way through the water and metal and glass to reach us in the control room.

All of those things were strange, but they were not the strangest thing. The strangest thing was the men that crowded the deck, waving their swords at us. They were barely more than skeletons, with their dark, leathery skin stretched over their bones, but they were clearly alive, even if they should have been drowning. At their forefront stood a man whose face was hidden in shadows, except for the sparks that burned where his eyes should have been.

"Damn it," I sighed.

Nemo looked at me. "And you claimed you had nothing to do with this," he said. "You know the ship." It was a statement, not a question.

"I'm afraid I do," I said as I watched it close in on us. "It's the *Revenge*."

"The *Revenge*," Nemo said, as if he didn't believe me. He looked back at the ship, which was leaving the light of the glowfish behind. It was close enough now that we could still make it out by the glow of its sails, though.

"It's Blackbeard," I said.

⚓

THE PIRATES' CURSE

I should probably explain about Blackbeard. We have a history. That would be the polite way of saying it, anyway.

Our relationship dated back to the time I tried to find the Holy Grail. I should have known better than to search for it. But you could say that about a lot of things I've done over the ages.

It happened after the whole Spanish Armada affair. There was an episode I didn't mention earlier, when I was telling you about my travels after escaping Noah. It's all rather embarrassing and I would have preferred to forget it. But here we are.

As it turned out, after I'd sacrificed Antonio to Noah and swum to the coast of Ireland, I'd stumbled ashore close to a camp of English soldiers. They were part of the army that was occupied with one of the many misadventures in the north of the land, but they were happy to break their routine of harassing the local villagers by chasing the survivors of the armada who managed to make it to land. I was out of grace and wearing the gear of the Spaniards, so they took me prisoner. They knocked me about a bit but otherwise treated me fairly well given the habits of the day. There's nothing like victory to fill you with charitable spirit. The English put me in an animal pen with some other Spaniards that had washed ashore here and there, although none had been from my ship and they didn't speak of Noah or his ark. Eventually they loaded us all aboard a ship that sailed back to Spain as part of a prisoner exchange.

The other former prisoners and I were taken straight from the dock to a bathhouse and cleaned up. Servants cut off most of our hair to rid us of the lice and such we'd picked up during our stay in the animal pens. Then we were dressed in soldier's uniforms and taken to the royal palace of *El Escorial*. We were paraded before King Philip in a great hall, where military officers told tales of our daring in the battles against the British. Philip sat on his throne in silence and stared at us until he eventually waved at the officers to stop talking. He stood and walked down the line of us, a few dozen survivors of the once mighty armada. Various members of his court followed him, and my eye was drawn to one of them. A plain-looking man with receding grey hair and fine clothes, but not too fine. An advisor, then. We looked at each other as Philip walked the line, asking each man what had happened.

When it was my turn, the king eyed me and sighed. "You are not even a true Spaniard, are you?" he asked.

"I am in spirit if not blood, your grace," I said. Even I knew enough of the proper things to say to stay alive in a royal court.

Philip nodded like he had expected the answer. "And what is your account of the armada's undoing?" he asked.

"A storm," I said. "A most unfortunate storm."

"An act of God, then?" he asked.

"No, your grace," I said. "More like an act of the devil, for God surely sides with us." But he was already moving on to the next man, which meant I didn't have to explain how the devil had triumphed over God after all.

I kept all talk of Noah to myself. None of the other prisoners had ever mentioned him, so I suspected I was the only survivor from the ships that had encountered the ark. I didn't think anyone would believe me if I told the true story, and I didn't want to be labelled a madman. Madmen weren't given free baths and shaves in those days.

The man whose eye I had caught walked past, following his ruler. He looked at me again and I knew what he was in that moment. An angel. I could sense the grace in him. He nodded slightly, and I understood that he knew me, too. Then Philip strode out of the room and we were ushered from the great hall into an immense dining room to celebrate our return to Spanish soil.

I ate and drank and exchanged small talk with my neighbours at the table. I made up a story about my ship floundering and sinking in waves higher than a church's steeple. I slipped away the first chance I had and went looking for the angel. I followed the feel of his grace until I found him in a small study, sitting alone behind an ornate wooden desk. The legs were carved to look like sea serpents and the surface was a sheet of gold. The walls were covered in maps of the known world at the time. More serpents lurked at the edges of the map.

He looked at me when I walked into the room but didn't bother to get up or even call for guards.

"And which one are you?" I asked. "I don't think we've met before."

"I am known here as Lucien, and so that is what you may call me," the angel said. "As for you, I know who you are. And I suspect there is more to your story than you told the king." He didn't look particularly worried that I had managed to track him down.

"I thought talk of Noah might get me thrown out of such pleasant surroundings," I said. "I wanted to at least partake in a meal first."

He nodded as he studied me. "I thought Noah might have had a hand in events," he said. "No matter. Tell me, did your meal satisfy the hunger within you?"

I smiled at him. "Not nearly enough," I said.

He didn't change expression. "You think you have found a gift from God in me," he said.

"I wouldn't call the angels a gift from God or anyone else," I said. "I know you all too well for that. "

"You will not kill me," Lucien said. "Not today, anyway."

"And why not?" I asked. I mean, there were the obvious reasons, like I didn't have any weapons and he was an advisor to the king of Spain in a castle full of soldiers. But those were minor obstacles in the overall picture. I had a feeling he was talking about something else entirely.

"You will not kill me, for I will give you the Holy Grail in exchange for my life," he said.

And that was enough to stop me from raising my hand in violence against him.

"Why would I care about that?" I asked, pretending as if I were not interested.

I'd heard about the Grail before, of course. The goblet that had been used to catch my blood the day of the Crucifixion. Well, Christ's blood. Judas had supposedly drunk from it when he'd visited Christ on the cross as he hung there, dying. This was shortly before I took up residence in this body. The Grail had been lost to time and, like most things associated with Christ, had taken on a mythological status. I had figured it was just another goblet that had been used to drink blood and then lost. History was full of such things, after all.

"Your blood soaked into the Grail," Lucien said. "On that unholiest of all unholy days. The Grail is now imbued with as much grace as the cross that bore your heavenly body. You could drink from it for a thousand years to replenish yourself and it would never grow empty of grace."

"So I let you keep your life and in return you give me the Grail."

"With the Grail, you may no longer have any need for my life," Lucien said. "Or the lives of any of the other angels."

"I'll be the judge of that," I said, but I had to admit I was intrigued. "How do I know you'll tell me the truth?"

"Why would I lie about such a thing?" he said. "It would be in my interest for you to find it. For many reasons."

"Fair point," I said. "Tell me where it is, then, and I'll be on my way."

Lucien's eyes wandered the maps on the walls. "It is nowhere you can find it now," he said. "I can only show you where it has been."

I followed his gaze to look at the maps myself. And I saw one of them changing. The continents on it were growing in size, as if viewed under a magnifying glass. They grew until they disappeared at the frame bordering the map. South America stayed in the middle, though, magnifying until the oceans around it disappeared and it filled the map. The mountains rose up to meet the eye, and I could see jungles and rivers growing clearer.

"You could spare all the theatrics and just tell me where the Grail is," I said.

"You should see what happened," Lucien said. "You should see what the angels see every day."

The map kept on magnifying until I could see individual trees in the jungle and flocks of birds flying above them. It was no longer a map but more a living picture of the world. It showed me a man walking through the jungle with a pack on his back. He had the look of someone who hailed from the Middle East. But even that changed as I watched. His skin turned golden, and his clothes melted away, replaced by bands of feathers and a simple loincloth. His pack transformed into a sack made of the scales of some beast. I could see the shape of a goblet within it. The Grail.

The scene filled most of the map now, as if it were a landscape painting. I knew who I looked upon. Judas.

As if he read my thoughts, he looked up at the sky, meeting my gaze. He grinned at me, showing off a mouthful of sharpened teeth.

I looked back at Lucien. "Is this happening now?" I asked. I wondered how quickly I could make it to South America.

"It happened some time ago," he said. "The maps are a form of archive, if you will."

I looked back at the map. Now the scene had changed. Judas stood atop a tiered pyramid made of stone blocks in a massive clearing in the jungle. The pyramid was lined with men wearing loincloths and brightly coloured robes, all looking up at Judas. The ones nearest the top wore feathered headdresses and gold circlets and rings. I took them to be the local priests, and I was confirmed in my belief when one of them at the top plunged a knife into the chest of a woman tied up and lying on the ground. He cut out her heart and offered it to Judas, who took it with another toothy smile. Judas ate the heart with relish and then reached into his bag and took out the Grail. It was a gleaming golden goblet encrusted with jewels. He bent down and filled it from the woman's body, then handed it to the man who had cut out her heart. He said something to the priest, who fell to his knees and touched his head to the Grail.

"What did he tell him?" I asked. Whatever it was, I knew I wouldn't like it, for it had the look of an order.

"He told him to keep it filled with blood," Lucien said.

Judas went down the steps of the pyramid and the crowd parted before him. He walked off into the jungle and disappeared without a backward glance. The scene suddenly sped up then, seasons passing in an eyeblink. There was a blur of people being dragged up to the top of the temple and cut open there, so that the priests could pour their blood into the Grail. Storms lashed the jungle, the sun rose and set several times a second, the victims died in the dozens and then the hundreds, and the Grail was always full of blood.

"Judas tricked them into believing he was a god," I said. "So they would sacrifice all those people. But why?"

"Because he is Judas," Lucien said. "Is that not enough?"

But the sacrifices weren't the only victims. The conquistadors came calling in a long column of men in armour carrying guns and swords. They marched through the jungle to the temple and shot or hacked down everyone they met.

"You sent them there," I said to Lucien. "To find the Grail."

"There were many reasons we went sent the expedition there," the angel responded.

A group of conquistadors fought their way up the steps of the pyramid, killing the priests who desperately swarmed them to defend the Grail. The pyramid ran red with blood. One of Lucien's men tore the Grail from the hand of the last dying priest and held it up the sky. To Lucien and me.

"But of course it wasn't that easy, was it?" I said.

"Not quite," Lucien said.

The conquistadors marched back into the jungle and made their way to ships anchored along the coast in but a few blinks of an eye. They set out to sea with great cheers and drunken toasts.

But something followed them.

A great winged serpent that erupted from the jungle and flew across the waves after them. It was as long as the ships, but it moved much quicker. It opened its mouth in a screech and the sails of the trailing ship burst into flame. The serpent fell upon the ship and snapped down the crew, one after another, ignoring the blades and musket fire of the screaming men.

"Xiuhcoatl," Lucien said. "An ancient god of the Aztecs that had been slumbering for centuries. All the blood that was spilled woke it. It wanted more blood."

"It's always the way with gods," I said.

Xiuhcoatl smashed its way through the deck of the ship to get at the crew belowdecks. By the time it had finally finished devouring them all, the ship was sinking. The serpent threw itself back into the air and went after the remaining ships. They split up, perhaps realizing they couldn't outrun the god, or perhaps just trying to draw it away from the Grail, so the ship carrying it could make an escape at least.

It didn't matter. Xiuhcoatl destroyed the other ships in the same fashion, one after another. Until there was only the ship carrying the Grail left.

Realizing they couldn't outrun the vengeful god, the conquistadors landed upon an uninhabited island they chanced upon. They left their boats on the beach and hurried into the forest, looking for some defensible patch of ground, as Xiuhcoatl winged its way toward them. But there was nothing, so they eventually turned to meet their fate as the serpent smashed its way through the trees.

You can imagine how things went from there.

The map suddenly reverted back to normal. The air in the room was the sweltering heat of the jungle, though.

"Where is the island?" I asked. I scanned the map but I no longer saw it.

"It doesn't exist in this realm anymore," Lucien said. "That is what happens when you wake slumbering gods."

"So how exactly am I supposed to find it?" I asked.

"You have shown yourself remarkably creative at finding things that didn't want to be found over the ages," Lucien said.

I shook my head. "Nothing is ever easy with you lot, is it?" I said.

"A life challenged is a life lived," Lucien said. He smiled at me. "No doubt this is the moment where you betray me and seek to kill me for my grace."

"I was thinking something along those lines," I admitted.

"Know then that the words I have spoken to you and what you have seen on the map are intimately tied to my very nature," he said. "Once I am gone, even the memory of them will fade with me. Think upon that before you act."

And then he got up and walked past me. He didn't even bother looking over his shoulder to see if I was going to attack him.

I let him go. I'm far too kind, sometimes. I didn't know if he was telling the truth or bluffing. There was only one way to find out, and I didn't want to risk losing my chance at the Holy Grail. So I left the room myself, only instead of going back to the feast, I went out into the night. I kept going, all the way to Haiti.

Once there, I visited a few of the markets until I found the person I was looking for. She was a woman whose eyes had been burned shut forever. I'd once offered to cure her blindness in payment for a favour, but she'd just grinned at me with broken teeth. She said having no eyes allowed her to see things the rest of us couldn't. She said she would take another favour in form of payment. I would have been better off gouging my own eyes out, but that's another story. This time I drank something that was like rum but wasn't rum with her, and she told me how to find what I wanted. When I asked her what she wanted in return, she just laughed like she knew something I didn't.

I rented a boat from a local and rowed out to sea on a night with a full moon. The woman with no eyes said the little trick I was going to perform wouldn't work on any night other than a full moon. Once I could no longer see the lights of land, I stopped and drifted on the waves. I dropped silver coins overboard from a bag I'd brought with me. They were the coins I'd won from sailors in gambling sessions on the trip to Haiti. I cut my hand open and dipped each coin in my blood first. The woman had told me gold would have been more effective, but I couldn't afford gold.

The silver worked anyway. I was most of the way through the bag when the ship came out of the night. A man-of-war that bore a flag of a skeleton holding an hourglass in one hand and a blade in the other. Apparently my time had come. The sails glowed with a green mist that shrouded them and trailed the vessel. Bones and the rusty shards of weapons were stuck to the side of the ship everywhere, like barnacles. The figurehead was the skeleton of a siren, and the ship's name was carved into the wood behind her, as if it had been gouged with a knife. *Revenge*.

The ship came up alongside my boat and the crew looked down at me. They were a worn-looking bunch, even by the standards of the sea. Their skin was sunken into their very bones—they looked as skeletal as the figure on the flag. Their eyes were as black as the night. They climbed up on the rail with cutlasses and pistols, but I didn't do anything to defend myself. I scanned their faces until I saw him. He wore lit fuses in his hair, and the blades of swords were broken off in his chest and stomach, though he didn't appear to be in any discomfort.

So I'd found Blackbeard and his merry crew.

I tied the bag of coins shut again and tossed it up to Blackbeard. He caught it without looking away from me. He had the same black eyes as the rest of his crew.

"That's the first part of my payment," I said. "You'll get the rest when you take me to my destination."

"I'll take you nowhere but hell," Blackbeard said, in a voice that sounded like a thousand winds all bound together. "And you'll be relieved to be there, because it'll mean you're no longer keeping my company."

He could have just been talking, but he could also have been telling the truth. The woman had told me that Blackbeard had learned the dark art of sorcery, which explained the ship and his crew. But he was first and foremost a pirate, and it was to the pirate I made my appeal.

"I seek the Holy Grail," I told him. "The holiest of all holy artifacts. The greatest treasure of all. So rich you cannot even measure its value."

They all looked down at me for a moment that felt much longer than a moment. Then Blackbeard spat into the ocean, and the surface sizzled where his spittle landed. He nodded and someone threw down a rope wet with what I hoped was just water. I climbed up onto the *Revenge*, careful to avoid the sharper pieces of bone and blade on the way. The pirates crowded around me when I swung myself over the rail, but none of them laid a finger on me. They all looked at Blackbeard instead.

"It has been a while since we've had a passenger," he said. "A paying one, at least."

I tried not to look deep into his eyes, for I suspected that way lay madness.

"You don't have the look of our normal passengers, either," he added, and for some reason the others all laughed at that, the sound of it like bones knocking together.

"Trust me when I tell you I'll be your most memorable passenger," I said.

Blackbeard smiled at me, showing off his mouthful of sharpened teeth. I was surprised there weren't more lit fuses among them.

"Give us the map to our destination and we'll set sail immediately," he said, even though the night was calm and there was no wind.

"If I knew the way to our destination, I wouldn't need you," I said. "I seek an island that exists yet doesn't exist. Much like you."

"Perhaps we'll just take your pitiful fortune and maroon you on the first island we set eyes upon," Blackbeard said. "It would be the pirate way, would it not?"

There were mutters of approval from the crew, but at least they didn't cheer. We were still in the negotiation phase.

"Consider the coins a token of my good will," I said. "I'll deliver your full payment when we reach the island. A sip from the Holy Grail for each of you. Who knows what power it will bring?"

Blackbeard stared at me with those dark eyes for a moment longer. Then he nodded.

"Set sail for the doldrums," he said, and the crew threw themselves into action, running about and pulling on ropes and generally doing the things sailors do, which have never interested me much.

A keening noise started over my head and I looked up to discover the sails were not made of cloth and canvas as was the fashion of the day, but from the skins of men and women, all stitched together. But these poor souls were not dead. Black eyes stared down at me and mouths writhed in the sails. The green mist emerged from their lips when they wailed and shrouded them even more. The sails were alive, in their own special way. I looked away before I could really register what I was seeing.

"You had best pray that we find what you seek at the isle," Blackbeard told me before stomping off to the ship's wheel, "or your very soul will be forfeit."

"I don't know if I even have a soul anymore," I told him, and then I went to the prow to watch the waves and keep an eye out for I didn't know what. I didn't want to look at those sails anymore. I didn't know if they were more of Blackbeard's crew or if they were his victims. I wasn't sure I wanted to know, because there was nothing I could do to help them.

I was happy we were under sail, at least. I hadn't been sure if Blackbeard knew where the isle was or not, but I suspected if anyone could find a ghost isle, it would be him.

There was no point lying to Blackbeard about the Grail. He'd figure out what I was after soon enough, once we found the island. I also assumed he'd betray me once we found the Grail. It was the treasure of all treasures, and it was the pirate way. But he probably knew that I knew he was going to betray me. In other words, it was business as usual.

A wind came up from nowhere and filled the sails, thankfully drowning out the noise they made. We travelled through the darkness for what seemed longer than a night. The full moon didn't change its position overhead, but the stars rearranged themselves into constellations I'd never seen before. I didn't know if that was a good sign or a bad one. The crew worked in silence, which I was grateful for, as I needed to come up with a plan for when we found the island.

After a time, the sea grew still and the wind died away. We continued to drift along, carried by momentum or perhaps something else. The sky was reflected in the water, so it seemed as if we were floating in a sea of stars.

Blackbeard came down from the stern and pushed past me. Instead of looking at the water ahead, though, he leaned out over the prow and whispered something into the ear of the siren figurehead.

She didn't reply, but now Blackbeard stared ahead, like she had revealed some great secret to him.

"There," he said, pointing to starboard, and the ship slowly turned that way.

I looked in that direction but I just saw more nothing.

"I don't see anything," I said.

"And that is why you sought me out," Blackbeard said, heading back to the wheel.

He spoke the truth, for soon an island came into view. It looked like all the other small islands that dotted the area: sandy beaches ringing a small, jungle-covered hill. Only it shimmered in and out of existence, like an image caught in a wave. The closer we came to it, though, the more solid it became.

The wind was completely gone now, and we drifted to a stop near a beach that many people would have called a good place to spend the rest of eternity. We dropped anchor and the crew lowered a boat over the side. Blackbeard and a handful of men climbed down ropes to get in the boat and I followed them.

"I trust this is the isle you seek," Blackbeard said. "If it's another ghost isle, then I know naught of it."

"Have you never set foot on it, then?" I asked.

Blackbeard grinned that sharp grin at me. "You might say I've learned my lesson about meddling with the supernatural and the unnatural," he said.

I glanced up at the sails, but they hung limp again. The eyes of the damned in them were shut once more, and they had ceased their mournful keening. I climbed down into the boat without saying anything.

When we drew near to the island a couple of the pirates jumped out and dragged the boat up to the shore. I stepped onto the beach and half expected to sink through it into the water below, but it wasn't an illusion. It was real.

Somehow it had become day without any noticeable dawn. I looked up at the sky to find it dark blue, much darker than it should have been. I looked back down at the jungle. It looked like normal jungle, even though I knew it wasn't.

"I've fulfilled my part of the bargain," Blackbeard said. "Lead us to the Grail."

I nodded and set out for the jungle, like I knew where the Grail was. How hard could it be to find on an island that didn't really exist?

As it turned out, the Grail wasn't difficult to find at all. We just had to follow the bones.

They started a few feet inside the jungle, scattered bits and pieces. I'd seen enough battles in my day to recognize them as human. They were mixed up with shards of broken armour and swords. The deeper we went, the more there were of them. The remains of the conquistadors.

"What befell this sorry lot?" Blackbeard asked from directly behind me. I tried not to think of the sword in his hand.

"Pick your curse," I said, thinking of Xiuhcoatl and Judas and even Lucien. It's always the way that mortals pay for the whims of others.

And then we came to the clearing with the giant pile of skeletons. The rest of the conquistadors. They were heaped upon one another in a mound that towered over our heads. Some of the skeletons were intact, but many were not. All of the swords were broken, as were the handful of muskets I saw.

"I'm beginning to think you haven't been entirely honest with me about this island," Blackbeard said. "If I recall correctly, you never said anything about a small army's worth of bodies."

I shrugged. "You never asked."

"I'm asking you now," he said. "Is there anything else we need to know before we start digging through the dead looking for your precious Grail?"

"I know you're planning on double-crossing me," I said. "But I'd advise against it."

Blackbeard fixed me with that dark gaze. "I'll take that under consideration."

So we pulled apart the pile of bones, looking for the Holy Grail. I had a plan for when we found it, but it wasn't much of a plan. My plans rarely were. That made it easier to adapt when things fell apart, which they usually did.

It wasn't Blackbeard or me that found the Grail, it was one of his crew. A thin man with an eyepatch and a hole in his stomach. He pulled the Grail from the grasp of one of the skeletons in the middle of the pile. It was the same golden goblet with gems fixed to its sides that I'd seen on the map. This close, it looked gaudy and cheap. The sort of thing some drunk noble would use to get even drunker. It hardly looked like a vessel worthy of the blood of Christ. Then again, I wasn't really worth the body of Christ, and here I was.

"Stop your search, brothers, for I've unearthed the treasure of the damned themselves," the pirate said. He danced a bit amid the bones, crushing them underfoot.

"Is that the Grail, then?" Blackbeard asked me.

"There's only one way to find out," I said.

"Aye," Blackbeard agreed and ran me through with his sword.

So far, things were going to plan.

I crumpled to the ground, sliding off his blade as I went. It wasn't nearly as smooth and painless as it sounds. Blackbeard grabbed the Grail from his man and held it to my wound. We both watched it fill with my blood.

"We'll have a sip of your life from the Grail and see what it does," he said. "If we like the treasure, I'll let you die easy."

"And if it doesn't do anything?" I asked, spitting blood at him.

He grinned at me again. "Well, we could use more sailcloth," he said.

The bones of the dead began to rattle and shake then.

"Beware!" Blackbeard cried to his men. "We are betrayed!"

Too late.

Smoke poured out of the jaws and eye sockets of the skulls in the pile of bones. The smoke writhed around Blackbeard's men, then coalesced into a shape. A giant, winged serpent that towered over the bone pile. Xiuhcoatl. Its scales were as blue as the sky overhead, and the feathers of its wings were every colour of the rainbow. But the shriek it made was nothing I'd ever heard before, and nothing I ever wanted to hear again. It made my nose bleed and my ears ring with strange cries.

I had known all along that Blackbeard planned to kill me on the island. Why let me escape with the Grail when he could have the treasure to himself? And I suspected he'd test my claims by filling the Grail with someone's blood—mine or perhaps one of his crew. I was counting on that blood sacrifice summoning Xiuhcoatl. Counting on it because I didn't have any other plan. Luckily, so far everything had gone more or less how I'd figured it would. Now I needed a new plan to get out of here with the Grail.

The pirates didn't waste any time. They attacked Xiuhcoatl before its cry had even faded away, hacking at its body with their blades. Black blood sprayed out like steam, scalding the pirates where it touched them. They didn't seem to care. Part of the sorcery, no doubt.

"You'll make my finest sail yet!" Blackbeard cried and threw himself at the serpent. It snapped him up whole in its jaws and swallowed him in what seemed like one motion. His crew didn't seem concerned, though. They just kept hurling themselves at Xiuhcoatl, opening up more wounds in its great hide. And I didn't think Blackbeard was the type to go down so easily—a hunch that was confirmed when I saw his blade thrust through the scales of the god from the inside.

I took advantage of the chaos to roll away, into the jungle. I took the Grail with me. The wound Blackbeard had dealt me was a mortal one, but I wasn't mortal. A little grace and I was as good as new.

I ran back the way we'd come, leaving the serpent god and the pirates to fight it out. When I reached the beach, I saw four more boats from the ship landing, the crew leaping out onto the golden sand. It looked like every single remaining member of Blackbeard's crew. The sounds of combat must have drifted out to them on the ship. I tucked the Grail under my shirt as I staggered out onto the sand.

"We need every fighting soul capable of wielding a blade!" I cried at them, before they could realize I was now the enemy. Well, one of the enemies, at least. "The treasure is defended by supernatural guardians that Blackbeard battles even now!" I waved at my bloody shirt to prove the seriousness of the situation.

Their thirst for a good fight overruled their suspicion of me and they charged past, into the jungle, following the sounds of the battle. I ran with them for a bit, like I was following them, but I gradually dropped back, pretending to favour my wounded side, and then I headed for the beach once more.

This time there was no one else in sight. I grabbed all the oars from the different boats and threw them into one. Then I pushed that boat into the water and began to row. I went past the *Revenge* because it was beyond my ability to sail it on my own. I knew, however, that as soon as the pirates realized I'd abandoned them they would give chase, and I couldn't out-row the ship. I had to disable it.

I summoned a bit of grace from inside me and blew a spark out my mouth. I watched it drift across the water and then catch a gust of air that carried it into the main sail. Within seconds, the sail was burning, the black smoke mixing with the green mist. The keening of the damned drifted across the water to me. I hoped the flames freed them rather than added to their suffering. I didn't bother watching the fire spread to the rest of the ship.

I dipped my hand in the water and used a bit more grace to stir up a current that carried the boat away from the island so I didn't have to row. I used the time instead to inspect the Grail.

And saw that once again I had been tricked.

The goblet was made of wood covered in gold paint. The gems were little more than pieces of coloured glass stuck into the wood. I knew the legends of the Grail said it was made of gold. What I didn't know was who had been the trickster here. Was it Judas? Or had Lucien somehow deceived me? Maybe the trickster was even someone else. It didn't matter. Once again, I had nothing. And I knew by the time I returned to the Spanish court, Lucien would be long gone.

I looked back at the island. Smoke from the burning ship hung over it now, and the jungle shook with the ongoing battle.

Correction. I had worse than nothing. I had new enemies that no doubt would plague me for years to come. But there was nothing to be done about it now.

Most of the blood that Blackbeard had caught in the goblet had spilled out as I'd run through the jungle, but there was still a splash left. I breathed some grace into it and turned it to rum, which I drank as I watched the burning island fade into the night, until I was alone in the ocean once more.

✝

BLACKBEARD'S REVENGE

So that was how we wound up with Blackbeard chasing the *Nautilus* as we carried God's bible to Atlantis.

"Blackbeard," Nemo said. He looked at the *Revenge* closing in on us, then at me.

"I'm afraid so," I said, staring at the pirates crowding the deck of the ship.

"I have heard the legends of the *Revenge* but never before seen it," Nemo said, still looking at me. "What would Blackbeard want with us?" It was a good question.

"He is sometimes attracted to treasure in the sea," I said, thinking of how I had summoned him originally. "I suppose there's no greater treasure than God's bible."

"Indeed," Nemo said. "Could there be any other reason he is pursuing us?"

"We may have a history," I admitted.

"What sort of history?" Nemo asked.

"It's a long story," I said, "and I don't really think we have the time for long stories right now."

As if to punctuate my statement, the wailing from the *Revenge*'s sails grew louder. It seemed I hadn't done the trapped souls any favours when I'd burned the ship the first time we'd met. The *Revenge* suddenly turned to port, much quicker than any regular ship should be able to. Especially a regular ship sailing hundreds of metres under the water.

"Dive!" Nemo snapped, and One-Eye's hands flew over his control panel. At the same time, the *Revenge* fired a full broadside at us. The cannons puffed more of that green mist, and white streaks shot through the water.

Thankfully, the *Nautilus* was not a normal vessel, either. We dove down as fast as a porpoise might, the deck tilting so sharply under my feet I had to grab on to the nearest control panel for support. The *Revenge*'s shots flashed over the *Nautilus*, missing by a few feet. There was a loud clanging sound from somewhere farther back, and the sub shook for a moment. One of the shots had struck us a glancing blow, I realized as the broken remains of a cannonball hurtled past the starboard window, sucked into the whirlpool by the current. The cannonball was no more normal than anything else in this encounter. It was as white as bone. That's because it *was* bone.

"Damage report," Nemo said. His voice was as calm as if we were discussing the weather.

"Minor surface damage," Scars said. "The armour deflected the shot."

"They're just bone," I said. "Your hull can withstand a few shots of bone, right?"

"There's bone and there's damned bone," Nemo said. "I suspect these shots are not the former."

He swivelled his chair so he could keep an eye on both the *Revenge* and the control room. "Bring us around," he said.

I could see men striding about the deck of the *Revenge*, brandishing cutlasses and pistols and walking through the water like it wasn't there. I could see the sails writhing and screaming as they created their own wind underwater. I could see Blackbeard's fiery gaze following us. In fact, all the pirates had fiery gazes now. That was new since the last time we'd met. I wasn't sure what it meant, but I figured it wasn't anything good. Meeting a person with fire for eyes rarely ends well in my experience.

The *Revenge* also came around, until both of us were headed back the way we'd come, the pirate ship a hundred metres or so above us but otherwise parallel with our course.

"Shouldn't we be taking evasive action?" I asked. I was no sailor, but that seemed like the sensible thing to do. "Or maybe trying to outrun them?"

"I don't think we'll be shaking that ship," Nemo said.

Blackbeard apparently agreed. He came to the rail of the *Revenge* and looked down at us. "Surrender to me the one known as Cross and I'll guarantee your deaths will be swift," Blackbeard shouted, in that voice of a thousand winds. Somehow it echoed throughout the *Nautilus* as if he were within the sub itself. "Fight me and I'll make you part of my damned crew, if not part of the *Revenge* itself!"

Nemo gave me a look again, then shook his head. "An agreeable sounding offer, but not just yet," he said. "Give them the eel, with a dose of ink and some starfish to wash it down."

"With pleasure, Captain," Scars said, her face showing no signs of pleasure whatsoever.

The *Nautilus* performed a series of maneuvers that left my stomach hanging in the air somewhere behind me, and made me grab on to the control panel like it was the only thing saving me from the whirlpool. When I dared look out the window again, we had reversed course once more, the sub shaking and straining against the whirlpool's pull. The *Revenge* was a few hundred metres behind, turning into our wake to pursue us.

Then a dark cloud blossomed behind the *Nautilus*, followed by a spray of twinkling metal starfish that hung suspended in the water despite the currents. Nemo ordered us into a sweeping turn to our port side, just as the *Revenge* sailed through the ink cloud.

"You cannot lose me anywhere in the living seas or the dead ones," Blackbeard thundered, his voice shaking the ship. "I'm as relentless as the tide itself."

The ink cloud wasn't an attempt to lose him, though. It was a diversion. The *Revenge* sailed into the net of starfish before Blackbeard could issue an order to evade them, and explosions lit up the dark sea. The *Nautilus* shook some more from the shockwaves. Pieces of the *Revenge* and members of Blackbeard's crew floated away in all directions, before they were quickly whipped away by the whirlpool's currents, but the ship kept sailing forward.

Just in time for us to pass it going the other way. The mines were the second diversion, apparently. Now came the true attack.

"Fire the cannons," Nemo said, as calmly as if he were ordering a tea.

"We have cannons?" I said.

The sea lit up again, as bolts of lightning erupted from the side of the *Nautilus* and swept across the *Revenge*. Wooden beams shattered under their force, but not the pirates. They staggered under the impact and their bodies erupted into flames despite the water, but they waved their weapons at us even as they burned.

"Give them a broadside and send them to hell!" Blackbeard screamed, his voice like a thunderstorm now, but it was too late. We were already slipping past them, and the *Revenge*'s shot only churned up our wake.

Nemo ordered us to keep turning, to come around behind the *Revenge*, where we could have our way with the other ship. But Blackbeard didn't let that happen. The *Revenge* suddenly stopped and spun about impossibly in place, and we were facing its cannons again.

"I would certainly like to learn the secrets of that ship," Nemo said. "Take us over the top." The *Nautilus* surged up, aiming for the gap between the sails of the *Revenge*. Not before Blackbeard ordered another broadside, though.

"Have a taste of the suffering that awaits you!" Blackbeard cried.

This time, the *Nautilus* shook and lurched as the bone shot struck it, and we developed a very noticeable drag through the water.

"I'll rip you apart, deck by deck, limb by limb," Blackbeard screamed as we slid between his sails. The green mist obscured the windows for a few seconds, and grappling hooks shot up around us but none caught. "I'll feed you to the great god myself!" he said, and I wondered which god he was talking about.

"We have three hull breaches in the lower decks," Scars said. "The flooded compartments are sealed."

"We've lost some maneuverability," One-Eye said, "so the rudder must have taken damage."

"We can't outrun him and we can't outmaneuver him," Nemo said, nodding. He looked at me. "Cross, given you two have a history, perhaps you have some ideas?"

I looked back through the window at the *Revenge*, which was following us once more. The wailing of the *Revenge*'s sails echoed throughout the *Nautilus*.

The sails. As long as the *Revenge* had those sails, Blackbeard could chase us around the oceans, above or below the water. But the sails were the weak point of any ship. Perhaps if I could somehow get rid of them, I could immobilize the *Revenge*. The only question was how to destroy enchanted sails made of the skins of the dead.

I did in fact have an idea.

The souls of the poor damned had been bound to those sails in some ritual unknown to me. But I knew my way around souls, so I didn't need to know the ritual to cause problems for Blackbeard.

I reached out in the ways one reaches out to souls and felt them all there, trapped in their dead skin, bound to each other with some supernatural thread. I tugged at a bit of the thread and loosened it, and one of the souls shrieked its gratitude as it fled its prison and disappeared to who knew where. I barely noticed the grace it cost me. Barely. But there were many more souls.

I did the same trick with a handful more, and now I felt the grace leaving me. But the *Revenge* started to slow behind us, and I saw Blackbeard turn his fiery gaze upward.

"I'm taking the wind out of his sails," I told Nemo. "Ready your cannons."

But then I saw a handful of Blackbeard's men clamber up the masts as fast as spiders. They carried what looked like bolts of cloth in their hands, but I knew it wasn't cloth. They tore the empty husks of the souls I'd freed from the sails and left them to drift in the wake of the *Revenge*. They unrolled their bolts and I saw they were indeed fresh sheets for the sail. Blackbeard's men sewed the new skins into the sails, and the ship surged after us again with wails and cries.

"I have a hold full of the damned," Blackbeard roared with laughter. "I'll wager we can repair our sails faster than you can free the poor souls trapped in them. If you could even free them all."

I stared at the *Revenge*, at the men lining the decks with grappling hooks, at the full sails, at the skeletal siren figurehead pointing at us like the blade of a knife.

"I am half inclined to give you over to him and cut our losses," Nemo said to me.

"I think I may have one more idea," I said.

I'd never attempted to resurrect anything like a siren before, but there was no time like the present. There might not be another time if I didn't try it. I reached out to her and gave it my best shot. I let the grace flow from me and into her, and I collapsed into my seat as I emptied out inside.

I was rewarded with watching the siren suddenly awaken on the prow of the *Revenge*, turning her skeletal head this way and that. The ship swung from side to side in the water as she looked about, like it was matching her move for move. Blackbeard's crew had to grab onto the masts and rails of the ship just to stay on board.

Then the siren ripped herself free of the ship and swam back into the midst of the crew, claws flashing. The *Revenge* rolled and spun about, as if caught by one rogue wave after another. A screeching sounded throughout the *Nautilus*, a sound I at first feared to be the hull failing before I realized it was the siren venting her wrath. I lost sight of Blackbeard in the chaos, but I heard him, even through the sounds of the siren.

"Damn your soul to the endless depths, you're a devilish one, Cross!" He sounded more amused than wrathful. "I'll have you in my crew yet!"

The *Revenge* began to drift deeper into the whirlpool now that it was directionless. It rolled and spun in the water. The crew that could manage to do more than hang on fought the siren, who swam through the mess of men, shredding them with her claws and knocking them overboard with her tail, where the current quickly carried them away. The siren continued to screech her rage as Blackbeard's men hacked away at her and sent shards of bone spinning after their lost shipmates. I hoped that her anger was contained to Blackbeard and the crew of the *Revenge*. An angry siren was clearly a force to be reckoned with.

Nemo brought the *Nautilus* around for another broadside. This time our cannons targeted the sails. The lightning tore into them and now the *Revenge*'s main sails came apart. Skins of the damned floated everywhere, crying out as they were swept away. Even if I couldn't free the souls from the sails, they'd be of little use to Blackbeard in pieces.

The *Revenge* spun faster, and now it began to move away from us, slowly at first and then quickly accelerating.

"The whirlpool has them," Nemo said. "They cannot escape now." He looked at me. "Are there any other secrets you're hiding?" he asked.

"Let's make sure we're done with this secret first," I said.

As it turned out, Blackbeard wasn't done with us yet.

The pirate strode to the rail of the *Revenge* and fixed his fiery gaze on us. He didn't seem to notice the wild movements of his ship.

"If I am off to Hell, I will see you there," he said. He raised his sword and then swung it down, chopping it into the rail of the *Revenge*.

"Evasive action!" Nemo said, his voice rising for the first time I could recall.

The *Revenge*'s cannons fired again, but this time no bone shells came forth from them. Instead, the cannonballs were made of that strange green mist. Only now the mist looked as solid as any shot I'd ever seen. They streaked through the water at us, but the *Nautilus* was already diving. Blackbeard's last shots were going to miss.

Then the cannonballs changed course to dive us after us.

"Interesting," Nemo said. "I wonder how that was done."

The cannonballs struck the *Nautilus* in several places, shaking the sub violently. Ice-cold water suddenly began to rise around me, pouring in through a massive hole in the starboard window of the control room. I saw One-Eye slumped in his chair, the back of his head gone. I saw Scars running her hands over the weapons controls, even as the water rose around her and blood jetted out of a massive wound in her neck. Her head had almost been severed by some flying piece of debris. I saw Nemo sitting in his chair, looking around and shaking his head at what he saw.

"To think it ends like this," he said, sounding as calm as ever.

And then the rest of the window exploded inward in a surge of water, and we followed the *Revenge* into the whirlpool.

THE WHITE WHALE

I resurrected to find an angel bending over me. He wore an undertaker's black suit and black hat, but I knew he was an angel because of his wings. I could see their shimmering shapes folded behind his back, even though they were rather intangible. They were made of white, glowing words swirling around and through each other. He had a halo, a glowing disk that framed his head and shone so brightly I couldn't make out his face. For a moment, I thought I was finally in Heaven. I cleared my throat and tried to think of a way to explain all the things I'd done over the ages.

Then I smelled the sea air and heard the familiar creak of wood and the snap of sails as the wind hit them. I was still at sea. The ship fell on the waves, and the halo rose up over the angel's head, revealing itself to be no more than the sun in the sky.

"You live once more," the angel said. "And just in time. We are nearly upon the logos."

"I don't know what you mean, but it doesn't sound good, whatever it is," I said, or at least tried to say. The memories of my death were still upon me, so I ended up mainly gasping for air and thrashing about as if I were still drowning. It usually takes me a bit of time to adjust to my new surroundings when I resurrect.

I must have managed to say something sensible, though, for someone else spoke then. "He means the word," a man's voice said. "We have nearly caught up to the word."

I finished flopping about like a fish on land and sat up. I was on the deck of a sailing ship, sitting in a puddle of water. My clothes were still wet, so I must have just been pulled out of the sea. There were a handful of people clustered around me, but none of them were Atlanteans. There was the angel, who I didn't know. A man with spectacles stood beside him. He wore the clothes of a gentleman rather than a sailor, and he clutched a leather-bound book in his hands. A man with bronzed skin covered in dark tattoos stood on my other side. The tattoos were illustrations of battles starring the man and various unnatural-looking creatures: giant sea serpents and winged monsters and the like. He wore only a cloth around his waist, with several long knives thrust through the rope belt. A harpoon made of what looked like bone was lashed to his back. The rope appeared to be made of the sinew from some great creature. Farther back, a bald man in black robes with smoke for eyes stood behind the ship's wheel, staring up at the sails. His lips moved in some silent speech that I immediately assumed I didn't want to hear.

There was none of the usual crew for the ship, despite the fact that it looked to be a full-sized schooner. The ship appeared to be sailing itself, more or less. Which didn't come as a real surprise, given the fact that there was an angel on board. An angel could sail a ship without the help of any of the others, which made me wonder why there were any others on the ship at all.

There was one more person aboard. A man wearing the clothes of a simple sailor, a deckhand at best. His hair was long and wild, and he also wore a beard that hid his features. His skin was bronzed and leathery, the sign of many a day spent at sea. I recognized him despite all that, anyway.

Ishmael. The monk that Sariel had cast down into the chasm in that monastery all those centuries earlier.

He stared at me but said nothing, even though I could see the recognition in his eyes.

I'd resurrected in plenty of strange places and circumstances, but this one was shaping up to be one of the more memorable ones.

"You are aboard the *Chains of Heaven*," the angel said as I stood and tried to find my sea legs again. "I am Ahab and this is my crew of lost souls."

"Melville," the man with the book said. "The tattooed

gentleman here is Queequeg. He's the harpooner. The, um, man at the wheel is . . . well, it's hard to pronounce. We just call him the Sorcerer."

"Sorcerer," I said, staring at the man. I wondered if he was any relation to Blackbeard.

"He supplies the wind," Melville said, gazing up at the sails. "And other things."

"And that one?" I asked, looking at Ishmael.

"That is Ishmael," Melville said, sparing him only a glance. "He's a simple sailor we plucked from the sea to man the ropes and such."

Ishmael stared at me and said nothing. There was no doubt he recognized me. I didn't say anything about our past because I was still trying to figure out the present.

I looked around and saw we were on stormy seas despite the sun in the sky. The ship rose and fell on large waves topped with whitecaps, and the sky ahead of the ship was a grey wall of clouds. I immediately had a bad feeling about things.

"I suppose I should thank you for rescuing me from the sea," I said, "but I expect I'm not going to be so grateful shortly."

"We pursue the logos," Ahab said, turning away from me and striding to the prow of the ship. "I have chased it across the known and unknown seas. I have crewed my ship with the lost and the damned, as befits such a quest. And now we have nearly caught it, thanks to your foul sin against all that is holy."

"You're going to have to be more specific than that," I said. "I've got a lot of foul sins to my credit."

"The logos seeks the bible," Ahab said, still gazing into the storm ahead. "It wishes to return to its home. Such an event would be cataclysmic without God properly binding it into place. But you have given it such a means with the gyre."

"The gyre?" I asked.

"I believe he means the whirlpool," Melville said. "The Sorcerer had a vision of it a few days ago. And then Ahab sensed the whale changing course for it. We are perhaps hours away. Ahab says we must stop the whale from finding the bible."

"The whale," I said.

"The white whale," Melville said. "We have pursued it across the world, through seas most strange." He looked out at the water, as if troubled by something.

I looked into the storm myself. I remembered the white whale I had seen breach the surface of the sea when I had followed the escaped word from God's bible through the desert, to the ocean.

"The logos is the white whale," I said.

"The logos is the word of God," Ahab said. "The white whale is the word of God unbound. It seeks the bible to return to God again. But without God to bind it, it will break the seals of the bible. It will release the rest of the logos. Who knows what madness would result?" He stretched out his wings, and the words swirled and twisted in the air behind him, as if alive. "We must find a way to bind it again."

"And how do we do that?" I asked. I wasn't exactly opposed to the idea, given I was the one who'd freed the word in the first place. But Ahab didn't answer me. He stared ahead of the *Chains*, as if he could see the white whale out there somewhere.

I turned back to Melville. "All right, so he's the angel trying to bind the word back into the bible," I said. "Queequeg here is obviously the muscle, and the Sorcerer, well he's a sorcerer."

"We found Queequeg in the stomach of a dead serpent," Melville said. "The champion of a people long lost. Ahab cut him out and found a spark of life still within him. The Sorcerer we found on a burning boat overflowing with the dead. He was the only one living, although I don't know his relation to the others." Melville's tone made it clear he didn't want to know much more about the Sorcerer.

"What about you?" I asked. "How did you come aboard the *Chains*?"

Melville stared out to sea. "I was aboard the *Pequod*," he said. "A whaler. We made the mistake of attacking the white whale. It sank us in a day I will never forget. I was the only survivor. The *Chains* sailed through the wreckage a few hours later. Ahab plucked me out of the water and said he had a need for me."

"And what might that need be?" I asked.

"We must have a wordsmith to record events," Ahab said from his spot at the prow. "If we can bind the story to our will, then perhaps it will help us bind the logos once more."

I looked at Melville, who stood there looking weak and mortal. I wondered if Ahab was perhaps a bit mad. He wouldn't be the first angel to have lost his mind in God's absence, after all.

"Lether manning tin'tar!" the Sorcerer suddenly shouted out of nowhere.

"And that one?" I said, turning my gaze to Ishmael, who had busied himself on the sails now. He clambered along the ropes with the ease of practice, despite the wind that was picking up and snapping the sails taut now.

"We found him aboard a lifeboat," Melville said, gazing up at Ishmael. "All alone. He said his ship had gone down in a storm that we knew had sprung up in the whale's wake. Ahab took that as a sign he was to become part of our crew."

I stared at Ishmael. I wondered what his true story was. It was clear Sariel had cursed him with some sort of immortality when she had cast him down into the chasm, if he was still alive hundreds of years later. But how had he come to be here? What did it mean?

"And then we came across you, floating on the surface of the sea," Melville continued. "And Ahab said our mad crew was at last complete."

"I'm no sailor," I said.

"No," Ahab said, "you are the lure."

He turned to look back at me and nodded. Only he wasn't nodding at me. He was nodding at someone behind me. I tried to spin around, because it's never a good thing when an angel gives a signal to someone behind you.

But I couldn't spin around because something was stopping me. And now I felt a great shock in my stomach, a shock that wouldn't go away. When I looked down, I saw the sharp end of the harpoon sticking out of my stomach, covered in my blood.

"Glab," I said, or something equally surprised. I mean, I'd only been alive for minutes since the last resurrection, and already someone had taken it into their head to kill me. And I didn't even know why.

"You're probably wondering why this is happening," Ahab said as Queequeg lifted me into the sky over his head, still impaled on the harpoon. He was impressively strong.

"Hnnnh!"

"We are closing on the logos, but we are out of time," Ahab said. "The Sorcerer says the logos is nearly upon the bible. We must distract it and lure it back to us. That is where you come in. You and your grace. We can only hope the logos senses God in the grace you have stolen from the angels."

With that he turned back to the clouds ahead of us. That seemed to be Queequeg's cue to throw the harpoon into the sea before the *Chains*, with me still attached to the harpoon. It should have been an impossible act, but he managed it. I had a feeling he did impossible acts most days. I flew through the air and for a moment I thought this is what an angel must feel like. Then I fell into the water, and the impact slammed the harpoon back and forth within me, opening up the wound some more. I curled around it like a baby for a moment as I sank in the ocean, then my lungs screamed for air and I managed to kick to the surface.

I rose up to a sea that had gone wild. We were suddenly in the storm. The clouds blocked out the sky and sun, and rain beat down upon me. The waves lifted me high and then dropped me back down, dozens of feet at a time. I could see the line still attached to the harpoon, trailing back to the *Chains* in the distance. I could barely make out the ship through the rain, although Ahab's wings seemed to shine as bright as ever.

"The logos!" Ahab cried. "Draw the logos to you or we are lost!"

"The hell with you!" I managed to say back, although I doubt anyone heard me. It was hard to speak, what with all the water splashing in my face and threatening to drown me, as well as the harpoon rammed through a good deal of my inner parts.

I drifted there for a while, struggling to stay afloat. I rose and fell on the waves, and after a while I couldn't see the *Chains* anymore. The harpoon's line stretched away into the mist and disappeared out of sight. I was alone in the sea. I began to slip under, my head dropping beneath the waves. I kicked back up and managed to find the surface again. But each time it took me longer and I felt more exhausted. My life was bleeding out of me and I was drowning at the same time. I hoped the next time I resurrected it was on the shore of a tropical island somewhere. I really needed a break from all of this.

Then I wasn't alone anymore. I sensed the presence beneath as much as I felt it. I looked down and saw something rising through the water under me. A great white shape. The whale. Or logos. Or whatever it was. It came up from the depths, aiming straight at me. I felt myself lifting up in the water as it came. Its black eyes were fixed on me, and then it opened its great jaws wide. I saw nothing inside its maw. No mouth or teeth or tongue. Or anything at all. It was as if the white whale contained a void within it. A void that was about to swallow me down.

Then the whale was knocked to the side by something that crashed into it below the water. A glowing shape that grabbed on to the whale's fluke and hung on. The whale breached beside me, lifting up into the air like the great leviathan it was. It hung in the air for a moment and I saw what had struck it. Ahab. He was climbing up that fluke now, digging his hands into the side of the whale like his fingers were knives. He looked it in the eye and screamed something I couldn't make out, and the words in his wings flared even brighter and swirled about faster.

Then the whale crashed down into the sea, and a great wave from its impact threw me away an unknown distance. I went under and managed to swim back up to the surface again, but just barely this time. I looked around and saw the *Chains* drifting my way. The crew lined the rail, looking down at me. Melville was scribbling furiously in his book with a quill he'd produced from somewhere. The Sorcerer was chanting something I couldn't make out. Ishmael looked down at me and smiled, which I didn't like to see at all.

Then Queequeg yanked on the line and ripped the harpoon out of me. I spun about in the water, screaming, then choking on my own blood. I was dying for sure and I didn't have enough grace left after resurrecting to heal myself. Yes, a deserted tropical island with no one else on it would be lovely.

Queequeg hauled the harpoon in and prepared to throw it. I spun in a slow circle, carried more by the waves than anything on my part, and I saw what he looked at. The white whale breached the surface again. Ahab was still clinging to it, riding its back.

No, he was doing more than that. He was sinking into its back. He was waist deep inside the white whale now, his body fusing into its head. He still clung to it with those hands that dug into the whale's flesh like knives. He spread his wings wide for balance. But no, that wasn't right either. He wasn't using the wings for balance but for something else. His wings were coming apart in the storm. The words drifted away from each other, somehow no longer bound. Or at least not bound in the form of wings. They fell down into the whale and burrowed into its skin. And then I saw the words moving about in the skin of the white whale itself, before it sank back down under the surface.

But not before Queequeg had cast his harpoon. It stuck into the whale's head beside Ahab, and Ahab grabbed onto the weapon with one hand. Then Ahab and the whale went under, and the line snapped tight. The *Chains* suddenly surged forward, and the crew all cried out.

Then things got strange.

The water began to rise from the ocean into the air, thinning out as it went. I felt myself slowly falling, but I was falling up. I spun about again, and I caught sight of the *Chains* hanging in the air a few dozen yards away. The crew had lifted off the deck and were flailing about. Then the ship began to break apart. First the masts separated from the deck, lifting off and drifting away. The ropes all untied themselves and hung loose in the air. The sails went slack. The planks and boards that made up the ship loosened, the tar and nails that held them together coming free. It was as if the ship was deconstructing itself as it hung there. Or maybe it was as if the world itself was coming apart.

I looked back around for the whale and saw it again in the water beneath me, the sea that I had just risen from. Only now it wasn't a whale. It was a great white serpent that Ahab struggled with. He was still fused with it, though. He held Queequeg's harpoon in his hand and struck the serpent with it, ramming the great blade into the creature's head. The serpent suddenly transformed into a white hydra with many heads, its skin flowing like water as it changed. The heads bit and snapped at Ahab and he struck at them with the harpoon. Ahab's wings were gone now, and the words ran everywhere in the creature's flesh. And now it was a squid that wrapped its many tentacles around Ahab. He roared and the words flared inside the creature and then the *Chains* came apart completely and fell back into the sea, along with the rest of us.

I saw dark rectangular shapes spill out of the *Chains'* hold as we fell, each about the length of a man. It was only when I hit the water and sank down that I recognized what they were. Coffins. The *Chains* was carrying a load of coffins. One of them plunged into the sea beside me, and I caught on to it. I let it lift me back up to the surface. I bobbed there amid the wreckage, surrounded by other coffins that popped up and floated all around me.

Ahab and the white whale were nowhere to be seen now. The water churned and heaved though, so I assumed the battle continued on somewhere in the depths.

Then the crew of the *Chains* began to surface amid the coffins. First the strange head of the Sorcerer appeared a few dozen yards away, gazing around with those smoky eyes. Then Queequeg burst forth an equal distance away on my other side, grabbing on to a coffin and hauling the unconscious Melville aboard. Finally, Ishmael surfaced beside me and grabbed on to my coffin. He gazed around at the others and then at me.

"I have often dreamed of meeting you again, but I have to admit I never saw it playing out like this," he said.

"I hope you'll at least grant me the favour of explaining things before I die," I said.

He looked down at the wound in my stomach, which had pretty much emptied me out by this point. "Yes, you're a dead man," he said. "But I know you, Cross. I have learned much about you since the day Sariel cursed me. And I know you'll be back."

"All right, you know me," I said. "You know what I am. But I don't know what you are. "

Ishmael reached into a pocket and came out with a coin. He grabbed hold of my head with his other hand. "I'm a devil and you're the one who condemned me to Hell," he said. He pulled my head back by the hair and I gasped. When I opened my mouth, he shoved the coin into it, forcing it down my throat. I tried to retch, but he'd lodged the coin in there too well. Now I couldn't breathe on top of everything else.

"And so I shall condemn you to Hell," Ishmael said. He laughed, showing me a set of fangs when he did so. That's when I understood what Sariel had done when she'd thrown Ishmael into that chasm. She had cursed him to a fate far worse than Hell. She had transformed Ishmael into one of the greatest monsters known to humanity. Somehow, by casting him into the abyss, she had turned him into a vampire.

And then Ishmael shoved my head underwater and held me there, and I drowned.

All in all, it wasn't one of my better resurrections.

☦

A CURIOUS ENCOUNTER
AMONG THE DEAD

Ishmael killing me during the battle with the white whale wasn't all bad. It was how I met Alice for the first time, and that is pretty important for a lot of reasons, including how this story ends.

After Ishmael drowned me, I resurrected to find a cold, hard hand reaching down my throat to pull out the coin he had lodged there. I opened my eyes to discover the hand belonged to a giant, skeletal man wearing a dark robe. He stood about eight or nine feet tall and he was completely hairless. His skin was white like a corpse's and his eyes were so pale as to be almost empty of colour. He pulled his hand out of my mouth and held up a coin that was covered in blood and other unsavoury fluids.

I sat up and looked around. I was in a long, black boat, drifting through what looked like a swamp. White reeds grew up through the water in clumps, and dead fish floated here and there. The sky appeared to be made of stone, and it took me a few seconds to realize we were in a vast cavern of some sort. The tall man kept his other hand on a pole that disappeared into the water. The pole looked as if it was made of bone. I spat blood overboard and then nodded at him.

"Charon, I presume?" I said. The ferryman of the dead. I mean, who else could it be?

He dropped the coin into a pocket in his robe as he studied me. "I know the dead, and you were dead," he said in a voice that was a mix of whispers and wind. "A mortal wound and drifting face-down in the water. A coin to pay your way into the afterlife.

Yet now you are alive. You must be the one known as Cross. I have long wondered when I would fish you out of the waters."

It was common knowledge among the Greeks and Romans that Charon would take their dead into Hades for the price of a coin or two. All you had to do was place the body into a boat, or even just the water, stick a coin in its mouth, and send it on its merry way. Charon would take care of the rest. It was less common knowledge that Charon would take any body with a coin, not just the Greeks and Romans. He wasn't discriminatory. Who knew why he wanted the coins? Maybe he just liked shiny things. I probably didn't want to know.

I did know what Ishmael had done, though. He must have heard enough about me that he knew I'd resurrect after he killed me. And he knew I wouldn't be too happy about that. He must have figured that if he couldn't kill me for good, maybe he could get rid of me for good. So he'd stuck a coin in my mouth and sent me out to sea, hoping Charon would find me before I resurrected. And lucky him. He'd come a long way since that first time we'd met. I wondered what had become of the other monks who had fallen into that chasm back in the monastery. Were they all vampires now, too? Or something worse, even? I hoped not, given I was at least partially to blame.

"What of the others?" I asked. "What of Ishmael? And the whale? And the bible, for that matter?"

"You were the only one to pay the fare," Charon said. "So I did not concern myself with the others."

I looked around the swamp. I saw shore in the distance, with some buildings half-hidden by a mist. There were people moving in the water, wearing tattered robes or rags and coming toward us, even though they sank to waist-deep and then shoulder-deep as they approached. Rock walls stretched around us to the vast ceiling overhead. There were more people climbing the rock, some of them even hanging from the ceiling. As I watched, one of them fell from above. He plummeted silently into the swamp and disappeared into the water with a massive splash. He didn't resurface.

"So this is Hades," I said.

"That has been one of the names for this place," Charon said. He pushed on the pole and the boat glided toward the shore.

"How much will it cost for you to ferry me out of here?" I asked.

"I only provide passage to Hades," Charon said. "I do not provide passage back to the land of the living."

"I had a feeling you were going to say that."

I looked at the people in the swamp. They were going past us now, some of them slipping under the surface as the water deepened.

"Looks like they don't need you to get out of Hades," I said.

"There is no current here, at the end of the rivers," Charon said. "The current grows stronger as they travel into the caverns. They will be carried back here. They are always carried back here."

The dead under the water didn't look up at us as we drifted over their heads. They just kept on to wherever it was they thought they were going. Someone else fell from the ceiling overhead, but I didn't look this time.

I sat up straighter and stretched the kinks of death out. I watched the shore approach. The city of the dead looked like any other ancient and forgotten city. I knew I'd find a way out of here on my own. The only question was how long it would take.

"If I recall my legends correctly, there should be a trail leading up to the mortal world," I said. "The one Orpheus used to make his entrance and escape when he tried to rescue Eurydice." The things one does when young and in love.

"The trail is closed now," Charon said. "Only the ferryman knows the ways out of Hades."

"There's really nothing I can do to buy my way out?" I asked.

"Hades will not give up its dead until the end of the world," Charon said as the boat ground up against the shore.

I didn't waste time arguing. When an infernal gatekeeper says no to you, they usually mean it. I hopped out of the boat and onto land. There was some sand that gave way to rock as the beach ended. The skeleton of a large dog with three heads lay on the beach. People in rags wandered past it to approach me, speaking in tongues I didn't understand.

"What are they saying?" I asked Charon.

"They are asking of the world they left behind," he said, pushing the boat back into the water.

"You don't want to know," I said, shaking my head at them. They stared at me with shell-shocked, gaunt faces, and I tried not to think of what it must be like to be trapped in a place like this for eternity. I pushed through the crowd and went deeper into Hades. If there was an exit, it probably wouldn't be right beside the entrance. Many of the dead followed after me, which I didn't really like. You never know what a crowd full of dead strangers is capable of until it's too late.

I went down the street, between rows of buildings with stone pillars and elaborate arches over them. They were the usual sort of thing you'd find in any ancient city, which is where the comparison ended, as the buildings shifted and changed even as I looked upon them. I walked past what looked like a temple, based on the number of masculine figures clutching lightning bolts carved into its facade. Cracks suddenly ran along the length of the building, through the gods and their lightning, as I looked upon it. Fragments of the pillars splintered and crumbled to the ground. I glanced back at the people following me, but they didn't seem to notice. Across the street, a building that may have been a bathhouse suddenly caught fire, great flames leaping out of the doorways. I threw myself to the side, away from the burning building, but my followers walked through the flames like they weren't even there. And maybe they weren't, because the fire didn't seem to burn or otherwise harm them.

It was like that with every building we passed, with the stone splintering and falling away or reforming itself into new shapes as we went, like I was watching the ages of any other place go by in seconds. I seemed to be the only one who noticed any of it. I wasn't sure what caused it, but maybe the buildings of Hades were reflecting the memories of the residents themselves, the ones trailing me through the streets now. Maybe the buildings were nothing more than memories. I couldn't decide if that made Hades better or worse.

The street underfoot at least stayed the same steady rock, worn smooth by the feet of countless souls wandering along it over the millennia. The souls following me now kept speaking in those tongues I didn't understand. I wished I'd spent some time over the centuries learning dead and forgotten languages instead of drowning my sorrows in whatever bottle or drug I could find. It would have made life a lot easier. Then again, it would have made life a lot less enjoyable. Sometimes you're just damned either way, so you may as well have a good time while you're waiting for things to fall apart around you.

If there were still any ruling powers left in Hades, they seemed unconcerned at my presence. They didn't make an appearance, anyway. Maybe they'd followed the example of God and made themselves scarce. I couldn't blame them if they had. The affairs of mortals were a constant mess and no amount of divine intervention was ever going to fix that. The whole race of humanity was the children who were never going to do good in their life.

That meant there was no one to perform crowd control duties, though, which was becoming a problem. There were around fifty or so of those people with the haunted faces following me now, and they were in danger of turning into a mob. They had started shouting things, and their body language had changed. I'd been in this situation often enough over the centuries to know I didn't have much time.

Then I found a building that looked to be a library, if the pillars carved to resemble rolled-up scrolls were any indication. I went up the steps and inside, even as those scrolls melted around me into the shapes of giant mushrooms. I've always found libraries a place of solace and quiet refuge. I was not cheered by the fact that the mob followed me into the building.

It was just as light inside as it was outside, which made me wonder for the first time where the light was coming from. There was no sky, after all, and I didn't see any torches anywhere. But it was one of those things best thought about later, when there wasn't an angry crowd following me wherever I went.

The library was circular in shape, with shelves of scrolls, tablets and ancient bound books lining the outer walls. The middle of the building was stone tables with benches. The tables and benches seemed to be carved out of the ground itself. There was only one other person in the library when we all entered: a woman wearing a formal dress in the style of the age it had been in the outside world when I'd died. The dress was unusual in that it appeared to be made of cobwebs all stuck together, but at least it wasn't the rags and tattered robes the others wore.

She was either someone important here or a visitor like me. She looked at us as we entered but didn't stop wandering the shelves, running her fingers along the scrolls and books. At least this room wasn't shifting and changing like the buildings outside. Not yet, anyway.

"I don't suppose you speak the local tongue," I said to her.

"I always speak the local tongue wherever I am," she said. "But I'm not always wherever I am."

"I see," I said, although I didn't. "What are you doing here now, then?"

"Reading," she said. "It's the sort of thing you do in libraries. Have you never been in a library before?"

"Not with so many angry people," I said, stepping away from the crowd and deeper into the room. Predictably, they followed me.

"They're angry because you're alive and they're not," she said to me. "They always get angry when they're reminded they're not. Maybe they think it will help them. But it won't." She nodded like she'd just spoken a self-evident truth instead of gibberish.

"Are you the librarian?" I asked her. Because it was the only thing that made sense at the moment.

She clapped her hands together like the thought of that excited her. "Oh no," she said. "I'm Alice. I wish I were the librarian, though."

"Alice?" I said.

"Not 'Alice?'" she said. "Alice."

"Are you one of the dead trapped here?" I asked.

"Oh no," she said. "I'm not a person. I'm a character from a book."

"And what book might that be?" I asked, playing along because I didn't see what else to do.

"I don't think I can tell you," she said, "because it's not written yet."

"How can you be from a book that's not written yet?" I asked.

"That's the magical thing about books," Alice said. "They don't have to make sense."

She was a character all right, but I didn't have time trying to figure out what kind of character. The crowd was really pressing in from behind me, pushing at me now and raising their voices.

I knew from experience that's always followed by the punching and kicking stage. The stage that comes next is usually determined by whatever makeshift weapons the members of the crowd have at hand. I didn't want to find out what sort of weapons they had in Hades. I didn't want to be trapped here in the memories of the dead

"I need to find a way out of here before this lot tears me apart," I said.

Alice giggled like I'd said something inappropriate or flirtatious or maybe both. "You can't do that," she said. "Only I can do that." Then she blinked several times, as if an idea had struck her. "At least I think I'm the only one who can do that. What if there are other Alices out there? Ohh, wouldn't that be fun!"

"Do you know a way out or not?" I asked.

"There's always a way out," she said. "Even when there's not." She offered her hand to me and I took it. The mob fell upon us instantly, because that was just the way things were going. But Alice pulled me through a gap in the bookshelves I hadn't noticed before, and suddenly we were running in between rows of more ancient books and scrolls. The restless dead followed us, but Alice pushed me through another gap, this one so narrow it scraped my body on both sides. We went down a spiralling staircase that was lined with more books that looked even older than the other ones. I heard yelling and crashing from up above as the mob followed us down the stairs.

The stairway ended in a small chamber lined with shelves holding stacks of papyrus sheets. There were six stone archways with hallways leading away from the chamber. Each hallway had shelves with more texts. One had scrolls, another folios, another yet more papyrus sheets, and so on.

"I can never remember which one it is," Alice said, "so let's try this one." She pulled me into a hall lined with stacks of stone tablets before I could look too far down the other ones. We'd run maybe twenty feet when the floor suddenly opened up underneath us into a pit. We fell into it before we could stop. Alice didn't even try to stop. She laughed and I screamed as we fell. The walls around us were lined with more scrolls and papyrus sheets and tablets. In fact, they seemed to be made of them. The floor at the bottom of the pit was a jumble of books. We crashed into them and through them and fell into the Hades library again, only we fell through a wall instead of the ceiling.

The mob was gone and the place was empty now. I picked myself up off the ground and looked back the way we'd come. The shelves of scrolls we'd crashed through were intact. I could see the stone wall behind them. There was no way we could have come that way. Yet here we were.

"How did you do that?" I asked.

Alice opened her eyes wide and covered her mouth with one hand. "I have no idea," she whispered.

"What happened to everyone chasing us?" I asked.

"You'd have to ask them," Alice said. "Shall I go get them?"

"Let's save that for later," I said. I looked around the library some more. "I thought you were going to get us out of here."

"I did," she said. "I got us out of the other here. Now we're in this here."

I went to the door and opened it a crack. Hades was still outside and a fresh mob was forming. I closed the door again.

"Is there anywhere else you could take us?" I asked.

"I could take us to another library," Alice said.

"And how do you do that?" I asked.

She chewed on the end of her hair and cocked her head like a bird. I could see spiders crawling around underneath the webs of her dress now.

"You just think about the one you'd like to visit and then you're there," Alice said. "Unless, of course, you're at another library."

"It's so simple I can't believe I didn't think of it myself," I said.

"Maybe you did," she said. "Sometimes people lose their thoughts and I find them in my head."

I nodded like that made sense to me.

"Well, let's begin our voyage, then," I said.

Alice clapped her hands with excitement and opened the door to the street. Instead of a mob of the angry dead outside, though, there was a great hallway of bound books that stretched away as far as the eye could see. Stairs led to higher levels of books, where more stairs led to even higher levels. I couldn't see an end to the library above us or in front of us. There were other hallways branching off from it, also lined with books. The light was golden even though I couldn't see anything casting the light. There were armchairs and couches and tables scattered here and there. It was the largest library I'd ever seen, and it appeared to be infinite.

"There are more books here than anyone could read in a lifetime," I said.

"And each book is its own lifetime!" Alice said. She took me by the hand and led me into the library.

☦

IN THE COMPANY OF MONSTERS

Alice and I wandered the strange library until we came to a great jumble of waterlogged books in the middle of the hall. They were piled up in a dripping mess, surrounded by a puddle. They were all of the ancient tome variety, and so ruined by the water I couldn't make out any of their titles.

"Oh, I'd forgotten about this," Alice said, skipping around the pile. "Or maybe I didn't even know about it until right now. I can't really remember."

"What is it?" I asked, studying the books. I was still wary about this place, and a mess of wet books where there was no source of water did little to reassure me.

"It's a door, silly, can't you see that?" Alice asked.

"It doesn't look like a door to me," I said. "It looks like a pile of garbage."

She stopped skipping and glared at me as she folded her arms across her chest. Spiders scuttled everywhere under her dress. "It's a door to the most important library in the world," she said. "I think it's the most important library in the world, anyway. I'm never really sure because the libraries keep changing what's important about them."

"What library are you talking about?" I asked. I looked closer at the books but I couldn't see a door hiding among them anywhere.

"I don't know," Alice said. "It hasn't happened yet."

"So when does it happen?" I asked.

"When you visit it," Alice said and pushed me into the wet books with a strength no young girl should have. I stumbled forward off balance, trying to regain my footing. When I stepped in the puddle, though, I sank down into it. Or rather, I sank into and through the puddle. Then I was falling somewhere, but only for a second. I landed on a cold, hard floor. A floor that was made of wooden planks rather than the stone floor I'd just been standing on. I pushed myself back to my feet and looked around.

Alice's library was gone, but I was still in a library. It was someone's home library, a small room lined with bookshelves. The shelves were crowded with leather-bound books and curiosities from around the world: a wooden face mask painted with strange symbols, a quill made of a long red feather, a handful of silver coins stamped with a crown I didn't recognize, and so on. The grey sky of early morning came in through the window, lighting up a desk in the corner. A stack of paper sat upon it, alongside a normal-looking quill and ink pot. There was no one else in the room.

"How is this the most—?" I asked, but then I saw Alice wasn't at my side anymore. There was no one else in the room. The only sign of the other library was a small puddle of water on the floor where I'd fallen. It drained away into the cracks of the floorboards as I watched.

I stepped over to the only door and opened it. A hallway of a house was on the other side. It was a regular-looking hallway, dark because of the hour. The other library was gone, as was Alice.

I closed the door again and studied the room. I didn't see what was so special about it. The owner was obviously a world traveller, though, so perhaps there was some clue hidden away. I went around the room, skimming the books, but they were the usual assortment of titles: some travel guides, the *Encyclopedia Britannica*, a dictionary, some Hawthorne and Tennyson—the sort of thing that any well-read gentleman would have in his library.

I looked out the window. There was a yard and trees in the distance, and a road. No other signs of life. I was in someone's country house. I went over to the desk and looked at the papers stacked there. There was a book's worth of them. That's because it was a book. The page in the centre of the desk was cut off in mid-story, the writer evidently having turned in for the night.

It told the tale of a crew pursuing a great whale. My eyes caught on the name *Ishmael*.

I lit a candle on the desk and sat down on the chair. Then I started reading from the beginning of the manuscript.

A few hours later, I heard the sounds of someone coming down the hall. I hadn't finished the book yet, but I'd read enough. I leaned back in the chair and waited.

The door opened and he came through. He stopped and stared at me sitting there. He looked older, weathered with age or experience or perhaps both. He had a beard that was starting to show grey, but he had the eyes of a thousand-year-old man.

"Hello, Melville," I said.

So Alice's door had led not only to a different library but also into the future. For it was obvious Melville had much aged since I'd seen him last, aboard the *Chains of Heaven*. Either that or I'd been in Hades much longer than I'd realized. I'd figure it out later if it mattered, and if it didn't, there was nothing to worry about.

Melville didn't say anything for a moment. He closed the door behind him and stared some more. He put a hand over his mouth and then dropped it again. I may have been just as surprised to see him, but I certainly hid it better.

"I thought you were dead," he said.

"I was. And now I'm not. It's complicated."

"Are you another monster like him, then?" he asked.

"I take it you mean Ishmael," I said. "Funny. He doesn't seem like such a monster here." I nodded at the pages in front of me.

Melville's eyes flicked to the manuscript, then back to me.

"It is a story," he said. "Nothing more."

"Not the real story," I said.

"No one would believe the real story," he said, which was probably true enough. "I am simply trying to capture the spirit of that time." He hesitated, then added, "I am driven to write about it."

"Well, that's not why I'm here anyway," I said.

"*How* are you here?" he asked me. "You sank beneath the waves like the *Chains of Heaven* itself."

"That's a different story," I said. One I didn't really understand myself. I didn't know why Alice had brought me here, or how she'd known about Ishmael and Melville and everything else. Or even what Alice was. But she was a mystery I'd have to figure out later. First I had to find out why I was in Melville's library, for surely this couldn't be a coincidence.

I got up and walked around the desk to stand before him, a little closer than decorum allowed. "I'm here because I want to know what happened after Ishmael killed me."

Melville stepped back, but the closed door stopped him.

I waited. I'd learned patience over the centuries. All right, that wasn't exactly true, but Melville wasn't going anywhere while I was standing there, so I could afford to be patient. Also, I didn't know where to go.

Melville cast a look over his shoulder, as if he expected someone else to walk through the door.

"Let me guess," I said. "Your wife."

He looked back at me and didn't say anything.

"Tell me what I want to know, and I'll leave without a sign I was ever here," I said.

He stared at me a moment longer, as if trying to decide whether or not he could trust me. Then he sighed and nodded. He pushed past me and collapsed into his chair. He gazed down at his manuscript with that far-away look.

"After the *Chains* sank and the sea swallowed up Ahab and that infernal whale for good, we were left adrift," he said. "Myself, Ishmael, Queequeg and that damned sorcerer. I do not know what became of Ahab and the whale. I suspect they perished fighting each other, but I cannot say for certain." He shuffled a few of the pages without really looking at them. "We drifted for days, at the mercy of the sea. We grew hungry. And thirsty. And Ishmael. . . ." He looked out the window now, and the rising sun lit up his face. "Ishmael was the thirstiest," he said.

"He fed on you," I said.

"He fed on all of us," Melville said, his voice barely above a whisper. "The Sorcerer was the first. He simply vanished during the night. Ishmael said a shark had taken him. As if a shark was any threat to one such as the Sorcerer. The second night Ishmael took Queequeg. The savage fought, but the monster was stronger. I had not believed it possible until I witnessed it."

"And then there was just you and Ishmael," I said.

Melville closed his eyes, as if remembering it. "He fed on me during the third night," he said. "He sang a song in a language I don't know. I'll never forget it. I hear it still. He was laughing the entire time."

"Why didn't he kill you?" I asked.

"He said he would spare me," Melville said. "So he could visit me again one day." He opened his eyes and looked at me once more. "As if that were sparing me."

I looked out the window, at the trees and sky outside. "We all have our crosses to bear," I said.

"That morning a schooner happened upon us," Melville said. "The *Grace*, it was called." He laughed, but it was an empty sound. "And so we were saved." He shook his head. "We told them nothing of what had happened, of course. Although we did tell them the truth, in a way. We said we were the sole survivors of the *West Wind*, the ship I had travelled on before it sank and Ahab plucked me from the sea. I said we had been drifting at sea since the *West Wind* had been lost. I suppose that I have indeed been adrift ever since."

"Where is Ishmael now?" I asked.

Melville shook his head. "I do not know," he said. "We made port in London and he vanished into the streets before I had even set foot on the docks."

"You haven't seen him since?" I asked.

Melville hesitated before answering. He took a handkerchief from his pocket and wiped his brow. "Only in my dreams," he said, crumpling the handkerchief in his fist.

"Well, that's interesting," I said. "Tell me more about that."

"From time to time I have nightmares," Melville said. His gaze wandered around the room, as if searching for something. "I am walking down the street or eating at a cafe or even praying in a church for the salvation of my soul. And he is there. Watching me from across the street. Bringing me my drink in the cafe. Lighting the candles in the church." He shook his head. "I am damned."

I thought for a moment. I'd never heard anything about vampires having the ability to stalk people in their dreams before. It was probably just residual terror left over from Melville's experiences at sea.

"Havana," Melville said.

"What about it?" I asked.

"The dreams always take place in Havana," he said. "I have been there in my travels, and so I recognize it."

I stared at him. "Every time?" I asked.

"Every time," he said. "I do not know why, but Havana is my hell."

"Why would . . . ?" But I didn't know how to finish the question. Things had started off strange when I resurrected, and they were getting stranger by the minute.

"I have seen many wondrous things in my travels," Melville said, "but nothing as wondrous as Ahab and the whale. I wish they had never rescued me from the sea. I wish they had let me drown. Sometimes I think that perhaps this is all my dying dream."

The whale. Perhaps the dreams were just another effect of the bible, something that had slipped into Melville during the battle with the whale. Perhaps they weren't dreams but visions.

Maybe they weren't anything at all. Maybe Melville's mind was slowly snapping. But I didn't have anything else to go on.

"The book is good," I said, nodding at the pages on the desk. "You should finish it."

"People will think me mad," he said, staring down at them.

"All the good writers are mad," I said. I went over to him and took the handkerchief. I put it in my pocket. Then I opened the door again and went down the hall and out the front entrance and kept going, all the way to Havana.

I didn't know where to look for Ishmael, so I had to make him come to me. I left the dock where I'd disembarked from the schooner I'd taken to Cuba and wandered the seawall that ran along the edge of Havana. As night fell I stopped at an open square where the locals were holding a dance. I sat on a crumbling section of seawall and took Melville's handkerchief out of a pocket. It was one of only two things I carried. The other was a knife I'd stolen from a sailor aboard the schooner. I left that in my pocket for now. I held up the handkerchief and let the wind from the sea blow it about in my hand. If I had more grace, I would have made the wind stronger, but I had next to nothing left after resurrecting. So I just sat and enjoyed the music and smiled at the locals. I watched the full moon rise and waited.

Eventually a drunk man staggered out of the crowd and fell more than sat beside me. He wore the sun-bleached clothes of a fisherman, and his skin was burnt and leathery. The face, though. He couldn't change his looks entirely. That was too much even for a vampire.

"You stink like Melville," he said. "I smelled you all the way across the city."

I slipped the handkerchief back into my pocket. If you can't be the hunter, then sometimes you have to become the prey. I knew vampires had a sense of smell like no other predator. Enough to catch the scent of a former victim from as little as a handkerchief.

"You're probably wondering how I managed to escape Hades," I said.

Ishmael nodded and spat on the ground. His spittle was bloody. If you didn't know better, you'd just think he was ill.

"I didn't think it would hold you for all eternity," he said. "But I thought it would hold you longer than this."

"You shouldn't have killed me," I said. "And you should have killed Melville."

Ishmael smiled as he watched the crowd. It was the sort of smile you never want to see directed your way.

"Well, it wouldn't be the first time I've made the wrong choice about killing someone," he said. "So why did you call me with Melville's little weeping cloth? Because I don't think you came here simply to get reacquainted. Is it vengeance you're after? Will you gut me in front of all these innocent people?" He snorted, as if the thought of that amused him. "I'd say we're even after what you did to me, but I don't think your one death even comes close to balancing that debt."

"I didn't do anything," I said. "I was simply enjoying a cup of wine in that monastery when you intruded on my moment. You started the chain of events that led to your own curse."

"This is why you called me here?" Ishmael asked. "To justify your actions? I am cut off from Heaven, for God would not allow a monster like me to enter such a holy place. How could you ever justify that?"

"I don't care about the past," I said. "Even if I were responsible for your curse, I've done far worse than that. No, I'm here to ask you something." I leaned closer, so we were looking into each other's eyes. I wanted to see his reaction. "Do you hunt your victims in their dreams?"

He stared at me for a moment, then laughed. He sounded just like any other drunken fisherman would laugh. He blended in well. Vampires always did.

"Why, you're mad," he said. "You didn't escape Hades unscathed, did you?"

I nodded, more to myself than to him. I had the answer I needed, the reason I'd held off killing him. Until now. He didn't know what I was talking about. Melville's dreams weren't caused by him. They had to be connected to the bible.

"You're right, I'm not going to gut you in front of all these people," I said. "I'm going to give you a head start. So you'd better get running."

"Are you sure there's not a bit of vampire in you?" he asked, grinning.

"Whatever's in me, it's far worse than a vampire," I said.

He looked back at the crowd and his gaze was like a cat watching a flock of birds. "I should have fed on you to find out what secrets you contain," he said. "The next time you're at my mercy, I'll not make the same mistake again."

"You don't even know how much of a head start I'm giving you," I said. "And here you are, still talking."

"Let's get on with it, then," Ishmael said and stood. He stumbled into the crowd, a drunk trying to rejoin the party. But I didn't miss how fluidly he moved in between the people, so they weren't even really aware of him. I wonder how many victims had never noticed him closing in on them until it was too late.

I gave him a couple of seconds, because anything more than that was too much time to give a vampire. Then I got to my feet and followed him.

When I emerged from the other side of the crowd, I saw Ishmael throwing himself through the open window of a house near the edge of the plaza. If it hadn't been for the full moon, I might have missed it. But I had timed my arrival well. I quickly scaled the side of the building, using the rough stone for handholds. I knew where Ishmael would go and I wasn't disappointed. He came out a doorway on the roof and I nearly had him. My fingers grazed the back of his shirt. Then he was leaping out into the night, and I leapt after him, to who knows where.

We landed in alley between houses, hitting the ground and smashing into the wall of the next house. He was up and running instantly, laughing as if he enjoyed this. Maybe he did. We went out onto another street that was empty of people and continued our game. At one point he turned and ran backward, looking at me. He was just as fast going backward as he was running normally. Then he sprang to the side, into a park. He scrambled up a tree, then leapt to another one. I followed underneath. I could have used some of the little grace I had left to jump into the trees with him. But I was saving it for something else. Besides, I was pretty sure he was just trying to get me to drain myself, so I wouldn't have anything for later. It wasn't the first time I'd fought a vampire, and I had some idea how they thought.

We went down some more streets that were conveniently empty. All the locals must have been at the dance. Then Ishmael leapt a fence and we were in a cemetery. It was an ancient one that must have been home to the wealthy of Havana, because the grave markers were all fancy, ornate statues and sculptures that towered above me, and the crypts were nearly as large as houses.

Ishmael slipped between the grave markers like they were doorways. He'd vanish behind one and appear beside another dozens of feet away. He looked back at me every now and then, but he didn't seem as concerned now that we were in the cemetery. So I knew this was where the trap lay. Because Ishmael wouldn't have come to me at the seawall if he didn't have a plan. Vampires always had a plan.

He darted behind a crypt but didn't immediately reappear anywhere else. A tombstone did fall over a dozen feet of so beyond the crypt, however. If you were just a mortal chasing him, you probably wouldn't even have noticed the thin line of string that was tied around the tombstone and which stretched back to the crypt. It was almost impossible to notice at night, even with the light of a full moon.

It was a nice trick, one that had probably worked before. But I had my own tricks.

I leapt up into the air, over the crypt. I used a little of my remaining grace to send my shadow in a different direction, around the edge of the crypt and toward that fallen tombstone. It didn't take much grace, as it was little more than a sleight. And even with a full moon, there wasn't much of a shadow to begin with. But Ishmael was a hunter, so he couldn't help but notice it. He lunged out from behind the crypt at the exact second the shadow suggested I would be stepping around the corner. He was all claws and fangs and snarling vampire.

And I wasn't there.

Instead, I fell upon him from above. His head snapped up as he heard me, and he threw himself to the side at the last second. Too late. I caught on to his shoulder and carried him down to the ground. I managed to get my elbow under his chin just before we hit, so I was able to both smash his head into the little stone fence surrounding the crypt and crush his throat with my arm.

That wasn't enough to stop a vampire, of course. He bit and clawed and spat at me. But I had my hand on his throat now, pinning him down and keeping those fangs away. I took out the knife with my other hand and buried it in his guts in a graveyard under the full moon. Really, it was a perfect moment.

Ishmael screamed in pain, then laughed again. "That was a most devious trick," he said.

"As was yours."

He stopped fighting and instead laid a hand on my cheek. "Well, what are you waiting for?" he asked. "I am enough of a hunter to know you have me at your mercy."

"I'm not going to kill you," I said.

"You'll forgive me for being skeptical given our present circumstances," Ishmael said.

"I will spare your life," I told him. "Under one condition."

"I'm listening," Ishmael said as blood ran out of the corners of his mouth.

"You are never to leave Havana again," I said. "Not without my permission."

His eyes narrowed and he studied me for a moment. "What is it you want from me?" he asked.

"I want you to stay where I can find you in the future," I said.

Don't get me wrong—I wanted to kill him. I wanted to kill him quite badly, in fact. But you never know when a vampire could come in handy. Like me, Ishmael was connected to God's bible, if Melville's dreams were any indication. And I had a feeling that the bible wasn't done causing problems.

"You'll spare me even though you know what I'll do to the good residents of Havana?" he asked.

I knew. But there's a price to everything.

"What you do in Havana is your business," I said. "Stay and live. Leave and die. The choice is yours."

I told myself that it didn't matter. We all die in the end, so what difference did it make? Most of you are even lucky enough to stay dead.

Ishmael gave me that cold smile again. "Well then, I suppose I'll stay and enjoy the Havana hospitality," he said.

"Don't get overly enthusiastic about that," I said. "I don't want to have to come back here to clean up your mess." I gave the knife a twist in his stomach, just to make sure there were no misunderstandings about the way I felt. He screamed some more and didn't laugh this time.

Then I stood up and left him there. I walked out of the cemetery and got on with my life.

✝

THE SECRETS OF THE SIRENS

And so it was that I lived and died and lived and died over and over again through the ages, until I found Penelope in the early part of the 20th century, then lost her at Hiroshima along with our unborn daughter, and then decades later watched as Morgana the faerie queen gave birth to that same daughter, Amelia, on the floor of an abandoned pub, and then I saved Amelia and Morgana and a few of the other faerie from the Hamlet ghost in the Forgotten Library, and then went on a solitary pilgrimage along the Camino, which led me to this moment, where I found myself talking to a dead man's head resting on the body of a giant squid floating in the ocean. A dead man who had just told me that Noah planned to end the world.

May you live in interesting times.

"I pray to the God that has abandoned me that Noah succeeds in his quest," Antonio said. "For you have transformed me into a monster, fit only to spend eternity in the bowels of other monsters." He looked around now, his eyes rolling in his head as he gazed at the ocean and up at the moon. "You have shown me the universe itself is naught but a monster we are all trapped within," he said.

"Speaking of that, how exactly did you wind up in this monster?" I asked. Finding him inside the squid I had caught with the strange copy of *Moby Dick* had to be more than a coincidence, but I still wasn't sure exactly what it meant.

"The last time you saw me, you gave me over to an abomination," Antonio said. He looked back at me. "As suits your nature, being an abomination yourself."

"I can't argue with you there," I said.

"After you abandoned me, Noah tore me asunder and cast me overboard," he said. "Where I became no more than a plaything for his pet horrors, like the creature you have freed me from. Limbless and lifeless but denied death. Cut off from Heaven because you cursed me with eternal life—if you can call *this* life."

I knew how he felt but decided against telling him that. I doubted he was in the mood for any bonding.

"That was an accident," I said. "I didn't intend to keep you alive after death." I must have given him too much grace when the ark was bearing down on us those centuries ago. Chalk it up to my drunkenness or the excitement of the moment. It was just as well, though, or I wouldn't have heard the latest news about Noah.

"I thought I was cursed to Hell for all my worldly sins," Antonio said. "But I had not even glimpsed Hell yet. Not like I have now."

"Tell me how this creature that bore you came to be here and I will free you," I said. I scanned the horizon again. Was Noah close even now? "I cannot make up what I've done to you, but I can end your suffering."

"There can be no freedom for me but oblivion," he said. "For even if I am liberated into the great afterlife, I will still have the memories of the horrors of this realm."

"Tell me how you came to be here," I said, "or I'll throw you back into the ocean for something else to eat." It was time for some tough love, or I'd be here all night listening to him complain.

"I have been consumed by all manner of nautical nightmares," Antonio said. "I would not know their thoughts even if I could. I cannot say how the infernal tides carried me to you once more. I only ask that you not cast me back. If there is any trace of humanity within you, you will show me the mercy of a final death."

So I did. I drew out of him the grace that I had cursed him with so long ago, the grace that had kept him alive all this time, despite having been torn asunder and his body parts scattered. I kept my hand on his forehead as I watched the life fade from his eyes. He smiled as he finally died. I don't know if he went to a better place or a worse place or any place at all. But at least he wasn't here any longer. I envied him that much, at least.

I took Antonio's head and dropped it into the sea, where it sank slowly down. I watched it go until it faded away, then I scanned the horizon. There was no sign of Noah. If the squid truly had been one of his creatures, then why was it here? I stared at the lights on the coast again. The encounter with Antonio and the squid hadn't given me any answers. I suspected they were just another sign, like the mysterious dust angel that had pointed me to the monastery and to Alice. Antonio and the squid were pointing me toward something else.

I looked around for the book, but it was gone now. Lost at sea. Maybe one of the dead sailors that filled the depths could use it for some entertainment to pass the ages. I just hoped it wouldn't cause any more problems wherever it had drifted off to.

I used the grace I had taken back from Antonio to pull myself up onto the surface of the water. I walked across it like I had in the old days. Blood dripped from my hand into the waves as I went from where the squid's beak had sliced my palm open, but I paid it no heed. There would be more blood to come before this tale was done. I left the squid floating where it was. The stories of its discovery would no doubt entertain the local fishermen for years to come.

When I made it back to shore, I turned and stared at the ocean. It was calm and quiet. The waves rolled in and out at my feet. The lights of an airliner blinked in the sky overhead. It was as if the battle with the giant squid and my encounter with Antonio had been a dream.

I have to admit, I considered forgetting all about the strange copy of *Moby Dick* then. I even considered forgetting all about Antonio and Noah. But I knew I couldn't. Alice's words still rang in my ears. *Who knows what you could catch with a book like that? Maybe an adventure. Maybe a pirate. Maybe even the end of the world.* Noah was one thing. But I suspected the *Moby Dick* book meant the white whale was likely somehow involved. And if the white whale was involved, that meant that God's bible might also be connected to what was going on. And if what was going on was Noah's quest to end the world . . .

I couldn't just walk away. I had to investigate. Whatever was happening might be my fault, after all. I couldn't go back in time and stop myself from opening God's bible. But maybe I could stop the end of the world from happening.

But first I had to find Noah.

The problem was I had no idea where to start my search. So I went to the ones who might know his whereabouts. At least they weren't that hard to track down. The trick with them has always been surviving once you do find them, though.

I walked through the night, letting the air dry my clothes. I came to a fork in the road. Left led to the village that was presumably home to the fishermen I'd seen earlier, and right led away from it. I took the right fork. I didn't want to go into the village after what I'd done to the boat. I walked and walked and eventually found my way to a town where I didn't think I'd made any enemies yet. I waited at the train station until dawn, when a yawning man opened the doors and another man who looked like he hadn't been to sleep yet sold me a ticket on the first train to Barcelona.

In the train car, I noticed the cut on my hand was still bleeding. Normally my body heals small wounds like that almost immediately, so it was a bit of a mystery. Maybe there was something in the water or the squid's beak. I went into the washroom and used a little grace to heal the cut. Only it didn't heal. Instead of fading away to a scar and then nothing but pink flesh, the cut stayed the same size and blood continued to ooze out. For some reason, my body wasn't cooperating.

I bit open the flesh on the palm of my other hand until it bled, and then I tried the grace trick again. That wound faded away instantly. So it wasn't the grace. It was something about the wound.

I stared at myself in the washroom mirror. I didn't know what to make of this. The grace had never failed me before. But I'd learned over the years that the world was full of surprises.

I wrapped my hand in fresh tissue and went back out to my seat. The businessman sitting beside me looked at my hand. "Cut myself fishing," I said, but he still didn't say anything. He just went back to composing a message on his phone without changing expression. He was an experienced traveller.

I went straight from the train station in Barcelona to the

airport. A few hours later, I stepped off a plane into Athens and the early afternoon heat of Greece. I rented a car at the airport and drove to a certain stretch of fishing villages that is best not to name here. I was wandering the waterfront of the first one by late afternoon, gazing out at the handful of boats anchored in the blue water that mirrored the cloudless sky overhead. A man was drying some octopuses on the rocks on the beach, while farther down another man was painting an overturned boat a brighter shade of red. It was like something out of a postcard, only it was real.

It didn't take me long to find what I was looking for. There was a restaurant near the docks, and it was crowded with weathered men who looked as if they'd spent their entire lives at sea. Fishermen who'd taken the day off or had already put in a full day and were seeking shelter from the sun now. They could have been the twins of the Spanish fishermen. I sent some grace out into my skin to give it the same leathery appearance as theirs and pulled up a chair. I nodded at the men and they nodded back. In places like these, fishermen come and go from the boats all the time. If someone is friendly to you, odds are you've met them before, even if you can't recall where or when.

This group of men didn't care too much that I mostly listened rather than talked. They spoke of storms that seemed to have risen from the bottom of the sea itself. They tried to outdo each other with sightings of strange things in those storms—ships with glowing sails, sea serpents longer than whales. They told stories of near-death experiences: capsized vessels and close calls with drownings. It was the usual fare for a mariners' bar.

At the mention of drowning, they all lifted their glasses in a toast.

"To Xander," they said, and I raised my glass to join theirs.

This is why I was here.

"He drowned?" I quietly asked the man seated to my left, and he nodded without looking away from his glass.

"He went out at night to fish for squid," he said. "He didn't come back. We found the boat, but he's still out there somewhere."

I took a sip of my drink so as not to react to the mention of squid.

"The second one this month," the man on my right said. "The sea is taking back its own."

"Where did these men go missing?" I asked. I lifted one of the bottles from the table and refilled their glasses.

They told me of a place where the tides meet and the winds turn into storms. I won't share the location. If you know it, you already know to stay away from there. And if you don't know it, you shouldn't.

I excused myself to go to the washroom, but once out of sight I kept walking, through the door and back to the docks. This time I stole a larger boat, one with a couple of engines. It wouldn't be missed, as long as I brought it back. I was pretty sure every fisherman in the area was drinking in that restaurant or working on the beach.

I took the boat out to the area they had told me about as the sun sank toward the water. It wasn't my final destination; it was only my starting point. I was searching for the sirens, and they can never be found in the same place twice. They move with the tides and other more mysterious currents. One of the ways to find them is to look where men have recently drowned. The trick is to find them without drowning yourself.

I knew I was close when I heard their song drifting over the waves. It sounds like the surf itself, so much so you don't realize you've been listening to it until you're in their spell. I've had enough dealings with them over the ages that I was prepared. I stopped up my ears with the wax of some emergency candles I found on the boat and melted a little. I used matches to light the candles because I was running low on grace. I was going to have to find another angel soon to replenish myself. First, though, I needed to find Noah.

The wax blocked most of the sirens' song. What was left was like a whisper in my mind. For a moment, I thought about slipping over the edge of the boat and into the water, under the waves, where I could hear the song better. I slapped my face a couple of times and opened up the engine a little more to drown out the noise.

I found the sirens on an island of bones. Or maybe it was a raft of bones. The bones were the remains of those who couldn't resist their song. There are very few beings who can. I didn't know if the bones went all the way down to the ocean floor or not. I didn't want to know.

There were three sirens in this little group. They looked vaguely like the drawings you see of mermaids, but only just. Take the basic premise of a mermaid and add scales as dark as the ocean floor, the teeth of a shark, seaweed instead of hair, and the eyes of the drowned, and you'll have an idea of what they look like. But only an idea.

They were sitting on the edge of their island, combing their weedy hair with finger bones, when they saw me. They cried out and slipped into the water. They surfaced around the boat an instant later, much quicker than they should have been able to travel the distance. I killed the engine because if it came down to it, I wouldn't be able to outrun them.

"The godless one has come back to us," the siren at the bow of the boat sang.

"The first to escape and return since Odysseus," the aft one sang.

"Stay for good this time and we will reward you with heavens even you can't imagine," the one swimming a little pattern beneath the boat sang. The water didn't stop her voice from reaching me.

"We know each other too well for that," I said, and they laughed together. It was like the sound of a ship breaking up as it goes under.

"I need your help," I went on, and now they circled the boat like sharks.

"What could we do that the son of God couldn't?" one of them asked. I wasn't sure which one.

"Why would we help the son of any God?" another asked.

The third one didn't say anything, just lashed the water with her tail, until the boat threatened to tip over. I hung on to a rail and managed to keep myself clear of the water.

"You know I'm not the son of God," I said. "And you'll help me because I'll give you something in return."

"A kiss," the one lashing her tail said.

"A kiss," the others agreed, nodding in unison.

"I don't think so," I said, shaking my head. The kiss of a siren is forever, and I had things I needed to do, places I needed to be.

I looked at the horizon. The sun was slipping under the waves now.

"I'll give you someone in my stead," I said. "Another sailor."

The words were like ash in my mouth, but I had no choice. There was only one thing the sirens wanted. There was only one thing they ever wanted.

"A mere mortal?" one of them asked. It was hard to keep track of them because they were sliding through each other's embraces and intertwining their tails now, like snakes.

"In exchange for the son of God?" another asked.

"We take all the sailors we want," the third one said. Or maybe it was one of the other two.

"And I won't warn the others to stay clear of this area," I added.

"We will drift to somewhere you have not been," one of the sirens said.

"Where the mortals have not heard of gods or sirens," another one said.

"Where we will turn the sea red with their blood," the third one said.

"What is it you want, then?" I asked. I hadn't thought it would go that easy, but you couldn't fault me for trying.

They fell silent, and there was only the sound of the waves. One of them pulled herself up on the bow of the boat to look at me. Her skin was covered in barnacles and other delights. "What is it you seek?" she asked. The others stayed in the water, watching.

"Noah," I said, and left it at that. There was no sense in telling them any more. You didn't want to share too much with the sirens.

"Noah," she said and laughed that terrible laugh again. "We do not know the whereabouts of Noah."

"You know everything in the oceans," I said.

"Noah travels on currents of his own making," she said, like that explained it all.

I shrugged and stepped back to the wheel of the boat.

"I guess we have no bargain then," I said. "And you'll have to move on to that mythical place you mentioned."

The sirens shared a look and a smile or a grimace. It was hard to tell which.

"We would have the *Revenge*," the siren on the bow said.

"You mean your revenge," I said, hoping I had misheard her.

"You know which revenge we want," she said. I tried not to let anything show on my face. I understood all too well.

"We would have our dead sister returned to us," one of the sirens in the water said.

"What good would that do?" I asked.

"Her bones are strong," the one on the bow said.

"Her spirit is stronger," the one in the water said.

"The island needs her," the third one said. She had somehow pulled herself up onto the stern of the boat without me noticing.

I looked at the island of bones. A countless number of skulls looked back at me.

"I'll do what I can," I said. Sometimes you have to make deals with the devil. And sometimes you have to make deals with things much worse.

The sirens all slid under the water and then popped up at different places around the boat.

"We have not seen Noah, but we have heard his voice on the winds and the waves," the siren on the starboard side said.

"What does he say?" I asked.

"The sunken city," she said and slipped back down into the water, out of sight.

"The sunken city at the end of the world," the siren on the port side said and also slipped under.

"The sunken city is the end of the world," the aft siren said and joined her sisters. A whirlpool opened up in her wake, the funnel stretching back in the direction of the island. I saw more bones at the end of the funnel, far beneath the surface. I wondered how many sailors the sirens had claimed over the ages.

I waited for the sirens to resurface so I could ask more questions, but they didn't come back up. They had told me all they were going to tell me.

The sunken city. There were dozens of sunken cities out there under the waves, if not hundreds. But I knew which one they were talking about.

Atlantis.

I turned the boat back to shore. On the way, I passed another man in a boat heading in the direction of the sirens. He didn't look at me, even though our boats were the only vessels in sight on the sea and we were close enough that our wakes rocked each other. He stared straight ahead, into the red glow on the horizon where the sun had once been. He was in a daze, no doubt listening to the song of the sirens.

I let him be and didn't try to warn him about his fate. I have many faults, and one of them is I'm a man of my word too often for my own good.

✟

A STRANGE RETURN TO
THE APOLLO CLUB

After I left the Sirens, I drove the car back to the airport and returned it to the same attendant who had rented it to me earlier. He eyed me for a moment and that's when I realized I'd forgotten to drop the sleight that made my skin look tanned and leathery.

"Ran out of sunscreen," I said and left it at that. If he had any more questions, he was experienced enough not to ask them.

I bought a ticket to Paris, but I had to wait a few hours for the flight. I spent the time wandering the airport until I found a washroom in a deserted section of the terminal. I went into a stall and dropped the sleight and came out a new man.

I washed the cut on my hand in the sink. It was a shallow cut, the sort of thing that should have started to heal by now even if I had a normal body instead of my body. But it was still seeping blood. There was definitely something unusual going on with the wound. The only thing I could do was carry on like normal until whatever the secret behind it was revealed itself. I bought some bandages at a convenience store in the terminal and covered the cut as best as I could.

I tried to sleep on the flight, but I was unsuccessful. The business with the Sirens had left me unsettled. Dealing with the Sirens usually did. I stepped off the plane in Paris and tried to ignore the exhaustion dragging my body down. I had work to do.

I took the metro to a part of the city that had seen better days. I went back up onto the street and walked to a neighbourhood that was almost forgotten by everyone. It was mostly warehouses now, with some slaughterhouses thrown in for variety, judging from the smells in the air. Which meant there was no one on the street this time of night. That was good, as I didn't want anyone to know where I was going.

I wandered along until I came to an old house tucked in between an empty warehouse with a lease sign in the window and a self-storage business that couldn't possibly have any customers here and so had to be a front. Which meant no one ever came this way.

I stood in front of the house and looked at it for a moment. It had been a great house in its time, but now all the windows were covered in bars. The glass was broken behind the bars, but someone had nailed up sheets of wood to seal the windows. The front door was a metal one, and it appeared to have been welded to its frame to prevent anyone from opening it. I didn't bother going around to the back of the house to check there. I knew every entrance would be sealed.

The sign was still over the doorway, although it hung loose on one side now, and you had to tilt your head to read it.

The Apollo Club.

It had been more than a hundred years since I had last been here, when Verne had sent me off on that disastrous trip with Nemo. I'd heard the club had been abandoned during one of the wars, although I couldn't remember which war. Someone must have been looking after the property, though, if it hadn't been destroyed or sold off.

They couldn't have been watching it that closely. I saw a couple of the bars on one window had been cut away. There was enough room for a smaller person to slip through. The broken glass had been cleared from that side, and the board pushed back a little from the window frame. Someone had gone into the house. I hoped they hadn't taken what I'd come for.

I didn't try the window myself. I figured if the opening was that obvious, it was probably a trap. Who knew what lay on the other side? I decided to enter like the honoured guest I had once been. Well, I'd been a guest, anyway. I'll leave it to others to decide my level of honour.

I went up the steps to the front door and put my hand on it. I channeled some grace into the door and let it flow to the edges, where the door had been welded onto the frame. The metal there turned red as it heated up, until it softened enough that I could push the door open on one side.

I slid through and shoved the door shut behind me, the metal still smoking around the frame. I thought about dispersing the smoke with some more grace. I didn't want anyone to wander past and call the fire department. I needed to be alone in here. But there was a good chance I was going to need that grace, so I saved it and let the smoke linger.

I stood in the entrance hall of The Apollo Club. There were closed doors on either side of me. I knew the one on my left led to the great room where the lectures were held, the one on the right to the lounge. Whoever had broken in here had come in through the window on the right side. I hoped they hadn't taken off with all the good brandy. I could use a drink.

It would have to wait, though. I sharpened my vision, so I could see in the dark, and then I went down the hall, past the empty chairs and dusty paintings on the walls, toward the exhibits room. Of course, it wasn't going to be that easy.

There was a body on the floor in front of me. Or rather, it had once been a body. Now it was a skeleton wrapped in the ragged remains of its clothing. A man, judging by the pants and hoodie and boots. He had fallen facing the door, as if he were trying to get back out of the club when he had died. I stepped over him and kept going, a little slower now.

I heard the snoring before I saw him sitting there in the dark, in that last chair before the exhibits room. The old man in formal wear who'd been sleeping in the same chair the last time I'd been in the club. I stopped and looked at him. An empty glass was on the table beside him. He didn't appear to have aged a day since I'd last seen him. That was good for him, as he didn't appear to have any days to spare. I suspected it wasn't good for me, though.

I cleared my throat to try to get his attention, but it failed to wake him up. I tapped him on the shoulder and then stepped back, ready for any sort of attack. He kept on snoring. I gave him a strong shake. He snorted a little this time but still refused to wake.

I shrugged and went past him, into the exhibits room. Maybe

he wasn't some sort of supernatural guard, like I suspected. Maybe he was just another part of The Apollo Club's collection of strange and wondrous artifacts.

It was somehow even darker inside the room, so I fumbled along the wall until I found a switch. I flicked it and was surprised when a couple of bulbs lit up inside their wall sconces. They were enough to light up the room, although it was mostly mood lighting.

I stood in the place where I'd last seen Verne, and where I'd met Nemo for the first time. I looked around for a moment, comparing it to my memory. It looked much as I remembered it, although there was more dust on the chairs and shelves. And, of course, there was no Verne or Nemo.

I cast about until I found what I was looking for. A bottle of brandy on a corner table. I went and poured myself a glass and sipped from it for a minute. Nothing sprang from the shadows to attack me. The old man in the chair kept on snoring.

I looked at the idol of the fish man, still sitting on the shelf on the wall. He looked back at me with those dead eyes.

"I don't know what people see in you," I told him, but he didn't deign to answer me. Idols are often like that.

I finished the drink and put the glass back on the table. I was tempted to have another, maybe even sit in one of the chairs and put my feet up. But I really needed to get what I'd come for and leave this place again, before someone or something came to see who was drinking all the brandy.

I went over to the idol and picked it up from the shelf. "I need a favour from you," I told it. I stared down at it in my hand for a moment, but nothing happened, so I stuffed it into one of my pockets. That's when I noticed the snoring in the hallway had stopped.

I turned to the doorway in time to see the old man shuffle into the room. He was yawning and blinking sleepily. His clothes were wrinkled from a hundred-plus years of slumber. He squinted against the light and looked around until he found me.

"Ah, Cross," he said. "I should have known it would be you."

There were many things strange about this moment. But perhaps the strangest thing was that the old man spoke with Verne's voice. As in he sounded exactly like Verne.

"Jules?" I said. "Is that you?"

"Partially," he said as he shuffled toward me. "But not enough, I'm afraid."

"Not enough for what?" I asked. I decided discretion was the better part of survival in this instance, and I backed away from him, putting a table and a couple of chairs in between us.

"Not enough to let you walk out of here with what you're trying to steal," he said, glancing down at my pocket. "The Isymuth Idol? Whatever do you want with that?"

"That's not really the important question to ask right now," I said. "The important question to ask is what the hell is going on." I backed up past the table with the brandy. I grabbed the bottle and took a long swallow of it, because why not?

"Ah, well, I thought it would be obvious," Verne said. "You've broken in to the club to steal something, and you've activated the sentry system. Which means you should probably be trying to leave with all haste."

"Why are *you* the sentry system?" I asked. "I mean, why are you in the sentry's body? Did someone trap your soul in there?"

"I'm not really me," he said, with an apologetic shrug. He suddenly grabbed the table in between us and flung it out of the way, with much more strength than a normal human should have. "It's rather difficult to explain," he added.

"Why don't you give it a try?" I said, and then I threw the bottle at his head. He didn't even try to duck, so it hit him square in the face. I've had a lot of practice throwing bottles at people over the ages, so I'm a pretty good shot when it comes down to it.

I can also throw a bottle pretty hard, like I did in this case. It split his nose open, and the skin peeled back, away from the wound. And then things started to make sense. It wasn't flesh and blood under the skin. It was metal rods and wires and gears.

"You're a robot?" I said, uncertain if I was understanding things correctly.

"I'm an automaton," Verne said. "And I was created to protect the club and its artifacts. So I'm afraid I'm going to have to kill you. Unless, of course, you can make your escape. I'd much prefer that."

I looked around for another weapon, but unfortunately the

room was short of swords and axes and assault rifles and the sort of thing you normally fight robots with.

"You could just let me leave," I said. "That sounds like a much more civilized plan of action."

"Unfortunately, my programming won't allow me to do that," he said, closing in. I realized he was keeping himself between the door and me the whole time. I'd have to try to get past him to flee. Unless I went for one of the windows. But they were boarded up and sealed with bars. I began to wonder if that was less to keep people out and more to keep people in.

"I don't understand," I said. "Are you Jules or are you the robot?"

"I am both," he said. He opened his shirt as he came, exposing his chest. There was no skin hiding his automaton self there, and I could see the metal rods of his rib cage, the gears spinning inside, and sparks flying in glass tubes.

And I could see his heart.

It looked exactly like a real heart, except it was made of crystal and was fused into the metal walls of his chest. It glowed with a strange light, a colour I couldn't quite pin down and which made me dizzy to look at.

"It's marvellous, isn't it?" he said. "Discovered in an ancient pyramid. It took us years to understand how it worked. That we could use it as a power source. As long as it had its own fuel, of course."

"And what might that be?" I asked.

"Why, souls, naturally," Verne said. He lunged at me, his hands reaching for my throat. I knew that if he caught hold of me, he wouldn't be letting go until I was dead.

There were only a few things I could do. I could keep stumbling backward, until I tripped over something and fell, at which point he'd have me. I could dodge to the left or right. Maybe I could even make it past him and to the hall outside. The same hall with the skeleton of the other man who'd tried to escape the house. So I did something else instead.

I leapt up into the air, sending some grace down through my legs to put a little extra height into it. I caught hold of the chandelier overhead and climbed up it, hanging on to the cable that suspended it from the ceiling. I was glad I hadn't wasted that grace earlier. I was out of Verne's reach now, though I doubted that would last. But I needed time to come up with a plan of action.

Verne stood underneath the chandelier and gazed up at me. "Very good," he said. "You always were full of surprises. Not like the last intruder I drained of his soul." He yawned again, like he was considering going back to sleep. "Not much to him at all." He shuffled over to the nearest wall and began to climb up it, like some sort of spider. This was all very much like a bad dream, and it was getting worse by the moment.

"The heart stole your soul?" I asked. "I can free you, Jules! Just give me the time to do it."

"I gave the heart part of my soul," Verne said, reaching the top of the wall. He dug his hands and feet into the ceiling, tearing through the plaster until he had a good grip. Then he came across the ceiling toward me. "Enough to make a copy of myself, in a way," he said. "For the automaton needs some guiding intelligence in addition to power. I'm afraid I am not the Jules you remember. I am simply a recording of him, if you will. I am sympathetic to your cause, but I am not your friend."

I realized the automaton must have been the security system Verne had said he was working on when I'd last seen him. I also realized Verne was exposing his weakness to me by telling me of his inner construction. But why? It could only be that the copy of Verne wanted me to succeed, even if his programming meant he had to try to destroy me. But how was I to defeat an automaton like this if I didn't even have any weapons?

"Imagine what I could do with a soul such as yours instead of a common thief's," Verne said, and he was nearly upon me now. "I would not need to sleep to conserve my power anymore. I could spend the rest of eternity awake and watching. Perhaps I could even resume my experiments."

And that was when I understood the secret he'd given me. I suspected the automaton's programming wouldn't allow Verne to directly tell me how to defeat it. But he'd given me a clue anyway. He knew I was here on a matter of great import, and he wanted me to succeed, false Verne or not.

"Thanks," I said, nodding at him and dropping back to the ground. I felt the impact in my knees and stumbled a little. I'm only human, after all. Sort of. "I'll leave a bottle of brandy at your grave," I said.

"Make it a fine vintage, please," he said and threw himself down upon me.

That was when I raised the dead man outside.

Resurrection is a simple enough process if you can manage it. You just call the soul back from wherever it is and into the body. There are a few variations to it: do you want the body to be alive when you call the soul back, or is it all right for it to be dead? That kind of thing. The main difference is how much grace it costs you—it takes a lot to raise both body and soul, but not so much if you don't care about the body. It also depends on how much screaming and other hysterics you're willing to put up with on the part of the newly resurrected. You can't really blame them—imagine if you suddenly woke up in your body again after you'd died. Now imagine you woke up in that same body, but that body was still dead, even though you were back in it.

I didn't care if the dead man outside came back screaming. In fact, that probably worked out better for me. A distraction would be handy right about now.

A distraction wasn't why I did what I did, though. I raised the dead man to strike Verne at the heart of his power, so to speak. If that crystal heart of his needed souls for fuel, then putting the soul back in its body might deprive the automaton of the energy it needed to kill me.

The first thing that happened was the immediate screaming in the hall. The second thing was that Verne froze up as he fell. I darted to the side and he crashed face-first into the floor without even trying to grab me.

I breathed a long sigh of relief and picked up the bottle of brandy. The neck had shattered and most of it had spilled out, but there was still enough left that it seemed a shame to waste it. So I finished it off and tried not to listen to the screaming in the hall.

That was when Verne pushed himself back to his feet. His face had completely split open from the impact with the floor, and now I could see all the inner mechanisms of his head. There was a metal skull surrounding more gears and glass tubes. One of the tubes was broken and sparking, and some of the gears were making grinding noises and producing smoke. One of Verne's eyes had fallen out of its socket and hung dangling from some red wires. The other one rolled in a couple of circles and then settled on me.

"Well done," Verne said. "Unfortunately, I still have enough reserve power to finish the job."

I ran for the door. I didn't even bother throwing the bottle at him this time. I just dropped it on the floor. It was clear I didn't have what it took to defeat the automaton. But I didn't have to defeat him. I just had to get out of there alive.

I went past the dead man in the hall. He was flopping around now and screaming as he came to terms with what I'd done. If you've never heard a skeleton scream, count your blessings. It's not a sound you want to hear.

"Sorry about this," I said as I ran past him. It was nasty business, even for me, but sometimes that can't be helped.

Verne thundered after me, his heavy tread shaking the floor. He was close behind.

I hit the front door with my shoulder, forcing it open. I slammed it shut again as soon as I was through and I ran my hands down the sides, sending out grace to fuse the metal into the frame a second before Verne reached it.

I felt the door shift just a little even as I still had my hand on it, as Verne tried to open it from the other side. But my new seals held. They were even stronger than the welding job from before, after all, for they were made of grace.

A section of the door near my head suddenly slammed outward in a roughly circular shape, with a sound like a gunshot to accompany it. A shape about the size of a man's fist. Verne didn't manage to break through the door on his first punch, but it was clear it wouldn't take him long.

I ran down the street, back the way I'd come, with the stolen idol in my pocket. I heard a few more sounds like gunshots, and then they stopped. I glanced behind me but didn't see the automaton in pursuit. A few seconds later, the shrieking suddenly cut off in mid-scream. I kept running, but that was the end of it. Verne didn't pursue me anymore. I figured his programming was willing to let me escape because there were still other artifacts to protect in the house.

I thought I may have heard a voice call out to me in the night as I ran. The voice may have said, "I hope you succeed in your quest, my friend. Whatever it is."

But it may have just been wishful thinking on my part.

I put what I'd done to the dead man out of my head as I left The Apollo Club behind. I wasn't proud of my actions, but I didn't really have a choice. And I had a feeling things were going to get much worse before they got any better. If they ever got better again.

⚭

IT'S ALWAYS RAINING IN INNSMOUTH

After I left The Apollo Club, I walked for several blocks until I could hail a taxi. I went to the airport, where I bought a ticket for New York. When I passed through security, I had to empty my pockets. I put the idol in the little tray along with the wallet I'd stolen from the taxi driver. The security screener looked at the idol, then back up at me.

"Family heirloom," I said, and she waved me through without saying anything.

The flight was a rough one, with turbulence the entire way. More than once I thought the plane was going to shake apart in mid-air. So did everyone around me, judging from the panicked gasps and muttered prayers. Like prayer has ever stopped a plane from falling out of the sky.

Usually when a flight gets rough, I look to the flight attendants for reassurance. If they're going about their usual business, smiling at passengers and handing out snacks, I know it's just routine turbulence. This time, they were strapping themselves in to their seats and looking at each other with worried expressions. One of them even crossed herself. I closed my eyes so I didn't have to see more. I really hoped the plane didn't crash. I never wanted to go through that again.

I figured the idol was probably to blame. I know it looked like it had more to do with the sea than the air, but strange idols are strange idols. You never know what they're going to do.

As it turned out, we landed at JFK Airport in New York without crashing or otherwise dying. It was one of those landings where everyone burst into applause, even the flight attendants. I joined in simply because I didn't want to draw attention to myself by not doing so. There was no other reason than that. I swear.

I went through the usual routine of renting a car with my stolen ID and credit cards. When the clerk informed me my card was no longer active, I nodded and told her to try again, and I blew a little grace out along with my words. She gave me the keys to a car without bothering to try the credit card again. Sometimes there are advantages to being who I am. Sometimes.

I won't bore you with the details of my trip, because it was long and tedious. Let's just say I left the city and made my way to the coast and leave it at that. I mean, there were lots of winding roads in between, with stops every now and then to eat and drink and check for signs of being followed while I put gas in the car. There may have been a bar fight with a couple of truckers that led to a police pursuit, and perhaps there was even some time spent hiding in a shack in the woods that may have also housed a ghost that loved Thoreau, but none of that has any bearing on this tale, so I won't bother telling you whether or not all those things happened.

Eventually, I found myself driving along an abandoned road that ran alongside the ocean. I'd left the highway hours ago and gone down a number of increasingly narrow and overgrown routes, until I found myself where I was now. A gentle rain was falling, and wisps of mist covered the road here and there. It was all very atmospheric—just the kind of thing that happens when you drive around with stolen idols in your pocket.

After a while I came across a police car with its lights on. It was blocking the road, but its doors were open and no one was inside. I couldn't see anyone in the trees around us. That was all right. I knew the routine. The cop car was just a way of keeping people from continuing down the road.

I got out of the rental and went over to the police car. I sat behind the wheel and ignored the blood all over the windshield. I put the vehicle in reverse and backed it up a bit, enough I could squeeze through with the other car. When I was done pulling the rental past, I got back into the police car and blocked the road again. I wanted to be a good guest. I came with a favour to ask, after all.

I kept driving down the road after I left the police car

behind. I followed it until it turned into a muddy path and the car eventually got stuck. By now I could see a church steeple covered in starfish poking over a hill, so I knew I'd arrived in Innsmouth. And when you arrive in Innsmouth, it's too late to turn back at that point.

Innsmouth could have been an easier place to find, but then other people might find it, and who wanted that?

I walked over the hill and down into the town. I knew no one would need to get past the car. I was the only one who'd be driving that road today. As for the residents of the town, they didn't go inland too often.

The town was just a scattering of old wooden buildings near the water. Some houses and a few stores, a warehouse, the usual kind of thing. None of the buildings looked as if they had been painted in decades, if ever. There weren't any other vehicles in sight, or roads. There weren't even any other people to be seen. The dock was full of boats, and gulls hung in the air overhead, screeching their rage at my presence. Or maybe they were just upset about being gulls.

I reached the town's only bar and paused. I told myself I really needed to start coming up with plans for situations like this, instead of just charging blindly into strange drinking establishments in strange towns. It wasn't the first time I'd told myself this. My shoes were bricks of mud by this point. I cleaned them off as best I could on the edge of the building, then I took a deep breath and went inside.

The place was as cozy as things got in the town of Innsmouth: there were a few tables and chairs, the floor was relatively dry and not flooded at all—there was even a small blaze struggling to survive in the fireplace built into one wall.

And then there were the customers. There were maybe a half dozen residents of Innsmouth scattered about the room. They all turned to look at me as I entered, and I took the time to look back at them. They wore the standard garb of fishermen—rain slickers and aprons and thick sweaters and the like. But their gear had personalized touches I'd never seen on any other fishermen before. One's man rain hat was decorated with barnacles and garlands of seaweed. Another man wore fish skeletons in his hair. The man behind the bar had a fish hook in his cheek. And so on. They stared at me with the dead eyes of sailors who have been underwater for longer than they can hold their breath, but they didn't say anything. I took their silence as an invitation to make myself at home.

I went over to a table where I could watch the room and the door at the same time. I sat down and picked up the menu on the table. It was made of cheap laminated plastic and was warped and stained in spots. The name at the top said it was from a ship called *Minerva*. All the tables had different menus. I put it down as the man behind the bar came over to my table, wearing the sort of polite scowl that only bartenders can manage.

"It's been a while since I've been here," I said. "What's good today?"

"We're out of everything on the menu," he said. "All we've got is fish and chips." It sounded like he was talking through a mouthful of water. The residents of Innsmouth have a very peculiar local accent.

"So nothing's changed since my last visit," I said.

"Fish and chips are very popular hereabouts," he said, as if challenging me to prove otherwise.

"I'll take the fish and chips, then," I said. "As cooked as you can make them." I'd learned my lesson the last time I'd visited.

"A drink?" he said.

"A drink for the whole bar," I said, loud enough for everyone to hear. He eyed me for a few seconds before nodding and shuffling back to the kitchen.

I looked around the room again. The other customers were muttering among themselves, but my offer to buy them a drink had kept them from pulling the knives from their belts and showing me that old-fashioned Innsmouth hospitality.

"I'm looking for a ship," I said to no one in particular, because I didn't like to meet any of their eyes for too long.

"There are more ships than you can count on the ocean floor," one of the fishermen at a nearby table said.

"And all free for the taking," another one said.

"Most worm food usually is," the one at the end of the bar said. The local drunk philosopher, maybe.

"I need a ship to take me to the *Nautilus*," I said.

Now they all fell silent and stared at me with those fish eyes some more. The bartender took that moment to deliver the free round of beer to everyone, which did little to improve the mood of the place. Things were going to get even worse when I had to admit to the bartender that I didn't have money to pay for all those free drinks.

The bartender put the last beer down before me, along with a plate of fish and chips that didn't look as if it had been made any time recently, let alone warmed up.

"That's the last of the beer," he said. "So you'll no doubt be wanting to go on your way when you're done."

I tried the beer. It was a bit salty for my taste, but I've had worse. Far worse. And I'll likely have worse again.

"Does that hook of yours ever get caught in anything?" I asked the bartender, looking at the fish hook stuck in his cheek. "Anyone ever try to pull it out?"

It was one of those moments where everything could change, where people drop the thin veneer of civilization and turn on each other. Or where people decide they're not that interested in a fight after all. Or where someone else feels the need to intervene, before things get out of hand. Which is why I'd said what I had. I couldn't care less what the bartender chose to adorn his face with. But I did want to move things along. The world was in danger of ending, after all.

"And what might you want with the *Nautilus*?" the drunk at the end of the bar asked.

"That's my business," I said. I wasn't sure where the townsfolk of Innsmouth might stand when it came to Noah, or Nemo for that matter. I didn't want to share too much with them. "But I'm willing to pay someone to take me to it."

"We don't have much need for money around here," the bartender said.

"Well, that's a good thing," I said, "but I wasn't going to pay you with money." I took the idol out of my pocket and set it on the table. And the dead eyes of everyone in the room came alive, just a little.

"A drowned man once told me our little friend here is of some import to you," I said. "I'm guessing from the looks on your faces that he was right."

They shifted in their seats and flexed their hands. As if

wondering how to get the idol from me.

"You take me to the *Nautilus*," I said, "and this is yours."

That was how I found myself on a fishing boat with the drunk from the bar, sailing away from Innsmouth on a wet, rainy day that was miserable even by Innsmouth standards. The boat was covered in barnacles and seaweed everywhere, even the roof of the cabin that was big enough only for one. The boat looked as if it had been recently raised from the ocean floor itself. Who knew—maybe it had been. Waves came from random directions, rolling the boat and threatening to capsize us, but my new guide didn't look concerned.

The other sailors had elected to stay in the bar and keep drinking the beer I'd bought with my non-existent money. The bartender hadn't bothered to bring me the bill. I guess he figured the idol would be payment enough. Or maybe he was just happy to have me out of his establishment.

The sailor took us toward a fog bank looming on the horizon. I didn't like the looks of it. It's been my experience that nothing good ever comes out of the fog.

"How far is it to the *Nautilus*?" I asked the sailor.

"Nothing over or under the waves is far from Innsmouth," he said.

"That's kind of catchy," I said. "You guys should think of rebranding the town into some sort of tourist destination."

"We have too many visitors as is," he muttered and closed the door to the cabin.

We went into the fog, which smelled like dead things. I thought I heard voices whispering out there somewhere, but when I glanced at the sailor it didn't look like he noticed them. The compass in front of him spun madly, and a little bit of St. Elmo's fire played about the instruments. I decided not to look in the cabin any more.

After a time the water grew rougher, and the boat swung this way and that as we continued on, as if currents were pulling us in random directions. We rode a large wave to its crest, then dropped down its backside and wallowed for a bit. The sailor came out of the cabin then and gazed into the fog ahead of us.

"Are we there already?" I asked. I looked around but I couldn't see anything except the water and the fog. The fact I couldn't see anything made me nervous. Who knew where Noah was at this very moment?

"I can take you no further without payment," he said.

I studied him for a moment, but if he was trying to trick me out of the idol, he wasn't showing it. That was the problem with the residents of Innsmouth: their faces always looked so dead you couldn't really read their emotions. I shrugged and took the idol out of my pocket and held it out to him. If this was a double-cross, there was only one of him. Of course, it was not like I had any idea how to find the *Nautilus* on my own. Or find my way back to shore.

"What do you guys see in this thing, anyway?" I asked him as he took the idol in both hands. He looked down at it for a moment. An uncomfortably long moment. I finally had to clear my throat to get his attention.

"What do you see in the angels?" he asked me.

"Let's talk about something else," I said.

"The *Nautilus* is lost," he said, fixing that flat gaze on me. "And its captain and crew are all dead."

"I know," I said. "I was the one who killed them."

That was the moment another great wave rose up over us and then fell down on the ship, hitting me with the weight of the ocean and washing me overboard. When I managed to thrash my way to the surface, I caught sight of the ship motoring along the backside of the wave, turned nearly completely on its side. The sailor from Innsmouth looked back at me and held the idol up in his hand, as if he were waving. Then another wave crashed down upon me. By the time I kicked my way back up to the air, both boat and sailor were gone.

Once again, I was adrift.

✟

THE SECRET OF *THE NAUTILUS*

After the sailor from Innsmouth left me in the middle of the ocean, I spent a minute or so treading water before the next big wave tried to drown me. I had to admit I'd gotten myself into a bad situation again. In fact, if I was being honest with myself, I had to admit that I'd gotten myself into a worse situation than normal.

I didn't know where I was, but I knew I was a long way from shore. I wasn't even sure which direction to swim. And who could say what might be lurking nearby above or under the water?

As if on cue, a series of waves rolled over me, forcing me beneath the surface. That was when I heard it. The howling in the depths. Something was in the water with me.

Thankfully, I recognized it before I panicked and started thrashing to get away from whatever it was. It was the same howling I'd heard when I'd been aboard the *Nautilus* all those years ago. The sound of its engine, Nemo had said. That sound could only mean the submarine was nearby.

I kicked back up to the surface and took several deep breaths of air. I looked around at the waves, which tossed me here and there without care. Then I dove back under and swam down, in search of the *Nautilus*.

The submarine was easy to find, thanks to the howling. I only had to swim seventy or eighty feet down. A hundred feet tops. Sometimes it's all right to be me.

The sailor from Innsmouth had kept his end of the bargain, no matter how things had played out after that. He'd left me adrift directly above the *Nautilus*. I fought the waves as I descended and managed to go down in more or less a straight line. On the sea floor beneath me was the *Nautilus*.

When I first heard the howling, I allowed myself a moment of hope. I thought maybe the *Nautilus* had somehow survived Blackbeard's final attack and the whirlpool when I had not. I thought I would find Nemo and his crew waiting to welcome me aboard with more of that fine liquor. Who knew—maybe the Atlanteans lived as long as some of my other acquaintances.

You'd think I would have learned my lesson over the ages.

The *Nautilus* was a wreck. It was half-buried in the muck of the ocean's floor. No lights shone in the control room windows, which were still broken. There were holes in its hull here and there along the length of it, where the *Revenge*'s spectral cannonballs had struck. And there was a giant tear in the middle of the sub, exposing the decks inside. The metal there was curled outward, rather than inward. It wasn't from the cannonballs. Something had ripped the *Nautilus* open from the outside.

I paused a dozen or so feet above the sub and looked around, but I couldn't see anything lurking in the depths, waiting to pounce on me. There weren't even any fish swimming about, which was unusual as fish usually love hiding out in wrecks. None of that meant much, as I couldn't see far beyond the ends of the *Nautilus* itself. If there was something waiting, it was probably best to get on with it anyway.

I swam down into that tear in the sub's side and entered the *Nautilus*. I hung there in the darkness for a few seconds, and then a low moan echoed throughout the sub. I turned and swam in what I thought was the direction of the engine room. I didn't have time to waste. I was already having to burn grace to keep oxygen in my system.

I came to a closed hatch and spun the handle open. It moved smoothly, as if the sub hadn't been sitting flooded on the ocean bottom all this time. Chalk it up to Atlantean technology. I swam through to the corridor on the other side and saw red emergency lights flashing on the walls above the brass power pipes that ran everywhere. They lit up the corridor with a bloody strobe effect.

I went past a room that had obviously once been the library. Shelves lined the walls but they were empty now. The books had all fallen to the floor, although a few loose pages lifted up into the air when I stopped in the doorway, disturbed by the current I'd made. A couple of plush chairs still stood upright, because they were bolted to the floor, and a bottle of that fine Altantean liquor rested atop a pile of books, the stopper still securely in the neck of the bottle. I was tempted to pause and have a drink, perhaps even look through the books to talk to Alice. But first things were first.

I continued on through another hatch and came face to face with one of the *Nautilus*'s crew. He floated in front of me, arms spread as if guarding the hallway. His silver eyes stared at me but I could tell they saw nothing. The rest of him was shrunken and drawn, as if he'd been left out in the sun rather than in the depths for over a century. He was more or less preserved, though. Maybe it was something in the water. I gently pushed him away, and he spun back, lifelessly bouncing off the walls. I felt for him, because I knew what it was like to drown.

I patted the dead man on the shoulder in sympathy and swam deeper into the *Nautilus*, until I came to the engine room hatch. I stopped there for a moment because I could hear sounds on the other side. A woman was weeping in the engine room. Then I heard the sounds of metal striking metal, followed by another howl. This close, I could tell the howling wasn't a mechanical noise. Someone or something alive was making the sound.

I opened the hatch and the water suddenly surged forward, carrying me into the engine room. My head bounced off the hard floor and I swore as stars flashed in my vision. That's when I realized the engine room wasn't flooded. The air was stale and foul, but it was air. I got to my knees and took a deep breath. Then I pushed my way through the rushing water, which was already up to my knees, and forced the hatch shut. I turned around, ready for anything. What I saw surprised even me.

The angel Sariel hung naked in the air in the middle of the room. She was suspended from chains that were wrapped around her hands and feet and bolted into the floor and ceiling. I'd never before seen chains that could bind an angel, but I figured the glyphs carved into the metal had something to do with it. They were symbols I didn't recognize, and they pulsed with a golden light, like a heartbeat. Sariel shifted in her chains to look at me, and the metal links clanked against their bolts. That was the source of the metal on metal sounds I'd heard.

The chains weren't the only things holding her. The brass power pipes that ran everywhere in the *Nautilus* also lined the walls in here. Several of them jutted out from the wall and went into Sariel's sides. They were jammed directly into her body and looked as if they'd been fused with her skin. The pipes lit up here and there with more glowing glyphs. I realized Nemo had told the truth when he said the howling was the *Nautilus*'s engine. Somehow the Atlanteans had incorporated Sariel into the submarine and made the angel a power source. I understood now why Nemo and his crew had seemed like they'd seen the angel before when we'd encountered the sand Sariels in the desert. As strange as that moment had been for me, it must have been even stranger for them.

It was only when Sariel turned her head my way that I saw she was missing her eyes. I knew she could see me anyway. She was an angel, after all.

"Hello, Sariel," I said.

"I thought I smelled the blood of an abomination in the water," she said. I couldn't help but close my wounded hand into a fist, to keep any more blood from escaping past the bandages.

"It's been a while," I said.

"It has been but a passing second in the great timeline," she said. "Although it has felt like eternity."

"I've often wondered what happened to you," I said. "But I never imagined it would be this."

Sariel turned her head away from me and looked at . . . well, I didn't know what she looked at with those sightless eyes. "I wandered for a time after we parted," she said. "And then I understood I had to be punished for my sins. So I gave myself to the Atlanteans, for I knew they would have the means to make me suffer for the greater good. And they have made me pay well indeed for my transgressions."

"What sins exactly are we talking about?" I asked, although I already had an idea.

"The sin of letting you enter the great library," she said. "For it would not have been destroyed if you had not entered. And if it had not been destroyed, then the greater sin would not have happened."

"The bible," I said.

"God's bible should never have been let loose in the world," Sariel said. She looked back at me. "I can never pay enough for such sins. I can only pray for the end of the world now. And it will be coming soon."

I took a deep breath of that foul air. I wondered how long it had been down here. The angels didn't need air like the rest of us, so it was likely untouched by Sariel. I could almost taste her screams in it, though.

No. I tasted grace in the air. I cast about until I saw one of the pipes halfway along the wall was cracked. Grace leaked from it, invisible to anyone but the angels. And me. I stared at the pipes in disbelief. They were full of grace. Grace that was obviously being siphoned out of Sariel to power the submarine. Unlike me, the angels could regenerate their grace, so she would recover from the loss. But it still had to be a drain on her.

I couldn't help myself. I went over to the cracked pipe and breathed deep of the grace, replenishing my depleted reserves. The more of it I took in, the more I began to feel sympathy for Sariel.

"How long . . . ?" I asked, but I didn't know how to finish the question.

"I've been trapped since the Atlanteans built this infernal craft and bound me to it," Sariel said. "I do not know how long it has been, but I have dreamed of death a thousand times over."

"Your grace powers the *Nautilus*." I said. I still almost couldn't believe it. The *Nautilus* was indeed infernal. I tried not to think about how long Sariel had been down here, trapped in the dead submarine. There were some fates even angels didn't deserve.

"I can no longer call what is within me grace," Sariel said. "I now see it as my damnation."

"I know what you mean," I said, nodding. I looked around to see if there were any other surprises, but there was just the usual sorts of machinery you see in an engine room, none of which I'd ever bothered to learn anything about. There were a couple of dead Atlanteans drifting in the water, but they didn't show any interest in joining our conversation. On one wall, there were air tanks and masks for emergencies, as well as some dive suits that seemed to be made of the same gelatinous material as the chairs in the sub's control room. I went over and tested the regulator on one of the air tanks. I was pleasantly surprised to find the air supply still worked. Atlantean technology may have been infernal, but it was reliable. I strapped on the tank and turned back to Sariel.

"Something ripped open the *Nautilus* from the outside," I said. "Was it Blackbeard?"

"Blackbeard," Sariel said and laughed. It was a laugh devoid of any humour, the sort of laugh one gives when facing a firing squad. "One far worse than Blackbeard visited the *Nautilus* after you left it."

"Who else was here?" I asked, even though I already knew the answer.

"God's greatest mistake," Sariel said and laughed again.

I grabbed a mask and pulled it over my head. When I turned to the hatch, Sariel realized I wasn't going to release her.

"Deliver me!" she cried. "If there is any measure of Christ left in you, you will end my suffering!"

It sounded much like what Antonio had said to me, but I couldn't afford to be charitable with Sariel.

"I'm sorry," I said, "but Christ and I never met." I went back through the hatch, forcing my way through the rush of water when I opened it again. Sariel's screams followed me as I swam back along the corridor. I did my best to ignore them, but it was hard now that I was full of her grace. The story of my life.

I made my way to the cargo hold that had held God's bible. The hatch had been ripped open, the metal around the frame peeled back as if to make room for someone or something larger than the space would permit. I looked inside the hold and saw the floor and walls were a melted mess of metal. The crates that had once been secured to the walls were somehow melted, too, and fused with the metal. Another effect of the bible, perhaps.

The bible was gone.

I could see the depression in the floor where it had rested in all its terrible weight. But there was no other sign of the bible. Someone had taken it.

Noah.

Noah had been here.

Noah had God's bible.

I swam as fast as I could to the control room of the *Nautilus* as Sariel kept on screaming. I passed a few more dead sailors along the way but left them alone. I stopped at the entrance to the control room and took a deep breath from the air tank. Then I opened the hatch and went in.

I expected the control room to be filled with floating bodies and wreckage, but it looked much like it had the last time I'd been aboard the *Nautilus*. The instrument panels and chairs were still largely intact, although the floor was torn up in a line that stretched across the room, starting from the shattered window and leading to a hole in the opposite wall. I assumed it was the path one of the spectral cannonballs had taken when it smashed into the sub. The crew still sat at their stations, dead but hands drifting over the controls, as if waiting for their next command.

That was why I was here.

I swam over to Nemo, who sat strapped in his chair. His head was slumped on his chest, as if he was sleeping. I laid my hands upon him.

A full resurrection would drain me of grace, which I figured I was going to need no matter how many angels like Sariel Nemo might have stashed in closets and cupboards around the *Nautilus*. There was also the fact that anyone I resurrected fully would instantly drown in the flooded submarine. So I settled for calling Nemo's soul back into his body like I had called back the soul of the would-be thief in The Apollo Club.

Nemo didn't react at all like most people who suddenly wake to find themselves in their own dead body. Instead, he just sat up in his chair and looked around with those shark-like eyes. He didn't seem surprised at returning as essentially a zombie, nor did he seem surprised to see me.

"Cross," he said, the word bubbling out of him. The last of the air in his dead lungs, no doubt. "I have been waiting for you," he added. His words were remarkably clear for someone speaking underwater. I wasn't sure if it was an Atlantean trick or some feature of the *Nautilus*. Or maybe I'd just had enough underwater conversations that I was used to it by now.

"It looks to me more like you've been dead," I said. I handed him the air tank so he could draw breath for more words.

He nodded and took several breaths before speaking again. Then he said, "I knew you would come. So I restrained my spirit to my body and waited for you to return and raise me." He gave me a look that seemed reproachful. "I should have known you would take your time about it," he said.

"You kept your spirit in your body?" I asked. I didn't even know that was possible. "On the off chance I would come back for you?"

"I know you are immortal," he said. "And I also know you always need help to solve problems you cannot handle yourself."

I took the regulator back for a few breaths of my own. I didn't return it to him in any hurry.

"So you didn't even try to stop Noah when he broke into the *Nautilus* and stole the bible?" I asked.

"Ah, that is unfortunate, but I was dead at the time," Nemo reminded me.

All right, so the Atlanteans weren't *that* special then, if Nemo couldn't rise from the dead to stop God's warden from boarding his submarine.

"Where is Noah now?" Nemo asked. "We must stop him before he does something reckless."

"It's a little late for that," I said. "I think he's headed for Atlantis with the bible."

Nemo sighed, air bubbling from his mouth.

"Tell me what you know," he said.

"I don't know much," I said. "The Sirens told me he was trying to find Atlantis. But what would he want with a sunken city?"

Nemo didn't answer for me a few seconds as we passed the regulator back and forth. He didn't even insult me. I began to grow worried.

"He should not be able to find Atlantis without help," Nemo finally said. "Not even him. It is lost to this world."

"Maybe the bible can help him somehow," I said. "What happens if he does find Atlantis?"

"Then we are all truly lost," Nemo said. He sat up in his chair.

"We must set course for Atlantis immediately."

"Take a look around," I said. "I don't think the *Nautilus* is in any shape to go anywhere."

"I can hear the engine," Nemo said as Sariel howled yet again. "As long as we have power, we can make repairs."

"Yeah, I found your angel," I said. "Neat trick, that. "

"Is the creature still bound?" Nemo said. "You haven't freed it or slain it in your ignorance, have you?"

I let the insult slide, because I knew there would just be another one if I didn't.

"You'll have to show me how you did it one day," I said. "That kind of knowledge could come in handy."

"Da Vinci was the one who came up with the method, in his own eccentric way," Nemo said. "We simply refined his procedures."

"If Da Vinci was involved, maybe I don't want to know," I said. "You may have a problem, though. I think Sariel has gone mad."

"She was mad before," Nemo said. "It's her madness that makes her such a useful engine." He unstrapped himself from the chair and stood.

"Enough of this talk," he said. "Now we must raise the *Nautilus* from the dead."

☥

ATLANTIS

I went about raising Nemo's crew just like I'd done with him. I started with Scars and One-Eye on account of our long history together. They were as calm and collected as Nemo had been when I called them back from death. Each one pulled an air tank from under their instrument panels and strapped them on as soon as I raised them, so they could draw breath for speech. They didn't bother with dive masks, maybe because they could see fine under water with those strange eyes of theirs.

"I didn't think you'd make it back to us," Scars said.

"Oh ye of little faith," I said.

"I thought you'd be drinking your latest life away somewhere," she said. Then she got busy with powering up the weapons controls and shaking her head at flashing lights I didn't understand.

It was almost like she knew me.

One-Eye went straight to work at his controls, too. I'll say this for the Atlanteans: they have a strong constitution. Things really got going when I raised Bad News. She'd lost most of the fingers on her right hand during Blackbeard's attack on the *Nautilus*, but that didn't stop her from hitting a series of buttons that raised new windows all around the control room. They slid up in the frames from recessed slots and sealed us off from the sea again. Bad News hit another button and air began to bubble into the room from vents around the ceiling. The water level dropped and it took me a moment to find more vents at floor level around the room, presumably taking care of the flooding.

When the water dropped down to my shoulders, I took off my

mask and sniffed the air cautiously. It was just as foul as the air in the engine room, and just as breathable.

"Good as new," I said.

"Let's raise the rest of the crew," Nemo said, heading for the door. I followed him, putting a hand on one of those power pipes to reassure me it was full of grace. I could feel it there, under my hand, waiting to be used. The glyphs flared up under my touch. I thought about tearing the pipe open and sucking the grace out, but I restrained myself. Barely, but I managed it.

"It's a good thing I found you or you'd all still be dead," I said.

"It almost makes up for you getting us killed in the first place," Nemo said.

Nemo and I went through the rest of the *Nautilus*, searching for his crew. We found them everywhere. I raised a couple of them in the corridors, as the water sank down around us to waist level. They were just as calm as the others. When Nemo ordered them to seal the holes in the hull, they just nodded and waded through the water to find some tools.

"Whatever happened to Atlantis anyway?" I asked Nemo as we sloshed along, looking for more of the dead. "It seems like you lot could handle anything."

"The ocean holds secrets too dire even for Atlanteans," he said, which did little to make me feel better.

I raised a half dozen dead we found in the forward weapons room. On a normal submarine there would be things like torpedoes here, and there were torpedoes, whole racks of them. But there were also other things: strange metal jellyfish devices hanging from chains on the ceiling, glass crabs with pulsing lights inside of them clinging to poles, metal starfish with wicked-looking spikes and antennae adorning their backs in crates on the floor.

"Interesting toys you have here," I said, watching the crew members I'd raised inspect the weapons for damage.

"These are the ones it is safe to look upon," Nemo said. "The others are in the sealed chambers, where they can't harm us."

We kept on, as the water level sank to our ankles. The sound of power tools echoed throughout the corridors. Sariel shrieked and howled as the lights flickered a few times and then came on and stayed on. I tried not to think about what she was going through.

We stopped in the cargo hold that had held the bible and Nemo stared at the wreckage for a moment.

"It's not your fault," I said, clapping him on the shoulder. "There wasn't anything you could do."

"I believe the entire set of unfortunate circumstances is your fault," he said.

"Let's move on," I said.

By the time we reached the engine room, I'd raised most of the crew. No doubt there were a few strays hidden away in nooks and crannies, but there'd be time for them later. Hopefully. Right now, I needed to replenish the grace I had used up.

"Don't drain her entirely of life," Nemo said, gazing upon Sariel. "We need her power yet."

"I do have some measure of self-control," I said.

"If that were truly the case, then I suspect we wouldn't be in this situation right now," Nemo said and left me in the engine room. The Atlanteans' insight into my nature was really beginning to annoy me.

I considered Sariel. I'd raised the dead Atlanteans in here, so we had some company now. They were working on the engines, and they threw some glances at me before returning to their labour.

"Tell me about Noah," I said. I wandered around her to inspect the pipes that ran into her body. They were joined with her so seamlessly they seemed part of her body now. I wouldn't mind learning how the Atlanteans had done it. I wouldn't have to bother with all the trouble of tracking down angels and killing them for their grace if I could just have one locked up in a room somewhere, like my own private power generator.

Sariel rattled her chains and the engineers gave me another look. They probably didn't like me messing with their main engine.

"Noah was a mistake," Sariel said. She looked at me again with that sightless gaze. "Not unlike yourself."

"I won't argue that point," I said. "But I'd like to say I've put my time on this earth to better use than him."

"That's a matter of opinion," she said. "I'm sure many of the dead would disagree with you."

"Tell me your opinion then," I said. "What do you think Noah wants with Atlantis?"

Sariel stared at the opposite wall, as if she were looking through it and searching for Noah somewhere out there in the seas. "Not even God can see into Noah's mind now," she said.

"Blasphemous talk for an angel," I said.

"Look at me," Sariel said, nodding at herself. "Bound to the will of an Atlantean, powering an infernal craft under the seas, entertaining questions from an abomination that was never meant to be. Look at me and talk of blasphemy."

"I'll grant you that," I said. "But you have to admit, in the grand scheme of things, Noah is a little worse than Nemo and me."

Sariel cocked her head at me. "Is he?" she asked. "Noah does not feed upon the angels. Noah did not conspire with Judas to betray the Risen."

"That was a misunderstanding," I said. "Judas can be tricky that way. Besides, Judas just wants to destroy humanity, not the entire world. Who knows what Noah will do with God's bible?"

"He will drown us all, of course," Sariel said. "Why else would he want it?"

"I kind of figured it would be something like that," I said. "Is that why you came to me on the trail at the Camino then? To warn me?"

"I don't know what you're talking about," Sariel said. "Although you are strongly in need of a pilgrimage such as that."

"The dust angel wasn't you?" I asked. "It looked just like the ones back in the desert."

"Perhaps it was one of my incarnations," Sariel said. "They have run wild since we abandoned the bible in the desert. I have no more influence over them than you do your shadow."

"Well, I'm here now and that's what counts," I said. "And you should be helping us to find and stop Noah."

"The end of the world is my only salvation," Sariel said, rattling her chains some more. "It is the only way I can be freed of my sins, for they are too great to ever be forgiven."

The Atlanteans powered up some of the machinery, which

came to life with a quiet hum. Sariel screamed in contrast.

"You should know Noah's intentions better than me," Sariel gasped. "You are bound by blood, after all."

"What's that supposed to mean?" I asked, but Sariel just smiled.

"Mean?" she said. "Nothing means anything anymore. Haven't you been paying attention?"

"Why didn't he take you when he was here?" I asked. "Why didn't he add the *Nautilus* to the ark?"

"He had eyes only for the bible," Sariel said. "What do we matter when the world will be no more?"

I stepped in close, so the engineers couldn't hear me. "All right, forget about Noah," I said. "Just let me know one thing. What is Nemo not telling me about Atlantis?"

Sariel smiled at me, like a grown-up might smile at a pacified child.

"You mean you don't know?" she whispered.

"If I knew, I wouldn't be here asking questions of a half-mad angel," I said.

"Oh, I am wholly mad," Sariel said. "I have never been madder. It is of great solace to me."

"Atlantis," I said. "What happened to it?"

"The city drowned itself," Sariel said. "It was host to a race of scientists and thinkers. They reached too far and discovered a terrible secret that meant their own end. A thing that even God chose not to think of."

"What did they find?" I asked.

"You'll soon find out," Sariel said. "We will all find out what the Atlanteans learned." She laughed again and this time she didn't stop.

I replenished my grace from the broken pipe, although I was tempted to kill Sariel and take it directly from her. I left her there, but it did no good. Her laughter followed me wherever I went in the *Nautilus*, until Nemo's voice came over to the intercom to announce we were setting course for Atlantis.

I made my way back to the control room and stood beside Nemo in his chair. The place was somehow dry again already, despite having been flooded for so long. I looked out at the water passing by, which looked the same as the water passing by usually did. At least some things were still normal.

"How long until we reach Atlantis?" I asked.

"Perhaps a day, given our current condition," Nemo said. "Nothing is far for the *Nautilus*. We could reach it sooner if not for the damage inflicted upon us by the *Revenge*."

"Any sign of Noah in the vicinity?" I asked, and Nemo shook his head.

"I don't believe he knows the location of Atlantis," he said. "Few have ever known it, and most of those are no longer of this world."

"How can you say for sure?" I asked. "When was the last time you were there?"

"We have revisited Atlantis many times since it sank beneath the waves," Nemo said, his voice growing quiet. "Trust me when I say it is lost to the world and history both."

"Maybe this is the time you should tell me what sunk it," I said.

"If the need arises for that, then we are probably already doomed," he said. He glanced at me and grimaced. "Now could you please remove yourself to the health station and bandage that wound before you cover the *Nautilus* in your blood?"

I looked down at my hand and saw it was dripping blood again. I was really going to have to do something about that once we were done saving the world. If we saved the world.

I left the control room and made my way to the health station, which, to be honest, sounded a little better than sick bay. It was near the middle of the submarine, and I'd raised a couple of Nemo's crew in it. They were gone by the time I got there, no doubt off repairing damage somewhere. I was able to find some fresh gauze on my own by going through all the cupboards, and I cleaned my hand and then wrapped it up again. I was tempted to try some of the pills I found in bottles in the cupboards, but I restrained myself. I lay down on one of the examination tables instead, and closed my eyes for a brief rest.

I was shaken awake what seemed a few minutes later. I opened my eyes to see Nemo standing beside the table.

"We have arrived at Atlantis," he said. "I thought perhaps you would want to be awake for this. Of course, I could be mistaken."

"Already?" I asked. "I just laid down."

"You've been asleep most of the day," he said, his tone indicating what he thought of people lazy enough to sleep.

I followed Nemo out of the health station, but instead of returning to the control room, he took me to an airlock, where there were a number of dive suits hanging from hooks. He selected one and tossed it to me.

"You'll need this to protect you from the cold and the pressure," he said. "We are at a depth that would crush you before you could drown."

"And the hull of the *Nautilus* is strong enough to hold up?" I asked.

"It was before Noah tore it open," he said. "Now we'll have to wait and see."

I couldn't get into the dive suit fast enough. It was lightweight and puffy, like wearing a snowsuit. It had a built-in mask and air tank, so I didn't need goggles or a regulator. Nemo pulled the hood over my head and made sure it was sealed, then nodded.

"If you drown now, it's no fault of mine," he said, his voice coming through speakers in the hood.

"How long have you had dive suits like these?" I asked. "They would have been useful to the rest of the world a few hundred years ago."

"We've had them long enough to know they're best kept out of the hands of the rest of the world," Nemo said.

Once we were both suited up, he let the water into the airlock, then opened the door. The suit stiffened a little around my limbs, which I figured meant the gel was taking the pressure so I didn't have to.

I saw the *Nautilus* was resting on the sea bed, tucked in amid some ancient peaks that towered over us.

"Where are we?" I asked, looking outside. I could see everything as clearly as day, but I knew there should be little light down here. The suit's mask must have had some sort of filter that enhanced my vision.

"Welcome to Atlantis," Nemo said and stepped outside.

I stepped out after him, my feet sinking into the muck past my ankles. I looked around but didn't see any sign of the city.

There were no gleaming towers, like I'd always imagined, and no ruins, for that matter. There was just the ocean and the peaks and the mud.

"Where is it?" I asked, but Nemo didn't answer. Instead he just walked away from the *Nautilus*, toward a gap between a couple of the peaks.

"I've got a feeling this won't end well," I muttered but followed him anyway.

We went into the gap and along the edges of the peaks. They were covered in a layer of muck themselves. There were no sea creatures down here, no crabs scuttling along the bottom or eels sticking their heads out of cracks or anything like that. There was no sign of life at all.

We emerged from the passageway between the peaks to find a large rock dome before us, surrounded by more rocky towers rising out of the sea bed. The dome was just as covered in muck as the rest of the area, but it looked too smooth and even to be a natural structure. There was something man-made under there. Or rather, Atlantean made.

Nemo confirmed my hunch by walking up to the edge of the dome and wiping some of the muck away with his hand. A glass surface shone through underneath, covered in symbols that had been etched into it: swirling lines, stars, things that looked like fins and jellyfish half-moons and so on. Nemo kept on clearing the muck and uncovered more symbols, clustered in sets that were themselves arranged in lines. I realized they were words, most likely in the Atlantean tongue.

Nemo cleaned away so much muck he almost disappeared in a cloud of it. Then he uncovered the doors. They were like the pages of books, covered in more of the Atlantean words.

"It's a library," I said. "The library of Atlantis."

"There's hope for you yet," Nemo said. He pulled open one of the doors and went inside.

"Not another library," I groaned and followed him once more.

The library must have been a magnificent structure in its time. We walked along a hall where bookshelves climbed high above our heads, accessed by winding staircases and ornate catwalks. The shelves were more of that strange glass with words etched into them. The books all still sat on the shelves, though they looked waterlogged beyond repair. I wondered if Alice had ever set foot inside this library.

Nemo was walking like he knew where we were going, and I hurried to keep up with him.

"What are we looking for?" I asked.

"Special collections," he said.

"I like the sound of this less and less," I said.

"I don't think anything we find here will reassure you," Nemo said.

We went down a stairway, to a hall that was empty of bookshelves. Even the walls were plain. It stretched on for perhaps a hundred feet or so, until it reached a door that was equally as plain.

"This doesn't seem up to the usual Atlantean design standards," I said.

"The area was kept as neutral as possible," he said. "So as not to disturb the contents of the room."

I just shook my head and didn't say anything. I wasn't sure I wanted to learn any more.

But there was no choice in the matter, as through the door we went. There was a large chamber on the other side, its walls made of stone rather than glass. It was almost completely empty, containing only a single pedestal holding an ancient tome that had been left open.

The tome was one of those ancient things that looked older than time and radiated menace. Or maybe I was just projecting onto it given the circumstances. We went over to it and looked down at the opened pages. Somehow, the water hadn't ruined them. Maybe it was the ancient, menacing tome factor. The pages showed a map of the world, drawn in what was most likely someone else's blood. All the ancient books were written in blood. People had to make do before they discovered ink.

I was pretty sure it was a map of the world, anyway. The continents were more or less recognizable, although the shapes weren't quite the same. And they were in different places in the oceans than they occupied now. There was also an extra one of them. It was a star-shaped thing in the Pacific, roughly the size of Australia. There was a rendering of a city in the middle of it, with more symbols scrawled around it.

"What exactly is this?" I asked. "Some sort of ancient atlas?" I reached down to turn the book to its cover, but Nemo knocked my hand away. "Do not touch it," he said. "To even look upon it is to tempt madness."

"Oh, so it's one of those books," I said. "I'm beginning to think there are too many of them."

"The library appears to have been untouched since last we returned," Nemo said, still gazing at the book. "Noah has not yet set eyes upon the map."

"And what if he does see it?" I asked.

"Then the world is lost," Nemo said.

As if on cue, Scars' voice suddenly came through the speakers in our dive suits.

"Captain, you had best return to the *Nautilus*," she said. "We have company."

☦

NOAH'S TRAP

We hurried outside and back to the *Nautilus*, not even bothering to close the doors of the library behind us.

"What about the book?" I asked as we went.

"We must leave it, for we cannot risk touching it," Nemo said. "We would not survive the protective measures, let alone the book itself."

"I'm beginning to see why the e-book thing caught on," I said. "It's nice to be able to read something without having to worry about whether or not it's going to kill you."

"I'm not sure I even want to know what an e-book is," Nemo said.

We went back through the opening between the peaks and saw the *Nautilus* still there, as undisturbed as before. I looked around for a moment, wondering what Scars had meant when she said we had company.

Then I looked through another gap in the peaks beyond the *Nautilus* and I saw them in the distance, right at the edge of my vision. An army of figures advancing toward us along the seabed. Even from this far away, I could see they weren't any regular army. There were lines of men and women, with swords and axes and all other manner of weaponry. They wore the tattered garb of soldiers and sailors from other ages rather than dive suits, but they didn't seem bothered by the depth. Other beings moved among them: a skeletal octopus larger than a man that seemed to be all bone, a giant that towered above the rest of the army and gazed at us with one red eye, a half-dozen or so men that seemed to be made of flickering green flames, and so on.

Noah had found us.

"It's a trap," Nemo said, and I knew he was right. "Noah has used us to find Atlantis."

"But how did he follow us here?" I asked. "Surely we would have noticed him before now."

"I don't know," Nemo said, heading back to the *Nautilus*, "but I suspect you are to blame."

And that's when I knew how Noah had done it.

The wound in my hand, the wound I could not heal. Sariel had said Noah and I were bound by blood. I hadn't paid attention to her words at the time, because they seemed no more than the ravings of a mad angel. But the angels move in mysterious ways and all that. Maybe Sariel knew something I didn't. And I'd been leaving a trail of blood wherever I'd gone. A trail Noah must have followed all the way to Atlantis.

The water around us darkened as we moved toward the *Nautilus*, and I looked up to see the distant glow of the surface far above fade away. Then lightning flashed through the water in between us and the surface, and the crash of thunder was so loud it left my ears ringing.

"It's the storm!" I cried. "The ark is nearly upon us!"

"We must stop them from reaching the library!" Nemo said.

We were moving along the side of the *Nautilus* now, going past the area where Noah had torn the submarine open to gain entry. Nemo's crew had fixed the rent in the hull by welding sheets of metal to cover it, but I knew they probably weren't as strong as the hull itself.

"Is this area sealed off from the rest of the submarine?" I asked.

"Of course," Nemo said. "It's standard practice to keep the hatches closed through the *Nautilus* at all times. Why are you asking me this now?"

I answered him by turning to the sub and punching a hole through one of those sheets of metal. I used to grace to harden my arm and the dive suit around it, so I wouldn't damage myself.

"Do you have the depths madness?" Nemo said. "Or are you in league with Noah?"

"Neither," I said. "I'm trying to save us."

I tore open the hole I'd made, until it was large enough that I could reach an arm through. I felt around along the inside wall until I found one of those brass pipes. Then I crushed it in my hand, freeing the grace inside. It flowed through my fingers and along my arm, into my body, like a current straight from Heaven.

I used it to unleash Hell upon Noah's army.

I cast my other hand in their direction and sent a wave of grace out. I turned it into a real wave, one that swept through the figures advancing toward us and sent them tumbling back. The muck lifted up off the sea bed in a storm of my own and spun about in a giant cyclone, catching more of Noah's creatures and hurtling them away from us. It was so strong I could feel the water tugging at me where I stood.

"To the airlock!" Nemo cried. "We must get the *Nautilus* moving before we are truly trapped!"

More of Noah's creatures came around the edges of the storm I'd made, still advancing upon us. I glanced about and saw others coming in from our other sides, flanking us. No doubt there probably even some closing in from behind us. I looked up and saw the dark shapes of ships arriving on the surface overhead. Noah was here.

"Cross!" Nemo cried from the airlock. "We are about to be undone!"

"Not if I can help it!" I shouted back.

I threw out my hand in a gesture again, but this time I created a wave that rushed out in all directions from the *Nautilus*. A wave so strong it swept away all before it. Water surged around me and the sub and tore the muck from the peaks rising over the scene, revealing more of that Atlantean glass underneath. I saw then they weren't mountains of rock but were in fact towers —the towers of Atlantis itself. They rose above us on all sides, gleaming spires that jutted out of the sea bed and reached for the surface far overhead. I realized then why I hadn't seen any ruins before—they were hidden in plain sight, covered up by the sea itself. We were amid the ruins of the sunken city.

The waves I had created kept sweeping outward, until I waved my hands in a circle. Then the water started spinning, creating a massive whirlpool around us that reached up to the surface far overhead. We were in a pocket of air in the centre of the whirlpool, and I could see the storm clouds where the sky should have been over us. Then a handful of ships appeared at the top edge of the whirlpool, teetering there for a few seconds. A galleon with shredded sails, a tugboat with a shattered cabin, a yacht covered in barnacles across its entire surface. More of Noah's monstrous army clung to whatever surfaces they could on the vessels. Then the ships plunged over the edge and swept around us in a great circle as the whirlpool caught them. Noah's creatures cried out and then disappeared into the maelstrom, even as the ships started to come apart from the force of the water. It took a lot of grace out of me to power the whirlpool, but I could feel more of it flowing through me from the power pipes of the *Nautilus*. I could do this for as long as Sariel had grace.

Then the ark itself appeared overhead. It slid over the edge like the other ships had and the front half of it hung in the air above us for a moment, like the blade of a giant sword. Noah himself appeared at the prow of the ship and looked down upon us. He raised a hand and then dropped it. And a great tentacle reared in the sky behind him and then crashed down into the water beside the ark. The walls of the whirlpool suddenly gave way, and the ocean fell upon us in a great waterfall.

"Secure yourself!" I heard Nemo cry, maybe to me, maybe to his crew, maybe to both. Then the waves crashed down and it was like a building collapsing upon the *Nautilus*. I had to use more grace to shield us from the force of the water, but it wasn't enough to stop the waves from washing us away. The *Nautilus* was suddenly tumbling through the ocean in a surge of debris and muck and bubbles and what felt like every wave in the seas. It was all I could do to hang on to the power pipe and the side of the submarine as we rolled and spun through the water. We careened into one tower, then another, and the glass spires shattered and gave way before us. I had glimpses of the towers falling, but then we were tumbling away again.

I had glimpses of other things, too—naked men with swords hacking at the hull of the *Nautilus* before the water carried them off, a ghost shark that left a shimmering wake in its trail as it snapped at the sub and left deep gouges in the metal, the cyclops suddenly looming out of the water nearby and reaching for me, his fingers brushing my suit before the sub spun once more, striking him in the side and hurtling him back into the storm.

The *Nautilus* finally settled back down onto the sea bed moments later, apparently alone. Nothing came out of the murk to attack us. I looked around but couldn't see anything—the water was too disturbed to see more than a few feet in any direction.

I swam to the airlock and found Nemo inside, stunned but still more or less half alive. I could see through the dive mask that the side of his face was caved in, the result of a losing encounter with some patch of wall or another. It looked to be the sort of wound that was generally fatal, but he didn't seem particularly concerned about it. I suppose that was one of the advantages of already being dead.

"Where is Noah?" he said as I helped him back up.

"I don't know," I answered. "He had the kraken send its own wave back at us, and I think it swept us out of Atlantis."

"We must destroy the library before it is too late!" he said.

We sealed the airlock and stripped out of our suits, then ran back to the control room to find the crew at their stations. Some of them bore equally fatal wounds as Nemo's, but were just as stoic as he was about it. I looked through the windows, but all I could see was churning water outside.

"Status report!" Nemo snapped, scanning the instrument panels.

"We have minor flooding from the aft hatch failing," Bad News said. She had a shard of metal sticking out of the side of her head now. "We've sealed the compartments and contained it."

"We've stabilized our position and our engines are operational," One-Eye said. "But we've suffered some damage to both the propellers and more damage to the rudder. We won't know how much until we're underway again."

"Weapons systems are functional," Scars said. She was my favourite member of the crew at the moment, actually, for speaking those words. She was largely untouched, except she seemed to be missing a couple of fingers on her left hand. "We are ready to engage with all systems."

"Where is Noah?" Nemo asked, but no one had an answer.

"More importantly, where are we?" I asked, and Nemo nodded.

"Let's get a clearer view," he said.

The murk around us faded as we looked through the windows, which I took to be the effect of another filter. Now it was like there was no water around us at all.

I saw right away we were no longer in Atlantis. The kraken's wave had washed out of the ruins. The city was visible on our starboard side, a distant collection of shimmering spires. The storm drifted down through the water toward it, and I saw the ark at its front, sailing impossibly under the sea. It surged into Atlantis, crashing through the spires and shattering them. The broken remains fell to the sea floor, no doubt to be buried in the muck once more.

"Ready all weapons systems," Nemo said. "Take us in at whatever speed we can manage."

One-Eye ran his hands across his instrument panel but the *Nautilus* did not move. He shook his head.

"We don't have enough power," he said. "The systems are too drained of grace. We'll have to recharge before we can move."

"We're helpless if he comes for us," I said.

"He's not coming for us," Nemo said. "He wants the library."

There were a series of explosions in the city then, rainbow flashes of light that lit up the scene. More towers toppled and fell. For a moment everything was still.

"Maybe your security system blew up Noah," I said.

"I'm not sure he can even be killed," Nemo said.

Sure enough, the storm began to move again a few minutes later. I expected it to come for us, but instead it surged back up to the surface, heading away from our position.

"He has found the map," Nemo said, slumping into his chair and watching the storm recede. "The world is lost if we cannot find a way to stop him."

"The city on that map, what place was that?" I asked. I couldn't help but notice the rest of the crew turn and look at us.

"It is the Sunken City," Nemo said. He said it in a way that I knew the words were capitalized.

"I thought Atlantis was the Sunken City," I said.

"The Sunken City is what drowned Atlantis," Nemo said. "And who knows what before that. And now Noah will be able to find it."

"Sounds like we've really got to stop him from reaching it," I said.

"The problem being we clearly can't beat him," Nemo pointed out.

"Maybe not on our own," I said. "Maybe we can with the help of an angel."

Nemo shook his head. "We need Sariel to power the *Nautilus* to have any chance at all," he said. "Besides, Sariel would welcome the end of the world at this point."

"I was speaking of another angel," I said.

Nemo turned away from watching Noah disappear, to look at me.

"And where would we find this other angel?"

"I'm not really sure," I admitted. In fact, I wasn't even sure if the angel in question was still alive, but I kept that part to myself.

"If you don't tell me what you're talking about, I will throw you out the airlock and leave you to drown in the ruins of Atlantis," Nemo said.

"Ahab," I said. "He may be able to help us in the fight against Noah. He chased down the white whale to stop the world from ending, so I imagine he'd be willing to help us chase down Noah and stop him, too."

Nemo kept staring at me. "It pains me to admit this," he said, "but I have no idea what you are talking about."

I remembered then that he had been dead when I'd encountered Ahab and the whale, and he'd still been dead when Melville had written his own version of those events, and he'd continued to be dead when the story of Ahab and the whale had become a literary classic.

"I can't believe I actually know something you don't," I said.

"I suspect there's a catch to all this," Nemo said.

"A small one," I admitted. "I don't exactly know where to find Ahab."

"I am somehow not surprised," Nemo said.

"But I know someone who may be able to help us," I said.

"Of course you do," Nemo said. "That's always the way with you."

"Cuba," I said. "We need to go to Havana."

"And what will we find there?" Nemo asked.

"The vampire who might just save the world," I said.

A CREATURE OF GOD

Eventually, Sariel provided the *Nautilus* with enough grace that the submarine could move again. It involved a lot of screaming and howling, but that's the way of things with mad angels. We set course for Havana and stared out into the depths as we cruised along. The sub made more grinding noises than before and lurched through the water every now and then, but at least we were moving.

I sat in an empty seat and tried not to pay attention to all the flashing warning lights on the instrument panels in the control room. I ran over what had happened in my mind.

The whole thing had been a trap for longer than Nemo or I had realized. It must have started the moment I'd fought the giant squid. Noah had probably sent the creature after me with the sole intent of inflicting a wound that wouldn't heal. A wound that would give him a blood trail to follow. Maybe he'd even put Antonio's head in its stomach himself, trusting I would seek out the sirens to learn what they knew once I'd talked to him. Perhaps Noah had spoken of the Sunken City into a wind that carried his words all the way to the sirens. And then all he had to do was wait for me to raise Nemo from the dead, so Nemo could lead him to Atlantis.

There was one thing about all this that still puzzled me, though. I never would have hooked the squid if Alice hadn't given me that strange copy of *Moby Dick*. I couldn't see any reason why she would betray me to Noah, but who knew what powers Noah had? Maybe he had found a way to control Alice.

That was a question that would have to be answered later.

Right now I had more pressing questions.

"There are things you haven't been telling me about Atlantis," I said to Nemo.

"You didn't need to know them before," he said. "And frankly, the less you know of Atlantis, the more comfortable I am."

"Whatever it is, I need to know it now," I said. "I can't help save the world if I don't even understand how Noah plans to end it."

Nemo was silent for a moment. Finally, he nodded.

"Our people were a race of scientists and explorers," Nemo said. "We mapped the seas, the land, and the air. We discovered many great things in our short time on the earth, and we created a civilization that has not been equaled since." He shook his head. "It will likely never be equaled. Not by your lot, anyway."

"There's always a but," I said, trying not to speak aloud any of the comebacks that sprang to mind. I didn't want to discourage Nemo from opening up to me like this.

"But we were not the first on this world," he said. "There were others here long before us. Others not of this world, or even of this universe. Perhaps they came from another realm. Perhaps they existed before the universe. It is unclear, even to me."

"The Sunken City that Noah seeks, it was their city," I guessed.

"If only that were the case," Nemo said, gazing out into the darkness pressing in on us. "The Sunken City is where they hid away their darkest secrets. It is more a tomb than a city."

"A tomb for what?" I asked, because I had to ask.

Nemo paused again, taking so long to answer me that I thought perhaps he wasn't going to bother.

"The only way to say for certain is to breach the gates of the Sunken City and enter it," he finally said. "We dared not do so. We dared not wake what slumbers within the Sunken City."

"How do you know something's asleep in the city if you didn't even go in?" I asked.

"We managed to capture one of its dreams," he said. Scars looked at him and then away. The rest of the crew stared at their instrument panels or out into the nothingness outside. "We thought perhaps we could understand what was in the city if we studied the dream," he said.

"How exactly do you capture a dream?" I asked, but Nemo just shook his head.

"The knowledge of that is too dangerous to share with the world," he said. "Atlantis is evidence of that. The dream of the Sleeper is what drowned Atlantis." He said it in a way that implied the Sleeper was definitely a proper name. "Our entire civilization wiped out because of a stray thought. Imagine if the Sleeper awoke. What would happen then?"

"What about whoever built the Sunken City?" I asked. "Can they help?"

There was a loud banging sound from somewhere at the rear of the *Nautilus*, and we slowed further in the water. Nemo didn't even bother with a damage report this time.

"From what we were able to decipher of the writing on the walls of the Sunken City, they left our world again after sealing the Sleeper within it," Nemo said. "Perhaps they will return one day, maybe if the Sleeper awakes. But the consensus among our best thinkers was that they brought the Sleeper to our world to rid themselves of it. I fear it is our problem and our problem alone."

"Whose brilliant idea was it to capture the dream in the first place?" I asked, shaking my head.

"It was mine," Nemo said, staring ahead. "I am to blame for the end of Atlantis. And now maybe the end of the world."

I didn't say anything else then, for I understood how he felt. For the first time, I had sympathy for him.

"From blood we are born!" Sariel suddenly shrieked, her words echoing through the *Nautilus*. "And in blood we will drown!" This was getting tiring.

Nemo didn't seem to notice Sariel's words. I guess when you have a crazy angel as your engine, you probably stop noticing the ranting and raving after a while.

"The Sunken City has remained hidden for so long only because it has been lost to the depths," Nemo said. "The continent that bears it has sunk under its burden. It is now at the deepest, most remote part of the ocean. Too deep for mortals to descend. The *Nautilus* could perhaps reach its gates in full operating condition, but I fear we would not survive the pressures in our current state."

"The Marianas Trench," I said, thinking back to the map in that library in Atlantis.

"A great wound in the world," Nemo said. "And festering away in the midst of that wound is the Sunken City."

"Maybe the depths are too great even for Noah," I said.

"And perhaps he doesn't even need to reach the city," Nemo said. "Perhaps all he needs to do is open God's bible near it, and it will wake the Sleeper with its own madness."

"Maybe we could just hijack a few subs and shoot some nukes into the trench," I said. "We could take out Noah and the Sleeper at the same time." Of course, nuking God's bible could cause some other problems, I realized.

"Do you really think mortal science will prevail in this instance?" Nemo asked. "Have you not learned the lesson of Atlantis?" He shook his head. "If we cannot find a way to stop Noah, then all the world will ever know are the waves that surround us now."

Right. No pressure, Cross. We cruised the rest of the way to Cuba on that cheery thought, Sariel and the *Nautilus* complaining the whole way. There's not much to say about the trip, unless you are really fond of descriptions of foul air and malfunctioning machinery and screaming angels, which I am not. So let's move along to the point where Nemo ordered the *Nautilus* to the surface and I saw the day had been replaced by night, with clusters of lights on the horizon.

"We'll take a launch in the rest of the way," Nemo said, rising from his chair. "We don't want to draw attention to ourselves."

"You might want to put on a pair of sunglasses, then," I said. I still wasn't used to those shark eyes of his.

Nemo didn't bother with a response. Instead, he ordered the crew to descend to a safe depth and make repairs while we were gone. He added that if we didn't come back, the crew shouldn't come looking for us.

"Take the *Nautilus* to the Sunken City and try to ram the ark if all else fails," he told them. "If the world must end, let it end on the memory of Atlantis." They nodded and all put their hands over their hearts but didn't say anything in response.

"You may as well finish off that liquor of yours while you're at it," I said. "It would be a shame to waste a good drink."

They all dropped their hands and went back to their instrument panels. Some people were just determined to not like me no matter what.

Nemo and I went back aft, to the chamber with all the boats. He hit a button on the wall and the hatch slid up to reveal the ocean on the other side. The lights in the room automatically dimmed, so we wouldn't stand out like a beacon on the water. I helped Nemo drag a battered rowboat through the opening and into the water. We got in the boat and Nemo closed the hatch on the *Nautilus* by running his hand over a section of the hull that looked no different from the rest. And so the heroes set forth to save the world in their leaky boat.

I looked at the shoreline in the distance. "It will take us all night to row in," I said.

Nemo tapped the bottom of the boat in a complicated pattern. The boat surged forward, propelled by some hidden motor underneath the boat.

"I should have known you'd have some trick up your sleeve," I said.

"And to think we are relying upon you to save the world," Nemo said.

We cruised in to shore, Nemo using the oars as makeshift rudders to guide us. I spent the time checking the fresh bandages I'd applied to my wound. They were already damp with blood. I kept my hand inside the boat, away from the water. Maybe it was too late, but I didn't want Noah to be able to track me any more.

Once we were at a safe distance, whoever was in charge of the *Nautilus* now took it slowly under, disappearing as gently beneath the waves as a drowning man who'd finally given up.

Nemo pulled a duffle bag out from under a seat and tossed it to me. "I am not aware of the current fashions," he said. "Is there anything suitable in here?"

I looked through the bag. There were some robes, a pair of breeches, a soldier's redcoat jacket and a couple of mariners' uniforms, neatly folded. I shook my head and cast a sleight on him, so he looked like he was wearing a pair of khakis and a T-shirt.

"This is how people choose to present themselves?" he asked, staring down at himself in a manner that I could only describe as horror. I shrugged and added a few holes to the T-shirt.

Before he put the bag away again, Nemo took out a pair of ancient looking glasses with green lenses. They were the sort of thing I hadn't seen since the 18th century or so.

"What are those?" I asked. "You look like some sort of dandy."

"They're sunglasses," he said, as if I were the one with no eyes.

I shook my head. The glasses weren't going to stop people from staring at him. But the lenses were dark enough that any curious watchers were unlikely to see the true nature of his eyes.

I cast about to see if Nemo had any bags of weapons as well, but the boat was otherwise empty.

"We'll just have to improvise," he said, as if reading my mind.

"I've had lots of practice at that," I said.

The lights grew and spread in front of us until I recognized the familiar sights of Havana. I suddenly wanted to smoke a cigar and enjoy a glass of rum, two things I didn't know I was missing until that moment.

"We'll need a safe place to leave the boat," I said.

"I'm taking us there now," Nemo said and changed course slightly, steering us away from the direction of Havana harbour and toward a marina farther along the coast. I recognized it: Marina Hemingway. I was never sure if it was named in honour of the writer or if it was a joke at the writer's expense. The Cubans had a knack for talking in code, courtesy of living under a repressive regime for all those years.

The marina lived up to its name, with a dangerous approach that was recommended only for the foolhardy and the drunk. We were a small enough boat to navigate the narrow approach without too much difficulty, though, and avoided grounding ourselves on the coral reefs on either side of the marina entrance. From there, we cruised through the marina until we found an empty slip between a couple of pleasure boats. We tied the boat to the moorings and we were on land and walking through the marina a few seconds later.

"Now all we have to do is find your friend among all these people before Noah reaches the Sunken City and ends the world," Nemo said, gazing at the lights of Havana stretching away before us. "How can you be confident he is here?"

"I have my reasons," I said. Even if I hadn't convinced Ishmael to remain the last time we'd met, Havana was still an ideal hunting ground for vampires. People stayed out at all hours of the night, and most were willing to do anything and go anywhere for money. Combine that with lax law enforcement and officials you can bribe, and you pretty much had paradise for the likes of Ishmael.

Nemo shook his head. "Perhaps if you associated with better people, you wouldn't get killed so often," he said.

"If I did that, the world would have ended ages ago," I said.

We walked into the city as the sun came up. At first we saw only a few late-night revellers staggering home. Then people passed us on bicycles, on their way to work. Then a couple of cars went by that made it seem as if we had been transported back to the fifties.

"We should bring some Cuban mechanics back to fix the *Nautilus*," I said. "They can get anything running."

"Let's forget about the jokes and just get on with saving the world," Nemo said.

We went past closed and locked storefronts until we finally found a general store open in a crumbling stone building. It was a meagre establishment, selling only the basics—a few bread loaves, some suntan lotion, soda and snacks, and a local paper, which is what I was really after.

I took it to the woman sitting on a stool at the front of the store, who looked up from the worn mystery novel she was reading. That's when I realized I didn't have any money. I looked at Nemo, who sighed. He reached into his pocket and pulled out some coins and offered them to the woman. She stared at them without taking them.

"Those are reals," she said.

"They are all we have," Nemo said.

The woman took one and looked at it. "It's from 1799," she said, squinting to make out the worn date on the coin.

"Perhaps they might be worth more than your local currency," Nemo said. "I confess I am not familiar with the current exchange rate."

The woman looked back at him. I didn't miss the slow movement of her free hand to rest upon something under the counter. My guess was a knife, as a gun probably wouldn't be in her budget.

"He says they're worth more than pesos," I said.

"In that case," the woman said. Her hand came back up and pocketed Nemo's reals. She turned her attention back to her novel and we left the shop with the paper.

"I forgot how long you were down at the bottom of the ocean," I said when we were out of sight of the shop.

"It has been a while," he said. "I'm not even certain of the year."

"Neither am I," I admitted. When you've lived as long as I have, you sometimes lose track. "We'd better hurry and find Ishmael," I added. "She's probably already called the police."

"Why would she do that?" Nemo asked. "We paid her more than the paper was worth."

"She was reading a mystery novel," I said. "And then along come a couple of strangers at the crack of dawn who pay her in a forgotten currency for a newspaper. She'd tell the police even if there wasn't a reward for reporting suspicious behaviour."

Nemo frowned but didn't say anything else, which gave me the time to flip through the paper, a local rag that delivered the regional news about Havana and thus wasn't as preoccupied with propaganda as the national papers. I found what I was looking for on the third page.

"Here," I said, pointing out the news story to Nemo. "Ishmael is still here."

The story was a brief about a teen girl found dead in an alley. She was the latest in a string of girls that had been found dead or gone missing. There was a photo of her from some family party or another, smiling at the camera. The story said she'd been found with her neck slashed open, just like the others. Police suspected the work of a serial killer and were appealing to the public for leads.

"How do you know it's your friend?" Nemo said, scanning the article.

"He's not my friend," I said. "And it's got Ishmael written all over it. Vampires like teen girls because they're easy prey.

There's always one of them in a crowd who has a thing for older men, and they don't put up much of a fight. So that's one clue. The other is that the throat slashing is a good way to hide the fact you've drained a body of blood. The authorities just think the victim has drained out. Some forensics people who know what they're doing might realize there's not enough blood at the scene, but the cops here . . ." I shook my head. "I told you, Havana is a good hunting ground."

"But how do we find him?" Nemo asked. "Does the newspaper tell you that, too?"

I read a line from the article. "The victim was last seen leaving the Havana Cathedral after her daily prayer session." I tossed the paper aside and looked and in the direction of where I knew the church to be.

"A good godly girl," I said. "The kind vampires like the best."

The Havana Cathedral was close to the harbour. By the time we reached it, the day had truly begun in the city. The sun lit up the buildings, which were covered in all shades of bright paint to hide the crumbling structures underneath. People walked or rode or drove around us in the streets. Most of the vehicles were older, from the fifties and sixties, but here and there were newer sedans and SUVs. Driven by government officials, no doubt. We could have reached the cathedral in short time if we'd been willing to take a taxi, but then we would have run into the whole local currency problem again.

We were sweating from our walk by the time we reached the cathedral, and the sun did nothing to cool us down. There was a small square beside the church with a few cafes that were already open to cater to the tourists. We walked among the tables for a bit, where I brushed up against chairs with jackets and purses slung over them. And just like that, the currency problem was solved.

We sat at one of the tables and ordered water and coffee from the waitress who came out of the crowd as soon as we laid some money down. I tipped her generously but not extravagantly, and then we watched the church as we rested and sipped our drinks.

"What exactly are we looking for?" Nemo asked.

"Actually, I was just admiring the architecture," I said.

"I can't imagine why," Nemo said. "But there will be plenty of time for that after we save the world."

"All right," I said. "I'm looking for Ishmael, then."

I know what you're thinking, but that myth about vampires being restricted to night is exactly that: a myth. I suspect it's perpetuated mainly by the vampires themselves, to keep people off guard. Although it does make hunting easier for them. Others are less inclined to run out of their homes and investigate screaming if it's dark outside.

"So where do we find him?" Nemo said.

"I've no idea," I said, settling into my chair and sighing with contentment. It felt good to relax for a bit.

"Cross," Nemo said.

So much for that.

"The paper said the girl was killed after leaving a prayer service at the church," I said. "So our only clue is the church. We watch the church until another clue shows up."

"Is this how you've made your way through the ages?" Nemo asked.

I shrugged. "I've learned there's no point in planning," I said. "The only thing planning leads to is disappointment."

As luck would have it, we'd arrived just in time for a service at the cathedral. A priest opened the doors and people began to file inside, first some of the locals and then clusters of tourists, curious about photo opportunities, no doubt.

I downed the remainder of my coffee and stood.

"Let us pray," I said to Nemo.

We sat in one of the rear pews. There was plenty of room to sit closer to the front, but I like to be near the doors in a church. They don't rank among my favourite places, for obvious reasons. Also, sitting at the back of a service gives you a good vantage point to keep an eye on the rest of the space.

Which is how I spotted Ishmael.

He was one of the priests. He was lighting the candles in the church's many candelabras when I noticed him. He looked younger than the last time I'd seen him, which wasn't surprising. Vampires can change their looks a little, like a chameleon, but they can't alter them completely. I knew it was him, just like I'd recognized him aboard the *Chains of Heaven*.

He finished lighting candles and turned around to perform

his next duty. His nose twitched and then his eyes skimmed over the people in the pews. His eyes settled on me for just a second before he continued scanning the crowd. But I knew he'd seen us.

He abandoned whatever his next task was and went over to another priest, a man with greying hair and glasses. Ishmael whispered something in his ear and the other man frowned at him, then nodded when Ishmael motioned at his stomach. Ishmael went through a door at the side of the nave without looking at us again.

"Well, he's made us," I said to Nemo. "Let's go back outside."

"What are we going to do out there?" Nemo asked. "We should keep an eye on him."

"He's going to run," I said. "The only question is which direction." And I hoped it was above ground. If there were any tunnels underneath the church, Ishmael would be able to lose us and we'd never find him again.

As it turned out, he wasn't hard to track at all.

We left the church in time to see Ishmael working his way into the crowd in the plaza outside. He must have gone right to a side exit in the church. It was hard for him to disappear entirely, though, on account of the robes he was still wearing.

"Don't get too close until the moment is right," I said. "I don't want to spook him in the middle of all these people." I knew from experience that a frightened, cornered vampire could make a real mess, and we didn't have time to clean up.

"When will the moment be right?" Nemo asked.

"Let's just hope we'll know," I said.

"The very randomness of your nature pains me," Nemo said.

"You and me both," I responded.

I wasn't sure which direction Ishmael was going to flee, but I was surprised when he went the way we'd come, walking down the same streets along the waterfront.

"We likely may have passed him on the way to the church," Nemo said. "Perhaps he was getting ready for his shift when we walked by his home."

"We could have saved ourselves a lot of trouble if we'd just looked through a few windows," I said.

I realized something wasn't right when Ishmael retraced our

steps exactly. He nodded every now and then at people who said hello to him, or at least hello to his robes. He didn't look over his shoulder for us once, but he had to know we were there.

"What game is he playing?" Nemo said as we followed him through the crowded midday streets. "How does he know what route we took?"

"He's a vampire," I said. "He can probably smell our trail." Which still didn't answer the question of what he was doing. He should have been trying to lose us. Instead, he appeared to be toying with us. I didn't have a good feeling about this. I never had a good feeling about vampires.

"I think we'd better get closer," I said.

We moved in on him, only to have him pick up his pace, as if he could sense what we were doing. Then I finally saw what he was up to, but it was too late.

We turned a corner and we were back on the street with the general store. Ishmael neared the store, then suddenly darted inside it. He had the roll-down shutter closed before we could even react.

"I think this is the moment," I said to Nemo and ran to the shop myself.

Ishmael hadn't locked the shutter, so I rolled it up enough to throw myself under. I leapt to my feet inside the store as Nemo followed me. We both froze at what we saw there.

Ishmael stood in the middle of the store, as if waiting for us. He looked unsurprised, calm even. He held the woman who'd sold us the newspaper in front of him. He also held the knife that had been under her counter. So I'd guessed right about that, at least. He had the blade pressed against her throat. She was trembling, but Ishmael was perfectly still. There was no one else in the store.

"If you would be so kind as to close that shutter," he said. "I don't think any of us want witnesses."

I didn't have to tell Nemo to roll the shutter back down. We looked at Ishmael and he gazed at us with the eyes of a lion. The woman in his grip had the wide eyes of a gazelle who'd realized its lot in life too late.

"I wasn't sure if I'd ever see you again," Ishmael said, looking at me. "I've heard stories of you over the ages. I was hoping maybe one of those deaths would stick."

"That makes two of us," I said. "Yet here we are."

"Who's your dead friend?" Ishmael asked, nodding at Nemo. "I thought all the Atlanteans were gone."

I didn't ask Ishmael how he knew about Atlantis. He'd been a vampire for a long time. He'd probably fed on all manners of mortals. No doubt he remembered the scent of each, like a sommelier could tell a bottle of wine by its aroma.

"How about we talk somewhere more private?" I said, glancing at the woman.

"Oh, you won't have to worry about her," Ishmael said. "She's not going to say anything."

"I swear it upon my husband's grave," the woman said, nodding as much as she could with a knife pressed into her throat. "I've seen nothing."

"Hush," Ishmael said.

"Oh please, God, please," the woman whispered, closing her eyes.

"God can't help you now," Ishmael said, and he grinned at me, showing those rows of fangs. "And neither can his son."

"There's no need for any innocents to get hurt," I said.

"Well, whatever brought you here can't be all that important, then," Ishmael said. "Not if you can't afford a few casualties. So why don't you leave Havana and never come back? You promise to do that and I'll leave this nice, God-fearing woman alone."

I sighed, because I saw the way this was going to play out. "You need to come with us, Ishmael," I said.

"I don't think I do," he said. "But I'm listening. Why don't you tell me why you need me so badly?"

"We have to find Ahab," I said.

Now Ishmael's smile faded away. "Ahab's not of this world anymore," he said. "If he ever was."

"That may be, but I still need to find him," I said. "Or there won't be a world anymore."

Ishmael shook his head. "I don't know where he is," he said. "The last time I saw him was the last time you saw him."

"Did you feed on him before the *Chains* plucked me from the sea?" I asked.

Ishmael stared at me for a moment. Then he chuckled. "How did you know?" he asked.

"The angel took everyone from that sea for a reason," I said. "You didn't have any useful role on the ship. So I'm guessing the angel thought your role might come later. I'm hoping he maybe foresaw this moment. Perhaps he saw the future and kept you around as an insurance policy."

It was a long shot, but angels sometimes played the long game.

The woman opened her eyes again. Now she stared at me with that prey gaze. I tried not to look at her.

"I was weak after they pulled me from the sea," Ishmael said. "I hadn't fed in some time. Ahab opened a vein in his wrist when no one was looking. That taste. . . ." He looked past me, at something none of us could see. "You can't imagine it," he said.

"I suspect I can," I said. "But this is not the time for baring our souls to one another. Find me Ahab."

"Ah, well, that's a problem," Ishmael said. "I was not joking when I said Ahab is no longer of this world. It's not so easy to find him as you may think."

"If I thought it would be easy, I'd just ask you for directions," I said. "There's a reason you're coming with us."

"And what if I say no?" Ishmael asked, as calm as ever.

"What do you think will happen?" I said. "I'm not letting you go. You can come willingly or you can come unwillingly. Either way, you're coming with us."

Ishmael thought things over for a moment. Then he shrugged. "Well, if you're not giving me any choice," he said. He drew the knife across the woman's throat as casually as if he were putting it away. She gurgled but couldn't say anything, couldn't even scream because the damage was already done. She looked down at the blood spilling out of her, as if she couldn't believe the way this day had gone. Your death never comes in quite the way you expect it.

Nemo took a step forward, but I put up a hand to stop him. Ishmael grinned at us.

"That's right," he said. "If you need me so badly, then you're not going to do anything about this one woman who means nothing at all in the grand scheme of things." And with that, he dropped his head to her neck to drink.

We didn't try to stop him. He was right, after all. We needed him and we couldn't afford to punish him for what he'd just done. Not now, anyway. Tomorrow was another day. If there was a tomorrow.

He drank from the woman while we watched and then he dropped her body to the ground. There was enough blood on her clothes and on the floor that no one would likely realize how much of it was missing. Ishmael was experienced at this sort of thing.

He licked his lips clean, then dropped the knife and put up his hands in surrender.

"Now, what would you have of a man of God?" he said.

✝

NEVER TRUST A VAMPIRE

We returned to the marina with Ishmael and set out for the *Nautilus* without further incident. Nemo and I didn't talk much beyond what was needed to get the boat untied and underway. Ishmael whistled a sailor's tune, something I dimly recognized but had no interest in learning again.

"So, what's the great rush to find Ahab?" Ishmael asked as Havana faded into the horizon behind us. "I would have thought the world better off without the likes of him."

"The world has seen better days," I said. "And worse ones to come if we don't get his help."

"Things must be dire indeed," Ishmael remarked, gazing around the water. We were far enough out there were few boats in sight now, and most of those far in the distance. I let the sleight I'd cast on Nemo fade away.

"There have been few times that they've been worse," I said.

We carried on in silence for a while, except for Ishmael's whistling. At least he had the decency to stop when Nemo turned off the hidden motor.

"We're almost there," Nemo said, scanning the water in front of us. "The *Nautilus* should be somewhere close ahead."

"Actually, it's on the port side," Ishmael said, waving vaguely in that direction. "About a hundred metres over and another hundred metres down."

We both looked at him and he smiled. "The crew smells of death as badly as your friend," he said to me. "Even up here." The smile faded. "There is another on the vessel," he said. "Someone familiar . . ." He frowned, as if trying to remember.

I was surprised he didn't recognize the scent of Sariel, but then I realized he hadn't become a vampire until after she had cast him into that chasm back in the monastery. He'd probably never encountered her since, so he'd likely never learned her scent. I kept my thoughts to myself because we had enough problems to deal with at the moment.

Nemo rowed us close to the spot Ishmael had indicated and splashed his hand in the water in a complicated pattern. A minute later the surface of the sea surged in front of us as the *Nautilus* rose from the depths. The hatch to the boat room dropped open before us, and we rode a wave into the *Nautilus*. Scars was there, a rifle at the ready. She hit the button on the wall that slid the hatch shut again before we even got out of the boat. She didn't take the gun off Ishmael when she did that. I liked her more and more. Ishmael grinned at her as I felt the *Nautilus* immediately descend.

He sniffed the air again as we all made for the control room. "Is there no one left alive on this ship?" he asked.

"There's me," I said. "And there's you."

"I hardly think we count," he said. He made a face. "It's a good thing I fed from that woman while I had the chance."

We reached the control room and the rest of Nemo's crew eyed Ishmael while Nemo and Scars settled into their chairs. Ishmael didn't seem concerned. He looked around the room and nodded to himself, as if it were what he expected.

I sat Ishmael down in an empty chair as Nemo listened to his crew update him about repairs.

"Don't try anything stupid or even smart," I told Ishmael. "We'll jettison you out one of the hatches if you're more trouble than you're worth."

Ishmael shrugged. "It wouldn't be the first time I've been adrift at sea," he said. "Someone always comes along to pick you up eventually."

"Not if we wrap you in enough weights," I said.

"That's a fine way to talk a member of the clergy," he said.

I nodded pointedly at the blood on his robes, and he waved me off.

"Fine, fine, I understand," he said. "Things are serious. I

will help you find Ahab. What happens after that is up to you, though."

Nemo finished with his crew and turned to Ishmael. "Where is Ahab?" he asked.

"He's in the Dead Sea," Ishmael said. "What does this do?" He reached out to push a button on the panel in front of him, but I slapped his hand away. I didn't know what the button did and I didn't want to find out.

"The Dead Sea in the Middle East?" Nemo asked.

"Not that Dead Sea," Ishmael said. "The real Dead Sea."

"Even I don't know what that means," Nemo said. "And I know all the seas."

"Oh my, you really do need me, don't you?" Ishmael said. "I should have fed on more people before we left."

"Ishmael, this is your chance to wipe the slate clean when it comes to us," I said. "And it might be your last chance."

He shrugged like he didn't care but then decided to answer us anyway. Maybe because he sensed how close to the breaking point I was with him. Who knew—maybe he could smell it.

"The Dead Sea is where those who die in the oceans drift to if nothing else catches them first," Ishmael said. "If they don't wash up on shore somewhere or get plucked out of the water by a ferryman." He smiled at me. "It is full of the drowned and the forgotten, and strange creatures the world has not seen for thousands of years. It is the final resting place for those truly lost at sea." He shook his head at Nemo. "And you call yourself a mariner."

"I never would have pegged you as a mariner," I said. "How do you know this?"

Ishmael looked back at me. "Ahab taught me much in the short time I spent with him," he said.

I wasn't sure if he meant Ahab had told him things or he had learned things from feeding on the angel. I didn't have time to ask, though.

"Where would we find such a place if it did indeed exist?" Nemo asked. I could tell from his tone of voice that he was having trouble believing Ishmael's story. I think we all were.

"It is not entirely of this world," Ishmael said. "But there is a current of this world that feeds it. It runs through all the seas. We must find the current and let it take us there."

I rubbed my eyes and bit back a curse. Just once I wanted a quest that wasn't impossible. Just once before the world ended.

"Very well," Nemo said. "Which way to the current you speak of?"

Ishmael lifted his head and sniffed at the air, like he was trying to catch Ahab's scent. Then he laughed and shook his head, as if he were joking.

"Take us to the Bermuda Triangle," he said.

"I'm waiting for the punchline," I said.

Ishmael leaned back and put his feet up on the control panel. "Many strange currents meet in the Triangle," he said. "Ships have disappeared there for ages. Ahab had a close call there once when we pursued the whale, although not with the Dead Sea current. There are other currents that run deep in the Triangle. Who knows where they lead?"

I wasn't quite ready to believe him yet. "What about the rumours of airplanes that have disappeared there?" I asked. "The currents couldn't have taken them."

"I have been many things in my life," Ishmael said. "A simple mariner. A simple priest. A simple vampire. But I have never been a pilot, simple or otherwise, so I wouldn't know about that. I don't like to fly. It leads to falling. And no good comes of falling." He smiled at me.

Nemo and I looked at each other.

"I don't see as we have much of a choice," I said.

"Set course for the Bermuda Triangle," Nemo said, and One-Eye got to work at his controls.

We locked Ishmael in the cabin that Nemo had once locked me in. How far I had come. Ishmael didn't protest. He must have recognized there would have been no point. Maybe he liked the looks of the bottle that was waiting for him inside as well. Nemo stationed a couple of crewmen outside the door, just in case.

I spent the time changing the bandages on my hand again and trying not to think about the fact that the Bermuda Triangle was not remotely in the direction of the Marianas Trench. We were losing ground to Noah with every minute. Judging by the silence in the control room of the *Nautilus*, everyone else knew it, too.

Eventually, Ishmael wandered back onto the bridge and put his feet up on the same instrument panel as before. Suddenly, everyone in the control room had guns out and were pointing them at him. Well, everyone but me.

"Oh, please," Ishmael said. "Your crew are fine. I'd hardly be a vampire if I couldn't get past a locked door and a couple of mortals." His words did little to reassure us, and one of the crew went back the way Ishmael had come, presumably to check on the Atlanteans who had been guarding him.

Ishmael looked out the windows and shook his head. "We need to be on the surface now. I have to be abovedecks for this to work."

"Aren't we more likely to find the current down here?" Nemo asked.

"I can't smell the Dead Sea from within this vessel," Ishmael said. "I can barely smell anything above the stench of all these dead sailors. I need to be outside, where I can tell one scent from another."

Nemo looked at me and I shrugged. I fully expected Ishmael to try something the first opportunity he had. But we were in the middle of the ocean, far from land. What could he do out here?

"Take us up," Nemo said to One-Eye, then nodded at Scars. "Come with us. Bring your weapon."

Ishmael shot one of those toothy grins at us. "What is the world coming to when you can't even trust a priest?" he said.

"Personally, I've never trusted priests," I said.

Scars kept her pistol aimed at Ishmael as the others more or less put their weapons away and got about the work of taking us to the surface. We broke through the water into a thick mist that limited our visibility to a dozen feet or so. Nemo and Scars escorted Ishmael to the near access hatch. I tagged along after them because I wanted to be near Ishmael when he tried something. I doubted the Atlanteans' pistols would make a difference, but maybe I would.

"What manner of futuristic weapons might these be?"

Ishmael asked, eyeing Scars' pistol as Nemo opened the hatch. "Tesla guns?"

"Tesla was on the right path," Nemo said, "but he didn't travel far enough down it." He climbed up onto the deck and motioned for Scars to follow him before it was Ishmael's turn. I followed Ishmael and then we were all standing on the slick deck of the *Nautilus* without incident.

We were still shrouded in mist. Waves lapped at the sides of the *Nautilus* from all directions, and we spun slowly to the port side, then the starboard as currents moved the vessel.

"Show us the way to Ahab and we'll set you free when we can," I said to Ishmael, but he just shook his head at me.

"Even I don't believe you," he said. "And I'm the one who should want to believe you."

"Trust me when I say a lone vampire is the least of our problems right now," I said.

Ishmael stared out into the mist for a time. Then he nodded. "Five degrees starboard," he said. "But slowly."

Nemo didn't say anything, but the *Nautilus* changed course appropriately. A neat trick, that. I'd get him to show me how he did that if I thought I'd ever take to the seas again after all this was over.

We drifted through the mist, with Ishmael calling out course corrections every now and then. First a few more degrees starboard, then a wide turn to port, then back to starboard again.

"It feels like you're taking us in one direction using a very crooked path," I said.

"You have to ride the current in just the right ways," Ishmael said.

"And what ways are those?" Nemo asked.

"Like you're a corpse," Ishmael said.

We left him to it. More starboard, until we had turned back the way we came, then we travelled in a straight line for a while, and then he had us simply spin in a circle a few times. Nemo and I exchanged another look, but we bit our tongues.

"Can you make your vessel roll a bit?" Ishmael asked, looking at Nemo. "You know, like a dead man caught in a wave?"

Nemo didn't say anything and Ishmael shrugged and looked back at the water. "Never mind," he said. "I'll do it the hard way."

I lost track of how long things went on like that, but finally Ishmael stepped back and nodded. "We are riding the current now," he said. "Change nothing and let it take us. We'll be in the Dead Sea soon enough." He turned to me. "I've given you what you want," he said. "Is this the point where you kill me now?"

"I'm tempted to do just that," I said. "But I'm a man of my word. You can keep on living for now, if you can even call what you do living."

"You say that as if we are somehow different at our base levels," Ishmael said. "We are not so unlike, you and I."

"We're very different," I said. "I've never masqueraded as a priest."

"We are both cursed by God," Ishmael said, and I said nothing to that.

Ishmael smiled and looked back out into the mist. "Ah, there it is now," he said, pointing. I looked in the direction he indicated. I saw nothing but more mist.

"What is it?" I asked.

"The Dead Sea marker," Ishmael said. "Do you not see it?"

"I see nothing," I said, taking a step forward and squinting into the mist. Too late I realized my mistake.

Ishmael was upon me before I could even turn to face him. He bit into my neck with that mouthful of teeth, but only for a second. Just enough for a taste. Then he threw himself off the deck of the *Nautilus* and into the water even as I pushed myself away from him.

Scars rushed to the side with her pistol raised, but I knocked her arm up into the air before she could fire a shot. "We may yet need him alive!" I said.

I turned and saw Ishmael in the water. He wasn't swimming but he was drifting away anyway. He was caught in another current, one that went in a different direction.

I stepped to the edge of the *Nautilus*, to dive in after him, but he shook his head. "I wouldn't do that if you want to find Ahab," he said. "Your only chance now is to keep riding the current all the way into the Dead Sea."

"And what about you?" I shouted at him. I put my hand to my

neck. It came away bloody. All these years of being so careful around vampires, and I'd been bitten by one as easily as if I were a schoolgirl.

"I'll just float along until someone picks me up," Ishmael said. "Someone always picks me up."

"It is a simple shot from here," Scars said at my side. "Even you could manage it."

"We can't shoot him and he knows it," I said.

"But if we don't shoot him now, we will lose him in the mist," Nemo said.

"The world is at stake," I said. "If we need him for something else. . . ."

Ishmael grinned at us as he drifted away into the mist and was gone.

"I am really sick and tired of vampires," I said.

"You're injured," Scars said.

"He fed on me," I said. "But it was just a taste."

"Why would he bother?" Nemo asked.

"Even a taste is enough to create a blood bond," I said. First Noah's trick with the blood and now this. I wondered if maybe Noah was part vampire. "He'll know wherever I am from now on. It's a handy way to hunt your prey. And to avoid your hunters."

"How long does it last?" Nemo asked.

"Until I kill him," I said.

"Let's hope he has set us on the right current, then," Nemo said, turning back to gaze into the mist ahead.

"Oh, I don't doubt that," I said. "The question is how we're going to find our way back without him."

☦

THE DEAD SEA

We drifted along until the mist faded away and we found ourselves in a perfectly calm sea. There were no waves at all. It was like floating in a bath. There wasn't any wind either. There was just nothing.

The water here was as black as an oil spill. It stretched around us in all directions, a flat, still plain. I could see a few feet down, but that was it. Light didn't seem to penetrate the water at all—maybe because there wasn't much light anyway. The sky was completely grey and featureless, no clouds in sight.

"This certainly has the look of the Dead Sea," I said.

"I have always wanted to explore all the seas," Nemo said, "but this is one I would have been content to never sail in."

I turned back the way we'd come. There was no sign of Ishmael anywhere in the water. The Dead Sea stretched to the horizon, where it met that grey sky. There was no current behind us either. There was only the dissipating wake of the *Nautilus*. Nemo had ordered the engines shut down, and now we were drifting to a stop.

"Things have gone more or less according to plan so far," I said. "Now we just need to find Ahab and the whale."

"Let's not forget discovering a way out," Nemo said, gazing around at the featureless sea.

"One thing at a time," I said.

Something found us before we could get around to finding all the things we were looking for.

There was a thumping sound from the front of the *Nautilus*, as if we had hit something. We looked that way in time to see a man pull himself up out of the water and onto the deck.

Make that a dead man, for he was clearly no longer one of the living. He wore the clothing of a Russian or eastern European sailor from the mid-20th century—striped shirt, dark pants—but his skin was the pale colour of one who'd spent a long time under the water. He stared at us blankly and then shambled forward, that dark water pouring out of his clothes as he walked.

"It appears to be a zombie," Nemo said, and Scars lifted her pistol.

"Technically, I'd call you guys the zombies," I said. "I think he's just dead."

There was no spark of life in the man's eyes as he came at us. He looked as slack and uncaring as any corpse. There was just the small matter of him walking across the deck of the *Nautilus* toward us.

"Dead or not, he doesn't look friendly," Nemo said. Scars pulled the trigger and a pulse of that strange light shot out and struck the man in the chest. The impact knocked him back, and he stumbled and fell. He hit the side of the *Nautilus* and slid over it, back into the water. There was no splash at impact. Instead, the sea simply seemed to swallow him.

Not for good, though.

I looked down over the side of the *Nautilus* as we drifted past, and I saw the sailor floating just under the surface, gazing up at us with those dead eyes. He reached out and pawed at the side of the submarine, searching for a handhold.

"I think you're going to need bigger guns," I told Nemo.

"And likely more of them," he agreed.

I turned away from the dead sailor to see what Nemo was looking at. Another dead man was pulling himself aboard on the starboard side of the *Nautilus*. This one wore the uniform of a Union soldier from the American civil war days. His face was just as blank as the other man's as he came toward us. Scars sent him back into the water. A burning smell filled the air.

But then other things started pulling themselves up onto the deck, things that weren't men.

A minotaur hauled itself halfway up the back of the *Nautilus*, and I quickly spun Scars around to shoot it off before it could get closer. Minotaurs are surprisingly fast if they have a good footing. The minotaur was followed by a woman in white robes who walked up the side of the *Nautilus* without using her hands at all. She also had black eyes, which I suspected had been that colour before she drowned. I didn't know what she was and I didn't want to find out. So back into the water she went, courtesy of Nemo this time. A siren even started to pull her way up before both of them shot her back down. I didn't know sirens could drown. It was probably a good thing she was dead, though, because she didn't seem interested in singing to us. That could have been a problem if she started up. I wasn't sure if Nemo and his crew were susceptible to the songs of sirens, seeing as they were half dead and all, but this didn't seem like the right time to find out.

"Maybe we should take the *Nautilus* under," I suggested, but Nemo shook his head.

"Who knows what is waiting for us under the surface?" he said. "We might never be able to ascend again."

Instead of ordering us below, he shouted down through the hatch to increase speed. The *Nautilus* surged forward through the Dead Sea, leaving many of our would-be boarders behind. The problem was more of them kept climbing up out of the water. There was a Roman centurion, somehow still in his full armour. A gaunt man in rags with a beard down to his chin, who looked like he'd been adrift at sea long before he'd found himself here. A woman in a ball gown with jewelled rings on all her fingers, probably the victim of some cruise ship disaster. They kept coming, and Scars and Nemo kept sweeping them off the deck with their guns.

"Maybe we need more crew up here," I said.

"We don't have any more crew to spare," Nemo said. "They're fighting boarders belowdecks too."

"What do you mean, boarders belowdecks?" I asked.

"They're trying to get in through the lower hatches and weapons tubes," Nemo said, looking about the Dead Sea as calmly as if we were on a sightseeing expedition. "We are at risk of being overwhelmed."

I really needed to learn his trick of knowing things without seemingly being told about them.

"What do you suppose they want?" I asked, but Nemo shook his head.

"I'd prefer not to find out."

And then the tentacles rose out of the water and wrapped around the *Nautilus*. Long, grey things with nasty-looking suckers on them. Scars and Nemo turned their guns on them, but this time the weapons did nothing. The tentacles just squeezed tighter, and I heard what I thought might be metal groaning under the strain.

"Everywhere we go, it's always the squid," Nemo said.

I wondered briefly if it was the squid I'd killed to start all this, then put it out of my mind. If it was, then things were probably going to get even worse.

"We'll need to step inside the *Nautilus* for a moment," Nemo said and dropped down through the open hatch. I hesitated for a second, trying to figure out which course of action was the lesser of evils that might befall me, and then Scars pushed me down the hatch and quickly followed. She slammed the hatch shut, but we didn't dive to battle the squid, like I was expecting. Instead, Nemo simply said, "Activate the squid field." He spoke in that same conversational tone of voice, but the crew in the control room heard him anyway.

There was a crackling sound from outside, and the hull of the *Nautilus* hummed for a few seconds. Then Nemo nodded and Scars opened the hatch and climbed out onto the deck again, followed by Nemo. I climbed up after them because what else was I going to do?

The tentacles were gone now, the squid having released its grip. The boarders were all back in the water too, bobbing along in our wake. For the moment, it was clear sailing again.

"What's the squid field?" I asked Nemo.

"It's like the guns, but on a much larger scale," he said. "It's standard defensive gear on all the Atlantean vessels. We tend to encounter squid wherever we go."

"So even the squid don't like you," I said.

"I don't think the end of the world is really the appropriate time for humour," Nemo said.

"I can't imagine a more appropriate time," I said.

Our reprieve was short-lived, though. More of the dead tried to pull themselves aboard, and the water surged off the bow as the squid came at us again, its tentacles reaching for the *Nautilus*. It turned out you couldn't really kill the dead, at least not in a sea named after them.

Then there was a massive surge of water around the squid and a great set of white jaws erupted through the surface and swallowed the creature.

The white whale.

It threw itself up out of the water, towering over the *Nautilus*. It had changed since our last meeting. It was no longer white. Instead, it was the weathered colour of bone, somewhere between white and nothing at all. Perhaps that was because it was bone and nothing but bone. Its skin and organs and all the other living parts of it were gone. It was just a skeleton now, a great bone whale. The squid writhed within it, trapped in a skeletal prison. And then the whale was gone, slipping back into the water without so much as a splash.

But not before I saw Ahab.

He rode the back of the whale, as if he were mounted upon a horse or some normal creature. He clung to the whale's skull with one hand, while in the other he held Queequeg's harpoon, blazing with green fire. The same green fire blazed in his eye sockets. He had shed his skin, too, and he was nothing but bone now. I recognized him by the black top hat and the undertaker's suit he still wore. His wings were gone, and I remembered how they had come apart, the words sinking down into the whale. Then he disappeared under the water along with the whale he rode.

They did not remain there long, though. They surfaced again behind the *Nautilus*, this time scooping up a mouthful of the dead that swam in our wake. The whale swallowed them down to join the squid, then went under once more. Ahab gazed at us with those burning eyes the whole time.

"That is what you want to help us?" Scars asked, staring at me.

"This seems mad even by your standards," Nemo said in agreement.

"That may be, but it's our only hope," I said.

The whale rose again, off the port side. It circled around us, swallowing every dead person and thing in sight. It slipped under and did the same with the dead that were trying to get aboard the *Nautilus* beneath the water line. When there was nothing left—at least nothing we could see—the whale surfaced in front of the *Nautilus*.

This time it remained there, regarding us with its empty eye sockets. We could see the squid and all the other dead thrashing around and climbing over each other in the whale's insides, trying to find a way out. The creature's bones were too strong for them, though, and they remained trapped inside it. Now that the whale remained on the surface, I could see the words flowing along the bones, white letters swirling inside them. The words from Ahab's wings. It must have been how he had bound the whale. Divine words to bind the word of God.

Ahab stood and walked along the skull of the white whale, the harpoon still in his hand. He dropped down onto the deck of the *Nautilus*, and the front of the submarine dipped in the water, as if something far heavier had landed on it. Scars raised her pistol as he approached, but I shook my head at her.

"I wouldn't," I said, so she dropped the weapon back down to her side.

Ahab strode up to us and then stopped about a harpoon's length away. He stared at us with those burning green eyes. I expected some sort of greeting from him, such as a death threat or vow to make me pay for all the things I'd done, but he remained silent. So it was up to me to break the silence.

"We've been looking for you," I said, stating the obvious.

"Have you run out of the living angels and must now seek the dead?" he asked. His voice was like rocks grinding together. "What of Sariel? We can hear her weeping in your vessel even as we speak."

"That's not why we're here," I said. "We need your help."

"And so you have found it," he said. "And just in time for you, it seems. The dead are intent on making you one of their own."

"Yeah, I'm not really sure what that's all about," I said. "Maybe they've got some grudge against me for something I can't recall."

"The grudge they bear is you are one of the living in the Dead Sea," Ahab said. "And then there is the matter of the abominations you have surrounded yourself with." He cast his gaze upon Nemo and Scars. It felt strange to be the most normal person in the scene. Well, the most normal looking, anyway.

"Speaking of abominations, we have a problem," I said. "Noah has gone mad."

Ahab looked back at me. "Noah was always mad," he said. "There is no place for sanity on the ark. Why should this concern us?"

"He has God's bible," I said.

The flames in his eye sockets seemed to flare as he stared at me.

"How did he obtain the bible?" he asked.

"It's a long story and who can really say who's to blame?" I said. "The point is he needs to be stopped."

"Noah is one of God's legion," Ahab said. "The bible should be just as safe with him as it was with Sariel. Perhaps safer."

"I don't know how to break this to you," I said, "but Noah is not who you think he is. Or what you think he is. He's on his way right now to the Sunken City to wake the Sleeper."

Ahab stared at me in silence. Out of the corner of my eye, I saw Scars inch her pistol upward again.

"He's going to end the world," I added, in case Ahab didn't understand.

"The world was always meant to end one day," Ahab said. "This is as certain as the Dead Sea is dead."

"He's going to open the bible and read it," I said. "If he hasn't done so already. He's going to release all the words and wake the Sleeper. The logos will be lost." I looked over his shoulder, at the white whale and its bellyful of the dead. "Imagine countless white whales, with no Ahabs to control them."

To be honest, I had no idea what Noah's plans were when it came to the bible. But now was not the time for honesty. I'm not sure if there's ever a time for honesty.

"We do not control the white whale," Ahab said. "We are the white whale."

That's when I realized why he kept saying "us" and "we." And why he was the same bone shade as the whale. Ahab and the white whale had somehow become the same entity. I guess that was how he had stopped it back when the *Chains* sank. I didn't know which one was in charge and the difference didn't really matter much at the moment.

"If the Sleeper wakes, it will destroy the world and the words of God will be lost," I said. "They are all that remain of him now. Noah seeks to destroy all that is left of God. We cannot let him succeed."

"We will stop Noah," Ahab said, the flames in his eyes flaring again. "We will protect the words of God."

The white whale suddenly sank down into the water, out of sight.

"Where's it going?" I asked.

"We are disgorging the dead," Ahab said. "We will take them deep into the depths of the Dead Sea and open our maw to allow them to escape. By the time they rise to the surface again, we will have travelled far across the sea from them."

"Why not take them all the way down to the bottom?" I suggested. "Make it a really long trip for them."

"There is no bottom to the Dead Sea," Ahab said. "Just as there is no end to the Dead Sea."

"All right," I said. "Let's get underway, then." I felt positively cheery. Things were shaping up for the better for the first time since, well, I wasn't actually sure when they'd last been good.

"Where would you have us go?" Ahab asked.

"I'm hoping you'll tell me," I said. "How do we get out of the Dead Sea?"

"There is no way to leave the Dead Sea," Ahab said. "As we said, it is boundless."

That cheery feeling started to fade. It had been fun while it lasted.

"What about the current that we rode in on?" I asked. "Can't we just go back the same way?"

"The current flows into the Dead Sea but no current ever flows out of the Dead Sea," Ahab said. "It is a whirlpool in time."

"I was afraid you were going to say something like that," I said. And now things were completely back to normal.

"So even an angel can't find a way out of the Dead Sea?" Nemo asked Ahab.

"We are no longer an angel," Ahab said.

"The white whale, then," Nemo said. "The white whale cannot find a way out?"

"We are no longer simply the white whale, either," Ahab said. "And no, we do not know how to leave the Dead Sea. We came here to never be found again, after all."

"So this is how the world ends?" Nemo asked. "Undone by a madman's quest and a vampire's trick?"

I gazed out across the Dead Sea. The white whale took that moment to surface again, its insides empty now. I thought about asking it to swallow me, about walking into that open mouth and just giving up and forgetting about saving the world and everything else. Some days, giving in to madness just seemed easier.

But today wasn't that day.

"I may have a trick of my own," I said.

☦

THE DEAD HAVE THEIR DAY AGAIN

I searched my pockets for money before I remembered I was as penniless as usual. I asked Nemo for more of the coins he had used to pay the shopkeeper back in Havana, and he shot me a quizzical look before giving me a handful of reals. I examined the coins, polished the one that looked the most presentable, and then put it in my mouth. I dropped the others into my pocket. You never know when you may need a little spending money.

"Someone needs to kill me," I said. "I'm not going to do it to myself."

The others didn't move. They all stared at me in the way you'd expect when you say something like that.

"Maybe there's a way out of the Dead Sea and maybe there's not," I said. "We don't have the time to search the place and find out for ourselves. But there's someone else who may know. Charon."

"Charon," Nemo said.

"The ferryman of the dead," Ahab said. "He plies the waters between myth and reality."

"I am aware of who he is," Nemo said. "I'm just not certain of his relevance in this instance."

"If there's anyone who knows the currents of waters that carry the dead, I imagine it's Charon," I said. "If we can draw him here, then perhaps he can lead us out back to the world we're trying to save."

Nemo looked down into the depths. "If you die here, you may not resurrect in the normal manner," he said. "You may instead become transformed into one of these living dead."

"I know," I said. "But what choice—"

I didn't have time to finish my sentence because Ahab stepped up and rammed his harpoon through my chest. It hurt in the impossibly vast way that harpoons and spears and other large objects do when they are thrust through your body. But there was another pain I'd never felt before. The green fire that ran the length of the harpoon. It burned inside of me like—actually, it's hard to describe because it even burned my mind. It hurt so much and in so many ways that I screamed, and I haven't done that for a while. When you get killed as often as I do, you get a little blasé about death. I'd prefer not to talk about it any more, if it's all the same to you. Scars and Nemo brought up their pistols, but I managed to wave them off.

"Let us wait for the ferryman," Ahab said, "or the end of the world."

I didn't have a witty comeback to that, because I was too busy slumping off the harpoon to the deck and into welcome death.

And the world grew dark for a time, as it does every now and then.

Let there be light.

I resurrected to the feel of something digging in my mouth, choking me. I instinctively reached up to my face and caught hold of a bony wrist covered in cloth. I opened my eyes to see Charon looming above me, wearing the same dark robe as the last time we'd met. His skin was as grey and gaunt as before, his eyes as empty. He drew his hand away from my mouth, and I saw the coin in his fingers. He dropped it into a pocket in his robe and stepped back to give me room to stand.

I climbed to my feet and saw more or less the same scene as when I'd died. I was on the deck of the *Nautilus*, with Nemo and Scars and Ahab around me. Some crew from below had joined us and they were helping fend off a new wave of the dead who were trying to board the submarine to do whatever it was they wanted to do to us. And there was Charon, of course.

The same boat he'd used to ferry me into Hades sat in the water beside the *Nautilus* now. The same pole was sticking out of the water as if Charon had simply stuck it down into a hidden bottom just beneath us.

I gave Ahab a look. "How about a little more warning next time you stick a harpoon through me?" I said. "Better yet, how about you use something smaller than a harpoon?" My chest still ached, even though it had healed.

"There is no point committing to death halfway," Ahab said. "You must fill your pockets with stones and dive to the bottom to find out what waits there."

"I don't even know why I bother talking to angels," I said.

"We are no longer an angel," Ahab said, but I ignored him and looked at Nemo instead.

"How long was I gone?" I asked.

"Only a few minutes," he said. "Your death seemed to increase the activity of the dead. They have been swarming us since you fell. And Charon arrived almost immediately." He gazed at the ferryman. "We did not see him approach until he was here. Strange, given the condition of the sea."

"Yeah, that's the strange thing," I said. I looked into the water, which was boiling with the dead. For some reason they left Charon's boat alone.

"A few minutes of death. That's quicker than I usually resurrect," I said. "Especially for a wound like that."

Nemo nodded. "I suspected as much," he said. "I imagine it is the nature of this place. We will have to return sometime and study it more."

"You have paid the ferryman's price, yet you live again," Charon said in that voice that was a mix of whispers and wind. "You are in the rare situation of choosing for yourself whether you will accompany me to the underworld."

"Actually, it's the other world I want to return to," I said. "That's why we called you here. We need a guide."

Charon didn't say anything. He was the strong, silent, eerie type.

"We're trapped here and we need you to lead us out of this place and back to the mortal world," I said.

There was a great splash in the sea behind me and I heard the sound of several of the crew's weapons. The air smelled burnt again. Or maybe still.

"Sooner is better than later," I added.

"I am a ferryman of the dead," Charon said. "I take people to the realm of the dead, not to the realm of the living."

"If we don't get back to the mortal world soon, there will be no realm of the living," I said. "Noah's gone mad and is trying to drown the world. If we don't stop him, Hades is going to be flooded with the dead. And worse."

"The world of the living and its problems are no concern of mine," Charon said. "I am a ferryman. No more, no less. I take payment in exchange for passage. Anything other than that does not concern a ferryman."

I didn't seem to be winning him over. On the other hand, he wasn't making any signs of leaving. So maybe I still had a chance.

There was more splashing and weapon noises behind me. Ahab stepped past me and struck something with his harpoon and the sounds subsided again.

"All right then, take us to Hades," I said.

"All of you?" Charon asked.

"Why not?" I said. "We're all dead in some form or another."

"Cross, perhaps we should discuss this," Nemo said.

But Charon had already turned back to his boat. He reached down and pulled it up onto the deck of the *Nautilus* in one motion, like it weighed nothing at all. Maybe it didn't to him. Then he grabbed the pole. He didn't take it from the water. Instead, he thrust it down deeper into the Dead Sea and pushed. The *Nautilus* surged forward.

"Cross," Nemo said again.

"Relax, I have a plan," I said.

"Your plans have not exactly saved the day so far," he pointed out.

"They haven't exactly sunk us yet either," I said, which wasn't entirely true. But I didn't want to think about Blackbeard any more.

I looked back and saw the dead splashing about in our wake, swimming after us. But the *Nautilus* was already moving quicker than them. The white whale followed us, plowing through the dead and pushing them back under. I imagined the dead would be talking about this for centuries in their underwater socials.

I moved over to stand beside Charon as he propelled the *Nautilus* along. He didn't pay me any attention. He just gazed ahead with no expression, like we were out for a leisurely Sunday cruise. Perhaps to a ferryman every day was a leisurely Sunday cruise.

"Maybe you can teach me all about all these special currents," I said. It would be handy knowledge to have for the next time someone stranded me in a place like the Dead Sea. Because if my past experience was any sign, it would certainly happen again. If we managed to save the world, that is.

"You cannot learn such things," Charon said.

"Forbidden knowledge and all that," I said, nodding.

"Your mind is like a stone in the water," he said. "The constant stream of life and death shapes you. But you are not part of life and death. You are not part of the stream itself. You could not understand the currents any more than the rock understands the water that slowly washes it away, until it is just one more grain of sand among millions, and then nothing at all."

I went back to stand by Nemo. "I never thought I'd prefer your company over anyone else's," I said.

We went on like that for a while, drifting across the featureless sea, and then some more fog came out of nowhere and we went into that. The fog seemed to be everyone's sleight of hand for hiding what they were doing. Think about that the next time you're wandering down a foggy path.

I kept a hopeful watch for Ishmael in the water, but there was no sign of him. With my fingers, I felt the wound on my neck from where he had bitten me, but it had already healed, unlike the wound in my hand. I wondered if I'd be able to sense Ishmael when he was near like he could now likely sense me. Probably not. There'd be no evolutionary advantage to that. Then I wondered if maybe the fact that I'd died would disrupt his ability to sense me. Probably not. There was likely no evolutionary sense to that either. I was the perfect meal, after all. He could drain me until death and I'd just keep resurrecting with a fresh batch of blood. It was a surprise the vampires hadn't banded together to hunt me down and imprison me in a dungeon somewhere ages ago. I was the cask of ale that never stopped pouring.

We came out of the mist and found ourselves in a river flowing through a cavern somewhere. It was dark as night but Ahab's blazing harpoon cast enough of an eerie light that we could see where we were going. Charon was still guiding the *Nautilus* with his pole, even though the river was a white water kind of affair. Most of the crew retreated belowdecks but Nemo stayed up with Ahab and me and Charon. I'm not ashamed to say I had the worst sea legs of the bunch. I sat down and dangled my feet through the hatch and hung on as best I could. I looked behind us again and saw the white whale still swimming along in our wake, like a faithful dog that didn't know when to give up.

"I take it this is Hades?" Nemo murmured to me.

I didn't have to answer, though, for just then the cavern widened and the water slowed its rush, until we were drifting along at a more sedate speed. The top of the cavern climbed higher and higher until it stretched above us like the night sky above the earth. I could see people hanging from cracks in the rocks up there.

I looked back down and saw the swamp from before, with the white reeds sticking up through the water and the shore in the distance. There was a crowd of people watching from the bank, and more coming to join them as we drifted closer. They had the same drawn, haunted faces that I remembered from the last time I'd visited here. I could see the buildings flickering behind them, as they shifted from one memory to another.

"You might want to get more armed men on deck," I told Nemo.

"Is there no place in the world you don't have enemies?" he asked.

"Usually enough people die that the next generation forgets about me," I said. "But that doesn't really apply to a place like this."

Nemo didn't call any men up to the deck, though. Maybe they had their hands full making repairs to the *Nautilus*. Or maybe Nemo was happy to hand me over to the good people of Hades in exchange for safe passage. It was a coin toss, really.

We went close enough to the shore that I could see the skeleton of the three-headed dog lying in the same place where I'd last seen it. I could see some of the people on the land recognized me as they stared at the *Nautilus*. Even a few of those under the water looked up at me with . . . I don't know what. Surprise?

Delight? Whatever it was, it didn't bode well.

"I should probably go below and stock up on some grace," I said to no one in particular.

Charon stopped pushing with the pole and the *Nautilus* drifted forward until the submarine ground up against the bottom.

"You have chosen Hades, and now Hades welcomes you," he said.

I looked at the people lining the shore. They all stared back at me. None of them had anything close to what I would call a welcoming expression.

"We should have stayed in Atlantis," Nemo said. "At least then I could have seen the end of the world in my own city."

"That's right," I said, nodding. "The world is ending." I turned to Charon. "And you know what that means."

He stared back at me for a moment. "The world has not yet ended," he finally said.

"Why wait until the last moment?" I said. "The end has begun. It began when Noah found God's bible. Isn't that enough?"

Charon stared at me some more, as if thinking. Then his lips twitched a little. Was that a smile? Did the ferryman of the dead just smile at me?

"Very well," he said. "Your argument has some merit." He began to move the pole in the water again. This time, though, instead of pushing it he swirled it around, churning up the water. The churning spread, until the entire swamp was frothing.

"Wait, did you just smile at me?" I asked Charon, but he ignored me and kept to his task.

"Would someone please explain to me what is going on?" Nemo said.

Now the water began to flow back the way it had come, back into the cavern we had followed into Hades. The dead on the shore cried out and rushed into the swamp, splashing past the *Nautilus* without paying us any more attention. Those under the water were whisked away by the sudden current Charon had created. The people hanging from the ceiling began to drop down into the swamp with joyous cries.

"The dead are trapped in Hades until the end of the world," I told Nemo. "Charon himself told me that the first time we met. Now that the world is ending, they are free."

A dozen or so cracks suddenly rent the walls of Hades, ripping the stone open to create more caverns. The water from the swamp flowed into them, too, with more of the dead that had been trapped in Hades all these ages.

"The dead can return to the world again," I said. "And so can we."

Nemo opened his mouth, but for once didn't say anything. And some people don't believe in miracles.

"You are free to travel anywhere you will in this end time," Charon said.

"Will you guide us once more?" I asked him.

He paused a moment before answering. The dead continued to flood out of Hades all around us, crying and screaming with delight at finally being freed. They filled the waters in a stampede now, and fell from the cavern roof like rain.

"I don't believe anything prevents me from guiding you back to the land of the living now that the dead are free once more," Charon finally said.

"I was hoping you'd say that," I said. "Wait here." I ran to the front of the *Nautilus* and jumped off, onto the shore.

"Cross, where are you going?" Nemo yelled after me.

"I won't be long," I called back. I pushed through the crowd of dead that were streaming out of Hades. They no longer looked haunted. Now they were laughing and weeping and shaking their heads as if they couldn't believe it.

"We don't have long," Nemo said.

I saved my breath for running instead of answering him. I made my way past buildings that changed shape like a dream as I went. A temple fell down into a jumble of ruins. A bathhouse disappeared in a cloud of steam that just as quickly dissipated, leaving what looked like a barracks in its place. A well in the street suddenly overflowed with bones. I found my way back to the library where I'd met Alice that first time I'd been here. The street was empty of the dead by the time I reached it. The building flickered as I walked through the door, for an instant becoming the cave that led to the monastery where I'd hidden from the demons all those ages ago. Then it flickered back to the library. Maybe I'd visited Hades enough that it was starting to treat me as a resident, and it was reflecting my own past back at me. The library was as empty as the street when I went inside. Empty except for one person.

She sat on one of the tables inside the library. Actually, she sat inside a bone cage on the table. It looked like the same sort of bone that the white whale was made of. The similarity was heightened by the fact that she wore the same funeral undertaker's suit and hat as Ahab. Her clothes and hair were wet, as if she'd just been swimming.

"Alice," I said. "I was hoping you'd be here."

"I'm always here," she said. "Except when I'm not. Then I'm here somewhere else."

"You need to come with me," I said. I looked for the door of the bone cage but there wasn't one. It was perfectly formed, with no entrance or exit.

"I can't leave," she said. "I have to stay in the library."

"This is no time for that," I said. I gave the bars a shake, but they were as solid as the whale itself looked. "The world is ending," I added.

"I know," she said, nodding. "I've read all the books about the world ending. In every one of them, you come here and try to get me to leave. But I don't go with you in any of them. So you're wasting your time even by being here."

I stared at her through the bars. Water dripped down her face from her wet hair. It looked like tears on her cheeks.

"How do the books end?" I asked her.

"Most of them end when Noah wakes up the Sleeper," Alice said. "I don't really like those ones."

"Are there any where that doesn't happen?" I asked.

"There's only one," she said. "And it isn't a very good book at all. I like that one the least." She pulled her hair over her face and now I couldn't see her eyes.

"One. Okay. That's a fighting chance," I told myself.

"You won't like it," she said.

"Alice, why did you give me that book in the monastery?" I said. "The copy of *Moby Dick*? If you hadn't done that, I never would have gone fishing with it. The squid would never have bit me and given Noah a blood trail to follow to Atlantis. He never would have found the Sunken City."

"Noah has squid looking for you in all the seas, but they don't matter to the story," Alice said. "He finds the Sunken City in all the books eventually, whether or not the squid finds you. He doesn't even need to find Atlantis in some of them. The only way to stop Noah is for everyone to come together against him. You and Ahab and the whale and Nemo and all those Atlanteans. And a few others. Even then, in most of the books Noah still drowns the world. The only chance to save it is to make the story about you. So I gave you the book so Noah would find you and you would find the story. Now we're in a book where you have a chance to stop Noah at least."

"I'm not even going to pretend to understand that," I said. "Come with me and help us save the world."

"Cross, the world is the library," she said. "Or maybe the library is the world. I'm never quite sure about that. Anyway, you look after one and I'll look after the other."

"All right," I said and held my hand up to the bars. I knew when I couldn't change Alice's mind. Alice put her own hand up against mine. It was wet and cold, like the hand of a corpse.

"I'll see you again when this is all over," I said.

"I don't know what will happen when this is all over," Alice said. "I won't know which book we're in until the end."

I ran back to the *Nautilus* without saying anything else, because I've never been the type for goodbyes and I didn't know what to say anyway.

The swamp was still a thrashing mass of people by the time I returned to the submarine, but the crowd had thinned on the shore. The water level had dropped by several feet already. I wondered if it would empty out completely. Thankfully, Nemo and Ahab and the whale had waited for me. So had Charon.

I climbed aboard the *Nautilus* and nodded at Charon. "Let's go," I said.

Nemo looked at me and frowned. "What happened on shore?" he asked.

I didn't say anything. I just turned toward the front of the *Nautilus* as Charon pushed us back into the water and spun us toward one of the new caverns. The water raged down it, but he guided us into it like it was a still pond.

"Noah seeks the Sunken City," I told Charon.

"I know of the Sunken City," he said. "I will take you as close as a ferryman can to it. The rest will be up to you."

I nodded. "Despite what everyone else says about you, I think you're all right," I said.

"You may want to go belowdecks," Charon said as we went past clusters of the dead swimming toward the cavern entrance. "The way ahead will be rough and unpredictable."

I wasn't sure if he was telling the truth or he just didn't want me around now that I'd seen him smile. Either way, I decided it was probably best for me to follow his suggestion. Nemo and the others of his crew elected to join me in dropping down through the hatch and sealing it tight behind us. Ahab was more inclined to climb back onto the white whale and enjoy the ride.

I accompanied Nemo to the control room, where he gave everyone orders to put on their dive suits. They pulled them out from compartments underneath their chairs and slipped them on. Nemo took one out for me and I pulled it over my own clothes before strapping myself into a seat. The others left their hoods off for now, so I followed their lead. I tried not to think about what Alice had said.

As Charon had warned, things got rough for a while. The water threw us around and the *Nautilus* bounced off the walls of the cavern enough times that I lost count. Whatever damage the crew had repaired, this part of our voyage had probably done more. But the water eventually grew calmer and then the control room's windows glowed with a light in front of us. There were no dead in the water now.

"The light at the end of the tunnel," I said, but no one laughed.

"Perhaps it is more like the calm before the storm," Nemo said.

The light turned out to be a mist that we sailed through for a time, and then the mist fell away to reveal a jungle on either side of us. The cavern was gone. I looked out the aft windows of the control room, but all I could see was more jungle and the river going around a bend.

"Any idea where we are?" I asked. "That river could have spit us out anywhere."

"The northern side of New Guinea," One-Eye answered, checking his instruments.

"Half a day from the Marianas Trench at our current top speed," Nemo said, leaning forward and gazing out the window. "And following in the wake of the storm."

I looked out the front window and saw the river flowing into the sea in front of us, and beyond that a grey smudge on the horizon. Noah.

"Can we catch him?" I asked.

Nemo shook his head. "We've repaired what we can but the *Nautilus* is too damaged. We can do no more without several weeks in dry dock. Even the technology of Atlantis has its limits."

"Push it as hard as you can," I said. "Or half a day is all the world has left."

Nemo nodded and the crew went to work on their controls. The *Nautilus* shook as we increased speed, and a terrible wailing started somewhere in the vessel's depths. Sariel sounded worse than usual. I tried not to listen. There were a lot of things I was trying to put out of my mind right now.

I glanced behind us again and saw Charon poling his way back up the river. He didn't turn his gaze to look at us. I waved a farewell to him anyway.

I saw the white whale surface directly behind the *Nautilus*, Ahab riding it once more. He stood and looked at the storm on the horizon. Then he dropped back down and the whale gave a mighty thrust of its tail and lunged at us, sending a great wave of water our way that drove us forward.

We surged out of the river and into the sea, through a rocky channel that no doubt kept all but the most foolhardy away from the river's entrance. And the most foolhardy often wound up in some hell or another anyway, so what was the harm if they found their way down one of the many branches of the River Styx?

"What are those mad creatures doing?" Nemo asked, as the white whale came forward again, forcing us to ride another wave.

"I think they're helping us move faster," I said.

It was true. Each lunge of the whale rocketed us forward,

like the *Nautilus* was a surfer riding a massive wave. A massive, unnatural wave. Ahab lifted his harpoon over his head and shook it, and I raised my hand in thanks.

Nemo settled back into his chair, but he didn't say anything else. This day just kept getting stranger and stranger.

We raced across the ocean that way, until I thought I was finally going to be seasick for the first time in centuries. But the storm grew larger and larger on the horizon, and then we could make out the dim shapes of ships moving within it, lightning striking all around them.

"Battle stations," Nemo said. "It's time to save the world."

⚓

THE SUNKEN CITY

Between the white whale pushing us forward and whatever torture the crew was inflicting upon Sariel to increase the power of the *Nautilus*'s engines, we drew within weapons range of the ark within a few hours. Now the hard part of our plan began: figuring out how to stop Noah.

"How close are we to the Marianas Trench?" I asked Nemo as he gave orders to ready various weapons systems. His orders went on for some time. The *Nautilus* had quite an impressive list of weapons. That is, it would have been impressive if we were about to fight anyone besides Noah.

"It lies just ahead but many fathoms down," Nemo answered. "If we can stop him on the surface, before he descends into the depths, then we may succeed yet."

But Noah didn't have any intention of stopping on the surface. The storm seemed to grow smaller in size before us, as if it were shrinking. Then I saw lightning flashing again—this time below the water.

"The ark is diving!" I said. Noah was taking his fleet under, just like at Atlantis.

Some of the storm clouds parted for a second, and I had a glimpse of the stern of the ark lift up from the water and point toward the sky. The hull was covered in the ark's equivalent of barnacles: skeletons and weapons stuck into the slimy wood. Then the ark slid straight down, into the water, the storm clouds following it under.

"Dive after them," Nemo ordered his crew. "Fire all the torpedoes and then reload immediately. Fire at will with the guns." He shook his head and looked at me. "Now would be a fine time for divine intervention if you are able to call in any favours," he said.

"I think I burned those bridges a long time ago," I answered.

The storm descended into the darker water below us, but it was easy enough to follow it down thanks to the constant lighting flashes. As we descended, I watched the torpedoes streak from the *Nautilus* and into the storm. Some of them went in a straight line and disappeared into the clouds, while others curved around and hit the storm from the sides. There were more flashes, and the *Nautilus* shook with the shock waves. The torpedoes were followed by those jellyfish things from the weapons hold. They swam into the storm at surprising speed and blue and yellow blooms of light erupted here and there, but this time there were no shock waves. None of our attacks seemed to do anything to stop or even slow the ark.

"I don't know if we're going to win the day here or not," I said to Nemo, "so I'd just like to say it's been an honour to sail with you." It was the sort of thing you were supposed to tell each other in grim moments like this.

"Of course," Nemo said. "That goes without saying."

I wanted to help, but there wasn't much I could do. I grabbed a power tube that ran into an unused instrument panel and cracked it open enough I could suck some grace from it. I had a feeling I'd be busy soon enough and I'd be needing all the grace I could get.

"We're having trouble locking on with the guns," Scars said, and Nemo nodded like he was expecting that.

"Fire into the clouds with a manta net spread," he said. "We're sure to hit something."

Scars ran her hands across the panel. Great bolts of lightning leapt through the water from somewhere on the *Nautilus* and joined the other lightning in the storm. It lit up the sea like it was day under the water, and the *Nautilus* shook some more.

"My prayers are answered," Sariel shrieked from the engine room. "Amen!" She said it with each explosion. "Amen! Amen! Amen!"

I looked over my shoulder to see what Ahab and the white whale were doing and saw they were no longer behind us.

"Hmm, did anyone see where our friends went?" I asked.

"Let's hope they have a plan," Nemo said, "for we are surely wanting of one."

Just then the clouds before us parted to either side, revealing the ark in all its horrible glory. The original ship had several holes torn in its sides and was burning in places despite being deep underwater. Several of the other vessels that had been grafted onto it had been blown free by the explosions, and they floated along in the ark's wake: a Roman trireme, a man-of-war, a Viking boat. Bodies drifted amid the wreckage, finally free of Noah. But he had more than enough crew left yet to deal with us. They lined the sides of the ark and the other vessels still attached. They shook their weapons at us, and I could hear their screams and wails through the water and the hull of the *Nautilus*. I didn't know if they were angry at us for trying to stop Noah or because we were failing to stop him.

Then Noah himself appeared at the rear of the ark, striding through the deck and knocking people and other creatures out of his way. They floated behind him like a misshapen, horrible halo. He was the same giant of a man as the last time I'd seen him, and he appeared to be wearing the same bloody robes. He was dragging the three angels on the chain again, but now the angels were all skeletons. They weren't dead, though. Even as skeletons they couldn't escape Noah. They carried God's bible in their hands, and they wailed as they came forward. The book looked unopened, though, so at least there was one good thing in all of this. I knew it wouldn't last.

Noah reached the rear railing of the ark and glared at us, then raised a hand above his head.

"Release the kraken!" he roared and dropped his hand. See what I mean?

The angels began to chant even while they kept on wailing. I almost felt sorry for them. Then a great wave buffeted the *Nautilus* underwater and I was thrown about in my chair. When I was able to steady myself, I looked out the window in time to see the kraken coming for us.

It's a hard creature to describe if you've never seen one. Think a giant squid crossed with, well, an even bigger giant squid. And maybe a cliff. And then the whole thing is thrown into a hook and spike factory. And then it's thrown at the *Nautilus.*

It reached out for us with tentacles the size of tree trunks and the length of soccer pitches. Each one of those tentacles was marked with giant suckers and hooks and claws, with more of Noah's captured crew melted into them, waving their weapons at us and shrieking their rage or horror or whatever it was they were shrieking.

"I thought the kraken were all dead," Nemo remarked, as casually as if we were watching a gentle sea turtle emerge from the depths. "I wonder how long he's had this one."

"Fire!" I shouted. "Fire fire fire!"

Scars was already on it. The torpedoes streaked out again and hit the kraken from all sides. It roared, enraged as explosions lit up all across its body, and I bounced around in my chair some more at the vibrations that shook the submarine. One of the blasts tore off a massive tentacle and it sank deeper into the depths, still writhing and reaching for us. The kraken's eyes, which were the size of houses, went red. Maybe with blood, maybe with bloodlust. The creature snapped its giant beak at us, and the sound of it echoing within the *Nautilus* actually drowned out Sariel's cries.

"Hit it with the cannons," Nemo said, but it was too late.

The torpedoes hadn't stopped the kraken. Instead, they just seemed to anger it further. One tentacle grabbed onto our stern, and another grabbed on to the bow. They tightened their grip and the metal groaned, then shrieked. The creatures trapped in the tentacles hacked away at the *Nautilus* with their weapons and claws and spikes. A man in a German submariner's uniform whose legs disappeared into the tentacle in front of us stabbed the window nearest me with a spear, scratching the glass, all the while screaming soundlessly. I couldn't help but notice the gold cross on a chain around his neck.

The cannons fired and lightning streaked along the kraken's body. The poor souls trapped in its limbs writhed in fresh pain, but it didn't stop the great beast. The tentacles flexed and twisted and then ripped the *Nautilus* in two.

The shriek of metal joined Sariel's shrieks and then various alarms joined the melody as we were thrown about the control room. I hung from the chair, which was now bolted to the ceiling, and the rest of the crew were suspended upside-down in their seats around me. I expected water to overwhelm us at any second, but the hatches held. Not that it was going to do us any good.

"Sound the call to abandon ship," Nemo said. We rolled in the water until we were right side up again, more or less. Nemo was as calm as if he were ordering us to set sail for some tropical island somewhere. "Set the weapons to autofire."

"Are you sure we want to go out there?" I asked, looking out the window as the alarms sounded and the lights flashed. The kraken was still clutching the two parts of the *Nautilus*, the creatures in the tentacles still hacking away at the sub's armour. As I watched, a sucker the size of my head slid over the window, scoring the surface with the hooks and spikes embedded in it.

"Our fighting capability has been somewhat reduced," Nemo said to me, rather pointing out the obvious. "We'll have to take the fight to them outside of the *Nautilus*."

"And how exactly are we going to do that?" I asked.

"I hope this is the point where you make yourself useful," Nemo said.

But instead it was Ahab and the white whale that saved the day, or at least the moment.

Through the rapidly deteriorating window I saw the whale rise up from the depths underneath the ark, smashing its way through the extended fleet and into the great vessel itself. I felt the impact in my bones, and a second later the shockwave lifted us as the whale drove the ark back up toward the surface. I caught a glimpse of the harpoon blazing in the chaos as Ahab struck at something, and then the windows were obscured with a wave of broken boards and body parts and bits and pieces of debris too small to identity.

Nemo pulled the hood of his dive suit over his head and the others of his crew did the same. I bowed to their experience and pulled the hood of my own suit over my head, managing to seal it. Thankfully, the suit's air system kicked in without me having to do anything.

"We must stop Noah and the ark from descending any farther at all costs," Nemo said through the speaker in the suit. "We cannot survive the lower depths, but Noah may be able to. If he reaches the Sunken City, all is lost."

Then he hit a button on his command chair and the windows blew apart as explosive charges went off in their frames. The control room suddenly became a raging torrent of water that quickly rose over our heads. We all waited several seconds for it to calm down, then we unbuckled ourselves from our seats and swam out of the *Nautilus*. I went past the German sailor writhing in the tentacle on the way, and I put some grace into a punch that shattered his jaw and likely most of the other bones in his head. I'll leave it up to you to decide whether or not I did him a favour.

I didn't like what I saw through the visor of my dive suit. The two halves of the *Nautilus* were falling through the water, trailing streams of air and oil and other things. Crew members were kicking away from the sub's remains in all directions, some with guns, others with swords. A tentacle swept through the area, the wave of its passage spinning me around. When I righted myself, a number of the crew had disappeared. I almost felt bad about raising them from the dead to meet such a fate. But things could get worse yet. Take, for example, the tentacle coming through the water my way.

Just then the *Nautilus*'s autofire system kicked in. The front half of the shattered submarine fired a broadside straight into the kraken's face. The creature writhed and screeched its pain, a sound like a hundred ships going down at once. The tentacle sweeping through the water toward me convulsed and missed, coming close enough that a man in a Roman centurion's gear managed to reach out and slash me in the side with his sword. A minor wound but a wound nevertheless. Now my blood joined everything else in the water. I frantically reached down to cover the tear in my suit before all my air escaped, but I saw the fabric had already fused back together. Atlantean technology at its finest.

Noah threw himself off the ark and fell upon the remains of the *Nautilus*. At least he left the angel skeletons behind. He grabbed the front end of the sub and ripped the metal open with his bare hands. He tore the guns out of their mounts and hurled them away through the water. It was a credit to their design that they were still firing when they disappeared in the distance.

Then Ahab and the whale struck again. This time they came from the far side of the battle and smashed right through the ark, crushing the smaller vessels before them and punching a hole in one side of Noah's original wooden ship before erupting from the other side. Debris exploded out in all directions: the remains of barrels, swords and spears and other weapons, even what looked like hundreds of books. Creatures spun madly in the water as they were thrown from the ark, trying to reach out and strike the whale with their weapons. Ahab speared a couple of them on his harpoon—a man in a diving suit with an axe and a strange being with crab legs and pincers for hands but the body of a man. The green fire of the harpoon flared up and turned them into burning torches underwater, and Ahab shook them free of the harpoon. They floated down, still burning and writhing, lighting up the scene.

Noah hurled the remains of the *Nautilus* away from him and turned to face Ahab and the whale. As the wreckage of the *Nautilus* sank down, though, a final volley of torpedoes shot up from the sub. They struck the ark all around the holes the white whale had made when it tore through the vessel. Explosions of every colour lit up the depths, and now the great ark was torn in half, the separate pieces drifting away from each other and burning with green fire.

"Do you really believe you can stop me from reaching the Sunken City?" Noah roared, his words like thunderclaps in the water. "I am one of the chosen of God himself!"

Ahab and the whale swam through the ruins of the ark and disappeared into the darkness again. "The chosen of God are few!" Ahab's voice cried. "We are the damned of God and we are legion!"

Noah looked around the scene and I did my best to hide behind the shredded body of a giant jellyfish thing that floated past. I didn't really want to attract his attention.

"Very well," Noah said. "If you would stop me from descending to the Sunken City, I will bring the Sunken City to me."

With that, he motioned to the angels floating amid the wreckage of the ark. They swam to him with the bible. It was all they could do to stop from sinking into the depths under its weight. They began chanting again, and this time Noah joined them. I didn't like the way this was going. It's been my experience that when a crazed, supernatural being decides to use a strange book in the middle of an epic battle, it's generally not a good thing.

Noah reached out and crushed the skull of one of the angels with his hand. He ground it into powder in his fist, and the angel stopped chanting. Noah grabbed the rest of the angel and tore it asunder. He took the bones in his hands and ground them to dust as well. The angel didn't resist, and the others didn't stop their chanting, not even when Noah churned his hand in the water and the angel dust swirled around to form a small whirlpool with the bible at its centre.

I cast about for a weapon, something, anything to stop whatever ritual Noah was performing. But everything had gone down with the *Nautilus*. The only things near me were a few paperbacks that had been cast out of the ark when Ahab had ruptured it. It was hardly the time for books. I could see a few of Nemo's crew drifting in the distance, but they looked either dead or stunned and weren't reacting to Noah.

Noah crushed the other two angels in the same manner. Their shackles fell into the depths and the whirlpool of bone dust stretched down after them. The bible hung suspended in the middle of the whirlpool. No, I didn't like the way this was going at all.

I felt something stirring in the water far below. It was hard to describe. A pressure from the deep that lifted me a little higher, pushing me up. The water grew even colder. And I saw glimpses of something moving far below, something I couldn't quite make out but that I knew instinctively was worse than the kraken.

And then Ahab and the whale came out of nowhere once more and smashed into Noah, driving him away from the whirlpool. Ahab slashed Noah's face with his harpoon, which was blazing with green fire like I'd never seen it blaze before. The blade sliced through the right side of Noah's face, and a cloud of black blood spilled out. The water boiled all around it, but Noah just laughed the laugh of the crazed.

"Too late!" he cried. "The Sunken City rises!"

The kraken surged through the ruins of the ark and latched

on to the white whale with a couple of tentacles. Instead of trying to get away, the whale swam closer to the great beast, so Ahab could strike it with his burning harpoon. The kraken's blood caught fire in the water, and the creature screamed some more. I had to cover my ears with my hands to save my eardrums. The whale hit the kraken with an impact that reverberated through the water. Both creatures tumbled away from me, Ahab still striking with his harpoon.

Then I saw it beneath me.

The Sunken City.

It was a great chaos of collapsed buildings and curved, tilting towers that pointed in every direction. It was all made of stone, looking as if it had been carved out of the cliffs of the ocean floor. The buildings seemed to melt into one another, like they were all one piece, frozen forever in the midst of a great disaster. There was something wrong with the angles of the buildings and the ways they bent back upon each other and through themselves, without ever breaking. My mind struggled to understand what it was seeing and failed. I grew dizzy just looking at the crazed towers as they rose out of the depths and toward us. It was like a mad dream of a city and I knew the Sleeper, whatever it was, had to be close to waking.

I looked back at Noah and saw him swimming down toward the Sunken City. All around him, the prisoners of his ark were closing in on the surviving members of the *Nautilus's* crew. I saw Scars and One-Eye floating back to back, firing their weapons on full auto into the mob of Noah's creatures. The Atlanteans were putting up a good fight, but it was just a matter of time and numbers. I'd been on the losing side of that equation often enough to know how it went. And Ahab and the white whale were still locked in a writhing struggle with the kraken, tentacles lashing and harpoon striking. It was up to me.

I burned some grace to give me extra speed and power, and I swam down in between Noah and the Sunken City. The dive suit pressed hard against my skin. The pressure at this depth must have been unbearable. Lightning and explosions lit up the water, and I saw Sariel drifting a few dozen yards overhead, with what could only be described as a happy smile on her face. I still didn't have a weapon.

"Join my crew, abomination," Noah said as he came at me, "and welcome the end of the world with all the other monstrosities."

I have to admit I didn't have a witty response to that one. But I didn't need one. Someone else responded for me.

Noah was suddenly thrown backwards, as something white streaked over my left shoulder and slammed into his chest. For a few seconds I thought it was maybe the whale again. Then I saw the shattered object drifting away in pieces from its impact with Noah, falling down to the Sunken City. It was a cannonball. A bone cannonball.

I looked over my shoulder and saw a ship sailing behind me, even though we were deep under the water. The *Revenge*. Blackbeard stood at the prow, gazing at us with his fiery eyes, as his crew manned the guns or stood at the railings, ready for combat. The skeletal siren was back as the figurehead, bound to the ship with chains now. She looked dead again, but I supposed that didn't mean anything on the *Revenge*.

"Cross is mine and no one else's!" Blackbeard roared at Noah. "You'll not be stealing my vengeance from me!"

His crew fired a broadside and the bone cannonballs tore into Noah's legion of the damned, tearing the limbs from some creatures and carrying others off into the darkness. A cannonball struck Sariel a glancing blow on her shoulder and she spun away but didn't stop laughing. Another cannonball flew at Noah but he batted it away with a hand that he then pointed at the *Revenge*.

A great mass of Noah's crew swarmed over the ship at his signal. Crab things and mermen fought dead pirates, and Blackbeard hacked his way into a crowd of men with shark heads, roaring and blazing away.

I saw more of Noah's crew swimming toward me, brandishing their various blades and fangs and other sharp things. I really needed to find a weapon soon.

Then reinforcements arrived.

More bodies fell from above, into the midst of Noah's army. Some of them wore robes or just rags but many wore nothing at all. Some were wailing while others were laughing. It took me a few seconds to recognize them as the denizens of Hades. There were hundreds of them falling from the surface, weaponless but making up for it in numbers as they swarmed Noah's creatures, grabbing on to their limbs and biting and punching and kicking them as they dragged them deeper. They seemed to have no trouble in the water despite their lack of dive suits or breathing apparatus. I guessed that was one of the bonuses of being dead already. I looked up and saw the silhouette of a boat pass overhead, a long pole reaching down from it and disappearing into the murk beneath me. Charon. He had returned with the dead from Hades. I imagined they were not so interested in seeing the world end now that they had their freedom again.

It still wasn't enough to stop Noah. He swung his arms wide, and a great underwater wave swept the fighters from both sides away from him. It was just like what I'd done at Atlantis. The *Revenge* rocked as the wave hit it. I was close enough to Noah that I was left untouched in between him and the Sunken City, which continued to rise. The towers were just beneath us now, almost within reach.

"The world was born in blood," Noah said as he bore down upon me. "It is fitting that it drowns in the same."

Blackbeard's crew managed to fire another broadside, and this time a volley of cannonballs struck Noah. He spun about wildly in the water at their impact, then righted himself and kept coming. I cursed God for what he had made. It wasn't the first time.

"Keep firing, you bastard, or he'll have me yet!" I shouted at Blackbeard, although I didn't know if he could hear me through the chaos or not.

I could see he wasn't going to be much help, though. His crew were barely holding their own against Noah's creatures, and now those who had been manning the cannons joined the fight against the boarders. Things were looking grim indeed.

Then a new force arrived on the scene. The air filled with a wailing that grew louder and louder, until it threatened to shatter my eardrums. At first I thought it was Sariel, but then I saw her floating at the edge of the scene, looking around from where she'd righted herself after being struck by the *Revenge*'s shot. For once, she was quiet.

They came out of the water from all sides. The sirens. A few dozen of them. They swam through the sea as fast as the

Nautilus's torpedoes, and they sang their song as they came. Perhaps they had been following me the same way Noah had, waiting for the *Revenge* to appear. Perhaps they could sense their dead sister on the *Revenge* like Ishmael could sense his prey, and they had just been waiting for the ship to arrive from wherever it was when it wasn't part of this world. Now wasn't the time to worry about how. Now was the time to use some grace to block out their song from my mind. The others were not so lucky. Members of Blackbeard's crew clapped their hands to their heads and screamed, as did some of the creatures they were fighting. Then the sirens tore into them.

The water turned even darker with blood as the sirens shredded Noah's creatures and Blackbeard's crew alike. They moved through the water as fast as the lightning bolts. I saw talons flashing in the murk, and teeth tearing at flesh. Blackbeard roared his rage and slashed around himself with his blade, keeping them at bay, but I knew there were too many sirens. It must have been all of the sirens left in the world. I thought I recognized a couple of them from my Greece trip, but I didn't wave.

They didn't confine themselves to venting their wrath on just those aboard the ship, either. They also fell upon Noah's creatures fighting the remnants of Nemo's crew, ripping the poor souls asunder. Which those damned might have seen as a final act of mercy before the world ended. A pair of sirens even latched onto Sariel, and the three of them tumbled away into the darkness, a screaming, laughing, flickering mess of blood.

The sirens stayed clear of Noah, though, as if they knew they could not harm him. And on he came, toward the Sunken City.

Then the scene lit up with a great golden fire, and the water boiled around me as a flaming serpent with wings reared over the deck of the *Revenge*. Xiuhcoatl. It rose up on tendrils of fire that reached down and into the crew of the pirate ship.

"Aye, you've gone and made him mad now," Blackbeard yelled, a great swath of fire blazing out of his eyes and rising up to feed the ancient god. That's when I understood what the flames in the eyes of all the pirates were. Somehow Xiuhcoatl had found its way into them all. Maybe Blackbeard had defeated and enslaved the god with his sorcery back on that ghost island.

Maybe the ancient god had defeated and enslaved the pirates. Maybe they were one and the same now, like Ahab and the white whale. Whatever had happened, the god was free and angry. It screeched its rage and struck at the monstrosities swarming the ship, swallowing down a crab thing with great claws and then some sort of merman thing with more tentacles than an octopus. It snapped its tendrils about like whips, and the sirens were knocked screaming off the ship. Blackbeard and his men cheered, and the serpent lunged at Noah, spitting flames through the water before it.

Noah's robes and hair caught fire and he burned in the water as the serpent wrapped itself around him quicker than my eye could take in, pinning one arm. I had a few seconds of hope, for surely if there was anything that could stop one of God's chosen, it was another god.

Then Noah grabbed the serpent by the neck with his free hand and choked it, as his entire body lit up with flames.

"You are not the first serpent I've caught!" he roared, and his other hand ripped its way through the creature to freedom. Blood and fire flowed into the water, and the serpent drifted away, writhing in pain. The tendrils that attached it to the pirates faded. Blackbeard and his crew cried out and dropped to their knees, obviously feeling the same pain as the god they had carried within them.

At the same moment, Ahab fell out of the sea above us and rammed his harpoon through Noah's chest. The green fire flared around the harpoon and ran over Noah's body, joining the fire from the serpent. Now Noah was burning with two mystical fires. It was something to see, but it still didn't stop him. I looked around for the whale, but it was nowhere in sight in all the madness.

"Fool!" Noah cried and struck Ahab with a fist. Ahab flew back and hit one of the towers of the Sunken City, which were rising around us now. He drifted away, unmoving. His harpoon remained in Noah, still blazing, but Noah didn't seem especially bothered by it.

"It would take all the forces of chaos and God combined to harm me!" Noah said. He ripped the harpoon from his body, and the flames flickered and nearly went out on the blade. He tossed it away—and I threw myself at it, catching it before it could sink and disappear. I finally had a weapon.

And I had an idea of how to stop Noah.

I threw myself at him and rammed the harpoon into his chest, in the exact same spot Ahab had impaled him. I channelled almost all the grace I had left through the harpoon and into Noah. The green fire blazed up again, and now the white fire of grace joined it. The two fires mingled with the serpent's fire, and then Noah went up like a torch as I kicked myself away from him. A holy trinity of flame, or maybe an unholy one, depending on your perspective.

Noah roared and writhed in pain as he burned. Impossibly, though, he kept coming.

"Abominations, all of you!" he cried. He pulled the harpoon out of his body again, and this time he threw it straight at me.

I tried to dodge it, but the water slowed me down. The harpoon scored my side in nearly the exact same spot the Roman soldier had earlier. My blood spilled out in a cloud around me. The suit sealed itself once more, saving my life again. I grabbed the harpoon before it was lost.

Noah swam down toward the Sunken City, still burning like a torch as he went. I could see streets carved out of the stone now, all of them leading to a massive structure in the centre of the city. It was a long, coffin-shaped building that all the other towers seemed to originate from, even as they spread out in all directions. There was a great set of doors in one side, also made of stone and sealed with a giant chain. It was toward those doors that Noah swam.

"Your sacrifice redeems you," he screamed, "but it does not redeem the world."

I swam after him with the harpoon, but I could barely manage a straight line. The crazed angles and shifting shapes of the Sunken City wreaked havoc in my mind.

Noah took hold of the chains on the doors with one hand and yanked. The chains strained in his hand for a second and then broke. Noah dropped the remains of the chains and reached out with both hands to open the gates to the Sunken City. The whirlpool of the angelic bone dust reached down toward the doors, spinning even harder now.

At the same time, I saw the white whale coming out of the chaos of the battle, streaking across the city toward Noah. Its tail smashed chunks out of the stone buildings and its jaws were open wide as it swam toward him. I could see words swirling in its bones, glowing brightly even in the murk. But how could it succeed where the rest of us had failed?

If this was going to be my final death, though, I was going down fighting.

I threw myself into the whirlpool. It whipped me about so hard I barely managed to hang on to the harpoon. The angel dust sparkled all around me with the last of the dead angels' grace. I saw flashes of the doors getting closer as the whirlpool dragged me down, and then they suddenly loomed in front of me. I drew all the grace out of the dust around me and used it to throw myself back out of the whirlpool just before it sucked me through those now open doors. I couldn't see anything inside—there was just darkness on the other side. But a great chill came out from that gate, and the water surged around me, as if something massive stirred in that darkness. I lunged at Noah as he began to step through the gate and into the Sunken City. I buried the harpoon in his back this time and used all the grace I had left to give me the strength to pull him back, away from the doors.

It wasn't enough. Even with the grace I wasn't strong enough to move him. But it was enough to hold him in place and stop him from fully stepping through the gates for a second.

And then the white whale took Noah.

It came along the side of the building and snapped its great jaws shut on his flaming figure. He tumbled into the whale's belly at the impact, with a great roar like a building collapsing.

And now the fire that engulfed Noah spread from him to the whale. The flames caught on the bones and raced along them, igniting the entire creature within seconds. But the fire didn't seem to harm the whale as it did Noah. Instead, the words swirling in the whale's bones flared brighter, and the bones seemed to thicken as I watched, growing even stronger as they burned. The words lifted out of the bones now and spread out, lashing through each other and forming chains that covered the whale's body, like some arcane skin. And still the whale burned with the flames of grace and the serpent god and Ahab's harpoon.

Noah battered at the sides of the whale as it swam past the gate and back up out of the Sunken City, but those bones held. I didn't think they would have been strong enough to contain him before, but the flames had made the white whale into something else, something that could hold even Noah.

"Release me, monstrosity!" Noah cried from inside the whale's stomach as he continued to blaze away and batter at the walls of his new prison, but the whale kept its jaws shut. It swam up to Ahab, who was stirring as he drifted in the water. Ahab reached out and caught on to the whale's side as it passed, pulling himself to his customary perch. He adjusted his top hat and he looked good as new. The whale swam in a circle through the wreckage of the battle, letting all see Noah was captured.

"The world must end!" Noah roared. "There is no meaning to any of this if the world does not end!" He hammered at the whale's ribs, but they held strong.

I made to toss the harpoon back to Ahab when the whale swam past me, but he shook his head.

"It is as much of you now as your own soul," he said. "Do what you would with thine own self." And now I saw the fire spreading from the whale to Ahab, the words swirling across his skeletal form like a new skin.

Ahab and the white whale swam away, into the darkness at the edge of the Sunken City as Noah raged inside them. They didn't look back as they disappeared into the sea. It took some time longer for the light of Noah burning to fade away, but eventually it did.

The storm was fading away too now that Noah was gone. The lightning had ceased and the clouds were dissipating. Noah's crew were scattering in every direction—crab creatures sinking into the depths, mermen swimming away, mortals like the centurions and simple sailors suddenly drowning and finally finding their release. Whatever spell Noah had over them was broken now.

I caught a glimpse of a great mass moving through the

darkness at the edge of my vision. Something writhed in the murk, and a great eye turned my way. Then a surge of water knocked me head over heels, sending me tumbling back from the open doors of the Sunken City and into one of the spires, as the kraken escaped into the sea.

Yes, there was still the problem of the Sunken City rising. I wasn't sure if the Sleeper inside would awaken if the city reached the surface, but I figured it probably wasn't a good thing to have it up there where everyone could see it.

I looked around, trying to find someone or something that could stop it. I saw the *Revenge* drifting directionless in the water. Blackbeard and his crew had managed to fight off their boarders, thanks to Xiuhcoatl, but the ship was in ruins. The deck was torn up and there were great holes in its sides where the cannons had been ripped out. The sirens had shredded the sails, so the ship had no wind to move it through the water now.

Blackbeard came to the rail and glared at me, but he may as well have been leagues away.

"I'll have you in my crew yet, Cross," he bellowed.

I should have come up with a witty response, but the truth was I had exhausted all my clever comebacks. And everything else. So I just watched as Xiuhcoatl stirred in the water and then writhed back to the *Revenge*. The god wrapped itself around the mast and then spread its body out, becoming a fiery sail for the ship. It reached down to the pirates with those flaming tendrils again, and they opened their arms to receive it. The *Revenge* moved away from the battle, and Blackbeard and his crew roared. I couldn't tell if it was a call of triumph or defeat.

So it was up to me to stop the Sunken City from rising. And I had no idea how to do that. I looked at the whirlpool, which still spun wildly down to the gates that Noah had opened. I could see a few sparks of grace still spinning in it, and I drew them all out, until the whirlpool was empty. I didn't know what I would do with the grace, but I had to do something.

I looked back up the funnel to the bible, which continued to hang in the centre of the whirlpool. The whirlpool had sucked in a cloud of other books from the remains of the ark, and they spun about it now. Ancient tomes and modern paperbacks and everything in between. Whatever ritual Noah had begun with the bible and the crushed angels, it hadn't stopped when the whale had taken him. But maybe there was a way to stop the ritual using the bible.

I swam over to the funnel and went up to where the bible hung there in the water. I knew I couldn't get rid of it on my own. But maybe there was someone who could help me.

I grabbed a book from the maelstrom and opened it so I could read the first line.

The year 1866 was signalised by a remarkable incident, a mysterious and puzzling phenomenon, which doubtless no one has yet forgotten.

The opening line of *20,000 Leagues Under the Sea*, by my old friend Jules Verne.

I stopped and looked around and I saw her.

Alice.

She hung in the whirlpool unmoving, the books flowing around her. No, that wasn't quite right, I realized. They were flowing *through* her. As if she were a ghost.

She was wearing a dress now, the sort of normal girl's dress that you saw in all the classic illustrations of the Alice in Wonderland tales. She smiled at me, but it was a sad sort of smile like I'd never seen on her face before.

"Alice!" I cried. "We must take the bible away from here!"

"I know," she said. "We try to do that in some of the books. It never turns out well, though."

"What else can we do?" I said.

"There's nothing else we can do," she said. "It's the only way the story can end."

"Open up the way to another library, then," I said. "As far away from here as you can manage."

Then I took a deep breath and threw myself into the whirlpool once more. I reached out for God's bible.

It was my fault the bible was here, causing all these problems. So it was my responsibility to get rid of it. I had a feeling it would probably mean my death or maybe madness like Noah to deal with the bible. But what choice did I have? Besides, Alice had already told me I wouldn't like the way this story ended.

I caught on to the bible and hung on like a drowning man clutching a life jacket. The whirlpool tried to rip me from it, but

I clung to it with all my might. I knew I had only one chance to do this. I was almost out of grace and I wasn't strong enough to battle the whirlpool for long.

Alice floated in the water across from me like the whirlpool wasn't even there. The books continued to hurtle through her even as they battered me. She laid her right hand on the bible and looked at me.

"If I had a world of my own, everything would be nonsense," she said.

"What are you talking about?" I asked. "Take us out of here."

And then the *Revenge* fired one last shot.

I turned at the sound and saw the green cannonball streaking away from the ship even as the *Revenge* disappeared into the darkness. It came at us and I threw myself to the side, to draw it away from Alice and the bible. If I was to die, maybe Alice could still somehow spirit away the bible.

Too late I saw I wasn't the target of the shot.

It flew straight toward the bible.

Blackbeard meant to shatter the seals of the bible and unleash its contents with his spectral shot.

We were undone.

The entire world was undone.

And then Alice was suddenly there in front of the bible, or maybe the bible was behind her. I wasn't sure. I didn't see anything move. It was more like reality had rearranged itself in the blink of an eye.

The cannonball struck Alice in the chest and there was a burst of green fire. Alice cried out and fell back into the whirlpool. She took the bible with her.

The whirlpool suddenly spun wildly, the funnel leaping away from the gates of the Sunken City and whipping about the water. I saw Alice spinning inside the whirlpool now, faster and faster. She looked at me and reached out her hand, the one that wasn't holding God's bible. Then the funnel streaked down into the ocean depths to the side of the Sunken City, and the cloud of books and ancient tomes were sucked down it. There was an explosion of pages as the books were ripped apart and then whipped downward. I thought I heard Blackbeard laugh from somewhere distant, but I may have imagined it. I saw Alice fall down into the depths and disappear into the darkness, still clutching God's bible. Then the whirlpool ripped itself apart, and there was only a cloud of the drifting remains of the books. Alice was gone.

"Alice!" I screamed. I put a hand against the spire to steady myself, and that's when I realized it was no longer moving. The Sunken City had stopped rising. Alice had somehow broken the ritual when she'd disappeared into the whirlpool with the bible.

I snatched my hand away from the spire, because even though it wasn't moving I still felt something from it. It wasn't like touching stone. It was like touching a sleeping person. I could feel the stone shift under my fingers, as if the Sleeper was beginning to wake.

I looked around and saw a great army of the dead drifting down into the strange streets of the Sunken City. There were hundreds of them: Noah's creatures, pirates, the damned of Hades that had been slain anew, some of Nemo's crew. Their bodies fell like rain upon the strange city, filling its streets.

There were survivors, though, and they were fleeing the scene. The sirens moved away slowly, carrying their dead with them. I saw three of them holding the skeletal one that had adorned the *Revenge* in their arms. They sang a mournful song as they went, something that you should pray you never have to hear. The dead from Hades who hadn't met their end in the battle swam away in all directions. Who knew where they were heading? Maybe back to Hades, but I doubted it. They were finally free, and I didn't imagine they had any intention of returning to their prison. I looked up for Charon but I didn't see his boat above us. No doubt he was already taking fresh souls back to populate the underworld again.

I felt something shift behind me, and I looked back to see the tower moving again. This time, though, it was descending rather than rising. The streets and other towers dropped down below me. The Sunken City was sinking.

I swam down to the gates that Noah had opened as quickly as I could. I pushed the doors shut. It was like pushing boulders, but I'd had some practice at that sort of thing. The chill faded from the water around me, and I no longer felt the sense of something stirring inside that coffin building. Once the doors were closed again, I slid the harpoon through the handles that had held the chains. I let the little grace I had left seep through my fingers into the harpoon, to fuse it to the stone doors. If the bone of the whale was enough to hold Noah, then maybe it was enough to hold the doors. The harpoon continued to burn with fire when I let it go. I didn't know if that was a good sign or a bad sign.

I could feel the pressure crushing me from all sides now despite the dive suit as the Sunken City continued its return to the depths. I let it go, floating where I was and watching the gates and then the buildings and towers recede beneath me. Everything except the harpoon disappeared into the darkness, but then even its flame dwindled to a torch, then a spark, and then nothing at all.

I looked around for Alice, but I didn't see her anywhere in the water. There were only the books that had spilled out of the ark and been caught in the whirlpool. I swam through them and grabbed one after another, reading the first lines and then letting the book go. Alice didn't reappear. That many books meant there had to be a library aboard the ark, though.

I swam over to the nearest section of ark and went through a hole in the hull. Shredded and mangled books floated in the water before me, like a trail. I followed them through a hallway of what looked like jail cells, only the bars were made of wood rather than metal or even bone. I couldn't see any point where they'd been joined to the floors and walls of the ark. It was as if the whole vessel had been carved out of one giant piece of wood. Or maybe it had just grown that way. The only one who could say for sure was Noah, and I'd heard enough from him for a while.

The doors to the cells were all open, and their inhabitants had either joined the battle or fled. There were no personal effects, but here and there someone had managed to scratch a picture into the walls of their cells. They were mainly of men and women, and a few creatures of indeterminate gender. But there were also other things. One whole wall was taken up with a carving of the Eiffel Tower. Someone else had covered their cell with crosses and passages from the Bible. I looked away from that one and kept going.

The trail of books led me through what I took to be Noah's

living quarters, on account that it was the largest room on the ark. It was empty of all furniture—there was no bed, no bar, no bookshelves. You know, the requirements of civilized living. Just four walls, a floor, and a ceiling.

Like some of his inmates, though, Noah had decorated his walls. They were all covered in scratches. They started off in neat rows on one wall, six vertical lines and then one horizontal one slashing across them. As they spread to the other walls, though, they grew more chaotic. The rows wandered in angles and loops. The horizontal slashes grew deeper, threatening to obliterate the other lines. Sometimes the rows were carved over other rows, vertical groups of lines carved over horizontal ones. It looked like the way some prisoners marked the days of their sentence. Or maybe it was the number of the damned that Noah claimed on the seas and imprisoned on the ark.

The ceiling was covered in more of the lines, but Noah had added a few words up there, carved deep into the wood.

He Is Not Coming Back.

I knew the feeling.

The books led to the rear of the ark, and the library, where the trail ended. The library was in another cell, but this one had shelves growing out of the walls, and more books drifted around the room. They looked to be from all ages—ancient tomes with gold on the covers, thriller paperbacks, textbooks, even a couple of e-readers. They probably were whatever had been aboard the ships that Noah had taken over the centuries and added to the ark. I went through the books here, too, opening them and reading their waterlogged pages before looking around for Alice. She didn't return to me, though. Alice was gone, along with God's bible. But where?

I left the remains of the ark again to see the survivors of the *Nautilus* collecting together in a small group nearby. There were only a handful of men and women left. I was surprised at the feelings I felt when I saw Nemo was among them. I was also strangely relieved to see Scars and One-Eye.

I swam over to them and they lowered their weapons when they saw it was just me. I gave Nemo a hug even though I could tell it made him uncomfortable. I did the same with Scars and One-Eye, with much the same response. It didn't matter.

We were alive. Well, I was alive. They were still somewhere in between life and death. But at least we weren't all dead.

"I guess the world didn't end after all," I said. "Not today, anyway."

Nemo nodded but didn't look particularly happy about the news. He stared down into the depths. I didn't know if he was looking for the Sunken City or the remains of the *Nautilus*. Maybe both.

"The gate is still secure?" Nemo asked, the words echoing brokenly in my suit. The radio must have been damaged in the battle.

"More than ever," I said.

"And the bible?" he asked.

"It's gone," I said.

"Gone where?" he asked, looking at me.

I could only shake my head. "I don't know," I said, and my voice broke on the words.

"What did you do this time?" he asked.

"I didn't do anything," I said. It was Alice. Alice had saved the world.

He stared at me for a few seconds longer, then looked back down into the depths.

"Perhaps we will find a way to bury the entire city for eternity," Nemo said. "Once we find a way to repair the *Nautilus*."

"How are you going to manage that?" I asked. "The pieces of your sub are at the bottom of the deepest part of the ocean, along with something that the world is better off forgetting."

"I am Captain Nemo of Atlantis," Nemo said, in a tone of voice that suggested I had somehow insulted him again. "I will find a way to retrieve the *Nautilus* and repair it. In the meantime, we will stand watch over the Sunken City to ensure no one else disturbs it."

"And when the *Nautilus* is repaired?" I asked.

Nemo gazed out into the sea surrounding us. "There are other things out there like the Sunken City. We will check on them all to make sure they remain undisturbed. And then perhaps we will restore Atlantis." He looked back at me. "It will take time, but I suppose you have given us that." It was probably the closest he could come to thanking me.

"Believe me when I tell you time is not a gift," I said.

"And what of you?" Nemo asked me. "What will you do now?"

"I don't know," I said, which wasn't exactly true. I had to find out what had happened to Alice and God's bible. I didn't want to think about the possibility that she was dead. And if she wasn't dead, that meant she was somewhere I could find her again. But I didn't know where to even start looking for her.

And she was just one of the many things I had to think about. I had to figure out a way to bind the kraken again. I had to take care of any other of Noah's former crew that might become a problem. I had to find Sariel, who had disappeared in the battle, before she made her way back to the world and stirred up trouble. There were fewer things worse than a deranged angel. I had to end my feud with Blackbeard and his crew. I had to find a way to cure the mysterious wound on my hand. Hell, I should probably keep an eye on the dead that had escaped Hades. Who knew what mischief they would cause returning to the land of the living after all this time? And, of course, I had to track down Ishmael and finally deal with him once and for all.

"I guess I'll go back up to the surface and then take it from there," I said. "One thing at a time." Sure.

"We'll meet again, then," Nemo said and offered me his hand.

"Stranger things have happened," I said, taking it.

"All the waves are part of the same ocean," he said. Atlantean wisdom, no doubt.

I took one last look around the scene, at the wrecked ark and other ships slowly sinking down, hopefully to be lost forever. Then I nodded my farewell to Nemo and Scars and One-Eye and the rest of the Atlanteans and swam up, toward the surface. It was hard going at first with all the weight of the water pressing down on me, but eventually the pressure eased and the water grew warmer around me. The suit finally ran out of air and I swam up the last hundred feet or so on my last breath. My lungs were screaming when I broke through the surface and erupted into the light.

I ripped off the suit's hood and floated there for a moment, gasping and gazing up at the sky overhead. It was grey and overcast, threatening to rain. I never thought I'd be so happy to see storm clouds again.

When I caught my breath, I looked around. I saw nothing but waves. There was no land in sight, no ships. I was alone, a castaway.

Then the books started surfacing all around. The first one popped up in front of me and bobbed along until I grabbed it.

Alice's Adventures in Wonderland. It was an old hardcover, with an illustration of Alice on the front. The book was heavy in my hand and probably shouldn't have floated, but it did.

More rose up out of the depths in a circle around me. I looked at them as well. *Through the Looking Glass. The Hunting of the Snark. Jabberwocky.* They were all books by Lewis Carroll, all old hardcovers with illustrations on the front. Maybe they were from Noah's library. Maybe they were from somewhere else. They all should have sunk but none of them did. They kept rising to the surface, different editions of the same books, until there were several dozen of them floating around me. I opened them and flipped through the pages to see if there was some sort of message, but they were all blank inside.

I knew they were a sign, anyway. Another sign from Alice. I didn't know what kind of sign it was, but then I rarely knew with her.

I lay on my back in the water amid the empty books and looked up at the sky full of nothing, and let the waves take me to who knew where.

☧

ABOUT THE AUTHOR

Peter Roman is the strange spirit that sometimes possesses Canadian author Peter Darbyshire and makes him write the Cross series. Roman is responsible for summoning the books *The Mona Lisa Sacrifice*, *The Dead Hamlets*, and now *The Apocalypse Ark*. Darbyshire, who wrote the award-winning and critically acclaimed novels *Please* and *The Warhol Gang*, is rumoured to be seeking out an exorcist.